THE REBEL AND THE CAPTIVE

THE
ReBeL
AND THE
CAPTIVE

KRIS K. HAINES

ISBN-13: 979-8-9926766-0-0

Author's note:

This book contains subject matter that might be difficult for some readers, including strong language, graphic sexual content, violence and gore, torture, colonial oppression, sexual assault (none of the main couples), references to parental abuse, depictions of mental illness, and suicidal thoughts. Reader discretion is advised. The mental health of my readers is of utmost importance to me. If you feel that there is a trigger that is not mentioned above, please do not hesitate to contact me via the form on my website: kriskhainesbooks.com.

For the rebel hearts.

Don't lose hope. Our fight lives on.

Pronunciation Guide

Characters

Cassandra Fortin - kah-SAHN-drah FOR-tin
Tristan Saros - TRIS-tehn SAHR-ohs
Cael Zephyrus - kale ZEFF-russ
Xenia Cirillo - ZEE-nee-ah suh-RIH-loh
Ronin Matakos – ROH-nihn mah-TAH-kohs
Mireille Valette – mih-RAY vah-LET

Aedelmar Burkhardt – AY-dell-mar BURK-heart
Ana – AHN-ah
Aneka - ANN-ih-kah
Arran Zephyrus - AIR-ahn ZEFF-russ
Aurelie Lambros – OHR-ah-lee LAMB-brohs
Belen Erabis - BAY-lehn AIR-ah-biss
Berstoh – BEAR-stow
Borea - boh-RAY-ah
Daena Geirdrios – DAY-nuh ghee-AIR-dree-ohs
Darius – DARE-ee-us
Eamon Erabis - AY-mahn AIR-ah-biss
Elodie Laskaris – EH-loh-dee lah-SKAHR-iss
Erik Zephyrus – AIR-ick ZEFF-russ
Felix Tanius – fee-LICKS TAN-ee-us
Helena – huh-LAY-nuh
Hella - HELL-ah
Ione - eye-OH-nee
Jonas – JOE-nahs
Layla Fetar – LAY-lah feh-TAHR
Leonard – lehn-erd
Leonin Erabis - LEE-oh-nihn AIR-ah-biss
Maksym - mack-SEEM
Mila Erabis - MEE-lah AIR-ah-biss

Mistress Ostere – [mistress] OH-stare
Ohan Stolia - OH-hahn STOH-lee-ah
Petra Zephyrus – peh-trah ZEFF-russ
Phidion Laskaris – FIH-dee-uhn lah-SKAHR-iss
Phaeban Erabis - FAY-behn AIR-ah-biss
Priya Burkhardt – PREE-yah BURK-heart
Reena - REE-nah
Remy Wormwood – REH-mee [wormwood]
Selene Matakos – seh-LEEN mah-TAH-kohs
Seraavi Pfania – seh-RAHV-ee PFAHN-ee-ah
Silas – SIGH-luss
Signys – SIG-niss
Skanisse – skah-NEESE
Sofia Hershon – soh-FEE-ah HER-shon Tomas
Zephyrus – TOHM-ahs ZEFF-russ Trophonios -
truh-FOHN-ee-uhs
Varuna Lykan - vah-RUHN-ah LIE-kan Viktor
Zephyrus – VICK-tohr ZEFF-russ Zosime
Laskaris – ZOH-see-may lah-SKAHR-iss

Places

Aethalia – eh-THAL-ee-ah
Akti - AHK-tee
Brachos - BROCK-ohs
Cernodas - SEHR-noh-dass
Delos - DEH-lohs
Denevrae – DEH-neh-vray
Diachre - dee-AHK-rah
Dordenne River - door-DEN [river]
Ethyrios - ih-THEE-ree-ohs
Icthian Mountains - ICK-thee-ahn [mountains]
Kheimos – KAI-mohs
Lebaedia – luh-BAY-dee-ah
Lodesvale – LOADS-vale
Meridon - MARE-ih-dahn

Nephes - NEH-fehs
Primarvia - prih-MAR-vee-ah
Rhamnos - RAHM-nohs
Staurien Pass – STAR-ee-ehn [pass]
Syvalle - see-VAHL-ay
Tartarus – TAR-tah-russ
Thalenn - THAH-lehn
Typhon Mountain - TIE-fuhn [mountain]

Terms

Adelphinae - ah-DELL-fee-nay
Aguaver - AAH-gwah-ver
Amatu - uh-MAH-too
Anaemos - ah-NAY-mohs
Aramaelish - ah-rah-MAY-lish
Delirium - duh-LEER-ee-uhm
Dienses - DEE-ehn-sees
The Delphine - [the] dell-FEEN
drachas - DRAH-kahs
Faurana - fowh-RAHN-ah
fieyrtes - fee-AIR-tays
Inom Than - ee-NOHM thahn
lui ganeth, lui cathona - lou-ee gah-NETH, lou-ee kah-THO-nah
Letha – LEH-thuh
Ma'anyu - MAHN-yoo
Nemosyna - neh-moh-SEE-nah
Stygios - STIH-gee-ohs
Teles Chrysos - TEH-less KREE-sohs
Thakavi - thah-KAH-vee
Vasilikan - vah-SILL-ih-kan
Vestan - VEST-an
Vestian - VEST-ee-an
Vicereine - vie-sir-EEN

Citizens of Ethyrios

FAE

Nearly immortal, magical, humanoid beings. Descendants
of the High Gods.
Divided into three sub-species.

Windriders: Winged sub-species, both of feather and of
flesh. Ability to fly. Ability to manipulate air and control
wind. Descendants of Anaemos.

Beastrunners: Sub-species of mammalian bi-forms. Ability
to switch between beast and humanoid forms at will.
Descendants of Faurana.

Deathstalkers: Venomous sub-species. Ability to paralyze
another Fae with a bite from their three-inch fangs.
A full Deathstalker bite is instantly fatal for humans.
Descendants of Stygios.

HUMANS

Mortal and non-magical. No sub-species.

Gods of Ethyrios

HIGH GODS

Anaemos: The Father, High God of Spirit and Sky

Faurana: The Mother, High Goddess of Land and Life

Stygios: The Reaper, High God of Death and Destruction

GODS

Letha: The Stranger, Goddess of Oblivion

Nemosyna: The Chronicler, Goddess of Memory

Dienses: The Jester, God of Merriment

Amatu: The Lover, Goddess of Love

Vestan: The Warrior, God of War

Thakavi: The Scholar, God of Wisdom

Ker: The Killer, Goddess of Violence

Adelphinae: The Creator, The Fallen Goddess*

*Adelphinae's story has been stripped from
Ethyrios's histories.

Territories of Ethyrios

CONTINENTAL

Akti: Southern coastal region. Capital: Rhamnos.

Brachos: Northwest region. Capital: Diachre.

Cernodas: Eastern region. Capital: Aethalia.

Nephes: Central region and home to the Imperial Capital, Delos.

Northern Territories: Northeast region. Capital: Kheimos.

Syvalle: North central region. Capital: Thalestria.

COLONIAL

Northern Colonies. Capital: Thalenn.

Northern Middle Colonies. Capital: Primarvia.

Southern Middle Colonies. Capital: Vaengya.

Southern Colonies. Capital: Meridon.

CHAPTER ONE

SNOW EXPLODED BENEATH TRISTAN Saros's feet as he landed in a forest overlooking the bone-white cliffs of Tartarus.

Across the lifeless valley, a swirling tempest of black shrouded the continent's legendary prison.

He stretched his aching wings as he trudged to a clearing, the icy wind plucking at his feathers. It was one of the few forces besides light that could penetrate the prison's powerful wards.

He suspected he wouldn't be able to breach them. But he wouldn't be able to live with himself if he didn't at least *try*.

Cassandra Fortin—his Daredevil, his *ma'anyu*, the brave, selfless little idiot who'd sacrificed her freedom—was trapped behind those wards.

The prison's intake tower stood atop a rocky outcropping, a lonely red-black spire at the edge of the known world. And no one in Ethyrios, save the damned, knew what lay within the obsidian mists beyond.

The weapons Tristan carried had been stolen from an Imperial soldier at a hostel in Cernodas. Tristan had left the male in pieces—a fleeting satisfaction—then stripped him of a Typhon broadsword, a stun pistol, and a snakebite. High-Gods-willing, the plum-sized bomb crafted with wind magic and Deathstalker venom would be powerful enough to tear a hole through the wards.

The frozen air needled his lungs as he summoned the wind and speared across the valley, the wards nipping at his power.

He pushed harder, his back muscles screaming. Warnings blared through his head to stop, to turn back before he plummeted to the valley floor. He ignored them, sights narrowed on that tower.

As he approached, his wind sputtered. He tucked his wings, barreling like a bullet toward the cliff-edge and smashing into it with nearly the same force.

Clinging to the rock, he began his climb. He dug his hands and feet into the cracks, trying to ignore the pain in his wrists, ankles, and shoulders. He grunted, inching slowly upward, the weight of his wings an increasingly heavy burden.

Once he reached the top, he dragged his grief-laden body up over the ledge, struggling to catch his breath.

The intake tower was a silent sentinel against the fading sun, several thousand paces ahead. As he heaved himself to his feet, he spied not a single individual, neither through the windows nor in the boulder-strewn yard. Was no one there? Or were the wards masking their presence?

He wondered how many had stood here before him. Had anyone, in the seven centuries of the prison's existence, ever been fool enough to break *into* Tartarus?

Tristan crunched toward the wards, noting a slight distortion in the air like looking through a thin wall of water. It buzzed against his hand as he pushed against their teasing pliability.

He unsheathed the Typhon broadsword from his back, then stabbed it into the wards. The air distorted around the tip, and for one relief-filled moment, Tristan could've sworn he saw a tiny tear forming. He pushed harder, but the wards fought back, the tear restitching as a red glow pulsed brighter at the contact point.

Tristan was blasted backward in an eruption of crimson sparks, his feet skidding through the gravel.

He peered into the yard, wondering if anyone could see him out here. He knew there were no guards—the *wards* were the guards—but could the prisoners sense him?

Could *she* sense him?

He pulled the snakebite from his pocket, then shot a tiny gust of wind—all he had left—into the bomb before tossing it toward the edge of the wards. He dashed off the cliff, grabbing the edge as he dangled over the side and nearly losing his grip when the ground-shaking explosion threw stones against his fingers.

As the smoke cleared, he pulled himself up—and his final ember of hope was snuffed out.

The snakebite had failed, evidenced by the perfect semi-circle of scorched dirt above which the shimmering wards were still intact.

Fuck.

He threw his head back and roared to the sky, then barreled into the wards, banging his fists, feet, head and shoulders against them.

He refused to believe he couldn't break through, couldn't get to her.

Seconds, minutes, hours ticked by as he beat himself against the impenetrable shield, the indifferent moon above the only witness to his crushing failure.

Until a burst of rainbow light flashed in his peripheral vision.

"You won't get to her that way."

The soft voice of Ione Saros, leader of the Teles Chrysos rebels—and his former lover—did nothing to quell his rage.

He cuffed her throat, a feral beast driven by instinct and madness, and slammed her into the wards. Her glistening white wings shuddered.

"Leave me," he growled, gnashing his teeth and exposing his sharp canines.

She snarled back, baring her own fangs, and the sight shocked him into releasing her. They were so different from the delicate human teeth he remembered. "You don't frighten me, Tristan. You never have."

Her indigo eyes gleamed with affection and, for a single moment, he was pitched back to the night he'd confessed his love for her. The night he'd attempted to Turn her.

The night he'd lost her.

She appeared only a few years older than she had then, her mortality inching glacially forward. He wondered if he looked any different to her. Had the centuries been as kind? Or could she see the buried scars her loss had inspired?

A violent, painful maelstrom seized his heart—past and present colliding.

She expelled a bitter laugh. "I confess, I thought you might have been a bit happier to see me after I rescued you from your brother. Or that you might have stayed in Akti long enough to thank me." She leveled him with a pleading stare.

He bit back his fury. Why hadn't Ione let him know she'd survived? That the Turning had been successful? What the *fuck* had she been doing for the past two centuries, and why had she only come for him now?

"We have so much to discuss," she said, as if reading every question written across his anguished face. "I will tell you everything, but you need to return with me, Prince."

"I'm not a fucking Prince anymore," he spat. "That dream died the moment Eamon took Cassandra from me. I don't want any part of a plan that doesn't start with getting her back."

Pain, envy even, flashed through Ione's eyes before she smoothed her expression and dared to place a hand on his shoulder. He shook her off. "If you want any hope of freeing her, I need you to trust me." She pulled a glowing fire opal from her fur-lined cloak. "*Please*."

Was it the plea of a long-lost love, desperate to rekindle their passion? Or was it the plea of a leader, determined to save her people and in need of a partner with the right title and history to do so?

He couldn't yet tell. He wasn't even sure he wanted to know. But what were his choices? Stay here and break himself against these wards? Flee from Ione again and traipse unprotected across a continent on the brink of civil war? Wait for his brother to capture him again?

Or take a chance on the female in front of him? A female who, once upon a time, he'd trusted with his most secret wishes for this world.

He gazed up at the tower, his shoulders dropping. "I never told her."

"Told her what?"

"That I loved her." He shook his head, correcting himself. "That I *love* her. She's trapped in there, fragile and frightened, without even the certainty of my feelings for comfort. I have to fix this, Ione. This world means fucking *nothing* to me without her. If I can't break through these wards myself, then I will raise an army to free her."

A forced smile crawled across Ione's face as she reached for him. "We have one of those."

He didn't know how to read her, but he grabbed her hand tight as she murmured the name of their destination into the opal and the world around them dissolved into strings of rainbow light.

CHAPTER TWO

*T*ODAY IS THE DAY. *Today is the* day.

Xenia Cirillo repeated the words to herself as she paced outside the entrance to Ohan Stolia's headquarters in downtown Rhamnos.

And though this particular mantra had failed her for the past week, Xenia still believed in the power of positive thinking.

After all, what was it if not her sunny determination—and maybe a bit of luck—that had helped her survive in this overcrowded, crime-ridden continental city?

When she'd first arrived at this address seven days ago, she'd been brimming with certainty. Ohan had already helped her once, at Cael's request, when he'd arranged passage for her to the colonies on one of his cargo ships. And though she'd abandoned that ticket, she knew, just *knew*, in her heart that Ohan would be moved by her desire to reunite with Cael. That the transportation magnate would find a way to get her to Brachos.

If only she could speak with him.

She hadn't yet achieved that part. Every day she'd been thwarted by the Deathstalker female who manned the front desk.

Daphne.

A tiny, elegant dictator with a golden nametag pinned to her crisp white blazer.

That first day, Daphne had taken one look at Xenia in all her bedraggled, frizzy-haired glory, and promptly used a commstone to call security.

Xenia had rushed out of the building before she was escorted out. Or worse.

That interaction *had* been a bit unlucky, even Xenia would admit that.

But afterward, what could it have been other than luck that had guided her to a human shelter mere blocks away, nestled between two skyscrapers? Perhaps it was the Goddess Letha smiling down upon her, grateful for all Xenia's years of service at her namesake Temple in Thalenn. Actually, the sparse, simple accommodations at the shelter reminded Xenia of her Temple quarters, and the two Beastrunner females who ran the place were the kindest Fae she'd yet met on the continent. They'd fed her, allowed her to bathe, and had given her a place to sleep in between attempts to breach the wall of Daphne.

Xenia had even made a few new friends among the other humans, mostly victims of the Fae traffickers. Some had escaped their bonds, others had been discarded by their masters. But to a one, they held out hope of returning to the colonies and to their families. Xenia promised to plead their case with Ohan as soon as she could gain an audience with him.

They'd all thanked her for the offer, even as they warned her away from her own plans. They were shocked she wanted to journey *farther* into the continent. Especially given the unrest from the burgeoning Teles Chrysos rebellion. They said the continent was more dangerous now for humans than it had ever been, despite the rebels fighting on their behalf.

They sounded far too much like Cael.

Xenia shrugged them off, fully believing in the luck that had seen her this far.

Luck that had delivered her a wonderful gift today.

Daphne was *gone*.

Xenia tried not to squeal with excitement as she entered the building, the automatic glass doors whooshing shut behind her. She crossed the sleek, marble-floored lobby, shoulders back, confidence soaring with every step.

She plastered on a friendly smile that wavered only slightly when Daphne's cream-winged replacement did not match it.

"Can I help you?" The Windrider's nose crinkled as he raked upturned black eyes over her filthy dress—the sky-blue one she'd been living in, sleeping in, for the past week. She couldn't tell if he was more insulted by her attire, her scent, or her humanity. Probably all three.

"I'm here to see Ohan Stolia," she said with only a slight wobble. She cheered herself for her courage.

The Windrider crossed his arms and rustled his feathers. "Do you have an appointment?"

"No, I don't. But I'm sure he'd want to meet with me."

The male pursed his lips to signal he wasn't sure of that at all. Xenia brushed her knuckles along the hilt of her dagger. Well, Cass's dagger. The one Cael had given her to return to her friend. The Windrider's gaze dipped to the weapon, tied at Xenia's hip with a crude piece of rope.

"Your name?" The words oozed off his tongue.

Despite his obvious disdain, Xenia's heart leapt. This was far further than she'd ever gotten with Daphne.

"Xenia. Xenia Cirillo. We share a friend in common—Cael Zephyrus."

A tiny flash of recognition lit up the male's face. He may not have heard of Cael, but he certainly knew Cael's last name thanks to his famous father—Arran Zephyrus, High Councilor of Brachos.

The Windrider whispered a message into his palm.

Xenia caught the phrase *young human female* and thought she heard him repeat her name, though she couldn't be sure.

He crossed his arms, glaring beneath lowered brows as he awaited an answer to his windwhisper.

Beneath his right ear, his violet commstone glowed and a forced grin exposed sharp canines. "Head on up. Twenty-fifth floor. He'll be waiting for you." He tapped a screen on the desk and the waist-high gate to Xenia's left opened. Before she could cross through, he snatched her upper arm. "Leave the dagger. No weapons allowed within the building."

Xenia hesitated, her fist clenched around the hilt. The weapon was more than just a means of protection. It was a token of hope. The gift she'd offer Cassandra if—no, *when*—she saw her friend again. Giving it up felt like abandoning that possibility.

"Hurry up," the Windrider spat. "Master Stolia is an extremely busy male."

Xenia sighed, then handed over the dagger. She'd tell Ohan, ask him to give it back to her. Right after she had a very long chat with him about his *rude* staff.

Her mood buoyed as she approached the bank of elevators. It was happening. She'd soon be on her way out of Rhamnos and on her way toward Cael.

She day-dreamed about their reunion as she waited for the elevator. Upon first sight, he'd likely be upset that she'd gambled with her safety. But he'd soften. She knew he would.

A male didn't kiss with such fervor, didn't do those *other things* Cael had done to her, if his feelings weren't genuine. And strong. She'd been fooled once before.

But she wasn't fooled by him. Not for a second. Not even when he'd left Ohan's ship, stubbornly insisting she was safer without him.

A soft ding sounded, breaking her reverie, and the middle set of doors opened.

Though she'd never ridden in an elevator—such things didn't exist in the colonies—she had a passing knowledge of how they worked, having studied Fae technology in the Temple library. She pressed the button for the twenty-fifth floor.

The glowing numbers ticked upwards, and her stomach dipped.

Fifteen.

Eighteen.

Twenty-two.

By the time they approached twenty-five, Xenia was vibrating with excitement. She'd made it. She'd gotten her meeting with Ohan. Soon, she'd be on a train to Brachos, she'd find Cael, and he'd be so touched that he'd—

The elevator doors slid apart and Xenia's excitement fizzled.

The male who stood in the hallway was not Ohan Stolia, the yak Beastrunner with the jovial laugh and avuncular manners.

This male had short platinum hair, a ruddy complexion, and a face that had been recently added to Xenia's all-too-frequent nightmares.

The fox bi-form who'd attempted to buy her from Cael last week.

She smashed the buttons in an attempt to re-close the doors, but it was too late. The Beastrunner snatched her arm with supernatural speed and yanked her into the hallway.

He pinned her arms, crushing her against his chest as a wicked smile transformed his vulpine features into something truly terrifying. "Hello again, pretty blonde pet."

Before she could scream, he crushed a wet rag over her mouth.

She kicked and flailed as he dragged her down the sterile hallway, her soles squeaking against the tiles as the overhead lights screamed their insectile buzz.

The bitter-scented liquid on the rag cocooned her mind in a cottony haze, and the Beastrunner whispered into her ear.

"Your Vestian should have taken my original offer."

CHAPTER THREE

*S*EVEN DAYS. LIFT. *THREE hours.* Stretch. *Forty-two minutes.* Lower.

Thwap.

Cassandra Fortin held her wings out and slammed a fist into the hanging bag, rattling its chain.

Seven days. Lift. *Three hours.* Stretch. *Forty-three minutes.* Lower.

Thwap.

Time was a funny thing. As a mortal woman, she'd had an ever-present awareness of its scarcity. As if life itself were a leaky bucket, another second lost with every drop.

But even now, in her newly immortal body, the seconds didn't feel any less precious.

Every moment she spent in this intake tower was a moment further away from Xenia. Further away from

Mama. Further away from Borea and the Shrouded Sisters and everyone and everything Cassandra had ever cared about.

Further away from Tristan.

Seven days, three hours, and forty-four minutes, to be precise.

Perhaps that was why she hadn't yet gotten used to her endless supply of time. Until the Emperor came to deliver her sentence, how could she know how much she had left?

She tried to focus on her exercises, the ones Ronin had shown her to strengthen her back muscles and ensure she could hold her wings properly. He'd instructed her to perform them wherever and whenever possible, so she spent the majority of the hours outside her cell in this empty training room.

Cassandra welcomed the physical distractions—the deep ache in her shoulders, the stiffness in her quads, the sting of her knuckles against the bag.

Lift. Stretch. Lower.

Thwap.

161803, the number on her gray linen shirt, shifted with her movements, rippling over her left breast. Right over that empty place where her heart should've been.

She hadn't yet tested her wind-summoning power. Couldn't, even if she'd wanted to. It had flickered out mere seconds after her Turning, thanks to the elemental magic suppressants woven into the prison's impenetrable wards.

But she could feel that she was stronger, even before she'd begun these exercises. Though that strength seemed as inconsequential as her missing heart and the two iridescent white wings springing from her shoulder blades.

The wings were a constant nuisance. It was difficult to get comfortable at night. Before she'd acquired these monstrosities, she'd been a back sleeper. Now, that position was almost painful, what with the itchy bedsheets pulling at her sensitive feathers.

Something she'd never considered before being Turned Fae—how the fuck to get used to a completely new sleeping position.

She *was* enjoying her newfound ability to curse.

She tried not to think about what had inspired it. That blissful night when she'd given Tristan everything—her heart, her body, her innocence. *Herself.*

What had happened to him after she was arrested? Eamon hadn't sent him here to Tartarus, obviously. Was he still his brother's captive? Or had Eamon already ended him?

Her anxiety about Tristan's safety was matched only by her anxiety about her sentencing. Not just what it would be, but how Eamon would react when he saw her. When he'd have no doubt about who had Turned her.

Lift. Stretch. Lower.

Thwap.

She attempted to quell her anxieties by running through the list of tasks that lay before her.

First, figure out how in the name of Stygios she was going to hide what she was from Eamon when he arrived.

Second, find Mireille Valette, Ronin's long-lost... *whatever*...to see if she had any idea of how they might escape the prison she'd been locked in for two centuries.

And third, after Cassandra, Mireille, Reena, Ronin, and Ronin's sister, Selene, accomplished said escape, find Tristan. Join the Teles Chrysos. End the Empire.

Those last three goals were so daunting that she didn't dare ponder them for long. When she did, her lungs seized, her head pounded, and her breath dissolved into a faint wheeze.

The clouds outside shifted, and a beam of sunlight speared into the room. Cassandra lowered her wings and opened the window, sniffing the crisp mountain air. Such a tease to feel the wind on her face but not be able to harness it. To smell her lost freedom.

Had Tristan lost his, too?

The thought stirred Cassandra's rage, and she volleyed a series of jabs into the bag.

"You done fighting that thing this morning?" Reena stepped into the room, her auburn hair glinting.

"It never fights back." Cassandra sighed, rustling her feathers.

"Come on." Reena held out claw-tipped fingers covered with white fur as her striped tail swished lazily behind her.

"Where are we going?" Cassandra asked as Reena dragged her from the training room.

"Ronin wants to talk to us."

"About what?"

Reena dragged a reverent gaze down Cassandra's feathered wings.

"About how we're going to hide those before the Emperor arrives."

Ronin Matakos sat before the roaring fireplace in the common room, chin propped on a tattooed fist. The dancing flames were stirring up memories.

Of another fortress full of violence and secrets.

Of another frigid landscape surrounded by impenetrable wards.

Of a majestic she-wolf covered in crackling fire.

He'd gotten quite adept at suppressing the memories. A necessity, really, since they made his chest ache fiercely enough to stop his heart.

In the earliest days after that final showdown with Mireille, he thought he might almost welcome such a fate. Better to embrace True Death than live with the unending regret over what they could have been.

But he'd be damned if he ever gave a female the power to ruin him like that again.

Instead, he drowned his feelings beneath an ocean of distractions. His two-faced role on the Imperial

Defense Council. His missions for the Teles Chrysos. Too many forgettable females.

You know as well as I do that no one will ever compare, his wolf piped up.

None of that, furball, he snapped back. *We agreed on our strategy if we run into her, remember? Cold indifference.*

His wolf shrugged. *That was before we found that gift she left us.*

She left that for Cassandra, not us.

You are a fool, his wolf laughed. *A fool in denial of his own feel—*

ENOUGH, Ronin roared.

His wolf retreated to the depths of mind with a frustrated whine and a softly muttered *Someone needs to get laid.*

The fire popped and Ronin jolted. Fuck, he was on edge. Maybe he *did* need to get laid. He wished he had a Delirium. He'd quit decades ago, but the cravings never truly went away. Shifting helped.

He'd done so this morning, his first shift since he'd arrived at the intake tower, and through his wolf's heightened sense of smell had immediately detected something in a barren corner of the yard. Its scent was painfully familiar—and centuries old if he wasn't mistaken—but he was still shocked at what he'd found beneath the gravel and packed dirt.

Soft footsteps and rustling wings broke through his musings.

"Well," he drawled as Reena and Cass shuffled toward him, "look what the big cat dragged in."

Cass snickered, but Reena rolled her eyes as the two took a seat on the rough stone bench across from him. Cassandra's face looked strained as she held her wings aloft—a show for the other prisoners in the cavernous room—but not nearly as strained as it had been a week ago. She'd been keeping up with her exercises. Good little soldier.

"Yeah, yeah." She rubbed her shoulder. "You summoned us?"

"Got a special surprise for you this morning."

"More exercises?" Cassandra grumbled.

"Way better." Ronin grinned.

Reena picked at her teeth with black claws.

"You shouldn't do that," he warned.

"Why?"

"It's a show of weakness."

A low growl crawled up Reena's throat. "Fuck off, Matakos."

Ronin shook his head, leaning forward and cradling the treasure in his hands. "Once we pass those mists, you'll need to put your fangs and claws away. If the other prisoners see them, you'll be challenged immediately. You show your strength in there by *not* showing it, you get me?"

"How do you know so much about the prison?" Cassandra asked.

Ronin raised a brow. "Nothing to do with the prison. Learned that lesson in the fighting rings of

Kheimos. Those with the loudest bark rarely had the strongest bite."

In truth, Ronin *had* been seeking information about Tartarus ever since Selene's arrest.

Maybe even far, far longer than that, if he were being honest with himself.

The problem was he hadn't been able to find a single former inmate anywhere. No one that could give him a sense of what awaited him nor help him imagine what Selene—and on his weaker nights, Mireille—might be going through within Tartarus proper.

"When do you think the Emperor will arrive to deliver our sentences?" Reena retracted her fangs and claws.

"Usually takes the Imperial Council about a week to deliberate." Ronin settled back in his chair. "Which means they'll be here any day now."

Cassandra's wings fell, her voice a panicked whisper. "So, we only have *hours* to figure out what to do about these?" She gestured to her back.

Ronin shot her an enigmatic smile. "Told you I have a surprise."

He lifted the vial he'd found nestled in that crumbling box in the yard, the clear liquid within glinting in the fire's flames.

"What is—" Cassandra asked.

"Veiling potion," Reena said reverently. "Where in Ethyrios did you get that?"

"Someone left it here for us." Ronin couldn't bring himself to say her name.

Cassandra extended him a kindness when she didn't say it either. "How long has it been there? And how did she know we would need it?"

Ronin rubbed at his scar, an incessant throb taking hold behind his eye-patch. "I have no idea. But from how deeply it was buried, it's been there for a very, *very* long time. She…"

Should he tell Cassandra what he knew? About her and Mireille being related? About what Mireille's father had told her in the Halfway? That Cassandra was Ethyrios's only chance for survival, and that Mireille was destined to help her?

He hesitated. He didn't want to add to Cassandra's already intense mental burden. Plus, if they *did* find Mireille beyond the mists, perhaps this was a story she should tell Cass herself.

Half of him couldn't wait to see those two together and the other half… He wasn't sure his soul would survive it.

"None of that is important right now," he said sharply. "We've got what we need to hide what you are during the sentencing. After that, we find my sister and we stay under the radar as we await our escape."

Reena snorted. "Oh yeah? Which cavalry is coming to save us then?"

"The Teles Chrysos are very close to achieving their goal of taking back Delos. Once they do, we'll *all* be getting out of here."

"Lucky us," Cassandra murmured. "So, what are we going to do as we *await our escape?*"

"Survive," Ronin answered.

He was surprised how easy it was, slipping back into command. A role he hadn't played since those bloody days on the battlefields of Aethalia. And though his forces were much, *much* smaller now, he still felt the same overwhelming sense of responsibility. To push them. To protect them.

"What about Tristan?" Cassandra whispered, her eyes shining. "Do you know what happened to him?"

Ronin shook his head sadly. "I didn't see. But the rebellion hinges upon Tristan's claim to the Crystal Throne. The Teles Chrysos have got members everywhere, including within the highest ranks of the Empire. They'll find him."

Cassandra smiled softly, her shoulders loosening. She looked so relieved that Ronin didn't dare tell her the news that could kill her hope. That Tristan's former lover, Ione Saros, was a key leader of the movement— and had been particularly vocal about how much she wanted the Prince by her side again.

But Tristan's complicated love life was none of Ronin's fucking business. He had enough of his own shit to worry about.

He handed Cassandra the vial, then rose from his chair.

"Where are you going?" Reena asked.

Ronin stared at the crackling fire. "I need to punch something."

"Me too." Cassandra stood, sliding the veiling potion into her pocket.

Reena heaved out a sigh and followed the pair out of the hall.

Hours later, even after he was sweaty and spent from pushing his body to the brink, his stubborn memories lingered.

And he had a bad feeling they were only going to get harder to ignore.

CHAPTER FOUR

T RISTAN FELL TO HIS knees and clutched his chest as the shimmering portal spit him and Ione out into a crumbling village square.

It was such an odd sensation, traveling via these opals. Felt like the Fallen Goddess herself had plunged her hand into his chest to drag him through space and time.

As he knelt on the warm, packed dirt—much warmer than the cold stone of the Northern Territories—Tristan heaved while Ione stood over him, waiting for him to regain his wits.

"You'll get used it to." She patted his shoulder before cupping a hand beneath his armpit.

The strength in her grip startled him. The Ione he'd known was a soft, delicate thing. Gaining the supernatural strength of a Fae, combined with whatever hardness had crept into her soul these many years, had forged her into something new.

The air in the small village was so thick and humid that Tristan began to sweat in his leathers. He unzipped his jacket, pulling at his white cotton shirt. Ione's gaze flicked to his chest, then bounced away.

He pretended not to notice.

A brick clocktower anchored a square ringed by vine-choked buildings. Narrow paths had been hacked through the greenery, and furry fingers of moss draped between the dwellings. A village lost to time, swallowed by the ravenous jungle.

"What is this place?" Tristan swatted his neck, then flicked a squished bug off his palm.

"Lebaedia." Ione waved at a cloud of gnats. "An old human village, abandoned when they fled the continent after the war." Tristan turned toward the sound of rushing water. "A small off-shoot of the Dordenne flows past here. It's close enough to fetch water and small enough that no cargo ships or Empire vessels can navigate it. We're well hidden. Plenty of fish in the river plus fruits and vegetables in the jungle. Anything else we need, we get from Rhamnos. The crew uses the opals to travel there. It's a much shorter journey than the one we just took. You might even be able to handle it without vomiting up your guts."

He snorted a laugh. "How long have you all been here?"

"This is just one of our various outposts throughout the continent. We stick to abandoned human villages; the Empire typically ignores them. They don't want to be reminded that two species once shared these lands." Ione sneered, removing her fur-lined cloak and revealing a white shirt over slim black pants. "We have several bases here in Akti. A few in Cernodas as well."

Tristan followed Ione across the quiet square. "Where is everyone?"

"Down in Rhamnos drumming up support for the cause. They'll be disappointed they weren't here to welcome you."

"Why?"

Ione smiled hesitantly, and Tristan's gaze caught on the small scar on her chin, the one she'd had since childhood. A lump formed in his throat. So her Turning hadn't washed away *all* signs of her previous mortality. "Some of them have been waiting centuries to express support for their Exiled Prince."

Something stirred in Tristan's chest. The something that had been stirring since he and Cassandra had that conversation in his bungalow what seemed like a lifetime ago.

He rubbed at his chest, warring emotions of excitement and terror flowing through him. He was on the cusp of becoming the leader of a movement he'd dreamed about since he was a boy. But was about to embark on it without the one woman who made it all worth it.

He would need to learn how to balance it. How to work for the good of the many when all he wanted was to dedicate his own cause to a single person. He knew how strong Cass was. Knew that Reena and Ronin would be there to protect her, too. He hoped that together they'd find a way to survive until he and the Teles Chrysos could get them out. He *forced* himself to cling to that hope.

Ione knocked upon a faded blue door, warped after centuries of exposure to the humidity. Exotic purple flowers dotted the vines blanketing the two-story brick rowhouse. From beyond the door came a faint whizzing and the steady metallic clang of a hammer.

Ione knocked harder and the clanging paused.

The Fae male who opened the door had a regal countenance. Certainly more regal than Tristan himself, even with his royal heritage.

Teal-blue eyes glowed in stark contrast to the male's ebony bald head, and a warm smile revealed a slash of glistening white teeth with two sharp, elongated canines. He raised an elegant hand, and Tristan raised his own to complete the greeting.

"Well met, Prince," the male said, a spotted tail undulating over his shoulder. "I'm—"

"Trophonios." Tristan breathed the name in a reverent whisper, and his hope soared. The inventor of Delirium was the most legendary scientific mind on the continent. If he was part of the movement...

Trophonios turned to Ione. "He looks shocked to see me. Why is he shocked to see me? Did you not brief him on anything before you brought him here?"

"We took a little detour," Ione answered, grabbing Tristan's wrist and breaking him from his stupor. "May we come in?"

"Of course, of course." Trophonios stepped aside and allowed Tristan and Ione to enter.

The ceiling soared above the eroded second floor, and metal shelves filled with glass jars lined the walls. The larger jars contained lumps of tissue suspended in liquid in increasing states of decay. Wormy trails of flesh swayed above the more deteriorated specimens. Tristan discouraged himself from guessing at the contents.

Three long tables ran parallel to the shelves, each brimming with polished tools and well-maintained contraptions.

At the back of the room, a blazing fire crackled in a large hearth, heating the room far more than necessary given the climate. Tristan wiped his brow, sweating even more profusely. Above the fire, several heavy iron pots released a variety of aromas—some earthy, some chemical, some iron-rich. A few were so pungent they stung his nostrils. He wondered if it was wise to spend a long amount of time in here.

As if sensing Tristan's discomfort, Trophonios chuckled, then opened a window. "Apologies. I'm used to the smells by now." He gestured to a worktable—the furthest from the hearth, praise Anaemos. "Come see what I've been working on. We made some wonderful progress while you were gone, Delphine. Just finished up the last of these beauties today."

Tristan jolted at Ione's title. The Delphine. The Goddess-blessed representative of Adelphinae on Ethyrios. He was reminded, yet again, of how much they still needed to discuss.

Trophonios plucked up a thin, silver cuff embedded with two specks of stone. One was a fire opal, the other a deep violet gem. Hundreds of similar cuffs gleamed from atop the table and in several barrels beside it.

"What do they do?" Tristan asked.

Ione glanced at Trophonios, raising a questioning eyebrow, and he answered, "By all means."

Ione nodded, then turned back to Tristan. "A demonstration is in order."

She snapped the cuff onto her delicate wrist, then placed a second on Tristan's before pulling him out of the workshop. As soon as they stepped into the sun, Ione disappeared in a flash of rainbow light.

Join me.

Her voice penetrated his mind and hummed through his body—far richer and clearer than any windwhisper.

He glanced at the cuff and saw the violet stone emanating a soft glow. "How?" he said out loud. "I don't even know where you are." His voice reverberated along his limbs, the gem pulsing with the cadence of his words.

Top of the hill just ahead of you. Imagine arriving there, then tap the fire opal.

Tristan closed his eyes and gently tapped the ice-cold opal.

Suddenly, that piercing sensation stabbed his chest and he was pitched forward, his eyes dragging open.

The world fractured.

Rainbow shards swarmed him, then reformed abruptly as he found himself standing atop a large hill overlooking the jungle. He didn't feel as ill this time, likely due to the short distance of the jump.

The canopy was thinner here, and fingers of brown water snaked through the greenery all the way to a shadowy mass upon the horizon—a portion of the Icthian Mountains, crawling along the Dordenne.

Tristan lifted his wrist. "What are these?"

"We needed a way to quickly move our forces throughout the continent. So Trophonios made us some new tools. And came up with the ingenious idea to add mentrite, so we can use them like commstones." Ione tapped the violet stone speck on his cuff. "The silver's conductivity increases the energy of the stones a hundredfold. That's why only small stones are needed. Trophonios has crafted enough to distribute throughout our forces."

"How many members do you have?"

"Fighting members? Thousands. Plus a silent majority within two of the major territories—Cernodas and Akti—who have pledged their support once we've achieved our ultimate goal."

"Which is?"

Ione squared her shoulders, a dazzling smile gracing her immortal features. "Taking Delos. And returning *you* to the Crystal Throne."

Tristan shook his head, in awe that not only had this rebellion grown while he was tucked away in the colonies, but that it was his former best friend and lover who'd been leading it the entire time.

"How... How has all of this happened, Ione?"

A sly smile spread onto her face.

"Are you ready to meet your people, Prince?"

CHAPTER FIVE

Fingers poked into Xenia's mouth, lifting her lips and examining her teeth.

She wanted to clamp down and bite them.

"Healthy gums," the male said. His dark eyes were set deep into a pudgy face covered with a thick black beard. "A good sign. Not like the last few I've purchased from you, Rankin."

The male removed his hands from her mouth, and Xenia dipped her head, twisting her wrists in her tight shackles.

She had no idea where on the continent she was.

After the trafficker, Rankin, had stolen her from Ohan Stolia's headquarters, she'd woken up in a truck bed covered by a canvas canopy. She'd spent the entire jostling journey—what had felt like days—alone and afraid, debilitated by the worst headache she'd ever experienced.

Today, they'd arrived at an abandoned storefront in some ramshackle little town in the middle of nowhere. The air was dry and hot enough to be on the edge of the Desolation, maybe? If so, that would put her somewhere in either northwestern Akti or southeastern Brachos.

As soon as the truck had stopped, Rankin had ripped open the canopy and dragged her out into the blinding sun, her legs stiff and her back aching.

"Look alive, pretty pet," he'd said. "This buyer has *drachas* to spend on a host gift. Asked for a pristine one." He'd dragged his gaze down her matted curls and filthy blue dress. "Hopefully he'll see the potential."

The Fae male before her now, another Beastrunner, stepped back to examine her. Xenia wanted to claw the hungry grin off his face. Fuck these shackles.

Rankin slapped a hand onto the male's shoulder. "Thoughts? I've got limited stock right now. Business is booming since Eamon Erabis took the throne. He's even less interested in upholding the Accords than his father was. Although I will say, I've rarely come across one as deliciously tempting. I've tasted her fear already and it was *divine*. Feel free to sample her before you make your decision. What kind of humans does your friend typically go for?"

Xenia froze, clenching her jaw. Her eyes prickled, but she refused to cry. These assholes didn't deserve her tears.

She wondered what Cael would say if he could see her now—in the exact scenario he'd warned her about. And the reason he'd wanted her to return to the colonies in the first place.

"Yes," the bearded male said, ignoring Rankin's question. "I think a sample is in order. But perhaps a different emotion would be a better test? Since you've already tasted her fear. I trust your palate."

Her head shot up as he approached, and she flinched from his hands, which were covered knuckle to wrist in coarse, sable fur. That combined with his round face, barrel-like chest, and the paunch jutting over his belt had Xenia guessing he was a bear bi-form.

Her shaking hands jangled her shackles as the male brushed her hair back and brought his nose to her neck.

He was all rancid breath and stale sweat, as if he too had been traveling for days. Xenia fought to suppress her gag reflex.

He sucked in a deep breath and the thread of anger woven through Xenia's fear, exhaustion, and anxiety blazed hot enough to scorch the desert outside.

Her wrists strained against her shackles and a throat-shredding roar tore past her lips. And though she knew her emotions were being manipulated, knew it was this disgusting specimen of a male heightening her anger, it felt *far* too good to deny.

Her chest heaved as she gnashed her teeth toward his ear, but he pulled away at the last second.

"Oh, you are a treat," the male chuckled. "Pity I'm not keeping you for myself."

The anger banked as abruptly as it had boiled, and an overwhelming wave of despair buckled her knees. She released a garbled sob.

Rankin backhanded her across the cheek.

The blow was a comfort, the pain far more real than whatever the other male had just pulled from her.

"Don't you fucking cry in front of a buyer," Rankin snarled. "If he wanted to feed on your sadness, he would."

"Now, now," the male said. "Don't frighten the poor thing. I'm not sure I'll be able to control myself on the journey if I'm tempted by the scent of it." He took a step back to study her further. "How much?"

"Five-hundred thousand," Rankin declared, crossing his arms as he too dipped his chin in a perusal of Xenia's body.

The male snorted, then turned to Rankin with an indignant glare. "I haven't paid that much for a human *ever*. And certainly not one I'm giving away."

"You've just tasted her. Surely you agree she's worth it."

The male stroked his beard. "Let me have a look at the rest of her."

Xenia blanched before Rankin grabbed her upper arm forcefully enough to inspire a yelp. "Come on, pet, no need for a struggle."

Xenia choked down an urge to vomit as Rankin unbuttoned her dress and pushed the fabric off her shoulders. It gathered around her waist, caught by her shackled hands.

She squeezed her eyes shut, willing the tears away. Reminded herself she was more than just a body. No matter how these Fae males were treating her.

She whimpered as rough fingers stabbed her collarbone, then traveled down her sternum before trailing along her breast.

"Tits are a bit small, but otherwise she's flawless," the bear bi-form said, pulling her dress back up. "But five-hundred thousand is excessive, by any standard. I'll give you three."

Rankin plucked at a whisker, running his tongue over a sharpened fang. "Four-fifty. I've already got an offer from a buyer in the Northern Territories. He's been begging me for a blonde. You know how rare they are."

Xenia thought he might be bluffing, remembered Rankin offering Cael two-hundred and fifty-thousand for her in that alley in Rhamnos. Wrath of Vestan, what she wouldn't give for Cael to come barreling in to save her now like he had then.

"Bullshit," the bear bi-form huffed. "Three seventy-five. That's my final offer."

Rankin's amber eyes glittered as he revealed a familiar, black-handled Typhon dagger.

Ker. Cassandra's dagger.

He must've retrieved it from the Windrider at the desk in Ohan's building.

"Four-hundred and I'll throw in this," Rankin countered. "You and I both know it's worth three times the difference. If I'm not mistaken, it's a blade from a Vestian Guard down in the colonies. A true work of art. The High Gods only know how this little kitten ended up with it."

The bear bi-form took the dagger, then swiped it through the air, admiring the whorled pattern on the blade. "Good balance," he murmured. "Though I'm not sure what use I would have for such a weapon."

He lunged and brought the edge of the knife up under Xenia's chin, nearly nicking her skin. Ice cold fear coursed through her veins.

The bear bi-form sucked in a deep breath, then chuckled. "It is quite handy for inspiring fear, though, isn't it?" He removed the blade from Xenia's throat and stepped back, flipping the dagger in his hand and thrusting the handle toward Rankin. "Deal. Wrap this and the kitten up for me. I'll meet you out at my convoy with the payment." He strode for the door, then turned back. "For the paperwork, put the name of her new owner. She's a surprise gift for the family I'm marrying my daughter into. Heading up to Diachre to see them now."

"As you wish, Laskaris," Rankin answered. "Whose name would you like me to put down?"

The bear bi-form, Laskaris, wrapped a meaty hand around the door frame. "Zephyrus."

Xenia's heart stalled.

"Arran Zephyrus."

CHAPTER SIX

CAEL ZEPHYRUS HAD FORGOTTEN that the forest-green velvet curtains in his childhood bedroom never quite shut all the way.

And even though Stoneridge, his family's lodge in Diachre, was in a near permanent state of gray, the sun still managed to peek through that crack and wake him from another night of numb, dreamless slumber.

He had no idea what time it was. Probably well into the morning. Well into the afternoon, even.

Just as he'd suspected, as soon as he'd returned to these suffocating log-paneled halls, he'd plummeted into one of his episodes.

He blinked as his consciousness slowly returned, bringing with it snippets of a conversation from what felt like eons ago.

I have...episodes. That pit of numbness I mentioned earlier? Sometimes it overtakes me, and I just disappear for weeks at a time.

He tried not to picture who had been on the receiving end of those words. But even covering his head with his pillow and shutting out the weak light couldn't stop visions of golden curls and emerald eyes from flooding his brain.

Not to mention the torturous memories of what had happened afterward.

Her taste lingered on his tongue, even now. He'd begun to wonder if he'd ever get that sweetness out of his mouth. Or if he'd carry it, as haunting as his lost wing, into this new, unwanted chapter of his immortality.

The things he'd told himself the morning after— that she was better off in the colonies, that she was safer there, that she'd be happier without him—had seemed true at the time.

Now, after a little over a week into this life he'd resigned himself to—one dedicated to duty, to his father, to Brachos—he could admit they were lies.

The door to his room flew open and, before Cael could brace himself, two heavily-muscled knees bracketed his hips and his pillow pressed down on his face.

"Were you always this lazy or did the Vestians teach you bad habits down there in the colonies?"

Erik's voice was muffled and only Cael's inability to breathe motivated him to swat his youngest brother.

Erik grabbed Cael's wrists in one hand and pressed them against his chest, using the other to keep the pillow in place. "Come on, big brother. Fight me off! I know you've got it in you."

Desperation tinged Erik's taunting words. As if the younger male was the only individual in all of Stoneridge who could see how much Cael was suffering. And the only one brave enough to goad him into returning to himself.

A big part of Cael wanted nothing more than to just lie here and let the pillow steal his breath. But some small spark, one that even in the darkest of his episodes had kept him clinging to life, flared in his chest.

He bucked his hips and pushed Erik off, his sole wing splaying out as he sat upright. Erik untangled himself from the sheets, laughing with relief.

As if he could tell how close Cael was to letting it all go.

Cael climbed out of bed to pull on a pair of dark pants and a loose white shirt. "What do you want?"

Erik's deep brown eyes—a gift from their mother—glinted with amusement. "Father sent me to get your lazy ass out of bed."

Cael whipped towards his brother, nearly toppling over. Even though it'd been weeks since he'd lost his wing, he was still getting used to the lack of counterbalance. "Why? He hasn't said a word to me since I've been back."

Erik crossed his arms, surveying the mess of Cael's room: the half-eaten plates of food, the empty bottles of wine, the sweat-soaked sheets. "He told me to tell you, using these exact words—" Erik cleared his throat, then let out a bone-chillingly accurate imitation of Arran "—*your wallowing is* finished, *Cael. Fucking clean yourself up and make yourself presentable for our guests.*"

Cael snickered, despite himself, and the sound loosened Erik's shoulders. "What guests?"

Erik stalked for the door, his fleshy gray wings bouncing. "I'd ask if you've been living under a rock for the past week, but all evidence in your room would suggest that indeed you have."

Erik gave Cael a mocking bow as he gestured through the door.

"Your fiancée and her family arrive tomorrow."

CHAPTER SEVEN

THE VASILIKANS WERE EVEN more terrifying than Cassandra remembered.

The Imperial guards had arrived at the intake tower this morning, black wings on display above raven-head helmets, broadswords clasped within gauntleted hands.

As Cassandra made her way across the yard, she tried to avoid the attention of the female at the head of their formation.

Vicereine Lykan's ice blond hair glowed in the early morning murk, her pale eyes raking a chilly gaze across the prisoners gathering before her. Her crimson lips twitched upward, and Cassandra fought the urge to cover wings she knew were hidden. She'd knocked back that veiling potion—a large enough dose to last several hours—as soon as she'd spied the first Vasilikan.

The prisoners gathered before the Vicereine, Cassandra flanked on one side by Reena, Ronin a brooding, tattooed wall of muscle on the other. If Cassandra weren't being watched so carefully, she might have asked where Eamon was.

The Vicereine's crystalline voice broke the yard's heavy silence. "You have all been accused of crimes against your Empire. Against your Emperor. The Imperial Council has found you guilty."

Cassandra bit back a scoff. They'd all been found guilty without any chance of defending themselves. Not that she was surprised.

A cruel smile revealed the Vicereine's fangs. "And I am here to deliver your sentences."

"Where's the Emperor?" A brave prisoner, a burly Beastrunner with shaggy black hair, piped up from the edge of the crowd. "He too cowardly to come here and show his face to his *subjects*?"

The Vicereine snapped her fingers and a Vasilikan flashed to the Beastrunner in a supernatural blur, delivering a heavy blow to the male's stomach. He crumpled forward, clutching his middle, but his sarcastic smile didn't falter. The Vasilikan rejoined the line with the other guards.

Cassandra glanced at Ronin, who quirked an onyx eyebrow. It was strange that Eamon would miss *her* sentencing. Perhaps this was just another of his ploys to throw her, prove how ineffectual she was. How unworthy of his presence.

"Matakos," the Vicereine spat. "You're up first."

Ronin clapped Cassandra on the shoulder, then squeezed. A show of solidarity as he sauntered over to the Vicereine.

"Take off your shirt," she commanded and Ronin obeyed, grasping it at the back of his neck and hauling it over his head. He kept the shirt clenched in his fist as two Vasilikans stepped out of line to wrap their gauntleted hands around his massive upper arms.

The Vicereine studied his bare torso, the aquamarine tattoos swirling across his chest. A mixture of attraction and disdain twisted her sharp features.

Ronin winked at her.

"Ronin Matakos," she said, upper lip curling, "you stand accused of conspiring against the Empire and undermining the interests of your Emperor with acts of treason. Do you have anything you'd like to say?"

Ronin's answering grin was feral. "He's not my fucking Emperor."

"Charming." The Vicereine's voice was cloaked in menace and power as she proclaimed, "You are hereby sentenced to life imprisonment within Tartarus."

A jet of red light burst from several feet behind the Vasilikans, seemingly out of nowhere. From the wards themselves?

It speared into Ronin's chest, right over his heart. Flesh crackled and popped as the smell of burnt hair and charred skin wafted through the yard.

Ronin sucked heaving breaths through clenched teeth, but to his credit, didn't make a single sound.

The light dissolved, revealing an angry, V-shaped brand that had burned away a section of Ronin's tattoos.

The Vicereine traced a hand up his stomach, her fingers rippling over the muscled grooves, then clucked her tongue. "Pity to ruin such a work of art." She pressed a thumb against Ronin's burn.

"Fuck you," he gasped, straining against the Vasilikans. "When I get out of here, I'm going to rip off your wings and feed them to your lover." He spat, the blood-tinged glob splattering at her feet. "Imperial whore."

She smiled and cupped his cheek. "Hold on to that anger as long as you can, Matakos. It might even serve you in there." She ripped the shirt from his hands and shoved it against his chest. "Get dressed and go wait by the gate while we deal with the rest of the dregs."

Ronin slipped his shirt on, wincing as the gray fabric slid over his wound, then turned to the towering obsidian gate across the yard. What fresh torments awaited the prisoners beyond those mist-shrouded doors?

The Vicereine performed the same show on the remaining prisoners, the wards branding each with a life sentence.

During Reena's turn, she elongated a claw and swiped it across the Vicereine's face, drawing a line of blood. Lykan didn't retaliate, merely offered Reena a crazed smile and made a snide remark about how quickly Tartarus would crush her spirit.

After what seemed like hours, Cassandra was the only prisoner left to receive her sentence. The rest of the group had joined Ronin at the gate, many collapsed, sobbing, in the dirt.

The Vicereine aimed a violent, gleeful grin at Cassandra, who sent back a matching one before the Vicereine crooked her finger, beckoning. "Cassandra Fortin. The *Savior* Sister. Come forth and receive your sentence."

Cassandra kept the smile on her face as she approached. She would not be broken by this golden-winged bitch.

The Vasilikans grabbed Cassandra's arms and held her in place as the Vicereine dipped her head so close that her nose caressed Cassandra's cheek.

Cassandra tensed, worried that Lykan might be able to scent the veiling potion, sense what Cassandra had become.

But the Vicereine gave no hint she'd uncovered the deception as she whispered, "It's a rather ironic title, actually. Since all the obliviates you *saved* have been re-obliviated and sent to the continent."

Cassandra's heart spilled a fresh wave of grief. All the work that she, Reena, Hella, and Borea had done to save those poor humans, undone by the monster this female served.

She didn't dare let anything show as she cast a stony stare past the Vicereine into the barren yard.

"Though you've always tried to raise yourself above your station, haven't you?" The Vicereine's laughter tickled Cassandra's cheek. "Thinking yourself worthy of the Exiled Prince. Though I can hardly blame you for trying." Her lips brushed Cassandra's ear. "Sometimes even *I* miss the feeling of him moving inside me. The pleasure he conjured with those skillful hands and that glorious tongue."

Cassandra's restraint snapped. She snarled, jerking forward to smash her forehead into Lykan's face. The Vicereine pulled back before she could manage it, her low chuckle boiling Cassandra's blood. She couldn't stop the question that ripped up her throat. "What has Eamon done with him?"

The sting of the Vicereine's slap did nothing to quell Cassandra's rage. "Tristan will be punished for his insolence. And do not *dare* speak of your Emperor so casually."

The Vicereine's eye twitched. The smallest of tells.

And the words she'd chosen.

Will be punished. Not *has been* punished.

The Vicereine grabbed Cassandra's upper arm, and the memory took over instantaneously.

Eamon Erabis, black wings askew and roaring in frustration as he tore apart an ornate, gilded room—decor Cassandra recognized from the Vicereine's palace. Lykan watched on helplessly, unable to soothe his anger.

Had Tristan escaped?

Hope blazed through Cassandra's chest, bright enough to dim the mists curling around the stone gate.

But before she could think on it further, or question how she was able to view the memory from touch alone and without Lykan noticing, the Vicereine ripped off Cassandra's shirt and tossed it into the dirt. Cassandra dipped her eyes to the bare space above her collarbone where Tristan's mark was still hidden by the veiling potion.

"Cassandra Fortin," the Vicereine intoned, "you are hereby sentenced, by order of his Imperial Majesty Eamon Erabis, to *death* for your crimes."

Cassandra barely had a second to breathe before the red light bolted from the wards and seared her chest. Her legs buckled, and the two Vasilikans gripped her arms tighter to keep her upright.

A scream sawed past her lips. She didn't want to give the Vicereine the satisfaction, but she couldn't help it. Fire tore through her chest and for a moment, she was worried she might pass out from the pain.

The light sucked back into the wards, and Cassandra glanced down at her pink, smoldering skin. At the letter inside the circle bubbling and blistering her flesh.

T. For *Than*.

Death.

The irony of her impending death—announced seconds after that vision that suggested Tristan might be free—was suddenly the most hilarious thing she'd ever heard.

Peals of uproarious laughter tore up her throat as the Vicereine snatched her chin. "Yes, *girl*, it is funny, isn't it? You'll find out exactly how funny very, very shortly."

The Vicereine shoved Cassandra toward the gate, and the stone doors groaned open, leaking clouds of night-dark mist.

"Give your executioner my regards," the Vicereine crooned.

Cassandra snatched up her shirt, then struggled back into it as she joined Ronin and Reena.

"Don't worry, Cass." Reena said, her face tight with fear as she looped an arm around Cassandra's shoulders. Seeing *Reena* afraid—one of the bravest females with the most *I-couldn't-give-less-of-a-shit* attitudes Cassandra had ever known—chilled her to the bone. "We'll figure it out."

Cassandra looked to Ronin, who wore a similarly horrified expression, but did his best to affirm Reena's statement with a stiff nod.

Cassandra tossed a glance over her shoulder, back toward the Vicereine and the Vasilikans. The Vicereine murmured something into the wards before the entire group vanished.

The obsidian gate fully opened, and several prisoners jumped at the boom that echoed across the yard.

While the others hesitated, Cassandra, Reena, and Ronin stepped forward.

They held hands as they crossed the threshold, swallowed by the swirling mists.

CHAPTER EIGHT

THE BLOWN-OUT CRATER BEFORE Tristan smoldered, the smoke stinging eyes already prickling with furious tears.

"There's an office building a few blocks away, right at the edge of the damage, that remained intact," said General Seraavi Pfania, the fuchsia-eyed Deathstalker who headed the Cernodas arm of the Teles Chrysos. "We've set up operations there, and any of our members with healer's training have been put on duty to assist the staff. All the surviving patients have been successfully transported, along with anyone wounded in the attack."

"I want to see them," Tristan said, peeling his gaze away from the Teles symbols crudely painted on the jagged shards of concrete that used to be a hospital in downtown Lodesvale. "They need to know we didn't do this."

Ione placed a hand on Tristan's forearm, and for the first time during this continental tour, his grief was too vast for him to immediately shrug her off. She pressed her advantage, sidling close enough to stroke his feathers with her own. "It's not the best idea, Prince. If word gets back to your brother—"

"Take me there," Tristan said, ignoring Ione and turning to General Pfania.

"It would be our honor, Highness." Ruby curls cascaded past Seraavi's shoulder as she bowed her half-shaved head. She picked her way out of what Tristan assumed had been the hospital courtyard, then called over her shoulder, "It's just a short walk this way."

Tristan followed, Ione on his heels.

Lodesvale was the third city they'd visited since leaving Lebaedia four days ago. The third city where he'd spent days conversing with the hopeful Fae who'd joined the movement. And the third city where Tristan had encountered a level of destruction that made him question how he and his brother could possibly be related.

"How long has he been doing this?" Tristan asked through gritted teeth.

"Months," Ione answered. "The more sympathy we gain among the population, the more aggressive his attacks."

Tristan nodded. "It's the same tactic he used in the colonies. Strikes that *he* orchestrated, then blamed on the Teles Chrysos."

Though in the colonies it had been empty banks and trade organization buildings. Not *hospitals*, for fuck's sake.

"Many Fae have fallen for it," Seraavi said, "but not all. Especially those on the ground who see our forces pour in to help rebuild. We wonder if he realizes how much he's helping our recruiting efforts."

"He's never attacked a hospital before," Ione piped up, echoing Tristan's thoughts as they picked their way through the rubble.

It was the identifiable detritus within the piles of smashed brick, broken glass, and twisted metal that hit Tristan the hardest. A crumpled bed sheet dotted with tiny pink flowers. A guitar with popped strings and a broken neck. A stuffed rabbit sporting a puff of white where its ear should have been.

He pinched the bridge of his nose, his sinuses stinging.

"He's getting desperate," Ione said, tripping over a concrete block and grabbing Tristan's arm for support. "We fear this specific attack was in retaliation for you joining us."

"Does he know I've joined?"

"You disappeared from that cell beneath the Vicereine's palace. I doubt he thinks you just vanished into thin air."

Seraavi turned a corner. "It's just up here, Your Highness."

The scene in the co-opted office building stoked Tristan's already red-hot fury to volcanic levels.

Stretched across the floor in defiance of the cubicle pattern etched into the carpet were rows and rows of cots. Fae of all three sub-species filled them, tended to by hospital staff and rebels. The severity of their wounds shouldn't have been possible, not with their supernatural healing abilities.

Tristan fought a wave of nausea, then turned to Seraavi. "Why haven't they healed yet?"

"Snakebites," Seraavi said with a shame-filled grimace. "The Deathstalker venom slows the process. It can take weeks, even months, to heal an injury that would typically be gone in less than a day."

Ione's wings drooped while Tristan fought an urge to punch his fist through the wall.

There were fucking *children* on those cots.

"How could he do this?" Tristan asked pointlessly.

"All he cares about is holding the Crystal Throne," Ione said. "And he's threatened by us. By *you*. He's trying to win public sentiment by dragging our movement's name through the mud."

Tristan was only half-listening, his gaze catching on a young male Beastrunner who looked to be the same age Tristan had been at his exile. The young male—some kind of hare bi-form based on the two furry ears flopping atop his tawny hair—fidgeted with his woven blue blanket as a healer checked his bandages. The look of cold, helpless fury on the young male's face no doubt matched Tristan's own.

"Do you have any idea where he plans to attack next?" Tristan asked.

"Our spies in Delos are keeping their eyes and ears open," Seraavi answered. "Most of the attacks have occurred here in Cernodas or down in Akti, the territories most sympathetic to our cause. We'll avert as many as we can before we're called upon to march with you, Highness."

"And when will that be?" Tristan turned to Ione.

"Soon," Ione said, grasping Tristan's hand. "There's something I'd like to discuss with you first." She nodded to Seraavi. "Thank you for your time today, General."

The Deathstalker bowed before loping through the maze of cots to assist with the healing.

Tristan's rage was still surging through his veins as Ione tapped her cuff and portaled them back to Lebaedia.

CHAPTER NINE

TRISTAN COULDN'T GET VISIONS of those wounded Fae in Lodesvale out of his head.

They drowned out nearly everything else, save for the ever-present longing in his chest for Cassandra. He wanted to solve the two problems simultaneously: save his love *and* his people.

Behind him, Ione banged around her kitchen chopping herbs, stirring pots, and softly cursing. She'd always been a mess while cooking. Far messier than Tristan. But somehow, her culinary sorcery always won out in the end.

Though as the bitter scent of burnt onions wafted, he thought perhaps he shouldn't judge anything yet.

As soon as they'd returned, Ione had invited him to dine with her. After everything she'd done for him, it didn't feel right to refuse. He'd offered to help her cook, but she'd insisted with something like hope crawling through her eyes.

Tristan hadn't commented on it.

Hadn't commented on *anything* since she'd rescued him. At least, nothing personal. Beside a few lingering looks and overly familiar touches on her part, things between them had been nothing but professional. And while Tristan was inclined to keep it that way, he had a feeling he was about to discover her true intentions.

He was more tense now than he'd been in that cell beneath the Vicereine's palace.

"Are you sure you don't want any help?" he offered over his shoulder.

"I'm fine!" she called back, cursing again. "Almost ready!"

Outside her window, the setting sun cast bands of gold and salmon across the vine-covered buildings. A softly cleared throat tore Tristan from the view, and he turned to see Ione standing by the table, two tapered candles flickering shadows across the feast she'd laid out.

"Dinner is served," she said quietly, tucking a strand of honey hair behind her ear and untying her apron. "Pour us some drinks while I change? Be right back."

Ione slipped down the hall and up the stairs to her bedroom while Tristan began perusing her wine rack.

For a rebel base in the middle of the jungle, she had quite a selection—buttery whites from the coasts of Akti, plummy burgundies from the hills of Nephes, and even a few sweet, fortified wines from the southern human colonies.

He looked toward the table, saw that Ione had prepared seafood, and selected a bottle of white. He popped the cork, then glugged out two glasses and placed them next to the opulent spread.

Ione had gone all out.

On a platter surrounded by roast potatoes and thick stalks of asparagus, an entire silvery-scaled fish peered up at him through a glassy eye. Next to it, an ice-filled plate held six oysters on the half-shell, a mignonette of shallots and vinegar floating atop the creamy flesh.

Tristan swallowed his discomfort. There was no way the oysters hadn't been a deliberate choice. Not only were they a known aphrodisiac, but they'd certainly come from Vaengya, the small colonial town where Ione's human parents had lived before journeying to the continent to work for Tristan's mother, Empress Mila.

They were also the source of that pearl ring Tristan had given to Ione lifetimes ago.

He took a gulping sip of wine, and then nearly choked on it as Ione returned from her room. Her freshly-brushed hair cascaded down her shoulders in two shining, golden sheets, and she'd changed into what looked more like a slip than a dress. As she approached the table, the sage-green silk shifted, barely held in place by two thin straps.

Certainly not an outfit one would wear for dinner with a mere colleague.

Amatu fucking *save* him.

He couldn't deny that she looked beautiful. She always had. And now as Fae, she was downright staggering. Any other male would've crashed to his knees and begged to worship at her feet.

But he'd rather be dining with someone else.

"Shall we?" Ione demurred, taking her seat and sliding three oysters onto each of their plates. She raised one toward him, a silent toast, and he did the same before tipping the shell to his lips and swallowing. The briny liquid combined with the acidic mignonette and sweet, creamy oyster was divine. But he'd expect nothing less from the woman who'd taught him to cook.

They finished the appetizer in silence, then helped themselves to the fish. He tried not to squirm. She was awfully silent since she'd laid this trap.

He broke first. "So…what's with all this?"

Ione cocked a pale brow, wrapping her lips around a piece of flaky white fish. She chewed softly, then swallowed. "What's with all what?"

Tristan sat back, swirling his wine. "The meal. The candles. The, uh, dress? I assume you're trying to seduce me."

Ione laughed, a pleasant tinkle. "As if such a thing were possible. Your heart is occupied elsewhere, is it not?"

"Yes."

She knew it was. He didn't want to talk about Cassandra with her. Wished she would let it go.

She didn't, of course.

"Why her?"

Genuine curiosity, maybe even a speck of disbelief, laced Ione's tone. She twirled the stem of her wine glass and Tristan glanced at her fingers. Short, scrubbed nails and rough, reddened knuckles. A warrior's hands.

Though this was a very different type of battle.

"Because she sees every part of me," he answered. "The good, the bad, and the messy. And embraces it without judgment. I feel the same about her. Our fragments fit together."

A sad smile crept onto Ione's lips. "You might have said the same thing about us once."

"Is that how love works then? She needs to possess some skill or attribute you don't so you can rationalize why I'd choose her over you?" Weeks of pent-up frustration shot for the closest target. "This isn't a meritocracy, Ione. I love her. I belong to her. And I always will."

They were silent for a few moments as the weight of his words washed over her. To her credit, she seemed to take it in stride, sipping her wine and tracing circles on the tablecloth, no hint of hurt or sadness on her face.

After a moment, he asked, "Has there been no one else for you in all this time? I find that extremely difficult to believe."

She let out a breathy little laugh. "I certainly wasn't celibate. I had my fun. Made my mistakes. But there's been no one important."

Just fucking say it, he silently begged. If she still wanted him, was angling to rekindle their affair, he was on edge waiting for her to come out with it. She was so outspoken everywhere else. High Gods, even when they were younger she used to boss him around the kitchen.

But the Ione he'd known had always been careful with her softer feelings. Back in Delos, she'd loved him in secret for just as long as he'd loved her. It was only when he'd finally confessed his feelings that she'd admitted to her own.

At the time, he'd chalked it up to fear. She'd been a human in love with a Fae. And not just any Fae—the Imperial Heir to the Crystal Throne of Ethyrios.

But they were *both* Fae now. "What do you want from me?"

She released a heavy sigh, then crossed her arms on the table. "It's not about what I want. It's about what the Goddess wants."

He recoiled, trying to keep the shock off his face. "What are you talking about?"

"Have you heard the prophecy?"

Tristan nodded. "Ronin told me. When he was trying to recruit me. On *your* behalf, I'm assuming. Why didn't you come down yourself? I've been wondering ever since you rescued me."

"Because you needed to make the decision on your own. And I needed to know if you still believed in your vision for this world. I didn't want…" She looked up toward the ceiling, tears staining her lower lashes. "*Two futures sown, one future known. Born from phantom wings and mortal bones, a new Delphine will rise.*"

She recaptured his gaze, awaiting his interpretation of the lines.

He'd been considering them since the moment he'd heard them in the Serpent's Den.

Ione prodded, "Two futures sown into one. Yours and mine. Your love Turned me into the Delphine, Tristan. And it's our love that will save this world."

She said it with such certainty that a headache began to form behind his eyeballs.

"*A new Delphine will rise* to..." Tristan insisted, knowing she'd left out a word. "No one knows the other half of the prophecy. Except maybe my brother, considering the Compendium's been kept within the palace for centuries."

"I don't need to know the other half," Ione said, wrapping her fingers around his. It took all his willpower not to recoil from her touch. "I know you think you love her, but she cannot be who the Goddess has intended for you. She is *human*. What's the point of promising yourself to her when you know you'll lose her?"

Tristan scoffed. "Would you have said the same about yourself two hundred years ago?" Had Ione washed her humanity away that easily?

"You may have already lost her."

Anger throbbed through his veins. He broke her gaze, gulping his wine and staring out the window.

"Tristan," she said, voice gentle, "you have a soft heart. It's what drew me to you in the first place. But sometimes, even a soft heart needs to make a hard decision. Would you truly choose a single mortal woman over the lives of everyone in Ethyrios? Because that is what will happen if you deny the Goddess's will. It may be painful for you, but imagine everything this world could gain." She dipped her head, stroking her fingers over his knuckles. "And would it really be so terrible? To learn to love me again?"

She knew exactly where to hit him—right in his guilt—to silence his protests. The corner of her lip curled, as if she knew the blow she'd landed.

"There's no need to make any decisions right now," she said, as if she hadn't just asked him to rip his fucking heart out and offer it to her on a platter. She sat back and closed her eyes, folding her palms across her chest. "We ask the Creator for guidance and safety, and that she may bestow her wisdom upon us."

His mind was swirling with everything Ione had said. Everything she'd claimed. When he'd decided to join the Teles Chrysos, to fight for his birthright, he never imagined it would come at such a cost.

Ione rose and began clearing plates. He grabbed her wrist to halt her.

"Let me," he said, rising from his chair. "You cooked, I'll clean. It's only fair."

Ione nodded. "I'll only say one more thing tonight. You need to consider her feelings as well. How fair would it be for you to keep her, for you to stay young and healthy while she grows old and frail? For her to know you will live lifetimes after her? Do you really want to subject her to that heartache?"

He knew it was cruel, but he couldn't help asking the question. "And what if I Turned her?"

Ione, Goddess bless her, didn't even flinch. "That's not possible."

"Why not?"

"Adelphinae would not allow it. She would have to bless your union. And she has already blessed ours. I wouldn't be in this body if she hadn't. I would not be the Delphine."

Tristan turned to his task as Ione slipped away from the table. He needed to pull himself together, needed to get some rest. Which, at the moment, felt like an impossibility.

And he certainly didn't feel like arguing with Ione anymore this evening. So he'd play along.

For now.

But he wanted that Compendium. Needed to hear the other half of that prophecy.

Needed to learn what consequences the ancient book might reveal for his anxious heart.

CHAPTER TEN

THE BLACK MISTS WERE so thick Cassandra could barely see a foot in front of her face. She'd lost all trace of the other prisoners besides Reena and Ronin.

She didn't know how long they'd been walking.

She didn't even know if they were walking in the right direction, though the ground beneath their feet sloped gently downward. As if it were funneling them somewhere.

Reena's muffled voice cut through the darkness, mirroring Cassandra's thoughts. "Where, exactly, are we going?"

Ronin grunted, rubbing at the brand beneath his prison shirt. "Don't know, but my..." He twisted his head to the side, cracking his neck and clenching his teeth. "But my wolf keeps harassing me to go *this* way. I think he senses something."

"Something?" Reena asked. "Or some*one*?"

From the tension in Ronin's shoulders, Cassandra guessed it was his former lover and not his sister.

"Stay close," was all he grumbled.

Cassandra plodded forward, dragging her wings across the dusty ground. High *Gods* it felt good to give her back muscles a break. Thankfully, Ronin hadn't seen fit to scold her about it when the veiling potion had worn off…minutes ago? Hours ago? Days ago?

It was difficult to assess the passage of time in this place. With no sun nor moon above and nothing but packed dirt beneath their feet, only endless black spread out in every direction.

Occasionally, Cassandra caught a looming silhouette far ahead. But no matter how many steps they took toward it, it never shifted position nor came any closer. Remained a hint of palatial shadow on the fuzzy horizon.

She rubbed at her stomach, wondering why she wasn't hungry or thirsty or tired. And why her other emotions weren't on overdrive.

She should be terrified of whatever lay beyond these mists. Hopeful that Tristan had escaped his brother's clutches. Anxious about her death sentence.

But the enveloping darkness dampened *everything*.

Were Ronin and Reena feeling as numb?

She couldn't even muster the will to ask.

So she just kept plodding forward through the void.

Minutes, hours, days later…

A scream tore through the mists, and the trio halted.

"What was that?" Reena asked, tone flat.

Ronin cocked his head, but only dreadful silence shouted back. He shrugged and the group continued forward.

No one said a thing when they came upon the body sprawled face-down in the dirt.

Ronin bent down to flip it over.

A Beastrunner male—the shaggy-haired prisoner who'd asked the Vicereine why Eamon hadn't attended sentencing.

His skin bore no marks, and his gray prison uniform, though streaked with black dust, was intact. The unnatural stillness of his chest was the only sign he wasn't merely sleeping. Well, that and his body was completely devoid of color, like a black-and-white photograph.

Cassandra couldn't tell if it was real or if the mists were affecting her vision.

Reena leaned down to touch the male's head and chest, murmuring a prayer. "What do we do?" Her voice sounded hollow. "We can't just leave him here."

"We can," Ronin said, and Reena frowned, rising to her feet. "And we will.

"Keep walking."

They kept walking and walking and walking.

And walking.

Nothing shone through the mists. No light. No sounds. No hint of a break in the darkness.

Cassandra wondered if this was what it felt like to go mad. Perhaps she'd died in the intake yard. Perhaps her body was still out there. Perhaps she was nothing more than a soul wandering through an eternal night.

A low hum bloomed to life between her ears.

At first, she thought it was the sound of her blood rushing through her veins.

But then it began to rise, both in pitch and frequency, before breaking apart into murmuring whispers. A susurration of voices.

Thousands.

Millions.

Billions.

She glanced sidelong toward Reena, whose eyes were closed and whose lips were moving unnaturally fast.

Cassandra grabbed Reena's arm, then snatched her hand back, hissing. Reena's skin was so cold it burned Cassandra's fingertips.

"Ronin," she croaked out. "What's wrong with her?"

The voices in Cassandra's mind grew louder and louder. So loud they rattled her brain against her skull. Ronin clutched at his shaved temples, squeezing his eyes shut, as if he heard them, too.

She was about to release a scream as agonized as the one they'd heard earlier—yesterday? A week ago? Ten years ago?—when the voices stopped, and the mists pulsed. Prisms shimmered in her peripheral vision, but disappeared as soon as she turned to catch sight of them.

Reena's lids popped open, revealing milky white in place of her familiar golden eyes.

Ronin shoved Cassandra behind him, muttering, "The chronomancer in…"

He trailed off and before Cassandra could ask what he meant, Reena's lips spread into a chilling, rictus grin, wrinkling her cheeks. When she spoke, her voice rang out in a monstrous echo.

"Her eyes have been called. The paths converge. He is searching for a way in."

"Reena," Ronin growled, "what the fuck are you—"

In a flash of orange and black fur, Reena shifted into her tiger, then dove into the mists, an iridescent shimmer trailing behind her.

Cassandra twisted out of Ronin's grip, then gave chase, shouting Reena's name into the shadows. Her feet pounded the dirt and her wings bounced against her back. The rainbow glow of Reena's trail faded the farther she ran.

A strong arm curled around Cassandra's waist and Ronin hauled her back against his chest, his fingers tangling in her feathers. "Let her go, Cass. Let her *go*. We need to get out of these mists or we're not going to survive. And we can't help her if we're dead."

Cassandra collapsed in Ronin's arms, too dazed to move. She raised a hand to her cheek, surprised to find wetness.

As soon as she recognized her tears, her suppressed emotions crashed upon her in a disorienting wave. Terror, anxiety, exhaustion, grief, agony, panic. So many, she could barely identify them all.

Those voices overtook her mind, morphing into screams so loud she clapped her hands over her ears. Before she realized *she* was the one screaming.

CHAPTER ELEVEN

CASSANDRA'S CONSCIOUSNESS SLAMMED BACK into her body, jolting her limbs and nearly toppling her to the ground before she felt Ronin's hands on her shoulders.

Her head pounded, her vision was blurry, and her throat felt like it had been scraped clean with a wire brush.

But the air was clear. Were they out of the mists? And where had Reena—

Reena.

Cassandra swiveled, half expecting to see the tiger bi-form standing beside her.

But there was nothing but a moat that stretched out so far in either direction that it disappeared into the black mist. Above, the moon shone bright on a cloudless night.

"Where..." she attempted, the words barely a squeak. "Where are we?"

A few paces away, an obsidian bridge crossed the moat to an unexpected sight. "Is that a—"

"It's a *city*," Ronin gaped.

It looked more like a sculpture.

On the far end of the bridge, rising up from the middle of nowhere, rings of buildings and cobblestoned streets spread out beneath a domineering castle crafted from the same black stone as the intake tower. Two sharp spires threaded with red polemite pierced the sky like blood-drenched fangs.

Ronin guided Cassandra along the bridge as she peered over the edge into the still, glossy water below. Were the large, shadowy masses shifting beneath the surface real, or was she still disoriented from her journey through the mists?

Her stomach grumbled, her missing hunger roaring to life and gnawing at her insides. How long had they been wandering? And where were the other prisoners from the intake tower?

Guilt pierced her chest; they'd *left* Reena behind. Although, if Cassandra and Ronin had arrived at this city, perhaps Reena had as well?

The faint din of voices grew louder as she and Ronin reached the end of the bridge. A towering wall of obsidian soared above them, and she caught a hint of movement beyond the lowered iron portcullis. Its holes were large enough for a human or Fae to pass through and she wondered why it was lowered.

What were they trying to keep out?

She glanced at those shifting shadows in the moat, then paused to pick up a small pebble. She tossed it over the bridge, and circles rippled out from where it plinked into the water.

Just as the waves flattened, an enormous, reptilian beast with a mottled brown-and-green scaled body burst upward, snapping a long snout full of sharp teeth inches away from the bridge.

"Guess we're not trying to escape via the moat," Ronin grumbled as three more beasts surged toward the bridge and laughter rang out above the city wall.

They'd gained an audience.

Spectators gathered on stone balconies and between the old-fashioned buildings. Whether they were Fae or human or a mix of both, Cassandra couldn't yet tell. Though she did spy a few pairs of wings, and also saw more color than expected. The prisoners were no longer wearing their gray uniforms.

The portcullis rumbled upward, and a thin male Beastrunner emerged, clapping. He had cropped brown hair and sharp features, all the more weasel-like with his pencil-thin mustache and goatee.

His dark eyes gleamed with amusement, and his nasally tone grated Cassandra's bones. "My sincerest congratulations on your survival."

"Are we the only ones who've arrived?" Cassandra asked, her heart in her throat at the thought of Reena alone and lost in that terrible emptiness.

The male nodded, pouting. "Even less than usual, I'd say. Remy Wormwood. It's a pleasure to make your acquaintance." He gestured backward as the portcullis clanged to a thunderous halt and the city yawned out behind it.

"Welcome to Tartarus."

It *was* a city. Cassandra could scarcely believe it as Wormwood led her and Ronin along the cobbled, upward sloping streets that wended toward the castle.

Candles flickered in lead-glass windows and flames danced in cast-iron streetlamps. Most of the timber-framed buildings seemed to be private dwellings. At least until they came upon the main city square halfway up the hill where two taverns occupied opposite corners.

The more opulent of the two bore a sign that read World's End in filigreed lettering. Red curtains hung in the upper floor windows above a gold-and-black striped awning and golden double doors.

At the south corner, a hand-painted side reading The Other Place hung above a dilapidated tavern. Outside, wearied Fae gathered in quiet conversation at chipped wooden tables. They were mostly Beastrunners and Deathstalkers, but she did see a scant number of Windriders with both feathered and fleshy wings.

What she didn't see were any humans.

Ronin scanned every face they passed. Searching for Reena? Selene?

Or Mireille?

"Keep up!" Wormwood called from the other end of the square, his whiskers twitching at his cheeks. "I am sure you are anxious to get some food and rest. All will be possible after he has reviewed your sentences."

Wormwood turned down another cobbled street, moving so quickly that Cassandra didn't have a chance to take in her surroundings. He sailed around a corner, arriving at a graveled courtyard that led to the castle entrance. It looked much larger than it had from across the bridge, the two spires rising at least ten stories up. Wormwood ushered them through a large archway. "Come, come, my friends! There's nothing to fear."

"Bullshit," Ronin grumbled.

Two obsidian staircases bracketed the soaring foyer, past which she heard the booming, sinister tones of gathered male voices.

Wormwood led them into a throne room trisected by lines of thick black columns. Fae males cloaked in furs and leather filled the hall, armed to the teeth with polished stone weapons hanging from their backs and hips. Tall, iron candelabras bathed the room in pockets of light and shadow, and at the far end, an enormous obsidian throne veined with red polemite sat empty atop a stepped dais.

The Fae warriors—Cassandra wasn't sure what else to call them; they appeared dressed for war and had an air of authority she hadn't sensed from the Fae in the streets—stilled as she, Ronin, and Wormwood passed, though they didn't pause their conversations.

Multiple pairs of eyes crawled over her glimmering white feathers. Reactions to Ronin were mixed, some faces pinched with distaste, while others widened in awe.

Wormwood clapped his hands, seeking the hall's attention, then arranged Ronin and Cassandra on either side of the aisle.

Flashing a slimy grin, he took to the dais. "Well, Brethren. What a joyous day! It has been some time since the Emperor sent us new citizens." He snickered, and the warriors—the Brethren—laughed along with him. "The ledgers confirmed there were more. May their eternal souls find peace within the Tartaran mists."

Cassandra's chest ached. She hadn't spied Reena anywhere within the city walls. She was losing hope that her friend had made it here.

Wormwood continued, "But these two fine specimens have survived! And I'm sure you're all as anxious as I am to reveal their sentences and see what the Koenig has in store for them."

The males roared, stomping their feet and pounding their chests.

Footsteps sounded from the entrance and the frenzied shouting was replaced by creaking leather as, to a one, every male in the hall swept to their knees and bowed their heads.

Next to the throne, Wormwood genuflected as well, snapping at Cassandra and Ronin. She dropped down, draping her wings along her back, then tugged Ronin's wrist, forcing him to reluctantly follow.

Keeping her head tucked, she dared a side-long glance at the hulking, shirtless Windrider male who stalked up onto the dais. Well, she assumed he was a Windrider. He certainly wasn't a Deathstalker—no tell-tale serpentine features—and he didn't have the musky, animal scent of a Beastrunner. But where his wings should have been, two long scars snaked down his shoulder blades.

He turned in front of the throne, then raised his palms to signal the kneeling crowd to rise. Wheat-colored hair fell past his broad shoulders and his sapphire eyes were ringed with smudged kohl. He was strikingly handsome, even with the vicious scars marring the bottom half of his face. As if the flesh there had been burned away. Above his leather pants, a baldric of knives crossed his chest and, from a strap on his back, he pulled a colossal obsidian warhammer. Markings in some ancient language were etched down the handle, and inlaid into the head was a heart-shaped gem of crimson polemite.

Despite the scars and missing wings, immense power flowed from the piercing gaze he swept across the crowd. It snagged on Cassandra's wings, and confusion twisted his ruined features as he leaned his hammer against the throne.

Cassandra swallowed, willing her heart to stop pounding. Could he tell what she was? What she'd been?

Wormwood spoke up. "As you may have guessed, I serve the Koenig. I act as a sort of…translator."

Cassandra didn't dare ask why the Koenig needed a translator, but Ronin had no such qualms.

"Oh, yeah?" Ronin crossed his own massive, tattooed arms and held the Koenig's flinty gaze. "He can't speak for himself?"

The Koenig's wide lips pulled back to expose a row of pearly white teeth. A shark's grin. Cassandra shuddered as a mangled lump of gray flesh rolled out between parted lips.

Someone had cut out his tongue.

Wormwood slithered down from the dais, his murky brown eyes drinking up Ronin's broad chest. "They took his tongue at the same time as they took his wings. But despite those limitations, he has managed to maintain authority in Tartarus through sheer force of will. And violence, of course. That's the only currency that matters here. You'll see. But we must warn you" —Wormwood leaned in close enough to touch his nose to Ronin's bulging shoulder— "he does not tolerate insolence. Nor insubordination. He may let you pass today because you've just arrived, but his patience is extremely limited. I would not advise testing it."

Ronin sniffed, uncrossing his arms and holding the Koenig's gaze as the male made a series of hand gestures toward Wormwood.

"Yes, yes." Wormwood bowed obsequiously. "My apologies for the delay, sire." He turned back to the prisoners. "Ronin Matakos, the Butcher of Aethalia. Your reputation is legendary enough to have slipped past these wards. So curious to find an Imperial darling here." Wormwood gestured toward Ronin's torso, raising a single brow. "Please confirm your sentence."

Ronin pulled aside his collar, exposing his V-shaped brand.

"Life. Wonderful. And your crime?"

"Treason," Ronin grunted.

Wormwood squeaked out a laugh. "Bold, given your history. Well, I don't need to ask about your skills, do I? You'll join the Brethren. The Koenig can always use another powerful male to add to his peace-keeping force."

At the throne, the Koenig nodded.

Wormwood glanced at Cassandra's shirt. "And you, prisoner 161803? What is your name?"

Cassandra bit the inside of her cheek, wondering if she should lie. But no one in here would've known her or that she'd been human before she arrived. "Cassandra Fortin."

Wormwood's whiskers rustled as he stared excitedly at her left breast. Cassandra blew out a breath and pulled aside her shirt.

"Yes, yes. Just as I suspected." He whispered in the Koenig's ear, and the male's kohl-lined eyes widened then darted to Cassandra, examining her more intensely. Her heart hammered so aggressively she was sure the Fae around her could hear it. "You've been given a death sentence."

Gasps scuttled through the hall.

"Yes," was all she said.

Wormwood scratched a whiskered cheek, his eyes sliding toward the Koenig. "Why?"

Cassandra shrugged. "Perhaps the Emperor is jealous that my wings are so much prettier than his."

Wormwood's face broke into wide grin. "They are that, indeed. A beautiful color, too. Rather rare."

Cassandra drew her chin up, waiting to see how this played out. She wasn't about to confirm or deny *anything*.

"Your sentence is rather rare as well. Did you know that?" Wormwood cocked his head. "In the seven centuries of the prison's existence, very few had been given a death sentence. What's the point? Life within the wards is akin to death. Even those who receive less than a life sentence typically choose to stay here rather than chasing their freedom in the mists."

"Who carries out the sentence?" Ronin asked, reaching for Cassandra's hand.

Wormwood shot the Koenig an amused smile. "Who do you think?"

Faster than Cassandra could blink, the Koenig tore a knife from his baldric and whipped it toward her.

A gloved hand appeared, seemingly out of nowhere, and grabbed it a hairsbreadth from Cassandra's heart.

Outraged shouts burst through the hall, and she fought to catch her breath as a cloaked figure stepped in front of her.

"Executioner's appeal," a lovely, melodic female voice said, barely audible above the din.

"Quiet!" Wormwood roared, silencing the crowd. "What did you say?"

The female turned toward the Koenig's translator, revealing a slice of her profile. Ronin blew out a long, ragged breath.

"Executioner's appeal," the female said, louder. "She demands an executioner's appeal."

Wormwood frowned. "Well, that's just absurd. Surely, we need not—" His words died on his lips as he faced the Koenig, whose expression was murderous. Murderous, yet resigned. As if hearing these ancient words from this tiny female, barely taller than Cassandra herself, had thwarted all his plans.

Wormwood regarded the Koenig's swirling hands with rapt attention, his indignation falling with each flick of his master's fingers. He loosed a heavy sigh. "Very well." He swept a judgmental sneer from Cassandra's head down to her toes. "Little good will it do her. Do you agree to this, prisoner 161803?"

Cassandra had no idea what in the name of Stygios she might be agreeing to. "I—"

"May I speak with her first, sire?" the female asked. The Koenig crossed his arms and gave her a curt nod.

Swiveling heads followed as Cassandra let herself be led into the shadows behind a column. Ronin remained by the dais, looking as if someone had punched a hole through his ribs and scooped out his insides.

The female removed her hood, and Cassandra finally got a look at her face. It was possibly the most beautiful she'd ever seen, all pale ivory skin and sharp cheekbones, full lips and glowing silver eyes.

"Mireille?"

Mireille didn't even question how Cassandra knew her name. "There is so much I need to tell you, but we'll have time for that later. For now, all you need to know is this. I've just given you the chance to defy your sentence."

"How?"

"By defeating the Koenig in armed combat."

Cassandra nearly doubled over in hysterics.

Mireille gripped her shoulders. "I know that sounds absurd, but it's how the Koenig himself earned his title. Every prisoner who is given a death sentence has the opportunity to thwart it and win that hammer." Cassandra glanced toward the black weapon with the glowing polemite heart. "Do you trust me?"

Cassandra scarcely knew how to answer that question. Ronin's story had not painted Mireille in the best light. But there was something strangely familiar about her.

Plus, she *had* just saved Cassandra's life.

The word *yes* fell from her lips before she could question it.

Relief softened Mireille's features as she closed her eyes and nodded. When she reopened them, Cassandra could've sworn she saw flames blazing within their mercury depths.

"I need you to listen to me very, *very* carefully," Mireille said.

"And then do exactly as I say."

CHAPTER TWELVE

A LL THE BLOOD HAD surely drained from Ronin's body, his head woolly and his vision blurred, as he watched Mireille—fucking *Mireille Valette* in the flesh—lead Cassandra back to the dais.

The she-wolf didn't spare him a single glance, and he was grateful for her inattention.

It allowed him the privacy to study her.

The stunning face that had haunted so many of his dreams—and nightmares—looked mostly unchanged since he'd last seen her. The icy indifference remained, though it held an even sharper edge.

A long, leather cloak hid her body from view—a blessing, he supposed—and as she brushed past, her scent washed over him. That unmistakable musk sweetened by ripe flowers. The same scent he'd caught on the vial of veiling potion in the intake yard. His wolf released a mournful howl before Ronin snarled back, silencing the beast.

Cassandra and Mireille paused before the Koenig, and Mireille whispered something into Cassandra's ear. Cassandra pushed her shoulders back, flaring her glimmering wings, and declared, "I request an executioner's appeal."

Wormwood grimaced, looking toward the throne for affirmation. The Koenig gave him another nod, stroking the handle of his warhammer.

"Very well," Wormwood said, narrowing his eyes at Mireille. "Such is your right. Step up here so we can seal it with a blood vow."

Cassandra darted a nervous glance to Mireille. Did Cassandra not know what a blood vow was? Mireille whispered into Cassandra's ear again, and Cass's steps faltered as she climbed the dais.

Wormwood snatched Cassandra's hand, then lifted it toward the Koenig. She hissed between clenched teeth as the Koenig dragged the edge of a knife over her palm. He sliced across his own, then clasped their hands together.

"You may select the weapons you'll be fighting with, *or* the date of your appeal," Wormwood said.

Come on, Cass, Ronin thought. *Choose wisely.*

"The date," she answered.

Good.

"As you wish," Wormwood said. "The latest you may choose is twenty-eight days from now, on the night of Vestan's crescent moon."

"Why?"

"Because that is as long as his mercy extends."

The Koenig's hand tightened on Cassandra's, spilling a fresh wave of blood from the wound. She didn't even wince.

Very good.

"Fine," she said. "Twenty-eight days."

Wormwood looked to the Koenig, who gave a dark smile. "Then you'll be fighting with broadswords. It's what he always chooses. He's nothing if not a traditionalist."

Now it was Ronin's turn to fight off a wince.

Broadswords, Creator help them.

Unless Cass had already been trained to use one—and he thought that extremely unlikely—twenty-eight days was not nearly enough time to gain the necessary skill to defeat a male who, by the looks of him, had been honing his craft for centuries. Even Ronin himself, a battle-tested warrior of five plus centuries, wasn't confident he could defeat the Koenig.

Cassandra had a virtually impossible task ahead of her.

Wormwood grabbed the hammer and thrust it between Cassandra and the Koenig, directly beneath their clasped hands. "Do you promise not to harm one another, nor to solicit any harm against one another, until the day of your appeal? At which time, one of you must die for the other to be declared victor?" Both Cassandra and the Koenig nodded. "Then feed the blood of your pact to the hammer, and the vow will be complete."

Four drops plinked onto the stone, the hall so silent that Ronin heard each one.

Once the fourth had fallen, tendrils of red light burst from the polemite heart and seeped into Cassandra and the Koenig.

"No Fae within Tartarus will be able to harm you until the appeal," Wormwood pronounced. "When you will battle the Koenig and two fighters of his choosing using broadswords on the night of Vestan's crescent moon. You may also select two individuals to fight alongside you. Your first choice?"

"Mireille Valette," Cassandra declared and Mireille bowed with a satisfied grin.

"The apothecarist?" Wormwood's eyebrows rose. "An interesting choice, but it is yours to make. Who will be your second choice?"

Cassandra surveyed the crowd. The Brethren avoided her stare, looking at their feet or toward the ceiling.

Cassandra's eyes landed on Ronin, and he knew what she was going to say before she opened her mouth.

Was *this* the role he was destined to play? The role that chronomancer in Kheimos had spoken of all those centuries ago? Through all his work with the Teles Chrysos, all the spying and the mind games, he hadn't felt as strong a tug in his chest as he felt now. As if something—or someone—was urging him toward this path.

"Well?" Wormwood said, exasperated. "Get on with it. Who is your second selection?"

Cassandra's fierce blue-gray eyes found his face, and his wolf yipped and pranced within him.

He'd barely finished nodding his acceptance before Cassandra sang out, "Ronin Matakos."

His name echoed through the hall, through his bones, through his soul.

"Ronin Matakos will be my second fighter."

At that, Mireille finally looked at him.

And smiled.

Mireille let Ronin and Cassandra into the small apartment above her apothecary shop.

"Cozy," Cassandra said around an exhausted laugh that matched Ronin's spirit.

Mireille hadn't said two words to Ronin since the trio had left the castle, directing all her questions toward Cassandra instead. Mireille had asked how Cassandra knew who she was, and the little traitor didn't even glance back for permission before she outed him. Told Mireille that Ronin had spilled their entire history at the intake tower.

Mireille tossed an annoyed look over her shoulder, but he didn't fucking care. It was his story to tell, too. He tried not to be insulted that Cassandra didn't even scold Mireille for taking his eye.

At one point, Cassandra stopped Mireille in the middle of the street and gathered her into a tight embrace. Tears lined her eyes as she thanked Mireille for saving her life.

Ronin had stood awkwardly behind them, scratching at the back of his neck, uncomfortable with the display of emotion.

Mireille had stiffened in the embrace. But as she wrapped her arms around Cassandra, carefully avoiding the wings, her gaze rose to Ronin.

And he swore he saw something like gratitude shining there.

For what, he didn't know. For protecting Cass during her sentencing? For helping her through the mists? For agreeing to this half-mad scenario where Mireille and Ronin would fight alongside Cass in a battle with a centuries-old, mutilated Windrider who controlled an entire city of the Empire's prisoners?

This was all so fucked.

But he didn't turn away from Mireille as she squeezed Cass tighter. Merely dipped his head in silent recognition.

He had a bad feeling it was about to be two against one.

Creator fucking spare him.

He shook off those thoughts as he surveyed the small, open living space. A scuffed leather couch and armchair were arranged before a stone fireplace. Beyond the sitting area was a wooden dining table with three chairs and a primitive kitchen. No stove, no refrigerator, none of the magical appliances he was used to on the continent. Though he did spy a faucet above the large porcelain sink, thank the Goddess. It had been centuries since he'd lived without the convenience of running water—not since he was a young pup in Denevrae—and he'd gotten quite used to the luxury. Hopefully that meant there was a shower as well.

Mireille piped up, "It's not much, but you'll be safe here. Not to mention you've got the protection of that blood vow upon you, Cassandra."

"You can call me Cass." She offered Mireille a warm, weary smile. "All my friends do."

That gorgeous blush that Ronin remembered well—*too* well—stole across Mireille's cheeks. She'd barely had any friends back in Kheimos and the clean, utilitarian space he now found himself in suggested that hadn't changed during her imprisonment.

Guilt and regret tightened his chest at the thought of what she must have endured here, trapped beyond the mists with these other prisoners for so long. It was almost enough to dampen the mistrust and anger he was still clinging to.

Almost, but not quite.

Mireille gestured down a short hallway. "The bathroom and two of the bedrooms are this way. One is mine. Then there's another one on the other side of the living room. You two can—"

"I'll take the one on the other side of the living room," Ronin grumbled.

"Right," Mireille said, lips tight, then turned to Cassandra. "Why don't you go get some rest? I'm sure you're exhausted after everything you've been through today. Borrow whatever you need from my closet. Tomorrow, we'll get you some training attire and more clothes."

"I don't have any… How do people *buy* things here?" Cassandra asked. "And where does it all come from?"

"From the Koenig," Mireille answered. "Gifted by the polemite in that warhammer. Some believe it's provided by Vestan the Warrior God himself."

Ronin's brows rose. He'd suspected for a long time that the Gods—both the Fae's High and the human's lesser—were not real. Just myths crafted by the Empire in an attempt to lure Ethyrios away from worship of Adelphinae, the true Creator. But the magic had to have originated somewhere.

Mireille continued, "It's why everything here appears from another era. Other than a few modern conveniences, the Koenig can only offer what he remembers from the time when he was free."

"Who *is* he?" Ronin asked, silently thanking whichever prisoner had convinced the male to upgrade to running water.

Mireille shook her head. "No one knows for sure. He's the oldest prisoner in here by centuries. And as you can imagine, he's not too keen on sharing his history. Adds to the air of mystery and power he's woven. There's no monetary system here. Nothing like *drachas*. The Koenig provides goods to each prisoner on a monthly basis, which can be used or bartered. If we desire something specific, we can make a special request of him or his Brethren. Sometimes they honor it, sometimes they don't. Depends on how generous they're feeling."

Cassandra's feathers rattled, as if she were bobbing her leg beneath the table.

Mireille sighed, then waved a hand and said, "Go on and get it over with. Ask me all the questions you have about this place. After tonight, your only focus is training."

Cassandra sucked in a long breath, then began her barrage. "Why is there a city here?"

"Fuck if I know," Mireille answered. "But mumblings around town claim it used to be home to a powerful magic wielder and their followers. The wards were allegedly created upon their death."

"For what purpose?"

Mireille shrugged, non-plussed.

"How long has the Koenig ruled?" Cassandra asked.

"Again, don't know, don't care."

"Why are there no children?"

"New life cannot be created within the wards. Just as elemental magic cannot be accessed."

"You mean wind magic?"

"I mean *all* elemental magics," Mireille said pointedly, flicking her eyes toward Ronin.

Cassandra didn't seem to notice. "If the Koenig and his Brethren are so terrible, why don't the other prisoners just rise up and kill them?"

Mireille snorted. "What makes you think they haven't tried?" Her cool facade returned. The one she'd always used to hide the feelings that made her uncomfortable: pain, shame, regret.

His blood boiled.

His worst nightmares over the centuries had been vivid speculations about what Mireille was enduring here in Tartarus. But seeing it now, seeing the results in person… He couldn't breathe.

"Anyway," Mireille said to Cassandra, "as challenger, you'll be given whatever you need leading up to your appeal."

"That's…oddly kind."

"Not really. They assume you'll be dead in a month, so what does it matter?"

Cassandra's face paled and her wings drooped.

Clearly, Mireille's small talk hadn't improved.

"Well," Cassandra huffed out, "on *that* cheery note, I'm going to try to get some sleep. I'll leave you two to…" Her gaze bobbed between Ronin and Mireille, who were both pointedly ignoring each other. "I'll leave you two. Good night."

Mireille nodded, tucking an escaped strand of copper hair behind her ear. "We're in this together now. For better or for worse."

"No pressure," Cassandra mumbled as she slid down the hallway, throwing a final wave over her shoulder and shutting herself in her bedroom.

Mireille's gaze remained glued to the table.

He couldn't believe he was actually standing here in front of her. Occupying the same space. Breathing the same air. This phantom that had stalked him for centuries, taunting him with visions of the life they could have shared. Snatched away with a single flick of her fiery sword.

He had so many questions. So many things he wanted to say to her. To *scream* at her. But he bit them back as she lifted her head, that familiar imperviousness shielding her quicksilver eyes.

"I…" she started, then blew out a long breath.

He crossed his arms over his chest, a protective measure, then planted his feet. He was here, in a physical place. He existed. He was *not* living some crazy nightmare crafted from his most bittersweet memories.

Mireille peered at him, her face unreadable, as she uttered a single word.

"Hi."

CHAPTER THIRTEEN

MIREILLE VALETTE WAS FINDING it incredibly difficult not to break down as she looked into Ronin's eyes.

Eye.

Fuck.

It was even more brutal than she'd anticipated, seeing the evidence of her hatred tracking from his black brow, down his cheekbone, and into his soft upper lip. Bless the Creator that the worst of the savage scar was hidden behind that eye patch.

If it wasn't, Mireille might very quickly lose hold of the control she was clinging to with every shallow breath, every stuttering heartbeat.

Her fury over his role in her father's death had cooled over the years—there were plenty of other things to be distracted by here in Tartarus—but it hadn't completely dissipated.

He hadn't apologized on the day they'd both discovered what he'd done.

Would it have made a difference then? Did it make a difference now?

The centuries-old memory was still crystal clear in her mind: Ronin kneeling in the pine needles, swearing that he didn't know the soldier he'd killed was her father. She believed him. But somehow, that had only made the betrayal worse. Her human father had been nothing but a nameless, faceless body on that battlefield in Aethalia. So inconsequential that Ronin didn't even remember him.

Her father hadn't mattered. Neither to Ronin nor to the Empire.

And if her father hadn't mattered, due to his humanity, what did that make Mireille with her half-human blood?

Sure, it had given her power for a short blip of time. That fire that flowed through her veins and coated her hide in swirls of crackling red and orange when she shifted. It had even crawled up the length of her sword to ensure that brutal scar remained on Ronin's otherwise perfect face.

But her fire had snuffed out the second she'd passed through Tartarus's wards. She'd become just another Beastrunner prisoner—capable of shifting into her wolf, if needed, but nothing more. Over the years, she'd found other ways to survive. She'd had to, in order to ensure she arrived at this specific night to meet the young girl her father had shown her in that vision in the Halfway all those years ago.

Ronin just stood there, stoic and silent.

She'd expected anger, hatred. Retaliation, even.

His indifference cut far deeper.

Her voice trembled on the question she'd been waiting centuries to ask him.

"Why are you here?"

He nodded toward Cassandra's bedroom. "Her."

"That the only reason?"

"Yes."

"You capable of giving me something more than a one-word answer?"

"No."

Her frustration spilled over. "Look, if she's going to have any chance of surviving her appeal, you and I need to put our past aside and help her. I knew she wasn't human anymore, but—"

"How? How did you know that? And how did you know we would need the veiling potion to get through sentencing?"

The name burned in Mireille's throat. "Gareth."

Ronin flinched.

Good.

She wanted Ronin wrecked by guilt at the sound of her father's name. "He's been visiting my dreams. Showing me visions of that meeting in the throne room. Helping me ensure all the players were in place."

"So you knew I was coming?" Ronin said, a bit breathlessly. Some hint of an emotion, finally.

"Yes." She raised her chin.

"And you know how this plays out?"

"No," Mireille admitted. "If he even tried to hint about what happens after the castle, I would wake up."

"Convenient," Ronin grumbled.

"Is it?" Mireille snapped, rising from the table and stepping into his space. She didn't dare breathe in, didn't need the distracting familiarity of his scent. "I think it's the Goddess who's waking me up. She doesn't want me to see how this could go. She wants me to…"

"Wants you to what?" Ronin's fingers tightened on his impressive arms. She remembered, all too clearly, how they'd felt wrapped around her. How safe and protected she'd been for the only time in her long, miserable life. A tiny blip of warmth in centuries of cold.

"To *choose* to fight for Cassandra without certainty of the outcome," she said. "What happened to her?"

"She was Turned."

Mireille rolled her eyes. "Yes, I had gath—"

"By Prince Tristan Erabis."

"*What?* How?"

"You don't know how Turning works?" A vein fluttered in Ronin's jaw. "He fell in love with her, they shared blood, and they fucked. Boom. A new Fae female is born on Ethyrios."

His bitterness shredded through her chest, even as she recognized the envy within it. A love so powerful that it could change a person's species? Mireille supposed that *was* the kind of love that would inspire envy.

The kind of love she and Ronin might have shared, before fate yanked it away.

Before they'd ruined each other.

Creator, she'd *promised* herself she wouldn't go down this path when she saw him again. A reunion she'd had ages to prepare for. Less than five minutes in and she was already breaking her own rules.

Fucking *focus*, Mireille.

She raised her chin, crossing her arms and mimicking his protective stance. "When did it happen? And does the Empire know?"

"I'm not sure that I should trust you with that information."

Mireille finally exploded. "She would be dead right now if it wasn't for me! Whatever intentions the Creator has for Cassandra, whatever help I'm supposed to provide her, preparing for it was the only thing keeping me going these past two centuries."

She didn't tell him how many times she'd wished for True Death. How many times she'd come so close to falling into that dark embrace. How it was only the thought of that young girl's face in the Halfway, so fragile yet so strong, that had Mireille clinging to some small shred of hope.

Whatever shit Ronin believed about her, she wasn't going to let it stand in the way of fulfilling her destiny. She couldn't. If she did, then everything she'd endured would have been for nothing.

"Her Turning happened very recently," he said, softening slightly at her outburst. "She transformed shortly after she was delivered to her cell in the intake tower. And thanks to the veiling potion you provided, the Vicereine only saw her as human. The Empire doesn't know what she's become."

Mireille jolted. "Varuna Lykan came to deliver the sentences? Not Eamon himself?" That was odd. Went against the protocol that had been established for new prisoners.

Ronin shook his head. "The gears of war are turning out there. The continent is poised to tear itself apart, and if we don't intervene soon we will all be destroyed. We need her to defeat the Koenig. And then we need to figure out how to get the fuck out of here."

"You don't have to keep telling me that. I understand how important it is that she wins."

"What are you going to do to help her, then?"

"I know the Koenig. I've seen him fight. And I know his Brethren. Some of them intimately. I can help her learn their weaknesses, prepare her for the battle."

"Good," Ronin said absently. As if still stuck on the word *intimately*. "She's going to need it. She's doesn't even know how to wield her new Fae strength yet."

"We'll prepare her as best we can."

Devastation flashed across his face, there and gone in an instant, when she'd referred to them as *we*.

He fidgeted, then spat out a question he couldn't seem to keep himself from asking. "Is that what you've been doing to inspire the Brethren's generosity? Fucking them?"

His judgmental tone landed a powerful strike, drawing rage instead of blood. "What would that even matter to you? Whatever promises we made to each other died outside that cabin. The choices I've made to survive in here are *none* of your fucking business."

Ronin snarled, hate simmering in his eye. She was wrong; this was so much worse than his indifference. "So, we'll be civil to each other to help Cassandra and that's all, right?"

She nodded stiffly.

He prowled in closer, towering over her, barely an inch of space between them. "Then stay out of my fucking business as well."

"With pleasure." She side-stepped as he shoved past her. She shouted over her shoulder as he stalked down the hallway, "I didn't ask for this, Ronin." His back stiffened at his name, and it felt like a small victory. "You play your part and I'll play mine."

"You were pretty good at that, if I recall," he said, refusing to look at her as his pounding footsteps faded.

His bedroom door slammed, and she dug her nails into her palms hard enough to break skin.

Well, her wolf purred. *That went well. You probably should have—*

I don't need your advice on how to handle him.

The beast licked her paw. *Are you sure? He seemed rather jealous when you mentioned the Brethren. Quite a strong response. Curious, don't you think?*

Mireille sighed. *It's not important. How we feel about each other doesn't—*

He looks just as delicious as I remembered. Maybe even more so with that glorious scar.

Mireille didn't have the energy to argue. Some small, starved part of her maybe even agreed. But the exchange had exhausted her. She'd been prepared to encounter his hatred.

But she hadn't expected it to hurt this much.

Ronin slammed his bedroom door, then leaned against it and dipped his head into his hands.

His wolf stirred.

Not one word, furball, Ronin growled. *Not one. Fucking. Word.*

Cold indifference, huh?

What did I just say?

The creature huffed. *You can pretend that you haven't been pining for that female for the past two hundred years, but I know the truth. And now you have a chance to fix what was broken. Don't let your anger stand in the way.*

Ronin snarled out loud. *What I do or do not do about her is none—*

You're a child. I thought maybe you'd grown up, but—

Stay OUT of it.

His wolf sighed and settled.

Ronin stripped off his shirt, wishing he could've taken a shower but too exhausted by this insane day to even consider it. Instead, he folded his massive body into the small, but comfortable bed.

And as he slipped off into a restless, tossing slumber, he couldn't help but wonder who would break first.

Him or Mireille.

CHAPTER FOURTEEN

TRISTAN LEANED AGAINST THE doorframe of Trophonios's workshop, hidden beneath his wings and awaiting his cue as Ione began her speech to the gathered rebels.

Tonight, Ione would officially turn leadership of the Teles Chrysos over to Tristan.

An impressive mix of all three sub-species of Fae had gathered in the village square, several sporting Teles symbols on their shirts or jackets.

Ione, wearing a sleeveless white tunic over flowy pants and crowned with a circlet bearing a fire opal, addressed the crowd. "I am pleased to see so many familiar faces. And even more pleased by the new. Welcome, friends and future allies." As a human, her voice had always been confident. Her Turning had honed it into something even more powerful—a dagger forged into a sword. It sliced through the square, demanding attention. "Already, we have shown you evidence of Adelphinae's pleasure with our work."

The festivities had commenced with an Anointment, a sight which Tristan would not soon forget.

Several long-standing members of the Teles Chrysos had bowed before Ione, all with mixed-species heritage; Trophonios himself had verified the human ancestry within their bloodlines. Ione had knelt with each supplicant and held their hands as they muttered prayers to Adelphinae.

Though Tristan agreed with the foundational principles of Adelphinae's dogma, he wasn't sure if he believed the Goddess was an actual living entity. If she was, Tristan might have some questions for her after everything Ione had claimed at dinner last night. A dinner that he hadn't said a word to Ione about all day.

But watching those Fae—the Anointed, as they were now called—show off their newly-restored fire, water, and lightning… Someone, or something, had provided it. If not the Goddess herself, then who? Or what?

He wondered what it might feel like to be blessed with a second element. To wield fire or lightning as easily as he summoned the wind. Futile musings, really. The Erabis line was the oldest and purest on the planet. Fae to the roots, not an ounce of human sap flowing through the family tree.

Ione continued, "Adelphinae herself, in her Compendium of Creation, stated that Fae and humans were created as equals. And that it is her wish that we share this world and her generous bounty. But that message has been lost over the centuries. Suppressed by greedy leaders who sought to invalidate her worship, to hoard resources for themselves and establish unnatural hierarchies between the species and sub-species. And in doing so, have dampened her elemental gifts."

Several rebels spat upon the cobblestones.

"With the increased support we've received these past decades, we are closer than ever to achieving our goal of taking back the Crystal Throne and restoring our Creator, so that all Ethyrians may thrive once again. Tonight, we thank you for your patience and ask for your continued support. But I would not do so without offering proof of our progress.

"We have gained the most important ally in our fight against the Empire. One that many of you will recognize. A leader who was stripped of his title, stripped of his *birthright*, before he could enact his plans for peace. Plans that caused his family to brand him a pariah and exile him to the colonies."

Ione glanced over her shoulder toward Tristan before turning back to the crowd. "It gives me the greatest honor to welcome the true leader of the Teles Chrysos. The male responsible for my own immortality. The male who Turned me into the Delphine and hastened my relationship with our wonderful Goddess.

"The rightful Emperor of Ethyrios—Prince Tristan Erabis!"

Shouts of joy rippled through the crowd as Tristan whipped his wings open and stepped into the square.

The Fae parted like a sea before him, many dropping to their knees and bowing their heads, others reaching for him with tears in their eyes.

He shook their hands and clasped their shoulders, murmuring greetings and words of encouragement. He made his way toward Ione, who sported a broad, boastful smile beneath the clock tower.

She snatched his hand, then raised their clasped fists into the air as a boisterous roar stirred the jungle.

All these Fae still remembered him. Shared his wishes for a better Ethyrios.

Not only that, they were willing to risk their safety—their *lives*—to achieve that goal.

Hope rattled his feathers.

He wanted to be worthy of their worship, worthy of their faith in him.

"They cheer for you, Prince," Ione muttered, drinking in the applause as she intertwined their fingers. "They cheer for *us*."

He faked a smile, stifled his heartache, and tried his best to project an air of confidence toward the crowd.

But how could *any* of this matter while he had the wrong female by his side?

Tristan smoothed a hand over his bloated stomach, dreaming of his bed. Rebel after rebel had approached him in the square tonight, toasting him with food and drink. He didn't have the heart to refuse a single one of their offerings.

And now, he was so full he could barely walk—and if he never saw another glass of aguaver for the rest of his life, he would die a happy male.

Trophonios ambled over and dropped a hand onto Tristan's shoulder. "The generals are ready for you, Prince."

Tristan groaned. "Remind me why I set a meeting this late?"

"Because you run as tight a ship as our Delphine." Trophonios winked.

When Ione had told him of her intention to turn leadership over to him, Tristan had crammed his days full of meetings and reports, gulping down as much knowledge as he could of the movement's history and future plans. He felt a tremendous amount of pressure— pressure he'd fully admit he'd put on himself—to get up to speed as quickly as possible.

He hefted himself out of his canvas chair, cursing past-Tristan for scheduling a status meeting in the middle of the night, then followed Trophonios to his war committee room.

Golden bowls filled with flames lit the corners of the dim, smoky hall, the fire provided by one of the Anointed. A large oval table topped with a fabric map of Ethyrios dominated the space. Ione was leaning over it, dressed in her ethereal white garments but without the opal-studded circlet.

Her chin rose when he entered, pure affection glowing in her smile. He returned a polite nod.

"Rebel Prince," she greeted, moving away from the head of the table.

Trophonios folded himself into his chair as the rest of the Teles Chrysos leadership filed into the room: Seraavi Pfania, the fuchsia-eyed Deathstalker who'd portaled down from Lodesvale; Felix Tanius, a rugged Windrider with persimmon-colored wings and long blond locks; Layla Fetar, a honey badger bi-form with pin-straight sheets of half-white, half-black hair and a glittering corset of throwing knives accentuating her waist.

Tristan had been pleased to discover the movement's key leaders were each a member of a different sub-species. Proof that the world they were fighting for would not hew to the hierarchies established by his father Leonin, who'd only ever put Windriders in positions of power. And as soon as it was possible—and safe—Tristan would be adding humans to this group as well.

Once everyone was seated, most of the eyes in the room shifted to Ione before recalibrating toward him. He could understand why. She commanded a tremendous amount of respect from the rebels. This former human woman who had somehow clawed her way back from death, now poised to help him take back his throne. Maybe even occupy it with him, if she was right about the prophecy.

His heart lurched in his chest, but he tried to ignore it as he addressed the room. "Our coup must be as bloodless and result in as little collateral damage as possible. Therefore, we have our sights set on a single location." He tapped his finger in the center of the map—right on the city of Delos. "If we can remove Eamon and his lackeys from the Imperial capital, with the support we have from Aurelie Lambros in Akti, plus the support of the Berstoh family in Cernodas, that leaves only Brachos, Syvalle and the Northern Territories to challenge us."

"Arran Zephyrus won't fight you," Layla piped up. "Not as long as you do nothing to diminish his wealth or remove him from power."

Ione's brows furrowed. "As long as he agrees to abide by our new laws, then I see no reason to do so."

Tristan snorted. "He's not going to like the '*treat humans as equals*' part. But I have an in with his family. His son Cael and I were Vestian Guards together. He may hold some sway over his father."

Tristan had no idea whether that was true or not. Sure, Arran Zephyrus had an obsessive, controlling sort of loyalty where his sons were concerned, but Tristan didn't even know where Cael *was*. The fucker hadn't returned any of Tristan's windwhispers. That could mean one of two things: Cael was going through one of his episodes again or…

Tristan didn't have the emotional capacity to consider the second option.

From what Tristan had gathered, Arran was somewhat of a free agent in this conflict, playing both sides. As long as his profits kept rolling in, Tristan didn't think Arran gave a flying fuck *who* sat on the Crystal

Throne in Delos. Tristan would use that indifference to his advantage now, then force the male to fall in line after.

"Assume Brachos won't be a threat," Tristan said, projecting a confidence he was trying to convince himself he felt.

Ione swept a hand across the Northern Territories. "Skanisse could be a problem. He's extremely close with Eamon."

Seraavi cut in. "Skanisse won't stand a chance against us. His is the least populous territory. His forces wouldn't even be a tenth of what we could conjure."

"What about the Imperial forces themselves?" Felix asked, ruffling his feathers. "The legions controlled by Eamon within Delos and Nephes?"

Ione rubbed a finger over her bottom lip. "They're loyal to the throne itself, not Eamon Erabis." Her indigo eyes shot to Tristan. "Once they have a new Erabis in the palace, they'll fall in line."

Felix looked skeptical. "That's a dangerous assumption."

Ione clenched her fist on the table, something passing between her and the blond general that made Tristan's wings prickle. A familiarity Tristan hadn't picked up on between her and any of the other leaders. "It's a risk we'll have to take," she said sharply, silencing him.

Seraavi scanned the map. "So that just leaves Syvalle and High Councilor Geirdrios. *Her* forces are not small. She could be a problem if she decides to side with Eamon." She turned to Tristan. "Your mother is a Geirdrios, is she not?"

"She is," Tristan answered. "Daena Geirdrios is my cousin. My mother's niece."

"Any familial affection we can exploit?"

Tristan shrugged. "I haven't seen her since I was a teenager." He felt Ione's eyes upon him, as if she was remembering him as a teenager—the young Fae male she'd fallen in love with. He shifted on his feet. "Where does my mother factor into all this? Or my sister Belen, for that matter?"

Trophonios leaned around Ione. "Our spies in Delos claim that Empress Mila is playing the part of the dutiful dowager at the moment. Supporting your brother publicly. As is your sister. But we have no idea how much either of them knew of Eamon's plans to capture you. Perhaps if you could speak to them..."

Tristan grimaced. Belen had been a young Faeling of only seven the last time Tristan had seen her. And he hadn't spoken to his mother in centuries. Not since the day Mila Erabis had stood next to her husband Leonin, dry-faced and silent, as the male had announced Tristan's exile. At the time, his mother's reaction had burned. She'd always been so loving, so affectionate. Had doted on both her boys. For her to not shed a single tear when her first-born had been sent away... Tristan had buried that pain long ago, had no interest in excavating it.

"I don't think we can count on either of their support," he said. "So we shouldn't count on Syvalle's, either. Assume it's hostile territory." Heads around the table bobbed. "We move forward with our plans then." He turned to Layla. "Is everything set for tomorrow morning's raid?"

"Yes, Prince," Layla said. "Our forces have set up camp along the cliffs above the Staurien Pass. They're ready to intercept as soon as the train exits the tunnel."

Layla had briefed Tristan on the details of the raid yesterday. The rebels had paid Arran Zephryus a nearly crippling amount of *drachas* to reveal the route of a missile shipment heading to Delos by way of the Staurien Pass in eastern Brachos. They wouldn't be able to take the city without them.

Delos was not only well-defended, but damn near unbreachable. The city itself consisted of a series of islands connected by narrow canals. A sieging army would only be able to capture the city with winged forces or water vessels. And, unfortunately, the Teles Chrysos didn't have any kind of armada floating around.

And speaking of weapons just laying around, he asked a question that hadn't occurred to him yesterday. "How do we know that Eamon won't have a few of those missiles aimed right back at us?"

"These are brand new," Layla answered. "A recent invention by Zephyrus's weapons manufacturing facilities at Typhon Mountain. They're filled with compressed dragon-fire, and take years to craft. Some wicked alchemy that even Trophonios can't figure out." The snow-leopard bi-form grunted at her side. "Eamon ordered all five missiles from Arran's first batch. The next five won't be available for another ten months."

"Good," Tristan said before he dropped the *other* proverbial bomb he'd been waiting to spring upon his generals. "Once the weapons are in hand, there's one more thing we need before we march upon Delos."

"What?" Ione asked.

Her confused smile transformed into a cold grimace at Tristan's answer.

"The final copy of the Goddess's Compendium."

"Respectfully," Tanius piped up, without an ounce of genuine respect, "it's too big a risk. Not to mention we don't need it to move forward."

Tristan cocked an eyebrow at the blond general, about to disagree when Trophonios's deep bass cut in. "That's not entirely true, Felix. There's knowledge buried within that book from the time of Adelphinae. There could be clues about how the wards of Tartarus were created. Clues about how to breach them, even. Such knowledge could be instrumental for my research team."

Blood rushed to Tristan's head, and he grappled with the urge to scream at Ione as he turned to her and asked in as professional a tone as he could muster, "Why did you not inform me of this?"

A mask settled upon Ione's features—the beatific one she used when she was about to invoke some blathering nonsense about her Goddess. "It is just a book, Your Highness. The Goddess provides us with her wisdom in myriad ways. Besides, as General Tanius has stated, to acquire it now would be too great a risk."

"Why?"

"Because," Ione said, still the picture of cool calm, "it's locked within a chamber beneath the palace.

"One that can only be opened by the blood of an Erabis male."

"Why didn't you tell me about your desire to retrieve the Compendium?" Ione asked, pressing in nearly close enough to trip Tristan as they left the leadership meeting.

Tristan stepped away, putting distance between then. "Why didn't you tell me Trophonios was researching how to breach the wards?"

Ione frowned. "Felix isn't wrong. You're the only one of us who can open the chamber. It's too great a risk to send you into your brother's orbit. Not to mention doing so could put our spies in danger of exposure. We can retrieve the book when we take the palace. It's the safest course."

While his head recognized the rationality, his heart fiercely protested. "Back in Thalenn, Ronin made it sound like you all were desperate to get your hands on it. I'm wondering why you changed your mind."

"I didn't change my mind, I..." Ione lifted her head, not looking at him and instead staring off into the middle distance. "You and I are fated, Tristan. Our love will save this world. We will rule Ethyrios together as Emperor and Empress and usher in a new era of peace." She stopped in her tracks and grabbed his hand.

"I don't need to know the other half of a prophecy to tell me that."

Didn't need the other half? Or was afraid of what it might reveal, given how quickly he'd abandoned her after she'd rescued him?

He dropped her hand, some selfish part of him relishing the hurt in her eyes. "I'm sorry, Ione, but I *do*. I need to know."

I need to know for certain that the Goddess is asking me to sacrifice my heart in order to save my people.

"I'd like to head to Delos as soon as possible," he said. "And I'm going with or without you."

Ione closed her eyes and let out a resigned sigh. "You'll have a better chance if I go with you. I spent decades down in those dungeons. I'll help you get to the chamber."

His expression softened. "Thank you, I—"

Someone shouted his name from across the square and they both turned to find General Fetar rushing toward them in a panic.

"Layla?" Tristan asked, gripping the female's forearm. "What's wrong?"

"Imperial forces," she snarled, flashing short, sharp fangs. "They've been spotted on the road through the Icthians that leads to the Staurien Pass."

"Head to the camp," Tristan said. "Now. Take as many members as we can spare. Go find Trophonios, he's got plenty of cuffs ready for travel."

"Yes, Your Highness," Layla said, scuttling off to the workshop.

Concerned for his rebels, annoyed that this meant delaying his trip to Delos, but grateful for the chance to work off some of his anger and frustration, Tristan turned to Ione.

"Wanna go smash some Imperial soldiers?"

CHAPTER FIFTEEN

THE FORMAL DINING HALL at Stoneridge was just as stuffy as Cael remembered.

Before he'd left to join the Vestians, he'd attended plenty of gatherings in the impressive space his father used to entertain far-flung family members, business partners, Imperial Council members—even Emperor Leonin and Empress Mila a time or two.

The hall was a perfect distillation of Stoneridge's lodge aesthetic, crafted from thick, shellacked logs and littered with hunting scene tapestries. A gallery of antlers decorated the south wall.

When Cael was younger, he'd sneak in here and run his fingers over the pristine bone. Try to figure out if his father's gruesome trophies were from true animals or Beastrunner Fae. It had been Cael's favorite, albeit macabre, game as a boy. He'd never been able to tell the difference, though he was convinced, even back then, that at least of few belonged to Arran's enemies.

The first thing he noticed this evening was how immeasurably his father's collection had grown. A century and a half ago, it had consisted of around twenty specimens. Now, there were over a hundred. And they were no longer limited to antlers. Yak horns and boar tusks, stuffed foxes and hares—even an ocelot stared back at him.

In the center of the mounted cemetery was a snarling grizzly bear head, its wrinkled muzzle pulled back over substantial fangs that gleamed in the candlelight. Which spilled from a chandelier made of antlers.

Though the estate was outfitted with the all the latest Fae technology, his mother had always preferred to dine by candlelight. Said it imparted a more intimate atmosphere, made her guests feel more relaxed. Whether her goal was mere conviviality or a lowering of defenses—loosened lips and spilled secrets—Cael could never tell.

Probably the latter, given the credenza full of ales, wine, liquors, and glowing bottles of Delirium.

Cael paused before the spread, deliberating. Given his mood, Delirium was the *last* substance he should be consuming. Sure, he'd get a burst of temporary euphoria. But as soon as that wore off, he'd be plunged into an even deeper despair.

It was tempting, though. To allow the elixir to dull the edges of the evening, to get him through this first meeting with his fiancée.

His *fiancée*.

Fucking Stygios take him.

His fingers trembled as he reached for a bottle. That sight alone had his better nature kicking in. He grabbed a glass mug instead, then filled it with ale.

A quick sip of the frothy, golden liquid settled his nerves, and he turned to find Erik caressing the tail of a frozen fox at Arran's trophy wall.

"I can't decide whether I find all this fascinating or horrific," Erik murmured. Cael couldn't tell if he was talking about the fox or the evening ahead.

"Can't it be both?" Cael shrugged, raising his mug again. The ale was bitter, but had a tart, refreshing finish. And went down far too easily. He'd have to watch himself. "Where's the rest of our illustrious family?"

Erik and their mother, Petra, were the only two Zephyruses for whom Cael's feelings were wholly uncomplicated. The rest of his familial bonds were barbed. Viktor, his oldest brother who had far too much in common with their father, had been harsh and cruel during childhood. And Tomas, the second oldest, had only tolerated Cael for a few years before settling into an alliance with Viktor.

His two older brothers had mocked him mercilessly. Cael cried too much, was too moody, was too much of a drain. It used to sting. Part of the reason he'd gone to the colonies in the first place was to prove them wrong. He used to dream of returning as a Vasilikan, more powerful and important and untouchable than they would ever be.

Standing here now, with his lone wing tucked against his back, he realized how foolish that plan had been. He'd become exactly what they'd always claimed.

Useless.

He buried that thought beneath another hearty gulp of ale.

"They're down in the foyer, awaiting our guests." Erik turned away from the gallery wall.

"Why aren't you down there with them?"

"Outcasts aren't worthy of the first impression." Erik's brown eyes flashed with something akin to hurt—pain Cael recognized. Was it selfish of Cael to have left Erik here to suffer their father and older brothers alone?

When Cael had first arrived in the colonies, he'd befriended Tristan because a part of him hoped that Tristan's openness and joviality would rub off on him. But the effects never took. And though Cael didn't *want* to end up like his father—someone who relished in and profited from the world's cruelty—sometimes he felt it was inevitable. A poison in the Zephyrus family blood that Cael was helpless to counteract.

He sipped his ale and surveyed his younger brother. That warm, open expression that was so much more Petra than Arran. Erik was the baby, after all. Maybe Cael *had* done the right thing by leaving and gifting Erik the full might of their mother's abundant affection. He'd often wondered why Erik hadn't left home yet. Perhaps he'd been reluctant to leave Mother alone with these cold, unfeeling Zephyrus males. Perhaps Cael should thank him for that.

The large wooden doors creaked open to reveal his father's deep, grinding voice. "And here are my other two sons."

Arran was accompanied by a paunchy Beastrunner of middling height with bushy black hair and a matching beard. The male's stomach preceded him into the room.

"Cael, Erik, this is Phidion Laskaris," Arran announced.

Laskaris extended a hairy-knuckled hand, his beady eyes crawling over Cael's sole wing.

Cael squeezed Laskaris's hand harder than necessary, inspiring a grunt of discomfort. "Pleasure to meet you, Master Laskaris. Welcome to Stoneridge."

Arran offered Cael an approving nod then turned to Erik, who executed a deep bow and pressed his forehead to Laskaris's proffered hand.

"Master Laskaris, your reputation precedes you. We are honored to have such an icon of continental commerce grace our humble estate." Erik delivered the speech to the ground and Cael swore he saw his brother's lips quirk faintly upward.

So *this* is how Erik had survived Stoneridge all these years—thinly-veiled sarcasm.

Laskaris didn't recognize the jab, his chest swelling with pride as Arran pulled Erik to standing with a look promising death.

Cael bit his lip to keep from laughing.

Petra bustled into the room, a Fae female on each arm. The female on her left was older—Laskaris's wife, no doubt. A beautiful, curvaceous Beastrunner with dark waves and glowing cheeks. She and Petra were laughing together.

The tall, lithe female on Petra's other arm wore a lilac dress that accentuated her creamy complexion. She smoothed back braided bronze hair as she aimed a shy smile at Cael.

"Here is my treasure," Laskaris said, his face beaming with pride. Cael's envy spiked—Arran had certainly never looked at *him* that way. Laskaris grasped his daughter's delicate hand between his mitts, then walked her over to Cael. "Master Zephyrus—"

"Just Cael is fine."

"—allow me to introduce my daughter, Elodie." Laskaris flashed him an indulgent smile. "She's been dying to meet you. Speculated about you the whole way here. Practically talked our ears off."

Elodie smacked her father's hand, ducking her head and releasing a breathy, embarrassed laugh before raising hazel eyes to meet Cael's. They were just as lovely as the rest of her.

But the shade was all wrong.

Nothing like those orbs of sparkling emerald that exposed every facet of his dark soul with their uplifting light.

Elodie lifted her hand and he took it, pressing his lips to her knuckles. "It's lovely to meet you. Would you like something to drink? I hope your journey wasn't uncomfortable."

Laskaris elbowed Arran in the ribs, and his father offered a strained smile.

Cael guided Elodie toward the credenza and her eyes snagged on the snarling grizzly bear head. He could've sworn he felt a shudder rack her thin frame before she leaned in to whisper, "My father's teasing me, but he's not wrong. I *have* been speculating about you. Ever since I learned they'd made this match for me. And I must say, I'm very pleasantly surprised. You're quite handsome."

Her candor coaxed a laugh from him. She pointed to a bottle of white wine, and he poured her a glass. She ran her fingers over his as he passed it to her.

"Yes, well, thank the High Gods for small favors," he chuckled. "The face helps distract from the lost wing."

She ran her tongue over her bottom lip to catch a drop of wine. A calculated seduction tactic that might have even worked on him before he'd... Before *her*.

"I think it adds to your charm." Elodie raised a saucy brow. "And I rather like the thought of you being grounded. You won't be able to fly away from me."

An odd joke, but Cael laughed politely as he led her toward the long mahogany dining table and pulled out her chair.

The families took their seats and the first breaking of bread between them commenced.

"How was the mood on your journey, Phidion?" Arran asked as he speared a roast duck breast and slid it onto Petra's plate.

Arran always served his wife at formal dinners. When Cael was younger, he'd believed it was an affectionate gesture. But now, he saw it for what it was—more evidence of Arran's control over the entire family. Petra didn't seem to mind, and only ever ate what Arran served her. Never requested anything different or asked for seconds.

"Turbulent," Laskaris said around a mouthful of potatoes.

The meal was far too abundant for the ten individuals seated around the table. Heaping platters of roast duck and seared trout, a terrine of squash soup, a mountain of glistening rolls, and three separate vegetables. Plus, several bottles of red and white wine from the credenza. If the turbulence Laskaris mentioned was disrupting the supply chain across the continent, it certainly hadn't affected the Zephyrus household.

"How so?" Arran prodded.

"Cernodas is awash in rebel activity, especially in the countryside we traveled through. Bastards destroyed a hospital in Lodesvale just last week. They've grown increasingly bold."

Viktor, Cael's oldest brother and the spitting image of their father with red-brown hair and piercing steel eyes asked, "What will that mean for your mining business?" Viktor's wife, Helena, who bore an uncomfortable resemblance to Petra, placed her hand on his forearm.

Arran shot Viktor a prideful glance.

Such a fucking kiss ass.

Cael knew their chief concern was what a continent at war with itself would mean for their profits. Arran was scheming to sell weapons to both sides. A risk he was willing to take, since he knew Eamon's Imperial forces weren't numerous enough to fight both the rebels *and* Arran's own Brachian armies. But, production would certainly be hampered if Cernodas fell to the Teles Chrysos and Laskaris couldn't get him any raw materials.

"Hard to tell," Laskaris answered Viktor. "The rebels have made no moves to shut us down, but if the conflict intensifies, shipping across the continent will be difficult. Our main supply route runs through Nephes, as you well know. Stolia and I have begun exploring alternate routes. I may need to raise costs."

Though Arran's face remained neutral, his knuckles whitened as he strangled his knife. Funny—and sad— that thinning profit margins made him angrier than his son's suffering.

The rest of the table quietly munched their dinner, watching the exchange between the two scions.

"Has the Emperor made any official statements?" Arran asked.

Laskaris huffed, a piece of gristle shining in his beard. "Not a word. Ever since he returned from Thalenn he's been quieter than usual. I assume you heard he canceled this month's Imperial Council meeting?"

Arran nodded brusquely. "He's informed all the High Councilors that he doesn't want us traveling to Delos. Too risky. He's concerned for our safety." The last was said with barely concealed disdain. "With a civil war on the horizon, one would think he'd want us in Delos to shore up a coordinated effort." He sliced off a chunk of duck, then tore into the blood-red meat with his sharp fangs.

"There are rumors that his trip to the colonies did not go as intended," Laskaris said. "He had some grand spectacle planned for his return, but canceled it at the last minute."

Cael dipped a spoon into his soup. He hadn't realized Eamon had visited the colonies. Had Tristan seen him? Cael might have known the answer to that question if he'd bothered responding to those windwhispers Tristan had sent. But he'd been so low on those first, horrible nights back at Stoneridge, he couldn't muster the energy to do *anything*. And now the thought of reaching out was too painful.

The less pieces of his old life that he clung to, the better.

"That's enough talk of politics and business," Petra said, placing a light hand on her husband's wrist. Arran's grip on his knife relaxed. "We've got more important matters to discuss." She turned to Laskaris's wife. "Zosime, we've made all the arrangements for the wedding. We didn't feel there was any reason to wait.

I assume you'll all be able to stay at Stoneridge for the next month as we prepare? It will be so lovely to have something to celebrate. Take our minds off this nasty business of war and rebellion."

Cael blanched. A *month*? He didn't realize it would happen so quickly.

"Yes, we're thrilled about the match." Zosime smiled at the couple. "We don't see any reason to wait either. This may be our last opportunity for cross-continental travel for some time." Her cheeks fell as tears pooled in her eyes. "Though it will be difficult for me to leave my baby here."

"Oh, Mama, you worry too much." Elodie beamed at Cael, placing a hand on his forearm. He resisted the instinct to pull away from her touch. "I'm sure my new husband will take very good care of me."

Her gaze bored into his cheek and he forced himself to meet it, but couldn't quite return her smile. He hid it by gulping his wine, letting the alcohol's burn dull his roaring mind.

Across the table, Tomas eyed Elodie with a predatory envy. Cael wondered why Tomas's own fiancée Constance, the Windrider daughter of close family friends, wasn't at this dinner. Purposefully uninvited, no doubt, so Tomas could pursue his philandering unsupervised.

"Wonderful," Petra cooed, her dark eyes shining as she gazed at Cael and Elodie. "It will be good for you, Cael, to have such a fine female at your side."

Cael understood his mother's subtext. *You need someone. You've always needed someone.*

He aimed a tight-lipped grin at his mother, and Elodie clasped their hands together.

"Elodie, I hope you won't mind helping to plan your own wedding," Petra said. "I wouldn't normally ask the bride to assist, but a month is not much time, and I'm afraid we're going to need all hands on deck."

"Not at all, Mother," Elodie said, and Cael nearly choked on his wine. She was calling her Mother already?

Petra snapped her fingers at Erik, who'd leaned his chair back from the table and was chucking potatoes into his open mouth. Arran shot him an annoyed glare, while Viktor and Tomas rolled their eyes. "You'll help, too."

The legs of Erik's chair clacked onto the floor. "How? Isn't this kind of thing better left to the females?"

Petra glared at him. "Now, now. Don't be so primitive. There's plenty you can help with."

Erik crossed his arms and aimed a petulant pout at their mother. "Why doesn't Cael have to help? It's his funeral, after all."

Tomas and Viktor laughed before Helena slapped her husband's wrist and Arran silenced them all. "I've got different work for him." Cael shot his father a questioning glance. Arran hadn't mentioned anything about any kind of work. "We'll discuss it after dinner in my office." He clapped his hands and a mortal servant came bustling into the room. "We're finished. Bring dessert and after-dinner drinks."

The man bowed at the waist, then whistled at the door, summoning a flurry of other servants.

The young woman clearing Elodie's plate dropped it into her lap, and a blob of gravy oozed onto her silk dress.

"Clumsy, stupid human!" Elodie shoved back from the table, flushed with anger, then raised her hand to strike the cowering girl.

Cael shot out of his chair and grabbed his fiancée's hand. No one else at the table had balked at her vitriol. "It was just an accident." He plucked up a napkin and patted at the stain.

The girl curtsied, then hustled, red-faced, out of the room as the rest of the staff cleared the table.

"Cael?" Petra cut in. "Why don't you take Elodie on a tour of the house while the rest of us have our dessert?" Her eyes widened—and not subtly.

"Of course, Mother." He'd lost what little appetite he had left anyway. Had choked down more of the meal tonight than he could stomach. To prove something—though he didn't know what—to his father.

"That sounds wonderful," Elodie preened, smoothing her skirt and reaching for his hand.

"Don't forget to show her the stable loft," Erik snickered, earning a smack atop his skull from Viktor.

The stable loft had been the sight of many a secret tryst by all four brothers over the years. And was the absolute *last* place Cael had any interest in taking Elodie.

But he led her from the room, playing the part of the dutiful fiancé.

He swallowed back his rising nausea. This role, this *life*, was rushing toward him faster than he'd anticipated.

He tried to resign himself to it as he toured Elodie through the estate, barely listening to her endless chatter.

Her plans for the wedding—what the fuck did he care.

Where she thought they might live afterward—wherever, what the fuck did it matter.

How many children they might have—enough for Cael to get his father off his fucking case.

Though briefly, the thought of becoming a father sunk claws past his ribs and he nearly had a panic attack outside the stables. He'd likely be just as shit at it as Arran was.

His future unfurled before him, an endless immortality of doing his father's bidding, raising children with a female he'd never love, and sinking deeper and deeper into his episodes.

This future was the price he'd paid for Xenia's salvation. He'd thought he could live with it as long as she was safe. As long as she had a chance at happiness, even if it didn't include him.

But as he walked the solemn grounds of Stoneridge, his fiancée prattling into the wind, he knew he'd made a terrible bargain.

CHAPTER SIXTEEN

XENIA WAS ONLY HALF-LISTENING as Mistress Ostere, the head of the human staff, lead her on a tour of Stoneridge's lower floors.

Xenia tensed every time they rounded a new corner. Every time the woman opened a new door. Every time they reached a new hallway.

But Xenia had yet to encounter what she was looking for.

Gray eyes, grumpy frown, lone wing.

When Xenia had arrived earlier, Master Laskaris had given her into the care of Mistress Ostere, who seemed kind enough, if not a little curt. Grumbled something about having to train new staff at a time like this.

"Here's your room," the woman said, opening a door at the end of a low-ceilinged hallway. The cramped nook contained nothing but a pine-framed bed and wardrobe.

More comfortable than Xenia's last cell, but still a cell.

"Shared bathroom's over there." Mistress Ostere gestured down the hall before opening the wardrobe to reveal three evergreen dresses and white aprons, plus several pairs of gray stockings. "Your new uniform." She pulled a box from her pocket and handed it to Xenia, who rattled the contents. "Hair pins. Keep that wild mane of curls tamed. From now on, you're invisible. Your goal is to blend in with the furniture. Do not speak to the Fae unless spoken to first. And even on those rare occasions, be absolutely certain a verbal response is desired. And keep *away* from the High Councilor's sons. Especially Tomas, the blond one. If he gets a hold of you, it's best to just let him have his way. Don't fight him. He's killed human girls for less."

Xenia shuddered, trying to find the positives of her situation and coming up empty. She was nothing but a piece of property—bought and sold to a new master. Barely different than the Shrouded Sister she'd been in the colonies.

Though there was *one* positive here.

Cael.

She needed to find him and convince him to…do what, exactly? Escape with her? Return to the colonies? Join the rebellion she'd heard Laskaris yammering about during their journey?

"Get yourself dressed, and pin back your hair," Mistress Ostere said, exiting Xenia's room to give her privacy to change.

"It's time for your introduction to the High Councilor."

Xenia stood in the darkened hallway outside High Councilor Zephyrus's office, pulling at the hem which barely passed the top of her thigh-high wool stockings. She didn't want to expose her thighs, especially not in front of Phidion Laskaris, whose growly voice echoed through the thick oak doors.

Mistress Ostere was already gone, having deposited Xenia here moments ago. She'd told Xenia to listen for a pause in the conversation, then knock to be let in. Xenia was a bit shocked to be left to her own devices.

Was the woman not concerned that Xenia might try to escape? She hadn't toured these upper floors yet, but they were as silent as the night outside. Perfect for prowling.

Xenia had already risked plenty to find Cael. Why stop now?

She'd only taken a few steps away from the office doors when someone shuffled up behind her and a deep, amused voice whispered into her ear, "What are you doing up here alone, little human?"

She spun to face a handsome Fae male with melted chocolate eyes and the same tousled hair as Cael. His wry smirk exposed a hint of fang, and his fleshy wings rose over his shoulders.

Xenia didn't know if she should answer or not. Had he seen her slip away from the door? And what had Mistress Ostere said? Don't speak unless spoken to.

The male was very obviously one of Cael's brothers. If she hadn't been able to tell from the hair, his long nose and sharp jawline would've given it away. His lips were fuller though, and he had an air of casual sensuality that didn't match Cael's severity.

He stepped closer. "Are you new here? You seem lost. You can answer me, you know." He held out a hand. "Erik Zephyrus. Third spare heir and indolent lay-about."

She shook his proffered hand. It was warm and soft, no hint of those warrior's calluses Cael sported. She couldn't be sure if she had anything to fear from Erik. He wasn't the blond brother Mistress Ostere had warned her about, but she had no idea if Erik shared Cael's tolerance of humans.

She dipped her head as she answered, making herself as small and meek as possible. "My name is Xenia. I just arrived today. Mistress Ostere brought me up here to meet the High Councilor."

"Come then, I'll introduce you." He lifted her chin. "But you must cower and pretend to be terribly impressed by my father, otherwise you'll bruise his fragile ego and he'll force Mistress Ostere to assign you some terrible task like mucking the stables or cleaning the toilets." He opened the door and, placing a hand on the small of her back, led her into the room.

The smell hit her first, a charred licorice scent she didn't recognize. And then there was the smoke—whipped cream clouds so thick she could only see seated silhouettes through them. Across the room, a massive oak desk was piled with folders, logbooks, and loose documents. A violet commstone had been discarded atop the mess.

"Ah, here's the gift I was telling you about, Arran." Laskaris swatted away the smoke, revealing his pudgy face, then pushed up from the leather couch and extinguished his cigarette. His pupils were so dilated, he could've been drinking Delirium. But she didn't see any bottles on the coffee table.

Erik nudged her forward, and Laskaris's palms fell upon her shoulders as he examined her face, hair, and uniform. His glazed eyes snagged on her skirt, and she fought an urge to tug her hem down again. "Yes, they've cleaned you up nicely."

He turned Xenia toward Arran, and she averted her gaze to the floor, suddenly terrified that Cael's father could see right through her. That he knew who she was, what she and Cael had done, and would punish her for it.

Or worse, punish his son.

Her brief glimpse had revealed braided copper hair, a long, groomed beard, and two enormous dusky wings tipped with sharp black talons.

Arran Zephyrus was not a Fae that *any* human would dare look in the eye.

Laskaris petted her hair. "Pretty thing, isn't she? And quite tall, for a human. When I saw her, I knew she'd be the perfect addition to your household. You don't have any blondes, do you?"

Xenia didn't dare look up, though she heard Arran's sniff before his voice cut through her, sharp as steel and twice as deadly. "No. We don't."

Her heart hammered as the toes of his thick boots invaded her line of sight, and she rubbed clammy palms on her apron.

Arran snatched her jaw, not gently, and forced her head up.

High Gods, those were *Cael's* eyes piercing her. Flint gray and unyielding.

He turned her face side to side, then released her chin to peruse the rest of her, grunting his disapproval. "This one will be a distraction. You really shouldn't have, Phidion."

Laskaris waved a hairy hand. "Nonsense. I asked around for weeks, trying to figure out what to give my oldest friend and most cherished business partner. And soon to be co-grand-parent, Faurana bless us." He wheezed out a laugh, spittle coating his thick lips, and Xenia's stomach churned.

She'd almost forgotten that she was the family's *wedding* gift.

"I don't usually allow pretty young women onto the household staff," Arran said. "Not after what happened to the last one."

Laskaris laughed. "Oh, I'll bet there's a fun story there."

Erik piped up from where he was leaning against the forest-green damask wallpaper. "Fun for Tomas. Not so fun for the human he impregnated."

Though his words were casual, irreverent even, there was a dark edge to his tone.

"Why?" Laskaris asked, picking a spot of ash from his beard. "What happened to her? When my humans get pregnant, we just add the child to the staff."

"That's not how we do things here," Arran growled, flaring his wings. "I took care of it. We do not sully our bloodline with half-human bastards." He bent forward, bringing his terrifying face far too close to her own. She was going to vomit all over his boots. "If you value your pathetic mortal existence, you'll keep your legs closed and stay away from my sons."

"Y-yes, sir."

Arran's hand was instantly at her throat. "Do not speak to me unless I explicitly tell you to do so. Is that clear?"

Xenia nodded furiously, her eyes stinging, trying to suck a breath past Arran's vise-like grip.

"She's turning purple, Father," Erik crooned. "You should probably let go before you waste the surely considerable amount of *drachas* Laskaris spent on this gift."

Laskaris laughed nervously. "A pittance."

Arran released her and she gulped down a breath as quietly as possible, not wanting to anger him further.

He strode to his desk and opened a drawer. The device he pulled out resembled a stun pistol, but the barrel ended in a thick needle-like spout. He placed something into the chamber, then racked the pistol. Xenia jumped at the terrifying click before he snapped his fingers at her. "Come."

She rushed over, didn't dare hesitate, and he grabbed her by the back of the neck. Before she could tense her muscles, Arran pressed the needle underneath her ear and pulled the trigger.

Fiery pain radiated through her jaw, and she clenched her teeth to muffle a scream.

"A tracking device," Arran whispered. "And if you try to leave the estate or remove it, well..." His bloodthirsty smile was the most terrifying thing Xenia had yet encountered on the continent. "Let's just say you wouldn't be very pretty anymore." Xenia quivered, lifting her fingers to the wound before Arran crushed her hand in his fist. "Don't touch it. It's coated in healing salve and will heal quickly. Return to your quarters."

Xenia darted for the door, trying not to think about how drastically her circumstances had just changed. A fucking *tracking device*? Oh, her mission to find Cael was going great.

She wrapped her fingers around the bronze handle and pulled the door open.

Then nearly collapsed to her knees in bone-deep relief when she saw who filled it.

CHAPTER SEVENTEEN

C AEL WAS HALLUCINATING.

He had to be.

An after-effect of the lethaphyll smoke that billowed from the open door of his father's office.

What in the ever-loving name of fucking *Stygios* was Xenia doing here? Wearing the uniform of the Stoneridge household staff, no less?

A smile ghosted over her lips, then died when he didn't return it.

Of course he didn't. Was she insane? Thank fuck the three other males behind her hadn't seen it.

Arran raised his head. "Yes? What do you want, Cael? Laskaris and I were just finishing up."

"I…" Cael started, but couldn't find his voice.

Xenia was here. In his father's fucking office. Nowhere near where she was supposed to be: safely ensconced in the Temple in the colonies.

She stared at the floor, wringing her fingers. Her hair had been pinned back into a low, puffy bun—a travesty. He ached to remove the pins, let her gorgeous curls spring forth with wild abandon.

Erik pushed off the wall and slapped a hand on Cael's shoulder. "Laskaris's wedding gift. A new human pet for the household staffs." He dipped his head, huffing a laugh. "I meant staff. Silly of me." His gaze bounced between Cael and Xenia, far too knowingly.

Cael trusted his baby brother more than anyone else in his family, but the thought of Arran interpreting whatever energy Erik had just sensed between him and Xenia…

Terror prickled down Cael's spine.

"Cael," Arran barked, breaking him from his stupor.

"Yes, Father, sorry, I… Hollins came to fetch me after I escorted Elodie back to her room. Said you were ready to meet with me."

Out of the corner of his eye, he swore he saw Xenia flinch at his fiancée's name. She'd need to learn how to control her reactions. Every thought, every emotion was written so plainly across her face. He adored that about her. But here at Stoneridge, it could get her killed.

"Hollins?" Arran asked.

"Your valet?"

Arran waved him off. As if he couldn't be bothered to remember the man's name. "Your work begins tomorrow. All new customer inquiries are now your responsibility."

Cael's wing twitched. "I'm not—"

"You've missed a great deal since you were off playing nursemaid in the colonies." Cael fought the urge to flick his eyes toward Xenia. Arran flung a packet of documents at him. "Not to mention I had to find a job you were capable of in your state." Arran dragged his disgusted gaze across Cael's lone wing. Cael wished he could say it didn't sting. "Review those and start arranging meetings. Time to prove your worth to this family."

Cael nodded, then glanced at Laskaris, whose heavy head dipped against his chest, his eyelids fluttering.

Erik pulled the male from the couch. "Come on, Phidion. I'll take you to your room. Cael, perhaps you can escort the little human back to her quarters?" A sly smirk, there and gone in an instant.

"Yes," Arran grumbled. "Get her out of here. Her mortal scent is growing pungent."

Xenia emanated a mixture of fear and excitement, tangy with a hint of peppery sweetness. Nearly as much of a tell as that small smile she'd given Cael.

She kept her head bowed as Cael approached. "Let's go," he snapped as he dragged her, as gently as possible, into the hallway.

The office door shut with an echoing thud, and down the hall, Erik and Phidion rounded the corner out of sight.

Xenia's head popped up and she opened her mouth.

He clapped his hand over it. "Not here."

He pulled her through the dark halls, then down the back stairs to the servant's quarters. "Which one?"

She raised a shaky hand, and he towed her into the last room at the end of the hallway. He cast a windshield around the walls to muffle their voices.

He leaned his head back against the door, staring at her from underneath slitted lids and trying to slow his frenzied heart.

She paused by her small bed, cheeks flushed, her breathing just as erratic as his own.

Her emerald eyes—that unforgettable, alluring color, Cael's favorite in the entire world—shone with teary relief. And apprehension.

His chest cracked open.

"Say something," she whispered.

He strode forward and grasped her soft face between his hands.

"You reckless little *fool*," he growled.

Then crushed his mouth to hers.

Relief pounded through Xenia, a heady release, as she whimpered into Cael's mouth.

She'd found him. Sure, it was in the most roundabout and dangerous way possible, the consequences of which hadn't even begun to be felt.

But she didn't care about any of that right now. Not with his hands and mouth on her.

Cael hoisted her up, wrapped her thighs around his waist, and slammed her into the wall. She broke their kiss, worried someone might have heard.

"Wind-shield," he croaked, his face so achingly close to hers. Everything she'd wanted since Rhamnos. Since far earlier than that, if she were being honest. "No one will hear."

The firm evidence of how much he'd missed her dragged along her center.

She had half a mind to scream at him. If he wanted her as badly as she could feel he did, why had he tried to send her away?

Her anger dissolved into rapturous shudders as he pressed soft kisses to her jaw, whispering her name like a prayer against her skin.

He moved back to her mouth, then stroked his tongue along the seam. She opened for him, tangling her fingers in his hair and tugging at the soft tendrils at his nape.

High Gods, *this* was why she hadn't stayed on that ship. She would've risked a thousand dangerous treks across the continent for just this single taste of him.

His fingertips trailed beneath her skirt, meeting her bare flesh far too briefly before he tensed and dropped her.

Her feet fell to the floor as she panted, undone by his kiss, and he pressed a fist against the wall above her head. "We can't," he eked out, eyes squeezed shut as if he didn't dare look at her. "They'll scent it."

She reached up to grab his chin. "Cael."

His eyes popped open, and she was skewered by the fear and longing in their thundercloud depths.

"What. The fuck. Are you doing here?" His breath pelted her lips and despite his barely restrained violence, he began gently tugging out her hair pins. "Why didn't you go back to the colonies?"

"I—" she started, then steeled her expression. "You know why."

"I really don't." He crossed his arms over his broad chest, his biceps straining his evergreen dinner jacket. "I told you there was nothing between us."

"I think you might be lying." Her lips curled as she darted her eyes toward the obvious bulge tenting his pants.

"This isn't a fucking joke!" he roared.

His fury coaxed hers to life. How fucking *dare* he?

"Isn't it?" She struggled to keep her voice level. "Over the past week, I've been abducted, thrown in the back of a truck, stripped bare, fed from, sold off, and had a tracking device implanted into my neck!"

Cael's face paled as he stepped into her, tilting her jaw to the side and brushing his thumb over the wound on her neck. "He put it in already?"

She nodded, tears welling.

He released her, then slumped onto the bed and dropped his head into his hands. "This is a disaster."

She wanted to step between his knees, rest his head against her stomach, assure him that everything was going to be okay now that they were together again.

But given his turbulent reaction, she didn't know if she even believed that herself.

"You were supposed to go back to the colonies," he muttered. "You were going to be safe there. I would've learned to live with it."

"Lived with what?"

Cael cupped his hands together, circling a thumb into his palm, eyes downcast. "The bittersweet agony of knowing you still existed in this world, but would never be mine." When he finally looked up, his anguish stole her breath. "I can't protect you from my father here. And now you're his fucking *property*."

"We'll figure something out," Xenia volunteered.

"I'm getting married in a month. And my new *wife* and I will be expected to get our own household and start pumping out heirs to shore up the bloodline. Even if he'd agree to have you transferred to my household, is that what you would want?"

He rose from the bed, a ferocious beast stalking its prey, and backed her against the wall again. He shoved a hand under her skirt to caress the skin above her stockings. "*Is* that what you want? To be my dirty little secret? The human mistress I fuck behind closed doors while my wife stands beside me in public?"

She shuddered as he inched his hand higher, tantalizingly close to her very bare, and very wet, sex. The weight of his body, his intoxicating scent— rainswept meadows and cool earth—the exploratory trail of his fingers… It was too much. In this moment, she would've given him everything, agreed to anything he asked. Even to being his whore.

He trembled as he grazed a fingertip up her slit. "*Fuck*, why aren't you ever wearing any underwear?"

Her knees nearly buckled as she choked out, "You are being extremely confusing right now."

He removed his hand from her skirt and dropped his forehead against the crown of her head. "That's because you confuse the fuck out of me." He cupped her cheeks again, gentle Cael making a rare appearance. "Why did you come back for me?"

"Because we're not finished with each other. And I missed arguing with you." He snorted an amused laugh and released her face. "Do you... Are you... Do you *want* to get married?"

"Not to her," Cael grimaced. "But even *if* I were to break off this engagement—which my father would never let me do—and find a way to leave Stoneridge, what will happen to *you*? He has the rest of my life planned out. If he thinks I'm straying from that path, he'll come looking for the reason. If he finds a single shred of evidence that it's you, he will kill you. And I will die before I let that happen."

Xenia rubbed at the small scar beneath her ear. "I—"

"*If* I were to even consider leaving here with you—" Xenia let out a small gasp of excitement and Cael narrowed his eyes, "—we would need to get that thing out first."

"How?" Xenia asked. "He said he'd be able to tell if it was tampered with or if I tried to remove it."

"He's right. Those things are bespelled against such interferences. We'll need to see what we can learn about them. Have they given you your assignment yet?"

"No, I've only just arrived this afternoon."

"You need to be extremely wary. Around my father, obviously. Around Laskaris. He looks at you like he regrets not purchasing you for his own household. And especially around my brother Tomas. Viktor won't look twice at you; he's inherited my father's distaste for humans. But Tomas…"

"I've been warned. What happened? Your father said something about Tomas getting a human pregnant and said he *took care of it.* Did he force her to get rid of the baby?"

Cael laughed bitterly. "No. He took a rather more permanent means of quashing the issue. He stabbed her in the stomach and slit her throat. Then strung her up in front of the estate. Left her there to rot as a warning. As much for my brothers as for the human staff. Arran Zephyrus never misses an opportunity to flaunt his cruelty. Toward humans *or* Fae."

Bile crawled across the back of Xenia's tongue, and tears pricked her eyes.

"Cassandra is probably going out of her mind with worry." Cael scrubbed a hand down his face. "The last I spoke with Tristan, I told him we would be back in the colonies in a few days. That was several weeks ago at this point."

"Have you talked to him since? Perhaps you can send him a windwhisper. Let him and Cass know that I'm safe."

"You're not safe," Cael grumbled.

"*Relatively* safe. Not dead at least."

Cael's face grew serious as he ran a knuckle along her jaw. She leaned into his touch. "I will do everything in my power to protect you while we figure out how to get that tracking device out. But we need to be careful. And we need to do this *right*."

Xenia wanted to say she knew that. Wanted to beg him to leave with her right now, tracking device be damned. To run away to some deserted area of the continent—if such a place existed—and let her heal him, body and spirit. But she knew it wasn't possible yet.

She yawned, covering her mouth with the back of her hand, her fear and adrenaline giving way to exhaustion.

"You should get some sleep," Cael said. "Lock the door behind me. I don't think anyone will bother you tonight. Thank the High Gods Tomas hasn't seen you yet." He flexed his hand, then balled it into a fist at his side. "Especially in that outfit."

Her heart trilled as he stepped over to cup her face again. He tilted his head down, and she closed her eyes, desire a hot pulse between her legs.

But his lips landed on her temple, not her mouth. Her shoulders dipped in disappointment.

He stepped around her, then waved away his windshield and strode for the door. Before he opened it and without turning to face her, he whispered, "I missed you, Blondie."

He exited the room and she shuddered out a relieved breath.

Despite the danger of her current circumstances, despite her terror and fatigue and anger, a small spark of her persistent optimism flared behind her ribs.

She'd found him again. Against all odds, and across a fucking continent.

If she could do *that*, Mighty Anaemos, she could do anything.

Even convince a stubborn, one-winged, century-and-a-half-old Fae male to run away with her.

CHAPTER EIGHTEEN

CASSANDRA FOLLOWED MIREILLE THROUGH the sun-dappled city, taking the time to review her surroundings. A luxury which Wormwood had not afforded her last night when she'd arrived.

This morning, there were more Fae—citizens? prisoners? Cassandra didn't know what to call them—gathered in weary groups on stoops and before storefronts. They lowered their conversations whenever Mireille and Cassandra neared, passing establishments so ordinary Cassandra nearly laughed despite her circumstances: grocers, tailors, salons and barber shops, even a bookstore.

Cassandra wondered where that inventory would have come from. Did the Koenig summon books with his magic warhammer, or were there authors behind the wards that supplied the stories?

Xenia would have been so curious.

That hole beneath Cassandra's ribs widened as thoughts of Xenia turned to thoughts of Reena turned to thoughts of Tristan.

All she wanted to do was return to Mireille's apartment, crawl back into bed, and slip into an unconsciousness where she wouldn't be forced to think about everyone she'd lost.

The *last* thing she wanted to be doing this morning was sword training.

So she was pleasantly surprised when they arrived at a bathhouse instead. "What are we... I thought we were starting training this morning?"

"We are," Mireille said flatly.

Cassandra's spirits dipped again as Mireille led her around the back of the building, then into a humid hallway lined with metal doors.

"What is this place?" Cassandra asked, swatting away steam.

"Used to be a gymnasium. The Koenig and his Brethren trained down here before they built themselves a grander space up at the palace."

"How do you have access to it?"

"I crafted a potion to soothe the proprietor's migraines and he was so grateful that he offered to let me use any room whenever I wanted."

Mireille opened one of the doors and gestured for Cassandra to step through.

It was a simple room with nothing more than a dirt floor and a rack of equipment on the wall.

Mireille plucked up two stone practice swords, then handed one to Cassandra. Her arm dipped.

"The real ones will be heavier," Mireille warned. "Did you exercise at all in the intake tower?"

Cassandra flared her wings in annoyance. "I was working on other areas. Trying to make sure I was capable of carrying these things so no one would be able to tell I've only been a Windrider for—" she canted her head, calculating "—two weeks."

"You'll need to work even harder to carry them through a fight."

"I know," Cassandra sighed.

"So, what kind of training *do* you have?"

"My father instructed me in hand-to-hand combat and dagger fighting when I was younger. Before he died."

Grief darkened Mireille's features, and Cassandra wondered if something had happened to her own parents.

She was on the verge of probing when Mireille cut her off. "Show me."

"What, just like, come at you?" Cassandra burbled a nervous laugh. She'd fought Fae before. Mostly Deathstalkers. But that was a lifetime ago. In a different city.

In a different *body*.

"Yes," Mireille said, lifting her sword. "Try to get a hit on me. Every time you succeed, I'll give you a five minute break." The corner of her mouth curled upward.

The smile died on her lips as Ronin padded into the room, then leaned against the wall and crossed his arms over his broad chest. Cassandra hadn't seen him since last night. He'd left the apartment this morning before she'd woken up.

"Glad you could join us," Mireille said, her eyes still focused on Cassandra.

"*Are* we glad?" Cassandra grumbled. "Not sure I want an audience for this."

"Ignore him. You'll have a larger audience during the appeal. The loudest of which will want nothing more than to see you lose. You might as well get used to it."

Ronin nodded subtly, and a little flicker of pride flitted through Mireille's mercurial gaze.

"All right," Cassandra muttered, raising her sword. "Here goes nothing."

It was, quite literally, nothing.

For nearly an hour, Cassandra attempted to get a hit on Mireille as the she-wolf parried and pivoted and knocked away every single strike, barking commands.

Keep your sword up! Stop signaling the direction of your blows! Plant your feet!

By the time Mireille called it, Cassandra was a sweaty mess. Her muscles quivered as she dropped the practice sword, then folded in half and rested her hands on her thighs.

Mireille hadn't even broken a sweat.

Cassandra thought she was in good shape. But maybe she'd only been in good *human* shape. And she cursed her new Fae body. What good were magical healing abilities if they didn't offer instant pain relief?

"Honestly, you did better than I expected," Mireille said with a wry smile, clapping a hand on Cassandra's shoulder.

Cassandra glanced up, breaths sawing through her open mouth. Her wings drooped on the dusty floor, her back muscles just as spent as the rest of her.

"I can tell you were trained for combat with a dagger and not a broadsword," Mireille said. "It's a different fighting style. You're trying to get too close. And you're overusing your thrusts. You're fighting against the sword."

"It's fighting against me!" Cassandra rose from her crouch and knocked away Mireille's hand.

Mireille's face hardened. "You must *embrace* it. So well that it becomes an extension of your arms, your body. We need to work on your muscle tone, too." She grabbed a bottle from her sack and handed it to Cassandra, who sucked down the entire thing, water streaming down her chin.

"And that's where I come in," Ronin chimed in.

Cassandra groaned.

Mireille toweled off, taking a wide path around Ronin as she walked toward the door. "Good luck."

"Where are you going?" Cassandra asked, panicky. She didn't want to be left alone with Ronin and his torture exercises.

"I've got catching up to do at the shop." Mireille jutted her chin toward Ronin as she left the training room. "She's all yours."

Ronin pushed off the wall, clapping his hands together. He looked exhausted. Like he hadn't slept at all. And she could guess what he'd been doing all morning. Searching the city for Selene.

She wanted to ask if he'd found any leads. Wanted to ask why he hadn't solicited Mireille's help.

But he cut her off before she could.

"Sword down, Cass," he said, with a hint of a weary smirk.

"Time to power up those new Fae muscles."

Later that night, Ronin eased into the apothecary shop, reaching up to muffle the bell. Was he doing it out of some generosity of spirit, not wanting to disturb Mireille and Cassandra from their rest? Or was it because he didn't want them to know he'd returned so late and ask where he'd been?

Or why he looked so disappointed?

He'd spent the entire day—except the hours he'd been training Cass this afternoon—canvassing the city for clues to Selene's whereabouts. Nobody he'd spoken with recalled seeing a petite white wolf bi-form with Ronin's coloring.

There'd been a flash of hope when his interrogations had led to a Deathstalker male who'd arrived around the same time as Selene's arrest. But whatever the male had seen during his journey through the mists had traumatized him. He could barely remember his own name, let alone the other prisoners he'd been sentenced with.

It was okay, Ronin assured himself. It was *fine*. This was a city of thousands. His search would not end today.

He could have asked Mireille, but couldn't bring himself to do it. Some stupid impulse to protect her. Though based on her chilly reception, he didn't know why he assumed she'd even care.

He tiptoed through the darkened shop and up the stairs, scenting dried mint, rosemary, lavender and other musty, earthy smells he didn't recognize.

He creaked open the apartment door, then stopped short.

Mireille sat at the kitchen table drinking tea, a chess board mid-game spread before her.

She tensed when he walked in, but kept her gaze glued to the pieces.

This was *fine*, too. She'd been absent from his life for far, far longer than she'd been present. Avoiding her, avoiding *thoughts* of her, had become second nature.

But catching her now, the long copper waves cascading down her black silk robe, the delicate fingers clutched around her mug, the shrewd eyes studying the board of a game *he'd* taught her to play...

For a moment, he forgot how to breathe. His control slipped, and the sense memories bombarded him.

Snow falling in giant, fluffy flakes against a cold, black night.

The smoky warmth of a fire.

Throaty laughter and ivory skin and quicksilver smiles.

And a feeling in his chest like he'd finally come home.

He stood in the doorway, struck dumb by the ghosts of their shared past, and scratched at his left pectoral.

"Close the door," Mireille said, not looking up from her game. "You're letting the heat out."

Ronin did as she'd asked, then turned toward his room.

"Did you find anything?" she asked quietly.

"How did you—"

"Cassandra told me." She took a sip from her mug.

"No. Nothing useful."

"I'm sorry."

And either she was the world's greatest actress—a remnant of her days as a spy for Imperial Affairs in the Northern Territories—or the sympathy in her tone was genuine.

"What are you drinking?" he asked, ambling over to the table.

"Vodka."

"Out of a chipped ceramic mug? Classy."

"Yes, etiquette is our chief concern here in Tartarus." She caught his gaze and the teasing smirk on her face raked nails across his heart. "Do you want some?"

He heard the subcontext.

Do you want to talk about it?

"I…"

He shouldn't. He *couldn't*. Cold indifference. That's what he'd promised himself.

It was the only way to survive her again.

His wolf whined and tore at his insides, making his opinion on Mireille's offer really fucking clear.

Ronin shook his head and turned down the hall. Behind him, Mireille let out a ragged sigh.

Before he entered his bedroom, he said over his shoulder. "You still play."

It wasn't a question, but Creator, it felt like one.

"I play every night after I'm done in the shop," she said.

"When do you dance?"

"I don't. Not anymore."

The admission sliced deeper than her teasing. She'd been so skilled—the most talented dancer in Kheimos. In all of Ethyrios, really. Not to mention, she'd loved it. So much that she hadn't given it up even when her assignments with the IA had monopolized her time. Why would she give it up now, when time was her most abundant resource?

He wanted to ask, but was too tired, too anxious.

Too cowardly.

It was probably his fault. All of this was. Mireille's incarceration, Selene's arrest, Cassandra's training failures, and—

"Check the taverns," Mireille said, cutting through his self-loathing. "Most prisoners have visited at least a time or two. Perhaps one of the bartenders or servers has seen her."

"And if they haven't?" Ronin's voice nearly broke.

Mireille turned her attention back to the game, her fingers lingering atop the white queen.

"Then you may have come to Tartarus for nothing."

CHAPTER NINETEEN

"LINE UP, EVERYONE!"

Mistress Ostere's clipped voice pulled Xenia from her breakfast of chopped apples and oatmeal. She pushed away from the table and joined the line of servants along the wall of the staff dining room on Stoneridge's lower level.

Feet shifted, stubble was scratched, and yawns were stifled as Mistress Ostere surveyed her charges. The staff woke early, long before the sun, in order to get the estate up and running for the Zephyruses and their guests.

"Stoneridge is going to be in a state of constant activity for the next month," Mistress Ostere said as she paced back and forth along the line. "Preparations for Master Cael and Mistress Elodie's wedding will take precedence over any of your regular duties. And I don't think I have to tell you that, should you be drawn away to work on something for the wedding, you will still be required to fulfill your regularly duties afterward."

The responding grumbles and huffs were quickly silenced when Mistress Ostere whipped her head in search of the source.

"It's going to be a long, hard month, but I trust you will all uphold the reputation of the household during that time."

Mistress Ostere stopped in front of Xenia. "I'd also like to introduce you all to Mistress Cirillo."

Xenia almost didn't realize the woman was talking about her. Mistress Cirillo was her mother. She was *Sister* Cirillo.

What an oddly out of body experience; being bestowed with a new title.

"She's new to the household. I trust you will all make her welcome and provide any requested assistance as she settles into her duties and learns the rules."

Something about the way Mistress Ostere said *rules* was quite ominous.

Xenia lifted her head, surveying the reactions of her new colleagues—a few kind smiles, a few lingering looks, even a wary glare or two.

Mistress Ostere folded her hands behind her back. "Off you go. Have a productive day, everyone."

The staff filed out while Xenia stayed against the wall, nodding her head and muttering *hellos* and *thank yous* to those who welcomed her on their way out.

Once the space was empty, she found Mistress Ostere staring at her, head cocked. "You're a bit more obedient than some of our previous newcomers. What's your history, then?"

Xenia rubbed at her right wrist, at the empty space where her tattoo had been. "I was a Shrouded Sister in Thalenn before I…came here." Such a simple way to describe her perilous journey.

"Praise Letha," Mistress Ostere said.

"Praise Letha," Xenia echoed quietly.

The woman stepped towards her, tugging at a stray curl. "You're going to be a problem."

"No, I—"

"It wasn't a question." Mistress Ostere's lips flattened. "The pretty ones always are." The woman's eyes flashed with concern. "What skills do you possess? I'm trying to figure out where I could best place you to minimize…temptations. Do you have any experience with gardening or landscape work?"

Xenia shook her head.

Mistress Ostere stood silently, waiting for Xenia to elaborate. When she didn't, the woman sighed heavily. "I'll have you assist with the housekeeping."

Housekeeping. Xenia could manage that.

"Keep your head down and do your work. You can start with the offices on the first floor. Master Zephyrus and his sons will be leaving on business for the day after breakfast." She gestured toward silver serving trays on the counter between the dining room and the kitchen, each holding a folded name card. "Then this afternoon, move to the bedrooms in the guest wing."

"Yes, Mistress." Xenia bobbed a curtsy and Mistress Ostere hustled out of the room.

Xenia lingered to examine the trays. Searching for one in particular.

When she found it, she peered into the kitchen, seeing if any of the staff had noticed her. They were all occupied wiping down appliances and cleaning dishes.

She plucked a pen from a cup, snatched the card with Cael's name, and wrote a message on the other side.

She snickered to herself, wishing she could be there to see Cael's face when he read it.

She returned the card to his tray and the pen to the cup, then smiled as she left the kitchen and headed to the upper floors to begin her first official day as a servant of Stoneridge.

The lingering scent of lethaphyll smoke crept up Xenia's nostrils as she paused before Arran Zephyrus's office.

She re-adjusted her bucket of cleaning supplies and pushed through the heavy oak doors.

Murky light spilled through the wall-spanning, two-story window, through which she spied a small army of servants landscaping the mist-covered meadow behind the lodge.

Preparing it for the wedding.

Xenia swallowed her deadline-inspired panic, placed her bucket by the door, and walked over to Arran's desk. It had been organized since last night, the piles of documents now corralled into mesh bins.

After a swift glance toward the doors, she began rifling through drawers.

When she found the golden pistol with the long, needle-like spout, she reflexively smoothed a palm over the tiny scar on her neck.

Next to the pistol was a small cardboard box full of what looked like translucent grains of rice.

She pinched one between her fingers and held it up to the light. There was a trace of orange in the center, but the device was cold, lifeless. Nothing like the faint sub-dermal heat in her neck.

She wondered what activated the devices. A living body, perhaps?

She slipped the grain into her apron and shut the drawer.

Suddenly, the door swung open, spilling her bucket of supplies.

"Oh! Oh, I'm sorry. I didn't realize—" A beautiful Beastrunner female with golden-bronze hair stepped into the room, freezing as she caught sight of Xenia.

Elodie.

Cael's *fiancée*.

The polite shock on Elodie's face melted into haughtiness. "What are you doing in here?"

Xenia wanted to throw her shoulders back and interrogate. Elodie had even less of a reason to be in here.

Xenia rounded the desk, eyes cemented to the floor. "Are you searching for Master Zephyrus, Mistress?" she asked in a meek voice. "I'm afraid he's left for the day."

Elodie scoffed, then crossed her arms. "Yes, of course I was looking for him. Why else would I be in here?" Xenia lifted her chin enough to note the unmistakable hint of panic in Elodie's hazel eyes.

"Would you like me to let him know you were—"

"No!" Elodie shouted. "No." She turned on her heel and rushed from the room, stumbling over Xenia's bucket. "And don't leave your things just laying anywhere!" She shouted as she scrambled, red-faced, out of the office.

Xenia ruminated on the odd exchange while she dusted bookshelves, polished the leather furniture, cleaned the window, and emptied the trash bin.

It was only as she was leaving the office, about to shut the door, that she realized what had thrown her.

Elodie hadn't knocked.

CHAPTER TWENTY

"So, is this where you bring all the girls?" Xenia asked, following Cael up a wooden ladder into the cramped stable loft. She flopped down onto a spiky bale, her head nearly touching the slanted ceiling.

"And boys." Cael winked, dropping into a cross-legged position in front of her.

And though the words were playful, Xenia could tell by his drooping wing and caved shoulders that his heart wasn't in them. He looked exhausted.

They'd agreed to meet here tonight to check in, and though Xenia had *plenty* of news to share, she questioned whether she should burden him with any of it.

Straws poked through her skirt, biting into the bare skin above her stockings, and the loft had a cozy, nostalgic smell. One she remembered well from her parents' farm in Primarvia: apples, hay, leather, and the sweet underlying scent of manure.

She imagined what it might be like had Cael lured her here for a different, more intimate purpose. How he might lay her down on the dusty boards. How strands of hay might catch in her curls. How he might slowly lift her skirt and trail his fingers up her—

"For the love of Anaemos, Blondie," Cael said, pinching the bridge of his nose. "You do realize I can scent every dirty thought running through your head, right?"

Xenia shrugged. "You never should've told me what you used to do up here."

Cael propped his elbows on his knees and placed his chin atop his folded hands. "How was your day? Where has Mistress Ostere assigned you?"

Xenia told him about her housekeeping duties, about how she'd spent the morning cleaning his father's office. She pulled the tiny grain from her pocket and handed it to him. "I found this in his desk."

Cael twisted the device in his fingers, holding it close to his face.

"What do you think that orange glow is?" Xenia asked.

"No idea," Cael muttered. "Did you find any documentation with it?"

"Yes," Xenia said, her tone dripping with sarcasm. "It was right beneath the box. And there was a sign on the drawer that said 'inside is the manual that explains how to deactivate my sinister tracking devices'."

Cael laughed, crinkling his eyes in a way that made him look a bit less tired. And had Xenia's heart soaring. She *loved* making him laugh. Could spend the rest of her life doing it.

"Stupid question. Been a long day." He expelled a weary sigh, and she couldn't help yawning in response.

"Djoo get my note?" she asked.

"*I don't have to give up on my hopes and dreams,*" Cael said with a smirk. "As affirmations go, that one was a little on the nose, don't you think?"

"Did you say it?"

He tossed a wayward curl off his forehead and looked up at her through thick, brown lashes. "Yes, ma'am."

Curse Amatu, he was so fucking handsome she almost forgot what they were talking about.

"How many times?" she asked.

"Five. More than the recommended dosage in your very thorough directions."

"Overachiever. How was *your* day? Did you find anything useful about the device?"

He blew out a long breath and dipped his head into his hands, scrubbing at his face. "I didn't have any fucking *time*. Father's got me running all over creation for these High-Gods-damned prospecting meetings. Waste of energy. No one's serious about buying anything. But he refuses to ignore them." Cael leaned his head back to stare at the ceiling, and his Adam's apple bulged. She wanted to sink her teeth into it. "I spent the half hour before I came up here listening to him shout about how incompetent I am that I can't find him any legitimate business." His eyes glazed over. "It was fun."

"You don't have to live under his thumb, Cael," Xenia whispered. She didn't understand why he assumed he had no other choices. He was a full-grown male, for fuck's sake.

Fear shivered Cael's wing. "You have no idea what he's like. *No* idea. Once Arran Zephyrus has mapped out your life, you thank him and you live it. Or suffer the consequences." He rubbed a hand over his mouth. "Sometimes I think he'd prefer I were dead than living outside his influence."

"Why'd he let you go to the colonies?" Xenia asked, picking straws from the bale.

Below, tails swished and horses nickered in the ensuing silence.

Cael dipped his head, tracing patterns on the dusty floorboards. "Because the path I was on would've given me—and by extension, him—power. Vestian to Vasilikan to head of the Imperial Guard."

"You wanted to serve Eamon Erabis?"

"I hadn't given him very much thought. It was more about the position. Moot point now, anyway," Cael said with defeated finality, rustling his wing.

Xenia didn't know what to say. When she'd tried to talk to Cael about his injury in the Desolation, he'd always shut her down. And he didn't seem any more inclined to open up tonight. So, she changed the subject.

"I ran into Elodie in your father's office."

Cael's head jolted upright. "Elodie? Why?"

Xenia shrugged. "No idea. She looked like she was going to jump out of her skin when she saw me. Then got all huffy and entitled. Like she was supposed to be there. Like she had business with your father."

"What business would *Elodie* have with my father?"

"That's what I want to know. She barged right into the room. Didn't even knock. Don't you think that's suspicious?" Cael lifted a shoulder, unconvinced. "And then when I asked her if I should tell Arran she was looking for him, she shouted *no* and ran from the room."

Cael shook his head. "I wouldn't worry about it. We've got more important shit to deal with."

Though Xenia bristled at his dismissal, his mood dissuaded her from pressing. But no way would she let it go that easily. She'd figure out on her own what his fiancée was up to.

He stood and helped her up. "You should get back to the estate."

"Okay," she agreed, though she didn't want to leave him.

"Go ahead of me. Best no one sees us together. If you run into anyone, just tell them Hildreth sent you out here to read bedtime stories to the horses. Stablemaster's a bit odd. And very attached to the animals. No one will question it."

Xenia nodded, opening her mouth to say more, though "Goodnight, Cael" was all she landed on.

He cocked his head, staring at her in a way that made her believe he wanted to say more, too. "Night, Blondie."

She exited the stables into the pitch-black night, ruminating on Cael's mood and Elodie's questionable behavior.

She was halfway up the path to the lodge when a deep voice slithered from the trees to her left.

"Well, what have we here? An escaped housemaid, creeping around the property in the dead of night?"

Tomas Zephyrus oozed out of the darkness. He was shorter than Cael, but slightly broader in the shoulders. Waves of golden hair spilled to his shoulders, and the path lights created ghoulish shadows beneath dark gray eyes that held not an ounce of kindness.

"I was just—"

Faster than she could blink, Tomas was upon her. "No need for excuses, pretty little maid. It's best when your kind keep your mouth shut anyway. Or use it for something other than talking." He tugged her off of the path. Toward the dark woods. "Walk with me."

Xenia pulled uselessly against his grip. Though the softness around his middle hinted at centuries of overindulgence, he was still Fae.

"Oh no, I don't think—"

"Tomas!"

Cael's voice boomed through the night and Tomas, startled, released her.

She stumbled backward, catching herself against a tree.

"I've been looking for you," Cael said, keeping his eyes on his brother.

Tomas furrowed his brow, glancing back at the lodge then over Cael's shoulder. Toward the stables. "Have you?"

"Father asked me to debrief you on my meetings."

Tomas leered at Xenia. "He's always spoiling my fun. Cael, have you met... What's your name then, little maid?"

Xenia didn't answer and once again, Cael saved her. "Let's *go*, Tomas. Leave the humans alone."

Cael shoved at Tomas's back and the two males took to the path, Cael's sole wing bobbing next to Tomas's pair. Tomas turned over his shoulder and mouthed *see you soon* to Xenia.

She waited several minutes before returning to the lodge to ensure Tomas couldn't follow her to her room.

That night, the monster in her nightmare had oily blond hair, blood-drenched fangs, and a rasping voice that whispered *little maid* over and over and over.

CHAPTER
TWENTY-ONE

TRISTAN STRETCHED OUT HIS wings as he stared at the twisted piles of metal that used to be a cargo train, now scattered throughout the Staurien Pass. Despite his sore muscles—and despite the loss—he couldn't deny how much he'd missed the focused fury of battle. Wielding steel and wind against a clear-cut enemy. Slicing limbs and stealing breath.

The Imperial soldiers who'd ambushed Tristan's forces had lingered for four fierce, bloody, brutal days. Days during which the Teles Chrysos had been *winning*. They fought with a fervor the Imperial infantry couldn't match. And the Anointed had been a sight to behold. Jets of fire had blazed through the pines. Imperial soldiers had spasmed on the ground, their bodies ringed with lightning. Others had drowned on dry land, choked by water magic.

In fact, up until the train cars had gone up in a flash of white followed by a cloud of black smoke, Tristan was sure his rebels would end the week victorious.

Instead, nearly a hundred had met True Death in the explosion and any hopes they'd had of acquiring those missiles had been destroyed.

A crushing blow, one that Eamon hadn't even been here to witness. Tristan might have thought his brother's absence odd if he didn't know what a spineless coward Eamon was.

A familiar voice rang out from the tent behind Tristan.

"What thinking about, little baby man?"

Hella clapped Tristan on the shoulder and he turned, attempting a smile that probably looked more like a grimace.

"They call me Prince now, or hadn't you heard?" He tried to muster his playful energy; it was more difficult than normal. But a good leader maintained good spirits. Even if those spirits were sometimes false. "I could have your head for such insolence."

"Will always be baby man to me." Hella's amber eyes crinkled with affection. "Come. They ready for you."

Tristan followed Hella into the tent, angling his shoulders to fit his wings through the flap.

On the second day of battle, Tristan had nearly wept with joy when Hella had appeared. She'd crashed down among a ring of Imperial soldiers then taken ten out at once in a blur of crimson feathers and swirling golden braids.

They hadn't yet had a chance to properly re-unite, and he had a million questions for her. Why had she left the Vestians? How had she fallen in with the Teles Chrysos? Had she left Aneka in Meridon with the Shrouded Sisters, like they'd planned? They'd shared nothing more than a fierce hug and a few teasing quips before they'd both lurched back into the chaos.

Tristan took the seat at the head of the oval table, scanning the papers scattered atop it—transcriptions of the windwhisper, commstone, and cuff messages that had been flowing in from Lebaedia.

Ione sat beside him looking mostly unharmed, save a bandage peeking through her collar. She must have been nicked by Typhon steel.

She'd been a glorious commander down by those tracks. Firm and compassionate with her soldiers, but never giving into their panic. She pulled back at all the right moments and pressed forward when she could tell the enemy was flagging. And throughout, she'd remained on the front line, not holding the rear while she asked others to take the brunt of the violence. It was no wonder the rebels respected her so much.

As if she felt the weight of his gaze, she lifted her head, gifting him a soft smile despite the worry crawling through her indigo eyes. She raised her hand toward his, then flattened it on her armrest when he didn't reach for her.

Hella flopped down across the table as Seraavi Pfania entered the tent. Tristan wouldn't soon forget the violent, inspiring sight of the pink-eyed Deathstalker ripping apart Imperial soldiers with her venomous fangs.

Layla Fetar, her black-and-white braids a frizzy mess, and Felix Tanius, persimmon wings tight against his back, were already seated.

"Gang's all here, Prince," Layla said. "Your show."

Tristan kicked off the meeting. "Do you have a full inventory of the weapons we'd hoped to gain from that shipment?"

Layla nodded. "Besides the five missiles, we lost two-hundred crates of snakebites, thousands of Typhon swords, daggers, and axes. Plus two pallets of stun pistols."

Hella emitted a low whistle as Felix muttered a drawn-out curse. Ione's face paled.

Layla plastered on a weary smile. "Bright side? The Empire won't be getting them either."

"How did the Empire know we were coming?" Ione snarled, turning to Seraavi. "Has someone in your group been compromised?"

"Never," Seraavi gritted out. "Our people are fiercely loyal to the cause. We would personally vouch for every single one."

"Why Emperor not show up himself?" Hella asked.

Felix ruffled his wings. "Our spies in Delos claim he hasn't left the palace since he returned from the colonies. Not since the Delphine stole his prize." A slow grin spread onto the male's face as he eyed up Tristan.

Tristan's hackles raised. Is that all Felix thought of him? That he was just a prize to be bandied about between sides? Had he not proven himself, fighting alongside them these past few days?

Tristan opened his mouth to protest before shame stilled his tongue. All the Fae in this room, with the exception of Hella, had been here on the continent laying the groundwork for this cause while he'd been down in the colonies doing what, exactly? A whole lot of fucking nothing.

As if she could sense the direction of his thoughts, Ione shot Felix a sharp look. "You will speak of your future Emperor with more respect than that, General Tanius."

Tristan shifted on his feet. "It's fine."

Her wings rustled at his voice, even as she stared down Felix, who bowed his head in a silent apology.

Tristan turned back to Layla. "What's the damage, do you think? How well stocked are the armories at our other bases? Can our plans to march on Delos withstand this blow?"

Layla grimaced. "Unlikely. Even with the weapons we have left, we don't have anything powerful enough to maintain a siege or force Eamon to surrender. We're going to have to come up with another way to take the city."

Tristan dropped his head, shoulders flagging as he blew out a long breath. The tent was silent as he pondered their options.

"Anyone have any ideas?" he asked.

Seraavi raised a brow at Layla. "Do you still have the relic?"

Layla jolted, sitting up higher in her seat and running a hand along the corset of knives at her waist. "Yes, but... It's never worked. We've blown it hundreds of times with no results. No one knows how Arran Zephyrus was able to—"

"You said you have a connection with his son, right?" Seraavi asked Tristan, cutting off Layla's protests.

"I do."

"How close are you?"

"He's my closest friend in the world."

His closest friend that he hadn't seen nor spoken with in weeks. Guilt squeezed his chest.

"Close enough that he'd be willing to perform a covert mission for you?"

Tristan furrowed his brow. "What kind of mission?"

"The dragon of Typhon Mountain. It's under Arran Zephyrus's control." Seraavi gestured to Layla. "Thanks to General Fetar, we are in possession of a relic of

Adelphinae—a flute—that may summon the creature away from him. But we need more information about how he's been able to keep it under his command all these centuries. Do you think your friend would be willing to help us ferret out that information?"

Tristan scrubbed a hand down his face, about to open his mouth to ask another question when Felix cut in.

"What use would the dragon be to our plans?"

Seraavi scoffed. "The creature decimated an entire territory with its fire. Enough fire to strike more fear into Eamon Erabis than five untested missiles, we'd say. He'll shit his Imperial pants if he sees us marching upon his city with the creature."

Everyone around the table laughed. Everyone except Felix, who grunted, color stealing across his cheeks as he folded his arms across his chest.

"It's risky," Felix ground out. "What happens if we can't figure out how to acquire the dragon? What's our back-up plan?"

Ione silenced him with a sharp glare. "There is no back-up plan."

Felix wouldn't let it go. And there was something petulant and personal in his tone. "What if we tried to contact Arran? Maybe he'd be willing to—"

"Even *if* we had enough *drachas* left to buy his cooperation, why would he risk his cash cow for us?" Ione spat. "He's playing *both* sides of this conflict, Felix.

He's not going to risk the exposure. And I'm not entirely convinced *he* wasn't the one who ratted us out."

The tips of Felix's ears were growing red. "That's all well and good, but—"

"Enough!" Tristan commanded, mashing his palm onto the table and making the entire group jump. "This is the plan." He stared down Felix. "You will escort me to Brachos tomorrow to meet with Cael Zephyrus." He turned to Layla. "You will give me the flute which I will give to Cael if he agrees to help us. And we should all pray to the Creator that he does. Afterward," he turned to Ione, "you and I will head to Delos as previously planned to retrieve the Compendium."

The finality in his tone brooked no room for argument, though Felix looked inclined.

"Any other objections?" Tristan swept his commanding gaze across the room. His stomach clenched when it landed on Ione, who was regarding him with enough heated awe to make him uncomfortable. "Dismissed."

He bolted out of the tent faster than she could follow, then tensed when a warm hand fell upon his shoulder.

"Take walk with me?" Hella asked.

Tristan relaxed, then nodded, following her out into the camp.

Bright stars twinkled across the black velvet sky, no ambient light from any surrounding cities to dull their shine.

"I hear what happen to Cassandra," Hella said, her golden eyes glued to the ground as she plodded along beside him. "So very sorry, Tristan."

He shuddered out a watery breath, eyes stinging. He'd barely had a moment to sit with his grief, and though working out his anger during that battle had helped, he was fresh out of distractions. The prospect of several uninterrupted hours with nothing but his thoughts was daunting.

"My first act as Emperor will be to get her out of there," Tristan vowed.

Hella paused before a small tent, regarding him carefully.

Tristan cocked a questioning eyebrow. "Why'd you join, Hella? The last we talked, you were heading down to Meridon to—"

The tent flap opened, and a familiar head of flaxen hair poked through.

"You're back," Aneka said through a relieved grin. Hella stepped over to cup her cheeks, and Aneka's sea-foam eyes scanned Hella's muscular frame for injuries. "I was worried that you—"

Hella dipped her head, stealing her lover's lips. Aneka whimpered. And though it was rude, Tristan couldn't help staring, envy searing his chest.

The kiss was fierce and deep, as if Hella were drinking her salvation from Aneka's mouth. It was a kiss of relief. A kiss that said *I will always return to you*.

Hella broke away and whispered, "Be right in."

Aneka glanced to Tristan, then back to Hella, a flush warming her cheeks. "Don't keep me waiting much longer."

Hella's crimson feathers rattled as she ran her thumb across Aneka's rosebud lips. "Never, my golden beauty."

But instead of stepping back into the tent, Aneka rushed to Tristan and threw her arms around him.

It had been weeks since he'd held anyone. Since anyone had held him. So he took a quiet moment to savor the contact as Aneka whispered against his shoulder, "I never thanked you. For what you and Cassandra did for me." At her name, that deep ache within him sharpened, so intense he nearly fell to his knees. He squeezed Aneka tighter before she pulled back. "Thank you. For saving me. You're going to be a wonderful Emperor."

He dipped his head in gratitude, though he wasn't sure he agreed with her. The thought of being responsible for an entire world, the very long and daunting path that lay ahead of him… It was all so vast he couldn't even grasp its edges. *One step at a time*, he told himself. *Just get through tonight.*

"That why," Hella whispered as Aneka entered the tent, then pulled the flap shut. "*She* is reason why." Hella turned toward him, golden eyes shining with resolve. "You understand?"

"Yes," Tristan said softly. "I do."

Hella's eyebrows knit together. "You okay?"

"No."

He may be faking it for everyone else in that war committee tent, but he was grateful he didn't have to fake anything for Hella.

She tipped her head back. "Maybe she looking at same sky right now. Maybe thinking same thoughts." Tristan glanced upward, but only the winking stars and glowing moon looked back. "Goodnight, Prince of Rebels."

The title echoed in his ears as Hella brushed into her tent. Likely to lose herself in Aneka's embrace, let their casual intimacies chase away all this death and destruction.

Jealousy blinded him as he tore away, not wanting to overhear their reunion.

Low laughter and murmured conversations chased him through the camp. He came upon a group of rebels gathered around a bonfire—four males and two females of varying sub-species. And despite everything they'd been through, the battle they'd just barely survived not to mention the loss of their friends and those missiles, they were laughing. Teasing each other. Clinking bottles of beer and wine.

Their camaraderie paralyzed him. How many would fall on the treacherous path ahead?

One rebel, a Beastrunner with two familiar pointed ears poking through his tawny hair—the young male from the hospital in Lodesvale—noticed Tristan watching. His laughter trailed off as his friends turned to see what had caught his attention.

They stood as one, angling their bottles toward Tristan. "To the new Emperor!" the long-eared Beastrunner proclaimed. The others echoed him, and Tristan bowed in acceptance of their toast, nausea roiling his gut.

He stomped away as fast as dignity allowed, then crashed through the tree line on the edge of the camp. He steadied himself against a cool pine, swallowing down breaths.

He was on the precipice of achieving everything he'd ever wanted.

And he was terrified.

What if he failed?

He sank down the trunk, his feathers catching on the rough bark, and looked toward the stars. Was Hella right? Could Cass see these same stars at this very moment through the wards of Tartarus?

Would they send her a message?

"I miss you," he whispered.

He leaned his head against the tree, picturing her in his mind. Her intelligent blue-gray eyes, her soft smile, the beauty and kindness and bravery that radiated from her every pore. It comforted him.

"They're calling me Prince and Your Highness and I...I've done nothing to earn those titles. The only sacrifice I've ever made is you." He swallowed the lump in his throat. "I'm not foolish enough to believe this path would be any easier if you were walking beside me. But I'd feel so much stronger if you were.

"I don't know how to do this without you."

He breathed deeply, bringing his awareness to the cool bark against his back, the damp grass below his hands. Grounding himself. Trying to purge his turbulent emotions. He knew it wouldn't work. He'd borne this type of grief once before, and it had ruined him. And though he was a little older, maybe even a little wiser, the burden of Cassandra's absence was infinitely heavier.

But blubbering about his lost love wouldn't get him anywhere. And if Cass could see him right now, she'd tell him to quit worrying about her and pull himself together. Focus on the goal. Focus on their *people.*

It was that thought which finally gave him the strength to rise and return to the camp. He paused in front of his tent, whispered into his palm and sent a message to Cael.

If he couldn't have Cassandra at his side, maybe the next best thing was a dragon.

CHAPTER
TWENTY-TWO

"KEEP UP," MIREILLE GRUMBLED over her shoulder. A few paces behind, Cassandra asked the same question she'd asked at least ten times since Mireille had dragged her from the shop. "Where are we going?"

"I told you, you'll *see*."

Was Mireille always this gruff? Or had her piss-poor reunion with a certain broody, muscular male put her in a foul mood? After a half a week in Mireille's company, Cassandra honestly couldn't tell.

The two females pushed their way through the cobbled streets, coming upon a crowd in the city square that was the largest Cassandra had yet encountered in the city—a roiling mass of Fae, cramming every side street and spilling out of the two corner taverns.

She kept her head down, ignoring whistles and hollers from passing Brethren. A male with a shaved head and upturned nose shouted that her days in Tartarus were numbered. She wanted to call back that yes, they were, because she was going to defeat the Koenig, win that hammer, then figure out how to get the fuck out of here. But she was worried her voice might tremble and ruin the comeback.

She shook off the taunts as Mireille led her toward Ronin, who was seated on a bench at the edge of the square. In the center, a rough wooden platform sporting ominously dark stains had been erected.

Cassandra flopped down next to Ronin, angling her wings over the back of the bench. Mireille took her other side.

"Hi," Cassandra said to his neck as he craned his head around.

"Hi," he clipped back, not looking at her.

Frenzied Dienses, both her chosen fighters were in a fine mood tonight. Though it wasn't much different than those excruciating training sessions. Or any of the time they'd spent together the past week, really. Whatever spectacle they were about to witness, Mireille had been tense about it for days. And Cassandra had barely seen Ronin, who spent every minute outside the training room trying to find Selene.

Cassandra ignored her gnawing loneliness and began scanning the crowd.

There was no sign of Wormwood nor the Koenig. And once again, Cassandra didn't spy a single human.

Their continued absence tightened the knot of dread in her stomach.

"You gonna tell me what this is all about?" Cassandra shouted into Mireille's ear over the din.

"It's called Harvest Night," Mireille answered, her voice tight. "It occurs once a month. A sacrifice to Vestan to restore the hammer's magic and allow the Koenig to refill the city's provisions."

Cassandra's stomach dropped. "What kind of sacrifice?"

Mireille schooled her features into a terrifying neutrality, her silence saying more than Cassandra likely wanted to know. She understood why Mireille had waited until the last possible minute to tell her about it.

While most of the prisoners seemed nervous and jumpy, the Brethren were downright delirious with bloodlust. Fights erupted, shouts pierced the night, and Cassandra clenched her jaw so hard she thought her teeth might snap.

"Apothecarist!" a booming voice called out from across the square.

Mireille's head whipped toward it. "Fuck," she muttered, her gaze landing on the meanest-looking Brethren Cassandra had yet seen. The hulking beast of a male had pale ice-blue eyes, and his waist-length hair was nearly as dark as the black fur draped around his shoulders.

"Hang on. I need to handle this." Mireille sauntered away, and a feral smile bloomed on the male's face.

Ronin tensed, his golden-blue eye tracking Mireille across the square.

She paused before the raven-haired male, wrapping her arms around her chest, and he leaned down to whisper into her ear. She shook her head, fingers digging into her biceps.

Faster than Cassandra could blink, the Brethren clamped an arm around Mireille's waist, hauled her against his chest, and clapped his other hand over her ass.

Ronin shot up from the bench, but reluctantly sat back down when another male beat him to Mireille's rescue. The lean yet muscular Windrider sported dove-gray feathered wings, closely-shaved dark hair, and a rumpled linen tunic that was very different from the attire of the blue-eyed Brethren he was arguing with.

The Brethren threw his hands up and finally stalked off to rejoin his peers, who were throwing nasty slurs and catcalls at Mireille.

The Windrider placed his hands on Mireille's shoulders and ducked his head as they conversed quietly. Whatever she said must have reassured him. After they parted, he returned to a diverse group of Fae gathered outside The Other Place.

"Who were those two?" Cassandra asked when Mireille sank down beside her.

"The Windrider with the gray wings is Silas. He's a friend. The long-haired Brethren asshole is Jonas. He is not. Or at least, not anymore."

Cassandra could've sworn she felt Ronin twitch, though he was very intensely pretending not to listen. "And what did they want?" she asked Mireille.

"Nothing." A slight tremor shook Mireille's hand as she raked it through her copper waves. Ronin's eye darted right to it. "They... It's nothing you need to worry about."

A hush fell over the crowd as Wormwood, who'd finally arrived, climbed the steps to the platform.

"Friends," he crowed. "Welcome to Harvest Night!"

Violent cheers rose from the Brethren, while most of the rest of the crowd remained silent.

Wormwood continued, "Tonight is a very special Harvest Night, as it will be the last before a spectacle which we have not enjoyed in over fifty years. There is a new challenger among us. A prisoner who arrived with a death sentence. And lucky for us, she has requested an executioner's appeal from our beloved Koenig!"

The Brethren erupted into uproarious laughter. A few of the other prisoners joined in. Cassandra's face heated.

Mireille squeezed her hand, whispering into her ear. "Fuck those bastards. They won't be laughing when you win."

Cassandra offered Mireille a wan smile, grateful that the female was trying to lift her spirits. But truthfully, Cassandra didn't know if they could get any lower.

"Challenger!" Wormwood called, his mousy brown eyes seeking her out. "Show yourself! Let the citizens of Tartarus say hello. And goodbye."

Cassandra steeled her shoulders, refusing to show her fear, then climbed on the bench and flared her wings wide.

The Brethren's hysteria pelted her as she stared down the crowd. But many regular prisoners offered subtle nods of approval.

"Let's hear it for Cassandra Fortin, folks," Wormwood crooned. "Prisoner 161803! And soon to be the Koenig's next victim."

The laughter reached a fever pitch, which Cassandra took as her cue to retake her seat. Mireille patted her thigh and Ronin squeezed her shoulder.

"You did well," Mireille said. "Don't give the Brethren another fucking thought. And when you *do* defeat the Koenig, you can decide whether to offer them mercy."

Cassandra nodded, her face and limbs numb, and wondered, for the hundredth time these past few weeks, how in Ethyrios she'd ended up here.

Wormwood raised his palms, encouraging the crowd to silence. "My friends, as I said, tonight is a very special Harvest Night. And as such, we have a different kind of fight than you're used to."

Mireille tensed, and Cassandra leaned over to whisper, "What does that mean?"

Mireille shook her head. "I don't know."

Wormwood continued, "In honor of our challenger, the Koenig *himself* has decided to participate in tonight's harvest!"

The Brethren jumped to their feet with a ground-shaking roar, and the Koenig paraded into the square. He acknowledged his subjects with dips of his chin, his shark-like grin plastered on his handsome face. He jogged up the steps, then took his place next to Wormwood.

Cassandra sneered, though he didn't look her way. An attempt to minimize her, surely.

One of the Brethren handed the hammer up to the Koenig, who swung it through the air. The polemite heart streaked ribbons of red through the twilight.

As Wormwood scanned the crowd, Cassandra scented new tendrils of tangy fear. He closed his eyes, his lids and lips moving as if he were doing calculations.

His eyes popped open. "Prisoner 628432! Join us on the platform."

Whispers echoed and heads swiveled as the spectators attempted to identify the selected prisoner. The chatter peaked in a corner where several prisoners were hugging a terrified Deathstalker male with pale blond hair and skin to match.

He trudged toward the platform, his sand-colored serpent's eyes glued to the Koenig. Once he'd climbed the stairs, he took a knee at the Koenig's feet. Wormwood pulled him upright, lifting his arm toward the sky, and the crowd peppered him with unenthusiastic applause.

"Prisoner 628432, Arseny Vasok!" Wormwood planted his hands on the male's shoulders. "Congratulations on being selected as tonight's sacrifice."

Vasok tittered. "What if we beat him?"

The Brethren laughed, though not as uproariously as they had at Cassandra.

"You will have the chance, of course. It's only fair." Wormwood offered Vasok a menacing smile. "And now, let the Harvest commence!" He snapped his fingers, then rushed off the platform.

Vasok trembled while the Koenig stood still as a statue, his hammer resting on his shoulder.

Vasok took his chance, popping his fangs and rushing for the Koenig, who didn't even bother using the weapon. He struck out a fist and knocked the Deathstalker to the boards.

Vasok cowered, wiping a bead of green from the corner of his mouth. The Koenig remained motionless above him, smirking at a group of females, before Vasok lunged and sank his fangs into the Koenig's calf.

Cassandra clasped Mireille's forearm, hope fluttering in her chest as she waited for the Koenig to collapse from the injection of Deathstalker venom coursing through his system.

"Is he—"

The Koenig's hissing laughter interrupted Cassandra's question. He shook Vasok off his leg and kicked him in the forehead.

Cassandra whispered, "He's *immune* to Deathstalker venom?"

Mireille nodded, brows pinched. "Built up over the years by letting his Deathstalker Brethren bite him. He's practically invincible."

A fresh wave of anxiety prickled the downy feathers at Cassandra's shoulder blades. Immune to Deathstalker venom. Well, that was just fucking *perfect*.

"Who *is* he?" Cassandra asked, but Mireille either didn't hear her or didn't bother responding.

Vasok staggered to his feet. His serpent's eyes had gone glassy, as if he'd resigned himself to his fate. His voice shook as he called out, "Put down your hammer and fight us as an equal!"

The Koenig lifted an incredulous eyebrow, and the Brethren swelled with whoops and hollers. He shrugged, then made a show of settling his hammer down gently onto the platform.

As soon as he raised his head, he barreled for Vasok.

The Deathstalker's eyes went wide as he realized his mistake.

And all the blood drained from Cassandra's body as she watched the Koenig tear Arseny Vasok apart with his bare hands.

This was a male who'd known nothing but violence for his centuries-long life.

Vasok's screams were unbearable as the Koenig crunched a fist into his skull, stomped through his leg, and in a terrible, final move, lifted his limp body in the air and cracked his spine.

The Koenig tossed Vasok's crumpled body to the boards. The Deathstalker was somehow still clinging to life, moaning faintly in a spreading pool of green blood.

The Brethren's ravenous chants of *Harvest! Harvest!* grew louder as the Koenig bent over to pluck up his hammer.

"Please," Vasok croaked at the Koenig's feet. "Please."

Cassandra wasn't sure if he was begging for help or begging for death.

The Koenig arced the hammer over his head, then brought it down upon Vasok's skull with a bone-crunching squelch. The Deathstalker's head popped like a ripe watermelon and though Cassandra desperately wanted to look away, she didn't dare. Didn't want to appear weak or squeamish in front of the Brethren.

Not to mention the Koenig had held her stare throughout that fatal swing.

He thrust the hammer into the air, green viscera and white skull fragments clinging to the black stone.

Applause exploded throughout the square as the Brethren surged to their feet.

Wormwood sidled up to the Koenig, his thin lips sliding into a grimace as he beheld the pile of mush that used to be prisoner 628432. "Let's hear it for our Koenig, folks!"

The Koenig lifted the hammer once more, and the polemite heart began to glow. Cassandra watched, awestruck, as Vasok's body dissolved in a flash of red mist.

Wormwood bowed his head and beside him, the Koenig did the same. The crowd followed shortly behind.

"Vestan, our Warrior God," Wormwood intoned, "please accept this sacrifice. A soul to add to your divine eternal army. He gave his life that we may preserve ours. And in your name, we give our thanks."

Red light flashed through the square, bursting through windows and flaring down side streets.

Barrels that had previously been empty filled with food—cuts of meat, root vegetables, leafy greens, fruits and grains, wheat and barley, and so much more. Casks of ale and bottles of wine appeared in front of the taverns and in shop windows.

The heart gem pulsed, bathing the Koenig's face in macabre red shadows. Combined with his kohl-lined eyes and wicked smile, Cassandra could've sworn she was gazing upon a demon risen from the depths of Stygios's realm.

And she couldn't stop trembling.

"Are you okay?" Mireille asked, trembling slightly herself. When Cassandra shook her head, willing her tears away, Mireille pulled her from the bench. "Let's go. The Brethren will be plenty distracted now that the feasting has begun."

"They'll think I'm a coward," Cassandra breathed out.

A few prisoners began fighting over casks of ale and Mireille offered Cassandra a rueful grin. "They won't remember much tomorrow anyway. Come on, we can sneak away before anyone notices." She turned to Ronin. "Are you coming?"

"No," was all he said before slipping into the crowd.

Mireille sighed, walking Cassandra—who was desperately trying not to fall apart in public—out of the square and back to her shop.

As soon as Mireille opened the door, Cassandra rushed up the stairs to the apartment and burst into the bathroom.

Then vomited up the meager contents of her stomach.

CHAPTER
TWENTY-THREE

THE ICY-EYED FEMALE DEATHSTALKER manning the door at World's End was a stone-cold bitch.

Ronin only managed a single glance into the thumping tavern before she slammed the door shut and shoved him away.

It made Ronin miss Charlie, the woolly mammoth bi-form from the Frosted Crystal in Kheimos. A friendly giant with a soft-spot for the ballet—and one very specific ballerina.

Ronin's single, stolen glance revealed barely-clothed females serving groups of drinking, shouting, leering Brethren. There looked to be another female dancing on a stage at the far end of the room, but he wasn't able to confirm.

He doubted he'd find Selene in there anyway. Or at least, he hoped and prayed he wouldn't.

He turned and ran straight into Wormwood, grasping the male's shoulder to keep him from falling backward.

"Challenger Matakos," the weasel bi-form crooned, dragging his beady eyes across Ronin's muscled arms. "How are you enjoying Harvest Night so far?"

"It's been riveting."

"Please," Wormwood chuckled through his nose, an invitation glinting in his dull brown eyes. "Call me, Remy." An odd request, since Ronin hadn't called him anything at all. "Care to join me for a drink?"

Though Ronin preferred females, he did harbor a few yet-to-be-indulged curiosities. But if ever *were* inclined, a devious, oil-slick male like Wormwood would be at the absolute bottom of his list.

Despite all that, he was tempted. Perhaps he could get Wormwood rip-roaring drunk then ask *him* about Selene. But Ronin didn't want to reveal such a weakness to the Koenig's steward.

Ronin frowned. "Not sure the challenger would appreciate me fraternizing with the enemy."

Wormwood's smile grew larger. "No, I don't suspect she would. Where *is* challenger Fortin? Thought I saw her run off shortly after the fight. I hope she wasn't too disturbed."

Ronin clenched his jaw. "She's fine. Rushed home to strategize since the Koenig was foolish enough to reveal his moves."

Wormwood's whiskers twitched. "Clever girl." He nodded toward the Deathstalker bouncer, who pushed open the door. "My invite stands should you ever change your mind, Butcher."

Wormwood crooned Ronin's nickname with far too much familiarity before entering the tavern to hoots and hollers from the Brethren.

Ronin stole another peek, spying the Koenig himself seated before the stage and surrounded by three beautiful Fae females. He lifted a mug toward his steward and—

The door slammed in Ronin's face and the Deathstalker angled her body before it, her popped fangs hanging below her chin in warning.

Messaged received.

So, Ronin ambled across the square to The Other Place and was welcomed by a far more subdued—and much shabbier—atmosphere.

The high wooden tabletops were cracked, chairs were missing legs, and steins were chipped. Even the bard warbling in the corner was off-key.

Despite the run-down digs, the patrons gave off a relieved energy—whether it was because their food stores had been replenished or because Wormwood hadn't called their names, Ronin couldn't say.

He sidled up to the bar, then leaned across the polished, pockmarked wood to signal the bartender.

An older Beastrunner with a flowing mane of gray-streaked blond hair and a missing canine ambled over. "What can I get ya?"

Ronin patted his pockets, realizing he had nothing to barter.

The bartender laughed, shaking his head. "Don't worry about it. First drink's on the house."

"Don't suppose you have any Delirium?"

"'Fraid not. You'll only find fresh feedings in Tartarus. And I can assure you, you won't get them in this establishment." The bartender cocked his head and eyed Ronin suspiciously.

Ronin hadn't seen a single human since he'd arrived, so he had no idea what the male was talking about. Still, he felt the need to confirm that he didn't feed from humans before he ordered a double-shot of aguaver.

As the bartender poured his drink, Ronin leaned across the bar and lowered his voice. "How long have you been here?"

The bartender puffed out his chest. "Been serving the thirsty citizens of Tartarus for four-hundred-and-fifty-two years. Almost as long as the Koenig has been in power, if ya please."

Ronin slid onto a barstool, settling in to grill the oldest tenured prisoner he'd met thus far. One who he hoped might provide him some clues to Selene's whereabouts. "I'm wondering if you might be able to help me find someone?"

The bartender hooked a thumb over his shoulder. "Nearest brothel's three blocks left of here."

"No, no, I... My sister—my twin sister—was arrested and sent here ten years ago. Her name's Selene Matakos."

The bartender studied Ronin's face as he slid him his drink, then shook his head. "Never heard the name. And pretty sure if I saw a female who looked like you, I'd remember."

Ronin wrapped his tattooed fingers around the cloudy glass, his shoulders slumping. "Cheers," he said before slamming it back, the burn of the liquor shaving off the sharpest edges of his disappointment. "What are you in for?"

The bartender leveled him with a glare. "Not a question one typically asks around here in polite company."

Ronin barked out a laugh. "I'm the least polite person you'll ever meet, friend."

An amused chuckle escaped the bartender's bearded muzzle and Ronin caught a whiff of a familiar scent. A tinge of decaying flowers that reminded him of Mireille.

Mortality.

Was the bartender part human?

If so, and he'd been here for centuries, perhaps he'd been locked up during or just after the war. During that time when Leonin Erabis and his Imperial minions had been determined to rid the continent of both humans *and* half-breeds. Ronin wondered how many other half-breeds were in here before returning to the subject of Selene.

"Is there a chance she's here and you've never met her?" he asked.

The bartender dashed his hope. "I know nearly everyone in Tartarus. Perils of the job."

"But she was arrested," Ronin said, twirling his empty glass and trying to decide if it was wise to order another. "So if she's not here, then…"

The bartender's bushy brows dipped with sympathy as he muttered, "The mists."

Ronin swallowed, his face going pale. There was no way. If Selene had been in the mists, Ronin was certain he would've sensed her. And if she'd died in there… Well, he and his wolf would know that as well.

Wouldn't they?

Ronin frowned, throwing back the rest of his aquaver and mulling over the hot load of *nothing* the bartender had shared. Perhaps Ronin would have to take Wormwood up on his offer after all.

But not tonight. His head was pounding, he was exhausted, and all he wanted to do was get out of this tavern, shift into his wolf for a quick run, then crash onto his tiny bed in Mireille's tiny apartment.

As he slid off his stool, a gorgeous Beastrunner female with a sleek blonde bob and a low-cut burgundy top leaned across the bar, signaling to the bartender.

Her eyes drifted to Ronin, then widened, her pupils dilating as her scent deepened.

Ronin knew what looks like that meant. If anything, he'd inspired even more since he'd started wearing the eye-patch.

The blonde's lips curved into a coy smile as she turned toward the bartender, but her body remained angled toward Ronin.

And Creator help him, he thought about it. For a second, he *really* did. About how easy it would be to throw her some half-hearted pick-up line and end his month-long dry spell with a quick, sweaty fuck against the tavern wall outside. He was partial to red-heads—for reasons to which he refused to ascribe any meaning—but he was desperate enough to make an exception.

But he just…

He couldn't.

And he wondered why? He'd been with plenty of females since he and Mireille had fallen out. Plus, she'd made it pretty clear she'd been fucking other people, too. So really, why did it matter?

You know why, his wolf offered as Ronin stalked from the bar, the blonde's disappointed gaze tracking him through the tavern door.

Ronin didn't bother answering as he slipped into the night, shifted into his wolf, and went for a run through the city streets.

He examined every face he passed, hoping against all odds that one would be his twin's.

He'd already lost one of the females who'd made his life worth living.

He couldn't stand the thought that he might have lost Selene as well.

CHAPTER
TWENTY-FOUR

CAEL USED A FIRE opal to journey to the church ruins in southeastern Brachos, just across the border from the Desolation, where Tristan had asked to meet today.

Cael had been on the brink of sleep last night when Tristan's message floated into his ear. He hadn't expected to hear from his friend again. Especially not after he had ignored all Tristan's previous windwhispers.

This was Cael's last stop of a very long day, as he'd spent most of his morning and afternoon meeting with prospective buyers.

Such a fucking joke of a job.

Visions of his soporific future unspooled daily: aimless meetings followed by his father's tirades followed by Elodie's inane prattling.

He wanted to escape more than he ever had. He'd leave tomorrow if Xenia didn't still have that fucking tracking device in her neck.

They'd made little progress over the past few days and therefore, he'd been in a foul mood this morning when he'd sifted through the new business inquiries. Though his mood had boosted slightly when he'd found another affirmation on his breakfast tray.

I am in control of my happiness and my destiny. Say it at least three times today, pterodactyl. Believe it.

He'd chuckled into his coffee as he'd read it. Again, the words were complete and utter bullshit. Cael had never felt *less* in control of his destiny. But he'd dutifully said the phrase when he left the estate and at the end of each waste-of-time meeting.

Said it again as he'd arrived in this abandoned stone ruin on the outskirts of nowhere.

Though he was looking forward to seeing his friend again, he wanted this meeting finished as quickly as possible so he could return to Stoneridge.

The thought of leaving Xenia there alone had his anxiety rising. Especially after Tomas had nearly made her his midnight snack the other night.

Before Cael had left this morning, he'd seriously considered asking Erik to watch over her. But the thought of confirming Xenia's importance to him, even to his younger brother, seemed too dangerous.

Cael's anxious thoughts were interrupted when a shimmery portal appeared in the center of the crumbling nave and two Fae stepped through it.

One, Cael didn't recognize, but the second...

Cael was shocked into stillness at the sight of Tristan, whose face broke into a broad grin as he swallowed Cael in a bone-crunching hug.

"Long way to travel over a few missed windwhispers," Cael croaked out, Tristan's vise-like grip squeezing his lungs. "You're not in the colonies."

"Neither are you," Tristan answered, pounding his friend on the back before pulling away, his face falling as it landed on Cael's sole wing. "What happened to your—"

"I'll tell you later. In private." Cael flicked his gaze to the other Fae male watching their reunion, then back to Tristan. "What are you *doing* here? Where's Cassandra?"

A devastated grimace stole across Tristan's face before he turned to the male behind him. "Business first. This is General Felix Tanius." The male flared his feathered wings in greeting, kicking up a cloud of dust. "An associate of mine with the Teles Chrysos."

Cael's brows rose. He'd heard the name of the rebel group who were weaving their influence throughout the continent. Had even heard about the few deals they'd made with Arran these past months, the money they'd paid his father for information about weapons shipments to the Empire. He'd overheard a conversation between Arran and Viktor regarding a shipment of missiles heading through the Staurien Pass yesterday that the rebels were supposed to intercept.

Based on the timing of this meeting and General Tanius's pinched face, Cael suspected the interception had not gone as planned.

He hoped they weren't about to ask Cael to convince his father to refund the *drachas* they'd paid for the intel. No fucking way would Arran agree to that.

Tanius stepped forward to clasp Cael's hand. "Master Zeph—"

"Just Cael is fine."

"Cael." Tanius nodded. "Thank you for meeting with us." His gaze bobbed between the two friends. "You served in the colonies together, that right? I thought you had to be able to fly to be a Vestian guard?"

"It's a recent loss," Cael said, baring his teeth. "What can I do for you both? Did something happen with the shipment?"

"You haven't heard?" Tristan asked.

Cael shook his head.

"They knew we were coming." Tristan dragged a hand along the back of his neck.

"Yes, someone must have informed the Emperor of our plans," Tanius said, side-eying Tristan.

Surely the male didn't think *Tristan* had given his brother that information.

Tristan ignored the look as he continued, "Hundreds of Imperial soldiers arrived to greet us. We held them off as long as we could, but they blew up the train. Chose to destroy those missiles rather than let them fall into our hands. Which, obviously, puts a damper on our plans to—"

Tanius grabbed Tristan's forearm, hissing. "Do *not* tell him anything. He's not a member of our movement."

Tristan's face hardened, and he reached down to pluck Tanius's fingers from his forearm, his voice lowering to a dangerous whisper. "First, do not ever touch me again without permission. Second—and you've been warned about this—you will treat me with the respect I am due as your future Emperor. Third, I would trust Cael with my *life*. With our Delphine's life. We would be lucky to have him in our movement, were he inclined to join us." He stepped closer to Tanius and flared his wings in a show of dominance. "If you'd like to question my judgment again—which is your right, of course—you will do so in private. Otherwise, I'll have you stripped of your leadership and you can join the rank and file. Is that clear?"

The air in the dusty church shifted and a spear of sunlight illuminated Tristan's blue-black feathers. Tanius took to his knees.

Fuck, Cael almost felt like he should do the same.

Tristan coming into his heritage, his authority—it was a mighty thing to behold.

"My apologies, Your Highness," Tanius said, sweeping his wings down his back in submission. "It won't happen again."

Tristan flicked his fingers, signaling for the male to rise.

"So," Cael began, trying to cut through some of the tension, "if this meeting isn't about the shipment, what's it about?"

Tristan placed his hand on Cael's shoulder. "How aligned are you with your father?"

"He's..." Cael schooled his features into neutrality. "My duty is to my family. To Brachos. And to my father, Arran." He didn't dare reveal his true feelings. Not in front of Tanius. And anyways, everything he'd said *was* true. For now at least. For as long as Xenia was his father's captive.

"Could you be persuaded to do something for us under his nose?" Tristan asked.

"What kind of something?"

"Arran has another weapon. A much more powerful one. One that could mean the difference between the Teles Chrysos's success or failure."

Cael remained silent as Tristan gave him an expectant look.

Then opened his mouth and dropped his bomb.

"The dragon of Typhon Mountain."

Perched on a rickety pew, Cael pinched the bridge of his nose, trying to will away the headache caused by everything Tristan and Tanius had just asked of him.

Tristan had sent the general outside to wait, requesting a private word with his friend.

Tristan crossed an arm over his chest, scratching his biceps. "Well. Will you do it?"

"I don't even..." Cael raked a hand through his short waves. "I've never even *seen* the dragon. I have no idea how my father's been able to control it all these years. Or how he was able to make it obey him during the war."

"This was part of it." Tristan pulled a silver chain from underneath his shirt. Dangling from the end was a small object thinner than a pinky finger and crafted of fire opal.

"What is that?" Cael asked.

"A relic of the Fallen Goddess that my father gave to *your* father. Claimed it could be used to call forth ancient monsters who watched over this world millennia ago. The Teles Chrysos believe he used it to summon the dragon."

Cael's brows furrowed. "How did the Teles Chrysos acquire it? I find it very difficult to believe my father would have lost or given away such a powerful object."

"Could be because it doesn't work," Tristan said. "The rebels have played it many times over the centuries, all to no avail. There's got to be another piece of the puzzle we're missing. We thought maybe there'd be some information up at Stoneridge. Documents or details that Arran's kept from when he captured the creature."

Cael shot his friend a pained look. "If this task only endangered me, you know I would do it for you in a heartbeat, Tristan. But I've got more than just myself to consider right now." Whatever Tristan heard in Cael's tone inspired him to crouch down and place a hand upon his friend's knee. "Xenia was gifted to my father. She's his property now. A member of the human staff at Stoneridge."

Tristan sucked in a sharp breath. "*What?* I thought she'd returned to the colonies."

"She was supposed to," Cael growled. "Brash little fool decided to take her chances on the continent instead. She was trying to get back to me. Ended up getting captured by a trafficker in Rhamnos who sold her to my fiancée's father as a wedding gift for our family."

"You're getting married?" Tristan said, taken aback.

"Not if I can help it. Arran placed a tracking device in Xenia's neck. She can't leave the estate or remove it without it exploding. I need to find a way to get it out of her before I say my vows in a few weeks."

"Why was she trying to get back to you? Did something happen between you two?"

"She's everything I'm not supposed to want." Cael exhaled a long sigh. "And everything I've ever needed."

Tristan closed his eyes. "I know the feeling."

"I will not leave her there alone with him. If we're not able to remove the device, I'll marry Elodie and convince her to stay at Stoneridge so I can watch over Zee. Protect her from my father and brothers."

"And never have a chance at true happiness with her?"

"What the fuck else am I supposed to do?" Cael roared.

"There may be a way we can help. Trophonios is a leader of our movement. If you can get a sample device for him to study, he may be able to figure out how to deactivate it."

Cael's hope soared, even as shock stole through him. "*Trophonios* is aligned with the Teles Chrysos?"

"Not just aligned. He's practically the founder of this modern incarnation. Started reviving the movement just after the war. The things he's been able to accomplish... Do you remember the elemental lightning magic Maksym possessed?"

"Hard thing to forget," Cael said, the color draining from his features. "He took my wing."

"*Fuck*," Tristan breathed out. "Why didn't you tell me, Cael? I'm so—"

"It's fine," Cael said flatly. "I'm...dealing with it."

I am in control of my happiness and my destiny.

Tristan cocked a skeptical eyebrow, but didn't push.

"And I made him pay for it." Cael rustled his sole wing, remembering how good it had felt to slice that Typhon broadsword through Maksym's matte green wings as the fucker begged for mercy. At least, it had felt good in the moment. "What *about* his lightning magic?"

"The Teles Chrysos have discovered a way to bestow it upon Fae with human heritage. The Anointed, they're called. A blessing from the Creator herself."

"You worship the Creator now?"

Tristan darted his eyes to the open door of the chapel, ensuring that General Tanius wasn't eavesdropping on their conversation. "I don't fucking know. The things I've seen these past weeks, they're certainly enough to make me question my faith in the High Gods, but... I don't know."

There was a weariness in Tristan's words, along with profound grief.

Cael stood, and Tristan crumpled, resting his forehead on Cael's shoulder as he spilled the story of Cassandra's arrest, Ione's reappearance, and his subsequent escape from Eamon. Plus, the rebellion's ultimate goal: return the Crystal Throne to Tristan.

Cael tried not to let his confusion show as he awkwardly patted Tristan's back. "And that's...a bad thing?"

Tristan lifted his head, jaw tightening. "No. No, of course not. It's everything I've wanted since I was exiled, but... What does it matter if Cassandra dies behind those wards? If I can't save her?"

Once upon a time, and not that long ago, Cael might have scoffed at his friend's romantic melodramatics. Fortunately—or unfortunately, depending on which day, which hour he was considering it—Cael understood now. All too well.

"She's strong, Tristan. She's a *fighter*. It will take a lot more than Tartarus to bring her down."

"I hope you're right. Anyway, placing me on the throne isn't all Ione wants. She also wants *me*. Believes we're fated by Adelphinae. Believes she's destined to be my Empress."

"And what do you believe?"

"I..." Tristan hesitated. "I'm not going to forsake Cassandra. And certainly not based on hearsay. Ione and I are heading to Delos tomorrow to retrieve the Compendium. I'm hoping it will offer some clarity. On many things."

Cael nodded thoughtfully, then jutted his chin toward the door. "What's with General Douchebag?"

Tristan snorted. "Can't tell yet. Fae dominance thing, maybe. I think he and Ione might've been together before she... Doesn't fucking matter. He's the least of my concerns." Tristan gripped Cael's forearm. "Will you help me, Cael? I need people I can trust, and they're in really short supply at the moment."

Tristan gave Cael that piteous, wide-eyed look that always worked to get what he wanted.

"Frenzied fucking Dienses, the future Emperor of Ethyrios is giving me puppy-dog eyes," Cael groaned.

Tristan smirked. "Still can't resist me, can you?" Cael rolled his eyes. "Or maybe it's not working because you've finally moved on and are mooning over someone else."

Cael crossed his arms and glared. "You have no fucking idea, Saros. No *fucking* idea. Or should I call you Erabis now?"

Tristan grimaced. "Not sure I love either option, but let's go with Erabis for the time being. I'll meet you back here after I return from Delos. Bring a tracking device and I'll give it to Trophonios. You can give me an update on the dragon then, too. Get Xenia to help. She's much better than you at research, if I recall."

Tristan handed him the flute, then gathered him into another fierce hug. Something glinted on his wrist. "Actually, here." He handed Cael a delicate silver cuff embedded with two gems: a small purple gem of mentrite and a speck of fire opal. "Give this to her.

Girls love when you bring them presents. She might be so grateful, she'll get down on her knees and—"

Cael snatched the cuff with an annoyed look. "It's not like that between us."

"Yet?" Tristan cocked an eyebrow.

Cael ignored him, examining the delicate silver. "What's it do?"

"It's like a commstone. She'll be able to receive your windwhispers. And send them back to you in return."

"How will that work? She doesn't have any internal magic."

"Works even on those without it. The silver increases the stones' power. Plus, she'll be able to use the opal to travel anywhere she wants."

"Anywhere within the estate," Cael grumbled. "But thank you. This…this actually will be helpful."

Tristan nodded, then headed for the exit. "Take care of yourself, Cael. And take care of Xenia, too." His expression was pained as he turned back. "Don't spend too long waiting for your *yet*. You have no idea how much time you'll have with her."

Cael looked down at the cuff. Fucking Stygios, Tristan always knew how to cut right to the core of Cael's issues. "See you in a few days, big boy."

Tristan winked. "Count on it."

He left the church, and Cael overheard the rumblings of a tense conversation between him and the general. Mutterings about why Tristan had given Cael the cuff. They must have worked it out, because no one came back in to take it from him.

Cael sighed, glancing toward the altar where a statue of Nemosyna, the human Goddess of Memory, stood. The Goddess's face was eroded—by time, by neglect. By indifference. By all those cosmic forces against which memory ceaselessly battled.

And in the battle between his father and Tristan, choosing a side was no choice at all. Cael would follow his friend to the edge of the universe and back.

As soon as he figured out a way to bring Xenia with him.

CHAPTER
TWENTY-FIVE

XENIA FIDDLED WITH THE pins that had worked their way out of her thick, unruly hair as she'd spent the afternoon tidying in the guest wing.

A few more guests had arrived this week: several siblings of Laskaris and his wife, along with their own large families.

Xenia thought it a bit excessive—the wedding wasn't for at least another three weeks—but she'd overheard mumblings about wanting to arrive at Stoneridge before the rebels made the continent impassable.

Why were Arran and Phidion were so keen to move forward with this wedding if war was about to erupt?

She pondered the question as she entered her final room for today's shift.

Elodie's room.

Xenia hadn't forgotten about that strange encounter in Arran's office the other day. And now she had the perfect excuse to snoop. The door closed behind her as she surveyed the messy space.

Pastel slippers were scattered across the floor while dresses in matching colors were strewn atop the unmade bed. An array of cosmetics and hair products sat atop the vanity, several containers tipped over and spilling onto the wood.

She rifled through the nightstands, the bureau, the vanity, finding nothing out of the ordinary. She had no idea what she was looking for, but assured herself she'd know it when she found it.

If she found it.

Perhaps Cael was right, and her jealousy of Elodie was clouding her judgment. Had her assigning suspicious motives to ordinary actions.

But Xenia couldn't shake the nagging sense that *something* was off about the beautiful Beastrunner female who was poised to take Cael away from her forever.

She stepped into the closet, and her gaze snagged on a small chest tucked away in the corner.

Purposefully hidden.

Adrenaline tingled through her limbs.

She crouched down on her heels, then pulled the wooden chest out and attempted to pry open the lid.

It was locked.

Of course it was.

She hadn't seen any kind of key during her initial search through Elodie's drawers, so she checked underneath the pillows, tore through the blankets, even looked under the mattress.

Nothing.

Shit.

She searched through the pockets of Elodie's scattered dresses, hanging them in the closet after each perusal, but no luck there either.

Venting a resigned sigh, Xenia returned the box to its hiding place, then began rifling through the dresses that were already hanging in the closet.

Her hand was deep into the pocket of a periwinkle silk dress when the doorknob turned and she froze.

"*What* are you doing in here?" Elodie stepped into the room, her nose crinkling as if she scented something unpleasant. "I've informed Mistress Ostere several times that I do not require housekeeping services." Elodie didn't bother closing the door. Merely crossed her arms over her chest, tapping her manicured nails against her upper arms. "Get out."

Xenia scrambled from the closet, her hand catching the pocket and ripping the silk dress in her haste.

"You *imbecile*," Elodie snarled, darting for the dress and shaking it in Xenia's face. "Do you have any idea how much this cost? Likely more than you're worth." Claws dug into Xenia's flesh as Elodie grabbed her arm. "Let's go. I'm sure the High Councilor will not be pleased to hear of your ineptitude."

Xenia didn't dare argue, blood pounding in her ears as Elodie dragged her through the hall muttering, "...don't need this ridiculousness when I'm trying to prepare for a *wedding*...going to be *punished* for this, surely... don't care how much my father paid for you..."

Xenia's body slicked with cool sweat as Elodie pulled her down the front stairs. Her feet slipped and she tumbled down several before Elodie reached for her again, her claws slicing two long, painful gashes into Xenia's upper arm.

Elodie snarled as she tugged Xenia upright, and something glinted at her collarbone.

A thin gold chain holding a brass key.

Xenia feigned falling again, crashing into Elodie and grasping for the key in the struggle and confusion.

"Get *off* of me!" Elodie shouted, pushing Xenia away, but keeping a firm grip on her arm.

Xenia cursed internally and bit back a whimper as Elodie's claws dug deeper into the cuts. Warm blood soaked Xenia's sleeve.

As soon as they reached the bottom of the stairs, rainbow light flashed and Cael appeared, his abrupt entrance stirring the white and green floral arrangement atop the foyer table.

Relief buckled Xenia's knees as Elodie stopped short.

"What's going on?" Cael asked in a low voice, his expression carefully cold. Though Xenia noticed his hands curling into fists.

Elodie's entire demeanor shifted as she released Xenia, who winced and clapped a hand over her wounded arm. Cael's eyes flicked to it, and a muscle ticked in his clenched jaw.

Elodie retracted her claws and placed a hand on Cael's chest, the picture of timid subservience. "I found her in my room. Rifling through my *dresses*. Who knows how long she'd been in there, touching my things. Ruining them with her human *filth*. I have half a mind to burn it all. I'm taking her to speak to your father. She needs to be reprimanded."

Cael's eyes darkened. "I'll handle it."

"But—" Elodie protested.

Cael stepped towards his fiancée, lifting her chin. "You needn't concern yourself with such trivial matters, my darling. Surely you have more important things to worry about than doling out punishment to a measly little human?"

Elodie melted against him, tipping her face up for a kiss, and jealousy, hot and heavy, seared through Xenia's chest. Elodie's eyes slid closed, but Cael stepped away, angling his body in front of Xenia instead.

Elodie's eyes fluttered open. "Yes, well," she said, flustered, "do make sure to tell your father exactly what I told you. I do not want her or any other servant in my room ever again."

"Of course," he demurred.

Elodie's expression softened, and she dipped her chin, gazing up at Cael through her lashes. "I'll see you at dinner later?"

"Until then." Cael offered a slight bow, which Elodie returned before floating up the stairs.

Xenia released a breath and Cael whirled on her, brows furrowed. "Are you alright?" He went preternaturally still at the sight of the small red pool at her feet. "What happened?"

"She wasn't lying," Xenia started. "I—"

Footsteps echoed from the hallway leading to Arran's office.

"Not here." He removed a handkerchief from his pocket and bent down to clean the blood from the floor. "Follow me."

He gently took her uninjured arm and rushed her up the stairs, turning toward the family quarters with a singular focus. He didn't even notice as they passed the open door to Erik's room.

Cael's brother was sprawled in a chair eating orange segments and flipping through a thick book. His eyes caught Xenia's and he raised a brow, though he didn't say a word as Cael pulled her further down the carpeted hallway.

At the end of the hall, Cael opened another door, then ushered Xenia into the room.

The door snicked shut behind them, and Xenia's limbs tingled when she realized where Cael had brought her.

His bedroom.

CHAPTER
TWENTY-SIX

XENIA'S HEART POUNDED FROM both the encounter with Elodie and the fact that she was alone with Cael in his bedroom.

It was larger than the guest rooms, with a wide expanse of window that overlooked the stables and paddock, as well as the lush evergreen woods beyond.

There was an unlit fireplace fronted by two low-backed chairs upholstered in a green-and-blue plaid. The two built-in shelves bracketing the fireplace held an array of books, their spines pristine. Cael wasn't much of a reader.

Occupying the other half of the room was a large bed with a dark wood frame and plaid linens that matched the armchairs.

The room was well-appointed and tastefully decorated to match the lodge's hunting aesthetic, but Xenia felt a pang of sadness that there wasn't a scrap of Cael anywhere. No art hung on the walls, no evidence of his own taste or hobbies. If she hadn't known any better, she'd think this was just another guest room.

At least it was clean. Bed made, no sign of Cael's breakfast tray. She *did* see the two notes she'd left him tucked against the brass lamp on his nightstand. She chuckled, wondering if he'd said his affirmations today.

"Come." Cael guided her into his bathroom, and Xenia cradled her wounded arm, trying not to bleed all over the black marble floor. "Take off your dress."

Xenia's insides sparkled to life at the deep command, though she knew he didn't mean it how she'd taken it. She untied her apron, then carefully shucked off her uniform.

Cael cupped her waist and hoisted her onto the light pine vanity, his cool fingers a brand on her hip through the thin silk of her chemise. He turned on the faucet, then grabbed a washcloth from underneath the sink. Gripping her forearm, his touch so achingly gentle, he began cleaning off her wounds.

She hissed when the warm water made contact with a bleeding gash.

"Sorry," he murmured, eyes focused on his task. "Why did she do this to you?"

Xenia choked back tears. "I was stupid. I just... I don't know what I was thinking. I didn't mean to rip her dress."

"I'm sure she has plenty." Cael cleaned the cloth under the running water, then knelt to grab something under the sink. It put his head perilously close to where it had been during their tryst in Rhamnos.

Phantom memories surfaced, the feel of his tongue and hands on her, inside her, and she pressed her thighs together to stop the warmth flooding her sex.

Dangerous. She didn't want to get him, or herself, into trouble with Arran.

Cael stood upright, shaking his head with a rueful smile, then began rubbing healing balm onto her wounds.

Her upper lip twitched. "This feels familiar."

"You can't seem to keep yourself from getting into trouble, Blondie." Cael's own lip twitched and Xenia's heart soared at her nickname.

"I need to get back in there."

The smile fell from Cael's face. "No. Absolutely not. I don't want you anywhere near her again. Why?"

"I found a locked box hidden in her closet. What do you think is in there?"

"Who the fuck knows? Or cares? Knowing her, it's probably a bunch of sappy love poems or something." Cael scoffed, his fingers tightening on her arm as he made another pass with the balm. "Your curiosity is going to get you killed someday. I'm sure it's nothing. Don't fucking worry about it."

"Why would she bother bringing it all the way here if it wasn't important?" Xenia countered, her defiance rising as Cael tried to dissuade her. "Don't you want to know what secrets your *fiancée* is hiding before you…before you promise yourself to her for the rest of your life?"

Healing complete, Cael placed his palms outside of Xenia's hips and leaned in, snaring her with his flint-steel gaze. His scent, that familiar mossy green freshness, washed over her as she tilted her head up, their lips nearly touching. Her heart slammed against her ribs as she fought the urge to open her thighs and wrap her legs around his waist.

"What's the matter, Zee?" he whispered, staring at her mouth. "You hoping to find something damning in there?"

"Yes." Cael's breathy chuckle caressed her lips. "And I don't trust her. She's petty and cruel."

"Then she and I are a perfect match."

She grabbed his chin, forcing him to look at her. "Bullshit. You are not cruel. You're a stubborn, bossy asshole, but you're not cruel."

His gaze softened, but underneath her fingertips, she could feel how tense his jaw was. As if he were clenching his teeth tight enough to snap them.

"You can't marry her," Xenia whispered.

Cael pushed up off of the sink, robbing her of their proximity.

"I know." He ran a hand through his hair, tousling it adorably. A sly grin spread onto his face and her heart leapt. "I had a very interesting meeting this morning."

Cael launched into an incredible story. One that filled Xenia with more hope than she'd felt since she'd been taken in Rhamnos. About how Tristan had returned to the continent. About how he'd joined with a group of rebels called the Teles Chrysos—of which Xenia's hero Trophonios was a member; so fucking cool.

"Tristan said Trophonios may be able to help us figure out how to deactivate the device. I'm meeting with Tristan again in a few days to bring him the sample you gave me."

"That's kind of them," Xenia said.

Cael dipped his chin. "We need to do something for them in return."

Xenia's excitement skyrocketed. "*We?*"

Cael nodded, then pulled a small flute made of fire opal from his pocket.

Xenia cocked her head. "What is that?"

He explained what it was and how the rebels hoped to use it to gain control over the dragon at Typhon Mountain.

Xenia blew out a long breath, shaking her head in wonder. "So you and I are going to be rebels together?"

Cael bit his lip, holding back an amused smile. "If you consider doing research rebel activity."

Xenia clapped her hands. "Research is my *favorite* kind of rebel activity."

Cael laughed, and Xenia responded in kind, peals of delighted giggles echoing off the marble around them.

Cael's brows pinched, and a look of such profound concern twisted his features that Xenia abruptly stopped laughing. "What?"

"I need to tell you something else." He stepped in closer, running a hand up over her jaw and cupping her cheek. "It's not pleasant."

Xenia squared her shoulders. "Tell me. Whatever it is, we can face it togeth—"

"Cassandra's been sent to Tartarus."

Horror plunked into Xenia's gut, displacing her excitement. Tears bloomed on her lashes and her throat pinched shut. She couldn't breathe. Oh High Gods, she couldn't—

Cael placed his hand on her heart, his fingertips caressing her collarbone. "Breathe, Zee. It's going to be okay. *Breathe.*"

She stared into his deep gray eyes, her anchor in a turbulent sea, and did as he commanded. She filled her lungs, pushing her chest into his hand.

"Good," Cael murmured. "Now exhale."

She released it slowly, Cael keeping his hand at her heart. And after a few more breaths, her panic subsided. She choked out a ragged whisper. "*Why?*"

Cael shook his head, looking as devastated as Xenia felt. "Eamon discovered what she was doing with those memories. Stealing treasures to help the humans in the colonies. At least, that's what he said publicly. More likely, it was a move to punish Tristan once Eamon learned how much she meant to him."

Xenia closed her eyes, clinging to Cael's shoulders and feeling like she might pass out. All her fears for Cassandra had finally been realized.

"What can we do?" Xenia said, her voice shrill as her panic flared again. "We have to leave. We have to go now. We'll go to Delos, beg the Emperor to let her out. I'll tell him it was my fault. I *helped* her, Cael. It's my fault. He can take me instead."

Cael's brows pinched, his lips a thin line. "You know that's not possible. The best thing you can do right now is be *strong* for her. Tristan and the Teles Chrysos will free her as soon as they take Delos. Focus on our own plan to get out of here and join the rebels so you can be reunited with her." He cupped her cheeks and brought their faces together. "*I am in control of my happiness and my destiny.*"

Xenia barked out a garbled laugh. "Since when did *you* become the positive one?"

Cael gave her a soft smile, stroking a thumb across her lips. "Someone once told me that positivity isn't effortless. You just have to dare to see the world the way you want to. So, dare to see this world with me. One where you and I are away from all this mess and with our friends again. Close your eyes and picture it."

Xenia did as she was told, her eyes sliding closed. And she *could* see that world. The four of them together again, laughing and hugging and crying. A lovely, tear-soaked reunion. She held the image in her heart, clung to it fiercely enough to power through these next weeks.

She popped her eyes open, capturing Cael's concerned ones, then pushed up from the counter and kissed him.

She tasted like sunshine and starlight. Like sin and madness. Like the decadent joy of the forbidden.

He eased himself between her spread thighs, and she let out a delicious little whimper as he probed his tongue into her mouth.

He shouldn't be doing this.

But Amatu fucking spare him, he couldn't help himself.

That stupid, selfish, primal part of his brain insisted he have her. Even if doing so meant putting her in grave danger.

He pulled back to study her: flushed, swollen lips; wild, rebellious curls; hard nipples poking through her thin white chemise.

His cock twitched as his eyes roved down to her legs. To those *fucking* stockings that drove him half-mad with desire.

He placed his hands on the golden skin just above, running his thumbs along the edges of the wool, and Xenia's thighs quivered in anticipation.

"Cael," she breathed.

He flicked his eyes back to hers, and the lust shining there ripped away the last shred of his sanity.

His hands roved higher, coasting over the crease of her hip. He dragged her chemise above the taut plane of her stomach, and she arched her back as his knuckles traced over her breasts. He tossed her chemise aside, then ran his thumb across a peaked bud while she writhed against the counter.

He leaned in, their mouths inches apart. "You want this?"

"You know I do." She grabbed his wrist and pushed his hand between her legs, to the wet heat waiting for him. He murmured a curse.

She surged forward and kissed him again, laying her hand atop his and grinding his fingers against her slick panties.

He was hard as a fucking rock, all rational thought buried. He needed to make her come. He needed to feel her fall apart on his fingers. He needed to give her something in return for her gentle words and buoyant spirit.

He wrenched his hand from underneath hers, and she huffed a frustrated breath against his mouth.

He pulled back and cocked an eyebrow at her. "Off," he ordered, dipping his eyes to her panties. "Now."

A thrill shuddered through her limbs as she scooted around on the counter, pulling them off and letting them fall to the floor. She went to remove the stockings, but he stilled her with a shake of his head.

"No. Leave those on. And open your legs."

Xenia leaned back against the mirror and obeyed his request.

Stygios *end* him.

Her flushed pink sex gleamed, and the sight of her bared to him in nothing but those wool stockings was the hottest fucking thing he'd seen in one-and-a-half centuries of life.

He spent a long minute admiring her. Committing the view to memory in case this was the last time.

She stroked her thighs, beckoning him.

He tried to draw up an ounce of guilt for what he was about to do. Technically, he was promised to another female.

But his selfish heart only wanted *her*.

The luminous little star splayed across his counter. His guiding light through the darkness.

He stepped into her, his cock throbbing behind his zipper, and slid a finger inside her at the same time as he cupped one small, perfect breast.

Her hips jolted forward, and she threw her head back.

She reached out to grab him, to pull him closer, but he caught her wrists in one hand and pulled them above her head.

"No touching," he murmured, running his lips down her neck as he continued to pump his finger in and out of her slowly. He didn't want her to touch him. He wanted this to be solely about her pleasure—and he might come in his pants if she did.

Her wrists strained against his grip. "Cael, *please*."

He squeezed them tighter. "No. Focus on how I'm making you feel. Don't worry about me."

He turned his hand, adding a second finger and pressing the base of his palm against her swollen clit.

"Oh, *f-f-fuck*." Her stuttering moan thickened his cock further. A bright bolt of pleasure that nearly pitched him over the edge. He'd thought of no one else since he'd left her in Rhamnos. Hadn't even touched himself. And that pent-up frustration was threatening to explode.

He pumped into her, circling his palm against her clit, feeling her inner walls ripple and shudder as she rolled her hips against his hand.

She was close.

"You can take more, Blondie," he growled against her neck, biting against her galloping pulse and drinking down the intoxicating taste of her skin, the scent of her arousal.

"*Yes.*"

He added a third finger, then switched out the base of his palm for his thumb, which he brushed over her clit in teasing, rhythmic strokes.

Her breathing stilled, her entire body taut as a bowstring. All her muscles tensed and released, then tensed again in shorter and shorter increments.

He released her wrists, traveling his palm up one of her hands and intertwining their fingers.

She brought her other hand to his face and cupped his cheek as he pressed their foreheads together, staring into her enchanting emerald eyes as he fucked her with his fingers.

And even though he was fully clothed, he felt stripped bare. An intimacy he'd never experienced with anyone.

He curled his fingers, stroking the tips across that spot just inside her entrance as he circled her clit with the pad of his thumb.

"Give it to me, Xenia," he breathed against her lips.

Her brows furrowed and her thighs pushed together slightly before they slammed back out again and she jerked against his hand, her sex pulsing around his fingers.

A scream tore from her throat, and he swallowed it with a kiss, devouring the sweet sounds of her climax as his own shuddered down his spine.

As she came down from the high, he removed his fingers, but continued to stroke his thumb over her clit. She squealed and pushed his hand away. "Too sensitive," she breathed as she fell against his torso, and he chuckled.

They spent several minutes like that, Cael holding her, stroking her hair. Her breathing returned to normal.

She pulled away and gazed up at him, satisfaction and wonder in her eyes. "What was that for?"

He tilted her chin up with a finger, and pressed a gentle kiss to her addicting lips. "That was for you."

Her eyes flicked to the wet spot at his groin. "Looks like it might have been for you, too."

He pinched one of her curls between his fingers. "I couldn't help it. I *crave* you. The sounds you make. The way you taste. I've been dying to touch you since the moment you came back to me."

He pulled the silver cuff from his pocket and placed it on her wrist.

She smiled up at him. "What's this?"

"Tristan gave it to me. It will help us communicate. Just tap the violet stone and picture me in your mind, and you'll be able to send me messages. Sort of like windwhispers. And the opal will allow you to portal wherever you like—within the estate, obviously. Though I wouldn't use that one very often. Only if you're completely sure that where you intend to land is empty. We should test it now; go back down to your room so you can put on a new uniform. Then I'm going to take you to see Mistress Ostere to have you reassigned."

"No," Xenia bit out, brows furrowed. "I need legitimate access to Elodie's room. And I need you to get me that key."

Cael scrubbed a hand down his face. "You're going to get caught, Blondie."

She shot him a sharp glare. "Cael."

"No."

"*Cael.*"

"I said *no!*"

She jumped down from the counter, her breasts jiggling, and he nearly forgot what they were arguing about.

She bent over to grab her panties and chemise, then hastily pulled them on. Her frustration was so adorable that he had to bite his lip to keep from laughing. High *Gods*, he was such an asshole. But if he broke, she'd resume her ill-advised campaign to spy on his fiancée.

Dressed again, she ran her fingers through her hair, pulling out the last few pins. "Thanks for the orgasm, pterodactyl, but if you're not going to get me that key, I'll do it myself."

She made to stride past him, but he caught her elbow. He didn't understand why she was so insistent.

"Zee, just *leave* it. There are far more important things to be doing." Cael leaned in again, brushing a strand of hair behind her ear. "And you're going to prefer your new assignment."

She cocked a brow. "Oh, am I?"

"Trust me." Cael nodded, then lifted her wrist and tapped the cuff, portaling them out of the room.

After a quick trip to Xenia's quarters to snag a clean uniform and ensure she could hide the cuff beneath her sleeve—and after Cael did some careful rearranging of his untucked shirt to hide the spot on his pants—he brought her to Mistress Ostere to secure her new assignment.

The Stoneridge estate library was a beautiful stone and glass building just inside the entrance gate and separate from the main house.

It wasn't as large as the Temple library in Thalenn, but certainly larger than one would expect to find within a private residence.

When he opened the thick glass door, Xenia's jaw dropped, her gaze gamboling through the hall.

The exact reaction he'd been hoping for.

"Told you you'd like it." He winked.

Flowing up to the coffered ceiling, three full floors of shelves were accessed by an iron spiral staircase. On the main floor, tufted leather couches and an arrangement of oak tables surrounded a floor-to-ceiling riverstone fireplace.

He placed his hand at the small of her back, savoring the contact. He wanted to steal her back to his bedroom and lock her away from the world. Keep her safe.

Keep her *his*.

But cocooning Xenia here among her beloved books, hidden from the prying eyes of Arran and Tomas—not to mention his fucking fiancée—gave him at least *some* sense of security. He could've kissed Mistress Ostere when she'd agreed to it.

He walked Xenia up to the main desk and the human librarian, a middle-aged woman with soil-dark hair and kind eyes, bowed at his approach.

"Master Zephryus," she said, "what a pleasure. What can I do for you today?"

"Good to see you again, Margaret." He pasted on his most charming smile. One that felt less fake than it might have a few weeks ago. Swore he saw Xenia bite her lip to stifle a chuckle. "This is Mistress Cirillo. She's new on staff and she's been assigned to the library."

"Wonderful." Margaret's eyes twinkled with genuine merriment. "I'll be happy for the help."

"She's also assisting me with some research." Cael leaned a forearm onto the desk. "I've been away from Stoneridge for too long, and I need to get up to speed on my father's business ventures. I trust you'll make sure she's not too bogged down with dusting and re-shelving to help me?"

Margaret sighed, enraptured by the full force of Cael's charisma. "Of course. Whatever you need."

"You're a doll, Margaret, thank you." The woman giggled, a peony blush staining her cheeks. Xenia was shaking with barely concealed laughter. "I'll show her around the hall, then leave her to your care."

Margaret dipped her head. "As you wish."

Cael tapped a hand against his heart, a gesture of gratitude, then led Xenia to the first row of stacks, loudly naming the section.

Once he knew Margaret couldn't overhear them, he cornered Xenia, placing his hands on the shelf behind her head and caging her between his arms.

"*Whatever you need, Master Zephryus,*" Xenia teased in Margaret's high-pitched voice. "High Gods, you had that woman—and Mistress Ostere, I might add—eating out of the palm of your hand."

He smirked, leaning in close enough to run his nose along her cheek. Fuck, she smelled damn-near edible. Especially with that lingering arousal still on her. "I can be charming when I want to be."

"Good thing I'm not silly enough to fall for it." Her eyes glittered with mischievous intent, and it took all of his restraint to not pull up her skirt, wrap her thighs around his waist and fuck her right here in the blissfully empty stacks.

"Oh, never," he grinned, feeling better than he had in weeks. Xenia coming on his fingers probably had something to do with it. "I was serious about the research though. I've given you the perfect cover. See what you can find about both the tracking device and the dragon while you're in here."

Xenia swiveled her gaze across the titles, a giddy child in a well-stocked candy store. Her grateful smile nearly stopped his heart.

"I've got to run," he said, reluctantly. "My father's expecting me to brief him on my meetings today. You'll be okay alone?"

"I will be now."

He narrowed his eyes. "Don't get distracted. You know what we're looking for."

"Yeah, yeah. Tracking device. Dragon. Flute. Any books on what a massive asshole your father is. Got it."

Cael chuckled, glancing left and right to ensure they lacked an audience, then kissed her temple. "Have fun, Blondie. Behave. Message me on the cuff if you find anything and we can meet in the stable loft."

She waved him away, then took off down the stacks, vibrating with excitement.

Cael shook his head ruefully as he left, thanking Margaret again, and trudged up the path to the main house.

With Xenia safely ensconced within the library, he felt like he could breathe for the first time in days.

It was unfamiliar, this thing blooming in his chest.

It almost felt like hope.

CHAPTER
TWENTY-SEVEN

SUNLIGHT SPARKLED OFF THE milky turquoise water as Ione pulled oars through the canal.

The fresh breeze on Tristan's face and the warmth on his feathers inspired flashbacks of a time two centuries ago when he'd been the one steering their boat.

"I can help, you know." He offered her a small smile.

"I know you can," she said, returning it. "But the exercise is good for me." She raised an arm and flexed her biceps, showing off the muscle tone of the mythic Fae warrior she'd become. "Keeps me big and strong."

Tristan huffed a laugh, turning to the floating city around them.

Delos was arranged on a series of islands, radiating out from the largest which housed the Imperial Palace. That one in particular was a *true* island, rising up from the seabed thousands of feet below. Very few of the others were connected to the land; most floated atop Lake Phaeban and stayed above the water by some feat of magical engineering. The islands were connected by curved bridges, underneath which flowed the canals that small boats used to traverse the city.

Delos had been built by a Beastrunner king from a time when the vast majority of Ethyrios, both Fae and humans, had worshiped Adelphinae. Legend had it the king and his wife were powerful water magic wielders and had decided to build their kingdom on the largest lake in Ethyrios. And they'd crafted the Crystal Throne in honor of their preferred element.

It was Tristan's great-grandfather Phaeban who'd taken the city. The Beastrunner king and his queen had passed by then, the water magic in their bloodline barely a trickle, so his progeny hadn't been able to challenge Phaeban, who renamed the lake for himself.

Yet another example of Tristan's terrible family taking whatever they wanted from whomever they wanted.

Tristan and Ione had used their cuffs to portal to a smaller island on the city's western edge this morning, where Ione had procured them this boat.

They wore hooded cloaks to hide their faces, and Ione had coated her feathers with mud before they'd left Lebaedia. Though white wings weren't rare, the shimmery iridescence of hers was, so she'd done her best to dull it. Tristan's black beauties were less of an issue, as they were sported by every member of the Erabis family including cousins and distant relatives still living in Delos.

There were plenty of boats on the canals, so he and Ione didn't inspire any more than a few passing glances. She guided them on a circuitous route, cutting back and passing the same islands multiple times to throw off attempts to follow their progress.

As the little boat glided across the water, Tristan drank in the sights and smells of this glittering jewel of a city: its winding waterways, its majestic multistory homes with their arched windows and ornate balconies. The opulent Imperial Palace perched like a bleached, bloated grande dame atop the center island.

He'd loved Delos as a boy. The Imperial capital was a cross-section of Fae from every continental territory, every sub-species. A city of strivers with grandiose dreams. Of artists and chefs, musicians and scientists, architects and storytellers. All who'd wanted nothing more than to showcase their talents in the most important city on the continent.

At least, that had been his impression at the time. Now there was something sinister about the wealth on display—a pristine facade masking a tormented history.

The tip of the boat bumped against the stony lakebed, and Tristan and Ione hopped out to drag it onto a small sliver of shore beneath a rocky cliff.

Above, Tristan could barely make out the white marble walls of the Imperial Palace. He was sure there must be Vasilikans up there on patrol, but the entrance was well hidden. The top of the cliff jutted out over the water, creating an overhang that led into a small cave where they hid the boat.

"This way," Ione gestured, tucking her wings. Her boots crunched along the pebbled cave floor as they came upon a circular wooden door. Ione rapped on it—three short knocks, followed by a single pound, followed by another two short knocks.

They waited several seconds before the door swung inwards to reveal a handsome Beastrunner male—a lion bi-form, based on his scent and his golden hair and eyes—wearing a red jacket and gold helmet. The telltale uniform of an Imperial soldier.

"Darius," Ione said, clasping the male's hand, then turned to Tristan. "One of ours."

Darius swept down to one knee. "Your Highness."

"Report?" Ione asked as Darius rose.

"The Emperor's been particularly unhinged these past few weeks," Darius sneered. "Worse than you can even imagine. Ever since the battle in Staurien Pass, he's been calling his soldiers back to Delos."

Ione's lips flattened. "Have you figured out how he learned we were after that shipment?"

"Not yet," Darius said, head bowed.

Ione turned to Tristan. "If someone from our group is feeding him information, he may know of our plans to take the city. Why else would he be concentrating his forces here?"

A thought crept into Tristan's mind, a flicker of something he remembered from the colonies. "He was having obliviated humans shipped here. Do you have any idea what he's doing with them?"

Darius shook his head. "The ships unload daily, herding scores of humans onto an island behind the palace. Every few days, he has several delivered to his quarters, but what happens to them there, we haven't been able to tell."

Tristan looked to Ione. "What's he planning? Could it be another weapon? Something even our Anointed couldn't combat?"

"I don't know," Ione said, frustrated. "Let's go before we lose our chance to get the Compendium."

Darius held the door open for them. "I was able to buy you a sliver of extra time. Sent the first shift guards away early. You've got twenty minutes. Make it count."

Ione slapped her cuff onto his wrist. "You too. Your assignment's over. Tell the others as well."

Darius reared back. "Why? It's the worst possible time for us not to have eyes and ears within the palace."

"And it's about to get far too dangerous for those eyes and ears. Especially if the Prince and I succeed today. I will not lose good people to Eamon."

Darius turned to Tristan. "May I speak freely?"

Ione gave an annoyed snort, but Tristan waved a hand, encouraging Darius to continue.

"I'll send the others back to Lebaedia, but I'd like to stay. You cannot take back your throne if you are blind to the goings-on inside this palace."

"Are you sure?" Tristan asked. "If he discovers what you've done today, he could torture you for information about our movement. You'd be a liability to us."

"I'd sooner die than break." Darius drew up to his full height.

Tristan glanced to Ione, who merely shrugged as if to say *your call*.

"Permission granted," Tristan said. "Use that cuff to get the rest out. And for Creator's sake, be *careful*."

"Yes, Your Highness." Darius bowed gratefully as Ione pushed past him into the hallway, Tristan a step behind. Ione slid Tristan a smirk, then wrapped her wings around her body, shaking them to activate her…camouflaging feathers?

Tristan tried to reign in his shock. He had no idea she'd inherited his Ghostwalking abilities. She grabbed his hand as he did the same with his own wings, then pulled him through the maze of marble hallways.

They passed a set of stairs, the bottom half of which was crafted of rough stone that led down into the dungeons. The marble upper half led into the palace proper.

A memory flashed through Tristan's mind, there and gone in an instant, of he and Eamon walking down those same stairs centuries ago. Back when they'd been close. Back when he was fretting about having fallen in love with Ione and Eamon had told him he may have a solution for him. Back before Eamon had betrayed him and he'd been exiled to the colonies, believing Ione was dead.

If Tristan had known she was alive all these years, how different would his life have been?

He shook those thoughts away—they would do him no good right now anyway—as they approached an opalescent door with a Teles symbol carved into the center.

Something hummed through Tristan's veins. Like every choice he'd made had led him to this moment.

Ione parted her feathers and reappeared before him as he did the same. She plucked a dagger—regular steel not Typhon—from her waist and grabbed his hand, raising a questioning eyebrow.

Tristan nodded his permission, then tried not to close his palm against the sting of the blade. A line of blood bubbled up from where she'd sliced across his Turning scar.

Her eyes darted toward his, glistening with regret, and though he couldn't remember the last time they'd done this—his memories of the Turning ceremony had been pulled by Shrouded Sisters before he was exiled—he wondered if Ione did.

She lifted his palm toward the door and pressed it against the Teles symbol. His blood seeped into the carving, and a faint rainbow pulsed through it before the door swept backward, then rumbled aside.

Ione glanced up at him, holding her breath.

"After you, Prince," was all she said before Tristan stepped into the chamber.

Not a chamber.

It was a chapel.

Though it looked very different from any other house of worship Tristan had ever visited.

He supposed technically he *had* visited this one before, though his memory of it was hazy.

The chapel was crafted entirely from the same opalescent stone as the door. Columns ringed the outer edges of the room and the soaring ceiling above showcased faded frescoes—pastoral scenes of various Fae sub-species cavorting with humans. The ceiling's center panel had been scrubbed raw, though faint traces of paint signaled there'd been a fresco there as well. Along the edge of the ceiling, just under where the dome began to curve, symbols were carved into the stone in a repeating pattern: an upright triangle, an inverted triangle, a lightning bolt, and a wavy line. Symbols of the elemental powers Adelphinae had bestowed upon her creations.

Ione dashed away a tear as she walked toward the center of the chapel. Tristan followed.

Concentric circular benches rose from the floor, and four aisles at north, south, east, and west flowed toward an obelisk carved with Teles symbols. And next to the obelisk was a single stone pedestal, atop which sat a book.

The book.

The Compendium of Creation.

He wondered why neither his father nor Eamon had destroyed it—the book or the chapel. They'd decimated the art, but had left this sacred space intact. He could almost hear chanting voices, could imagine the Fae gathered around a priestess of Adelphinae, who would have been on the same level as the congregation rather than up at a pulpit preaching downward. A difference in the Goddess's principles, versus the hierarchies imposed by the religion of the High Gods.

As they approached the pedestal, he couldn't help thinking that the book looked so *ordinary*. And small. Tristan didn't recognize the words embossed on the cover—an ancient dialect from the days of the Fallen Goddess, no doubt. When Eamon had shown Tristan the book in their youth, he hadn't known how to read the language either. They'd figured out the Turning ceremony thanks to crude drawings that represented the process.

Ione's hand hovered over the book, afraid to touch it lest it crumble to dust. "I… It doesn't feel real. How can so much knowledge be captured in such a tiny package?"

"What language is that?"

"Senskrish," Ione answered, her mouth wrapping confidently around the word. "An ancient dialect of Aramaelish."

"You can read it?"

"I can speak it, too. I've been studying it. Some of the older Teles Chrysos members who were alive before the war had texts written in it."

Holding her breath, she plucked up the small book, then nestled it in her sack. She glanced to the cuff on her wrist.

"These won't work within the palace," she said. "We need to return to the boat and clear the shield around the Imperial island before we're able to—"

A boom cut off her speech.

The chamber door had shut.

Sealing them within the chapel.

CHAPTER
TWENTY-EIGHT

TRISTAN AND IONE SCRAMBLED down the aisle, Tristan reaching for the dagger sheathed at her hip. She stilled his wrist. "It won't work from this side." She gestured to the smooth stone. "There are no carvings."

Tristan pressed his ear against the stone. In the hallway beyond, footsteps thumped and broadswords clanked. If he had to guess, nearly half the palace guards had come down to confront them. Shuffling sounded, as if the soldiers were stepping aside, followed by the clack of slow footsteps.

He'd recognize that gait anywhere. Unhurried. Self-assured. Arrogant, even.

A crazed laugh, bordering on hysterical, burst through the door. "There's only one other person in Ethyrios besides me who could have entered this chamber."

Tristan's feathers shivered at the clarity, the *proximity*, of that voice.

"Hello, my dear brother," Eamon said.

The last time Tristan had seen Eamon, he'd been taunting Tristan about how Tartarus was going to rip Cassandra to shreds. Taunting him about how he'd planned to sacrifice Tristan to shore up his own claim to the Crystal Throne.

If he were capable of it, Tristan would blast through this door and use his bare hands to peel Eamon's flesh from his bones.

"Ironic, isn't it?" Eamon continued. "You managed to escape one cell only to end up locked in another. Is that bitch Ione with you? She's been making such a hassle for my citizens."

"Fuck you, Eamon!" Ione shouted and Tristan fought the urge to clap a hand over her mouth.

"She *is* with you," Eamon chuckled. "My lucky day."

"How many guards can you take?" Tristan whispered. "We should have suspected that he—"

Ione pressed a hand against his chest. "There is something we can do..." she trailed off, searching his eyes. "A way to call for the Goddess's assistance using the connection we forged during the Turning ceremony."

"How?"

More shuffling sounded beyond the door followed by the metallic hiss of a broadsword being unsheathed.

Eamon about to spill his own blood to open the chamber?

Shit, they had *seconds*.

"It doesn't matter," Tristan whisper-shouted. "Whatever it is, just—"

Ione grabbed him by the back of the neck and hauled their mouths together, pressing her body into his.

And though her lips were warm and soft, familiar even centuries later, he felt nothing. No passion. No stirring in his groin. No urge to wrap his arms around her.

He pushed her away with a soft snarl.

Then shock barreled through him as beads of water formed along his palm. He raised his hand, then looked to Ione, who wore a similar expression of astonishment. Lightning crackled at her fingertips and sparks flashed through her indigo eyes.

"What…" Tristan croaked out, "…what's happening to us?"

"It worked," Ione said, relief and awe softening her words. "I was worried that since you…" She shook her head. "It doesn't matter. It *worked*." She tucked her sack inside her cloak. "But we'll only have the power temporarily. We can work together to create a storm."

"I've never wielded water. How does it—"

"Don't think, just *feel*. Like how you call upon the wind."

Tristan planted his feet and lifted his palms, reaching for his wind. It swirled around him in a thrashing cyclone, but other than a few small bursts of water, he couldn't get a handle on the new magic.

"It's not working!" he shouted over the roar of his wind and the sizzle of Ione's lightning.

"Water responds best to peace and calm!" Ione yelled, honey-colored strands whipping across her face.

How the fuck was he supposed to find *calm* when his brother and a hallway full of Vasilikans and palace guards were waiting on the other side of that door?

A memory pierced his panic, one he could've sworn was sent by the Goddess herself.

Blue-gray eyes. Soft, supple skin. The scent of honey and rosewood. And a warm body moving atop him.

I'm yours, Tristan, a gentle voice whispered. *For as little or as long as you want me. I'm* yours.

His own response rang out through his head, his heart.

His soul.

For eternity.

A tidal wave crashed through him, filling his veins and bursting from his fingers. He mixed the streams with his gusts, crafting a cyclone of wind and cloud and water.

A wicked grin spread onto Ione's face as she seeded it with lightning in the rapidly darkening chapel.

The door pushed inward, then slid aside.

And it was *epically* satisfying to see Eamon's smugness distort into wide-eyed shock as he and his guards were blown backward, swords crashing and helmets clattering.

Torrents of rain, cracks of lightning, and gusts of wind filled the hallway, ripping at Tristan's wings as he pulled Ione to his side and they rushed out of the chapel.

Eamon rose, his wet black clothes plastered against his body, and erected a wind-shield around himself to block the storm. His Vasilikans and a few Windrider guards did the same. The Beastrunners and Deathstalkers were unable to rise against the battering wind and thrashing rain.

"Follow them!" Eamon shouted.

Tristan and Ione tore down the hallway, feeding their magic into the storm at their backs.

A blast of energy whined through the din and Tristan turned back to see it ricochet off a gust and take down a Vasilikan brandishing a stun pistol.

They reached the wooden door they'd entered through, and Tristan shattered it with a concentrated blast of wind. He helped Ione through the jagged hole and into the stone passageways beyond.

He looked back over his shoulder. "Let's end him," he ground out. "No one else has to get hurt if we just kill Eamon now. Our storm—"

Ione's lips parted to answer, but before any sound came out, she was seized by the surge of a stun pistol. She crumpled, paralyzed, at his feet.

Tristan cursed low, watching as his brother and the guards clanked toward the blown out door. He couldn't fight them off alone *and* protect Ione.

He swore again, then hauled her over his shoulder and raced through the labyrinthine tunnels beneath the palace. Behind him, the storm fizzled while ahead, light began to glow.

The cave entrance. And just beyond, their boat.

He glanced over his shoulder, wiping rain from his eyes. Eamon and four guards were right on his heels.

Tristan burst out of the cave and tossed Ione into the boat. He redirected his wind into the water, a makeshift motor that powered their progress as he guided the little boat through the canal and into the open waters of Lake Phaeban.

The cuff at his wrist heated the moment they passed through the shield.

Brother! a voice roared into Tristan's ear via windwhisper.

Eamon stood on the shore hundreds of feet away, wings splayed, dark hair in disarray. Far enough away that neither he nor his guards would be able to reach Tristan before the cuff could portal him back to Lebaedia. Eamon seemed to discern as much as he whispered furiously into his palm, then waved over another message.

Tristan pulled Ione into his arms as his brother's words floated into his mind.

I hope you've prepared for this particular ending.

There was a manic edge to the message, but in typical Eamon fashion, it was cryptic fucking nonsense.

Tristan chose not to respond. At least not with words.

A crazed smile burst across his face as he lifted his middle finger to his brother.

Then tapped the opal on his cuff and disappeared in a flash of rainbow light.

CHAPTER
TWENTY-NINE

CASSANDRA COULDN'T SLEEP.

No different than any of the past nine nights she'd spent in Mireille's apartment, tossing and turning as the seconds ticked by.

Once her frustrating training sessions were finished each day, she, Ronin and Mireille would return to the apartment for a tense, silent meal, after which Mireille would work in her shop and Ronin would leave to roam the city in search of Selene. And it was during those lonely hours—after Cassandra had showered, dried her wings, and put herself to bed—that her mind came alive.

It couldn't stop tabulating the long string of poor decisions that had led her here. Stealing memories, leaving the Temple, restoring obliviates, defying the Emperor, getting tangled up with an exiled Prince. And though she didn't regret that last one, not for a single moment, the weight of Tristan's absence only compressed her anxieties.

She bore most of the consequences of those decisions on her own—her Turning, her death sentence. But now, others might suffer for her choices. How could she drag Mireille and Ronin into this appeal with her? High Gods, what if something were to happen them? What if they *died* because of her?

She couldn't stomach it. Couldn't just lay here in this claustrophobic little room with these excruciating thoughts after doing nothing but fail at training day after day after day.

There was one thing she thought she could fix. Something she'd dreamt about fixing since the day she'd arrived.

And the idea of taking some action, righting at least one of her many wrongs, was far too tempting to ignore.

Cassandra dressed in her training leathers and slipped out of the quiet apartment into a night dark enough to cloak her next decision.

The mists surrounding the moat seemed murkier than they had two weeks ago.

And as soon as Cassandra stepped off the bridge, they surrounded her like a night's cool kiss. She kept her footfalls gentle, listening for those voices she'd heard before Reena had run off.

Nothing called to her as she walked. And walked. And walked. And *walked*.

No break in the darkness, no sound except her own breaths and the steady beat of her heart.

After several hours, her legs were aching, even with her new Fae stamina. She had no idea where she was, this second journey just as disorienting as the first.

A debilitating wave of panic stole through her. If she got lost in these mists, who would even know to come looking for her? Would she spend the rest of her immortality wandering through nothingness?

She took several deep breaths in, and just as she was about to berate herself for her impulsivity, a faint, far away growl echoed through the mists.

Reena.

Cassandra headed toward the sound. Whenever she lost track, spinning in a search for her bearings, the growl sounded again. Slightly closer each time.

The growls began to mingle with that familiar buzz between her ears. The hairs on her limbs stood on end, the downy feathers at her shoulder-blades prickling, and her teeth vibrating with electric pain. The sensation was so intense it felt like her brain might explode.

She clapped her hands over her ears, and a faint pop echoed in her mind.

The mists cleared.

Heat kissed her cheeks and she shielded her eyes as a whipping wind tossed tiny grains of sand across her face.

A hundred yards away, nestled between two giant red sand dunes, a glittering pool of ink-blue water was surrounded by the strangest, most beautiful trees Cassandra had ever seen.

Thick, stark white trunks supported fluffy, near perfect balls of leaves in every color of the rainbow.

And right in front of them, head bowed and drinking from the pool, was a large tiger.

"Reena!" she shouted, though her voice was stolen by a violent wind that flung sand in her eyes and stole strands from her braid.

She dashed through the sand, her feet slipping. "*REENA!*"

The tiger lifted its head, amber eyes reflecting in the pool, then sauntered through the white trunks and disappeared.

"No," Cassandra blubbered as she reached the oasis.

The wind ripped through the trees and a single blue-black leaf tore free. As soon as it kissed the surface, the water came alive.

Strained whispers echoed from the ripples. A female voice.

And a male one that, even laced with fear, made the feathers lining her wings stand at attention.

A firm, powerful voice that she would recognize anywhere, in any time.

Tristan.

She knelt at the edge of the churning, boiling pool and as she peered into the water, the blurry vision upon its surface crystallized with life-like clarity.

She couldn't tell where he was; the background looked like some kind of church.

What she *could* make out was that the female with him was stunning.

Honey-blond hair fell to her waist in a thick braid, and her indigo eyes showcased an almost divine confidence.

But it was the two white wings at the female's back that had Cassandra sitting back on her heels in stunned silence.

Ione.

Cassandra felt two intense emotions at the exact same time.

The first was profound relief.

Tristan was *alive.*

And the second was gut-wrenching envy.

He was with his first love. The woman he'd Turned purposefully rather than by accident.

A female who radiated such grace and power that she looked like Adelphinae herself reborn.

How had Ione found him?

Had she—

Cassandra's relief curdled in her chest as Ione launched herself at Tristan, wrapping her arms around his neck and snaring his lips.

Cassandra's chest hollowed out and her breathing went shallow.

She barked out a choked sob. "Tristan?"

At the sound of her voice, the vision dissolved and the pool went still.

"No," she cried. "No, no, no. Bring it back."

She scrambled to her feet and leaned out over the edge, begging the pool to return the vision to her. As soul-crushing as it was to see Tristan kissing someone else—not just someone, but *Ione*—Cassandra needed to see what happened next.

She leaned out farther, shouting Tristan's name into the still pool.

Then the sand beneath her feet crumbled and she crashed into the water.

CHAPTER THIRTY

"I THINK SHE'S WAKING UP," a deep male voice said.

"Yeah, thanks. I can see that," an annoyed female voice answered, closer by.

Cassandra's lids fluttered open, her eyesight adjusting.

Ronin was leaned against the dresser in her bedroom at Mireille's, arms crossed, a worried expression tightening his features.

Mireille was seated next to the bed. "What happened?" The concern on her face belied the lack of sympathy in her tone.

"I...I don't..." Cassandra started, her mouth dry and her tongue thick. Mireille handed her a glass of water from the nightstand. Cassandra pushed up, electric pain sparking in her head, but took the glass and gulped down half. "Where did you find me?"

"Nowhere you were supposed to be," Ronin said, eye narrowing. "You were laying at the end of the bridge into the city. At the edge of the mists. What were you thinking? Why did you go down there?"

Cassandra handed the glass back to Mireille, then circled her fingers against her temples, willing away her headache.

Willing away the vision she'd seen in that pool.

Tristan.

With Ione.

Kissing Ione.

Those fissures in her heart deepened and she wished she could slip back into unconsciousness. Maybe forever.

She crashed back onto the pillows. "I went back for Reena. I thought—"

"Foolish," Ronin snarled. "Why didn't you tell me? I would've gone with you."

And even though she knew where his frustration was coming from—his search for Selene had yet to bear fruit—she bristled. "I wasn't aware I needed your *permission*."

Cassandra looked toward Mireille, expecting to find the same anger she'd heard in Ronin's tone, but instead found a soft understanding.

Ronin ignored Cassandra's jab. "Obviously you didn't find her. What. *Happened*?"

Cassandra told them what she'd seen in the mists, the red desert that Reena had led her to. The vision in that pool surrounded by the multi-colored trees.

"How is any of that possible?" she asked.

Ronin and Mireille shared a wary glance.

"It sounds like you may have visited the Halfway," Mireille said carefully.

"The what?"

"The Halfway. The realm between worlds ruled by the Creator. It's where our souls go when we die. While we wait for Adelphinae to deliver us into a new body in a new world. Some believe that the black mists surrounding Tartarus are made up of the souls of prisoners who've died here. That they've been trapped since death, unable to breach the wards."

Cassandra shuddered, remembering those voices she'd heard. She turned a panicked glance to Ronin. "Reena was there. In the Halfway. Does that mean she's…"

"Was she glowing?" Mireille asked. "Was there a multi-colored halo around her?"

"No, not that I—"

"Then she was just a visitor. She's not dead," Mireille said. "Perhaps the Goddess asked Reena to lead you there. Showed you that vision on purpose."

At the moment, Cassandra couldn't imagine what that purpose could possibly be.

She turned to Ronin, her heart squeezing though she forced herself to ask the question. "Ione Saros," she said, the name burning up her throat. "She's alive, then?"

Ronin gave her a stiff nod. "She's the leader of the Teles Chrysos. Along with Trophonios."

Cassandra slumped back against the pillows, shock stealing through her. "Trophonios?"

"It's a long story. They've been working on the continent together for centuries. Preparing for Tristan's return. Ensuring he would have enough support throughout the continent to take his throne back from Eamon."

"So, she's been…" Cassandra could barely finish the sentence.

"Waiting for him for centuries," Ronin said, his voice softening. "She is the Delphine the Goddess's prophecy speaks of. *Born of phantom wings and mortal bones.* Turned by the very Prince whose cause she's dedicated herself to."

Cassandra squeezed her eyes shut, a tear stealing down her cheek, and Ronin sat down on the end of the bed.

"Why didn't she come to the colonies in all that time to find him? Why now?" Cassandra asked.

He placed a hand on her ankle. "She felt it was safer for him down there, to be out of sight and reach of Eamon and Leonin while she and Trophonios worked to grow the movement. Once they'd amassed a sizeable enough force, she sent me to recruit him. You saw how that plan ended. She must have had some final trick up her sleeve after Eamon arrested him."

"So, they're what?" Cassandra asked, her throat closing. "Fated to one another?"

Ronin shrugged. "She certainly seems to think so. But no one knows how the prophecy ends." He gestured to Cassandra's wings. "And his Turning *you* as well has certainly called the entire thing into question. Too bad no one outside these wards knows you've been Turned."

"Why didn't you tell him that Ione was alive?" Cassandra snapped. "When you met with him at the Serpent's Den?"

Ronin dipped his head. "She asked me not to. Wanted him to come to the decision on his own."

Cassandra ran a hand through her damp, tangled hair. High *Gods*, she needed a shower. Needed to shut the entire world away.

All those fears she'd had back in Thalenn, before she'd given herself to Tristan, had been confirmed.

Tristan wasn't *hers*.

And even though she believed that the feelings he'd expressed at the time had been genuine, what did they matter in the face of the all-powerful Goddess who controlled their fates?

Perhaps *that* had been the purpose of the vision; Adelphinae showing her Tristan's true destiny.

And encouraging Cassandra to let him go.

Her heart began to pound, and she felt like she was suffocating. How was she supposed to continue training, continue working toward her appeal, if Tristan wasn't waiting for her on the other side?

Mireille said gently, "The only way to know the truth is to survive. Win that hammer. And hope we can *get out of here*."

Cassandra scoffed. "I'd actually have to defeat the Koenig to have any chance of that. And we only have twenty—"

"Nineteen," Ronin chimed in.

She shot him a glare. "Nineteen days left to train. It seems…"

She couldn't get the word out.

Impossible, that's what it seemed.

She pushed up out of bed, her head swimming. "I need to shower. Then I'd like to be left alone, please."

Mireille grimaced. "We should really continue training—"

"It's *pointless*!" Cassandra shouted. "I didn't ask for any of this. Not to be Turned, not to be sent here, not to be given this death sentence that's only giving you all false hope. I can't do it. And the sooner you both accept that, the better off we'll all be."

Ronin and Mireille exchanged a weighted glance as Cassandra stormed past them and out of the room.

"If Tristan is meant to be with Ione," her voice nearly broke and she didn't dare look at them as she reached the door, "if that is what's going to save this world, then the best thing I can do for him, for *everyone*, is to just accept my fate. Let the Koenig end me. One less complication for everyone to deal with."

"Cassandra," Mireille whispered, reaching for Cassandra's hand, "you can't—"

As soon as their fingers touched, Cassandra's eyes slammed shut and a memory ripped through her mind.

One of Mireille's memories.

Mireille was…in the backyard of Cassandra's childhood home?

And holy High Gods. That was Cassandra's father she was looking upon.

She didn't know how it was possible to feel any more grief than she already felt, but the sight of her father—his crinkled blue-gray eyes and long braided beard—debilitated her.

There was a haziness to the memory, and Papa was surrounded by a kaleidoscopic halo.

She nearly croaked out his name before Cassandra herself—spectral, but not multi-colored—rushed over on spindly pre-teen limbs wielding her wooden practice dagger.

Mireille had seen a vision of Cassandra and her father in the Halfway? And she'd never told her?

In the memory, Mireille turned toward another glowing presence: a man with dark hair and familiar smoky eyes. The view immediately shifted.

Something pierced Cassandra's chest, and she jolted into a different mind.

A mind in the present, not a memory. She could tell the difference.

Memories had a long-simmered flavor that deepened with age.

This vision tasted fresh.

Whoever's mind she occupied was sharpening a broadsword with a skull-head pommel on the porch of a cabin in a snowy, moonlit forest.

Wind bit her cheeks and the soft stillness smelled of frosted pine needles.

The view shifted and Cassandra jolted back into her own mind.

"—give up on yourself like that," Mireille finished, as if no time at all had passed. Her features twisted with confusion at Cassandra's shocked expression. "What?"

Cassandra's grief morphed into the most righteous fury.

Mireille had been hiding things. And Cassandra's powers were changing, more quickly than she could keep up with.

It was all too overwhelming.

She ripped her hand out of Mireille's grip, then fled to the bathroom, slammed the door, and turned on the shower.

She stripped off her clothes and sank beneath the spray.

And wished for the water to melt her into oblivion.

Ronin drummed his tattooed fingers on the dining table while Mireille fiddled around in the kitchen.

"What happened when she touched you?" he asked.

"I have no idea," Mireille admitted, not turning to him. "There was a tickling pressure in my head. Honestly, if her expression hadn't changed so dramatically, I'm not sure I would have even noticed it. It almost felt like... like she was tiptoeing through my brain."

Ronin chewed on a fingernail. "She'd been restoring obliviates in the colonies. Her power had been evolving even before she was Turned. Between becoming Fae and whatever happened to her in that pool in the Halfway…"

Creator, he felt terrible. Cassandra was navigating this confusing transformation—not to mention the devastating news she'd learned about Tristan— with two strangers she'd just met.

And he'd scolded her the minute she'd woken up.

Fuck, he wasn't very good at offering comfort when someone was in pain.

Or he wasn't anymore. He'd done so once, for the female heating a pot of water over the hearth. Though the stubborn she-wolf had barely wanted to accept his help at the time.

"I don't know what to say to help her," Ronin said on a ragged exhale.

Mireille placed a steaming cup of tea in front of him, the comforting, herbal scent settling his nerves.

"I don't either," Mireille said, blowing the steam off her own mug. "Did you know about Tristan and Ione being fated to one another?"

"Of course I did. But the minute I saw Cassandra with those wings, knew who'd Turned her and what it could mean… Everything the Teles Chrysos and Ione believes is now uncertain. Cassandra could be even more important than any of us ever thought. If she breaks here, if we can't find a way to get her through this…"

He didn't need to finish the sentence. Saw the same anxiety steal across Mireille's striking features. Still the most striking he'd ever seen.

"She needs something to fight for," Mireille said. "A reason to hope after everything she's just learned. Something stronger than the heartache trying to drag her under."

The familiarity in Mireille's tone, as if she'd had to do the same in here, stirred his anger.

How fucking *dare* she allude to her own heartache after she...

He shook away those useless thoughts. They'd do nothing to help him, or Cassandra, get through this mess. And if he were being *really* honest with himself, he was so fucking tired of holding on to this anger. Didn't know what to do with it.

I know what you could do with it, his wolf chimed in.

A memory bubbled to the surface of Ronin's mind. Of the punishments he'd once delivered to Mireille. Of her flesh reddening beneath his palm as she quivered in ecstasy across his lap.

He snarled at his wolf, pushing the vision away, though not fast enough to stem the powerful wave of *want* that tore through him and shifted his scent.

Mireille's nostrils flared, but she didn't acknowledge it. Dipped her eyes to her mug and took a short sip.

So he wouldn't acknowledge it either. Just let it sit there between them. A writhing beast he didn't have the strength to tame alone.

"How did *you* do it?" he asked, tentatively.

She raised her eyes, and he nearly roared at the centuries of fatigue dulling them.

At one time in his life, he'd wanted nothing more than to remove any shred of fatigue or anger or disappointment from those eyes. Fuck, maybe he *still* wanted to.

"It was never about me," she said, shaking her head sadly. "Never about what I wanted. I *knew* I needed to survive. To prepare myself for her." She nodded her head toward the bathroom.

The water had been running for too long. Maybe he should go check on Cass. But he knew as well as anyone that sometimes a person needed to shatter in private.

"And that's the secret, isn't it?" Mireille whispered, sipping from her mug and brushing a strand of copper hair off her face. He could almost feel it running through his fingers. Liquid silk. "We don't do it for ourselves. We need something bigger to fight for. Something that makes us forget our petty wants and selfish desires."

Ronin leaned back, cracking his knuckles and trying to imagine what might relight Cassandra's spark, give her the courage to fight. Or to at least *try*.

"Have you told her who she is to you yet?" Ronin asked.

Mireille scoffed. "And when, exactly, would I have had the time to do that?"

Mireille had had *plenty* of time to tell Cassandra about their shared ancestry. He knew that wasn't why she'd been hesitating. She'd never been good with the interpersonal stuff.

He shrugged. "Might help."

"Maybe," Mireille said thoughtfully, cupping her mug. "What was she like in the colonies? Before she was Turned."

"She…" Ronin hesitated. He hadn't known Cassandra for very long. Hadn't spent much time with her in Thalenn. But he'd heard the rumors of the risks she'd taken as the Savior Sister. "She lifts up the lowest of us. Fights for those who cannot fight for themselves. Often to her own detriment."

A dazzling smile spread across Mireille's face. A spear to his heart he wasn't prepared for. He looked away.

Her soft whisper floated across the table, laden with the barest hint of hope. "I think I know how to help her. But I'll need a few days to prepare."

Ronin had led soldiers onto and off of the battlefield. Was very familiar with those numb, twitchy looks that signaled a mind nearing the breaking point. Cassandra had worn far too many of those looks tonight.

"Good," he said. "Give her a few days to rest. To grieve.

"Then show her why the world is worth fighting for."

CHAPTER
THIRTY-ONE

THE OTHER PLACE WAS loud. And hot. And smelled like a wet dog.

And Cassandra didn't want to fucking be here.

She'd protested during the entire walk, a blocks-long torture she could barely power her legs through. By block five, Mireille had stop responding to Cassandra's whining. Had turned around and given Cassandra an icy stare that promised death if she didn't shut up. So Cassandra just grumbled her protests in silence.

Ronin hadn't been kidding about Mireille being even more terrifying than he was.

Cassandra didn't want to be this person. She'd *never* been this person. She hated the whiny, mewling, lazy brat she'd become since she'd seen that vision of Tristan and Ione kissing. Even just thinking their names in the same sentence tore a blazing hole through her chest.

She never thought she'd let any man—or male—affect her like this. She'd seen what had happened to her mother after her father's death, how Mama had stopped living. In order to avoid the same fate, Cassandra had vowed to never get involved with anyone.

But then, like the fucking *fool* she was, she'd let Tristan creep into her heart with his goodness and bravery. His compassion and intelligence. Not to mention his wicked smirks and playful ribbing. His addicting lips and tempting body. And those beautiful wings.

She'd been a goner since the night she'd stolen his memory at the Pagonis Manor. Back when she thought he was nothing more than a stupidly handsome Vestian Guard.

She should've known the minute she'd discovered he was Fae royalty that she could never hope to keep him.

Then maybe she wouldn't be stuck here in this foul, backwards city with these useless wings on her back less than three weeks away from a literal fight for her life.

Ronin and Mireille had let Cassandra wallow for a few days. Long, endless hours crying in bed, barely getting up to drink tea or broth or to relieve herself. They hadn't pushed, despite her appeal creeping closer.

But by this morning, their patience had run out. Ronin had barreled into Cassandra's bedroom, torn her from her sweat-soaked sheets, and thrown her into the bathroom, growling at her to shower and get dressed.

She'd barely finished washing her wings when Mireille had dragged her out of the apartment and marched her here to the tavern.

Mireille grabbed a table in a corner, then planted Cassandra in a creaky chair while she went to the counter. She came back with two mugs of beer and two bowls of some kind of creamy stew that made Cassandra's mouth water.

Okay, fine, she could admit she was hungry.

She dug her spoon into the stew, surveying the patrons of The Other Place. Not even that silly name could make her chuckle today.

There were no Brethren present. Instead, the tavern was filled with a drowsy mixture of the city's regular citizens wearing dull clothes and tired frowns.

Mireille sipped at her frothy mug, then licked the foam from her lip as Cassandra shoveled in mouthfuls of stew.

It tasted incredible. Though she thought she'd better slow down before she gave herself a stomachache. She'd barely eaten anything these past four days. Could Fae get stomachaches?

She set down her spoon. "Why did you bring me here?"

"So it *can* do something other than cry or whinge," Mireille said, lip curling as she placed her mug down on the sticky table. Her silver eyes twinkled with amusement, and if Cassandra wasn't mistaken, maybe even a hint of relief. "Because you're on a deadline. And you'd been given the customary amount of bereavement time. Four days. No more, no less."

Cassandra snorted. "Who made that rule?"

Mireille braced her forearms on the table, flames flashing through her narrowed silver eyes. "I did."

Definitely more terrifying than Ronin.

Mireille swirled her spoon through her own stew. "What happened the other night? When you touched me?"

Cassandra darted a wary glance toward the other patrons.

Mireille waved her off. "Don't worry about them."

"I…" Cassandra swallowed. "I'm not sure how I did it. It's like I was able to see into your memories without pulling them. It happened once before. At the intake tower during sentencing. I saw one of the Vicereine's memories when I touched her, but—"

"Do you know what triggered it? You've touched Ronin and I plenty of times before and it's never happened, right?"

"Right," Cassandra admitted. "I don't know. Both times, I was feeling out of control and overwhelmed."

"Do you think you could do it again?"

"Not really capable of feeling anything at the moment," Cassandra lifted her shoulder, non-committal.

"What did you see? In my memories?"

"I saw myself."

Mireille's poker face betrayed her with a slow blink.

"And my father," Cassandra continued. "He was glowing. So was the man standing next to you. When you looked at him, I… I think I jumped into his mind. His *present* mind. I could tell it wasn't a memory. He was…in a cabin somewhere. Maybe on the continent? It… I don't know how to explain it, but it didn't feel real."

Mireille cocked her head, considering, then laid her hands upon the table, and speared Cassandra with an important look. "That was *my* father. In the Halfway. His name was Gareth Fortin."

A bolt of icy hot adrenaline tingled through Cassandra's limbs, and a multi-faceted voice stole through her mind. The one she'd heard during that vision she'd had when she'd been trying to un-obliviate her mother.

Find her.

At the time, Cassandra had thought the voice was telling her to find Adelphinae, the Fallen Goddess. Perhaps the voice meant a very different *her.*

Mireille continued. "I never knew him in life. Our first meeting was when he showed me that vision of you as a child with your own father. He said I was destined to cross paths with you. That the Goddess had called upon me to help you."

Cassandra's feathers shivered. "Help me what?"

"Live," Mireille said with a finality that echoed through worlds. "He told me that you are our only hope for salvation."

Cassandra swallowed, her stew a lump in her stomach. If she had thought she couldn't bear the weight of her burdens before…

But getting out of Mireille's shop and into the fresh air, moving her body more than a few inches, even getting some food into her system… It had all helped. A bit. She wouldn't go so far as to say that she felt *better*, but she did at least feel…not worse. Even with the terrible importance of what Mireille had just shared.

"If your father was a Fortin," Cassandra began, "that means—"

"I'm half-human." Mireille said theatrically, and the entire tavern came to a screeching halt, utensils dropped, chairs turning.

Mireille smiled, summoning the closest group, who joined Cassandra's table, mugs in hand.

And Cassandra spent the rest of the afternoon learning the sad history of Tartarus's mixed heritage prisoners.

"Most of us were locked up during or just after the war," said Silas, the handsome, ochre-skinned Windrider Cassandra recognized from Harvest Night. "But I'd been fortunate enough to evade that fate for centuries. Penelope and I were well-hidden, I thought. Well past the danger."

He ran a finger through the foam trailing down his mug as a sad smile ghosted over his lips.

"We weren't, of course. A squadron of Imperial soldiers arrived at our farm, and I thank the Creator every day that my wife wasn't there to see them haul me away." He took a sip of his beer. "She'd gone to visit her

Fae parents—she was full-blooded—and I was supposed to join her the next day to share the good news. We'd just found out she was pregnant with our first." A tear plunked onto the tabletop. "And only."

Cassandra blinked back her own tears as Mireille shifted in her seat.

The Other Place was nearly empty now, the flaming sconces the only source of light since dusk had fallen.

Silas was the last patron Mireille had conscripted to…what, exactly? Talk some sense into Cassandra? Prove that everyone had their own trauma to work through? Appeal to her martyr complex?

Damn the sly, copper-haired she-wolf, it was working.

Silas tipped his moss-green eyes up to Cassandra's. "Eighty years and it never gets any easier. People might say 'well, this prison isn't so bad. There's no manual labor. There's access to resources.' But the Koenig and his pure-blooded Brethren keep the best of Vestan's gifts for themselves. And Wormwood guarantees that only we mixed-species Fae ever get selected as Harvest Night sacrifices. It's the same fucking system of power perpetuating itself, whether on the Ethyrian continent or trapped beyond the Tartaran mists. What's the point of authority if there's no one to rule?" He raked a hand across his stubbled chin. "I've survived *all* that, made my peace with it even, and still the worst pain is never having known my child."

He drained the last of his ale and leaned back in his chair.

Cassandra sat back in her own, shell-shocked by all the heartbreaking stories. No one in the colonies had ever spoken of the atrocities that Leonin Erabis and his Empire had committed against Fae with human heritage. Parents and children torn apart, spouses separated, even entire families locked away to rot.

And all because they had the potential to be Anointed by Adelphinae. To gain the long-dead elemental magics the Empire viewed as a threat.

"Thank you, Silas," Mireille said. "I know it's not easy to talk about."

"If any of what I said helps you win your appeal," he said to Cassandra, "I'm happy to help."

He stood and she shook his roughly callused hand before he exited The Other Place, leaving Mireille and Cassandra alone.

Mireille pushed up out of her seat. "We should get going. Only fifteen days left until your appeal. We really need to get back to training tomorrow."

Cassandra stayed in her seat. "Where are all the humans?"

Mireille pressed her lips together.

"I *know* there must be some," Cassandra insisted. "The Empire sends humans here. Surely a few of them must've survived the mists over the years."

Again, Mireille kept silent.

"Tell me." Cassandra glanced up. "Please."

Mireille released a heavy sigh, then turned for the door.

"I might as well just show you."

The first thing Cassandra noticed was the smell.

It whipped her in the face as soon as Mireille opened the door to the squat building shoved up against the city wall.

Human excrement. Unwashed bodies. Rot and infection. Scents she recognized from Thalenn's slums.

But beneath those familiar scents was something sickly sweet and putrid.

Despair.

So thick she almost choked on it.

She slammed a hand over her nose and nearly dropped the basket of apples she'd insisted they pick up on their way here.

Until this very moment, she'd forgotten she could scent human emotions.

Her sinuses burned with angry tears.

All was quiet beyond the door. Quieter than she'd anticipated. But her new Fae hearing caught the subtle shift of bodies, the soft hiccup of tears, the slow, rattling breaths.

Cassandra made to step over the threshold, but Mireille grabbed her upper arm. "Are you sure you want to see this?"

"I'm sure," she said, her voice tight with restrained fury as she stepped through the door and her eyes adjusted to the darkness.

Iron-barred cells, barely six feet deep, lined the narrow enclosure and the only light came from two glass oil lamps bracketing the door. There weren't many cells, maybe thirty in total, fifteen along each wall.

Mireille hung back as Cassandra approached the first and peered inside. Its occupants—four human women with barely enough room to lie on the floor without piling on top of each other—shrank back.

"It's okay," she said softly, crouching down. "I'm not going to hurt you. I brought... I brought you some apples."

Her throat closed and she could barely get a breath down. Apples? She'd brought these poor souls *apples.* When they clearly needed so very much more.

A level of fury she hadn't felt since her sentencing rose, a fiery knot unfurling in her stomach and glowing incandescent.

Pale, thin fingers curled around the bar, and a young woman who didn't look a day over twenty-five blinked at Cassandra. Her brown hair fell in matted clumps and purple bruises marred what was likely once a very pretty face.

But when Cassandra offered her an apple, she shook her head.

"The others," the woman croaked. "Give them to the others in the back cells. They don't... They are not called upon as often as we are. They rarely get a chance to eat."

Cassandra laid her own hand over the woman's fingers. "I am going to end this place. And free you. I swear it."

The woman grimaced, then pulled her hand away and burrowed back under the ripped, threadbare blankets with her cellmates.

Cassandra strung the basket over her forearm and walked down the aisle toward the darker cells in the back.

Each step added another brick to the pile on her chest. There were so many humans. Men and women—but praise Anaemos, no children—growing older and feebler the further back she traveled.

When she reached the end of the aisle, it was so dark she could barely see—even with her Fae eyesight—and the scent of despair was far more concentrated.

She crouched before the final cell, and tapped her fingers on the bars.

An old woman with sunken gray cheeks and wisps of white hair creaked out from underneath a blanket.

Cassandra didn't say a word—if she opened her mouth, she was sure she'd burst into body-wracking sobs. She held out an apple.

The old woman reached for it with wobbly fingers and wide, shining eyes, her tongue rolling over her cracked lips.

"It's okay," Cassandra whispered. "I'm not going to hurt you. I'm here to help."

The woman's features twisted into a grotesque mask, and she slapped the apple from Cassandra's hand. It went bouncing down the center aisle before rolling into another cell.

"I don't need your charity, do-gooder," the old woman rasped in a voice that sounded like it hadn't been used in decades. "You preening Fae come down here with your food and your potions, acting like you're kinder than the ones who did this to us. The ones who locked us up in the first place. And why? So you can feel *better* about yourself?"

Cassandra scrambled back from the bars as the woman lunged for her, much quicker than Cassandra would have expected.

The woman barked out a breathless laugh. "Fuck back off. And quit peddlin' your cruel hope."

Oily shame coated Cassandra's tongue as she saw herself as the woman saw her. The two feathered wings sprouting from her back. The sharp beauty of her ethereal features. The small fangs that, even now, pressed into her bottom lip.

She shuffled away from the cell, then emptied the basket into the next before fleeing down the hallway. She would come back here. Every day. Multiple times a day, if necessary, to bring these humans food, water, healing potions, whatever she could.

At least until she ended the fucking male who'd corralled them here in the first place.

Mireille materialized from the darkness. "They call it the Kennel."

"This is horrific," Cassandra said. "And so much worse than I could have imagined."

Mireille's head dipped. "I know. I visit as often as possible. So do many of the Fae you met in The Other Place today. A few decades back, two of them petitioned the Koenig to let the humans go, stop treating them like livestock."

"Livestock is treated better than this," Cassandra scoffed. "What happened to the petitioners?"

"What do you think?" Mireille said, her face a mask of cold fury. "No one has asked since. The Brethren come down to *borrow* them sometimes. For feedings, and—" Mireille shook her head, as if shaking away some terrible vision. Cassandra didn't want to know.

"This could have been me," Cassandra whispered. "If I hadn't... If Tristan hadn't..." Rage hardened her voice. "This could have been me."

Mireille did nothing but nod. What else was there to say?

"We cannot allow this to continue," Cassandra said fiercely. "Not here. Not *anywhere*."

Mireille placed her hands on Cassandra's shoulders. They were about the same height, Mireille slightly taller. Their faces were in line as Mireille's silver gaze bore into hers, reflecting the same fierce determination.

"We won't," she vowed. "But the only way to ensure that is to win your appeal and get out of here."

Cassandra nodded, gripping Mireille's forearms.

"They're my people, too," Mireille whispered.

Cassandra cocked her head. "What was he like? Your father?"

Even in the dim light, Cassandra could see the love and pride that glowed in Mireille's eyes. "I imagine he was very like *you*. Kind. Brave. Righteous. I wish...I wish I'd gotten to know him in life rather than only in death."

Cassandra squeezed Mireille's forearms tighter. "He regrets it, you know." Mireille flinched, understanding that Cassandra now spoke of a different *he*. "It was painfully apparent while he told us your history. Obvious that he still—"

"Don't say it," Mireille breathed out. "It doesn't matter anymore. And even if he did, it would be nothing but a distraction in here. We need to focus on surviving the appeal. Everything else is extraneous."

High *Gods*, Cassandra wanted to meddle. Wanted to mediate. Wanted to fix what was broken between Mireille and Ronin. Especially since she couldn't fix her own broken heart.

Mireille grabbed Cassandra's hand and pulled her toward the exit. "Come on. You need sleep."

Cassandra glanced over her shoulder, wishing she had more time, more food, more supplies.

Mireille squeezed Cassandra's hand as she nudged her through the door, her smile a thing of delicious savagery.

"Training resumes in earnest bright and early tomorrow morning."

CHAPTER
THIRTY-TWO

SWEAT DRIPPED DOWN CAEL's temple and beaded on his wing as he followed the forgemaster down a narrow tunnel.

The heat had been a constant companion throughout Cael's visit to Typhon Mountain, the manufacturing site of both Ethyrios's most treasured steel and the other weapons his father sold throughout the territories—stun pistols, snakebites, even those new dragon-fire missiles the Teles Chrysos had been trying to get their hands on.

Cael used to think the output was impressive. Now he just found it tragic, the sheer number of ways the Fae had invented to kill each other over the centuries.

"It's just ahead," the forgemaster—a short, stocky mole Beastrunner with a wrinkly bald head and lengthy incisors—grunted over his shoulder. "Mind the ceiling."

Cael ducked down, tucking his wing and trying to ignore the forgemaster's glance at the lonely appendage. He wished he could say it didn't bother him. But the pitying looks weren't the only inconvenience he'd dealt with today.

Normally, he would have taken this journey by flight. Would have enjoyed being up in the sky, any anxious, depressing thoughts ripped away by the roaring wind and misty clouds.

Instead, he'd been forced to use one of those blasted opals. Sure, it had been quick, but traveling that way made him queasy. When he'd first appeared in the forgemaster's office, he'd nearly vomited up his breakfast. Not wanting to show weakness in front of his father's employees, he'd swallowed it down and put on his cold, stoic mask. He didn't need anyone questioning why he'd shown up here.

In truth, he wasn't supposed to be here at all. He'd met with Arran this morning and convinced him that a surprise inspection of the facilities would keep everyone on their toes. Arran had offered a rare, prideful look in response to Cael's devious proactivity.

His true reason for the visit was, of course, quite different. He needed to see the dragon for himself. He'd never had the nerve as a boy, though Arran had brought both Viktor and Tomas for occasional visits. The thought of such a majestic creature being locked up and forced into centuries of servitude rankled Cael's sensitive nature as a boy.

It still bothered him now. But if the Teles Chrysos were right, and he could find some way to free it, he was determined to try.

"Few more steps," the forgemaster said, his beady eyes tracking the sweat on Cael's face. The mole biform didn't display a drop. "You get used to the heat."

Cael swiped a wrist across his forehead as he followed the small male around a corner. A fresh wall of heated steam blurred his vision as they clomped onto a metal walkway bolted to the wall high above a deep pit.

Across the cavernous space, a veritable hive of forges were carved into the stone. Each was manned by several Fae workers, their hammers clanging a metallic symphony.

"Don't usually have this many forges running at once," the forgemaster shouted over the din, "but High Councilor Zephyrus has insisted we maintain a high level of production, what with the rebellion and all. We've been running three shifts a day, many of us working overtime." He side-eyed Cael with a hint of annoyance. "Hope it's worth the—"

A ground-shaking rumble tore up from the pit, the walkway rattling so violently Cael feared it would tear away from the rock. The metal railing scalded his fingers as he peered over the edge.

Down below, two enormous, membranous wings were folded against a body the size of a steam ship, covered in black scales. Two heavy chains criss-crossed the creature's back and wings, connected to an iron collar around its neck.

Cael watched in horror as a group of workers circled the dragon, poking the soft spaces between scales on its belly and haunches with sharp metal rods.

Another bellowing roar shook the facility before an explosion of fire burst from the dragon's maw, then flowed through an intricate system of tubes into the forges. The hammering ceased as the workers took advantage of the increased flames to heat their steel.

Cael couldn't take his eyes off the dragon as its roar dissolved into a whimper, its wings straining against the chains. As if it were trying to protect itself when the keepers moved in again with their rods. Another powerful blast of fire surged through the tubes and Cael's chest constricted.

"Quite a show, isn't it?"

Cael nearly jumped out of his skin as the forgemaster shouted into his ear.

"Amazing," the male said, looking down and shaking his head. "The fire never runs out. You could prod that bitch every minute on the minute all day long and the fire will be just as hot the hundredth time as the first." Cael choked back his horror. "Come. I'll show you the forges."

"Actually, I'd rather go down to the pit floor. See the creature up close. Who here is responsible for its care? I'd like to speak with them."

The forgemaster raised a bushy brow. "Your father never goes to check on it. Last time he did, about eighty odd years ago, she broke one of her chains and nearly melted him alive. Took twenty keepers to subdue her. Since then, whenever High Councilor Zephyrus visits, he only inspects the forges. Are you sure you want to go down there? You share his blood; she might react just as violently."

"I'm sure," Cael said firmly.

The forgemaster muttered, "Your funeral. Turn around. We need to go back the way we came."

Cael stepped aside, letting the forgemaster pass by him before he followed along the walkway, then down a set of metal stairs.

As they descended into the pit, Cael realized the dragon's scales weren't black at all. They were coated in soot. Shimmering white streaks shone through in several places.

They reached the bottom, a circular expanse of stone floor to which the chains were bolted. The keepers gathered against the wall, chatting and laughing as if they hadn't just been torturing the poor thing. Cael wanted to rip their limbs off.

The dragon lay on her side, eyes closed, her wounded belly expanding and contracting with her steady breaths. A substance oozed from the punctures, unlike any blood

Cael had ever seen—goopy and translucent with an iridescent shimmer.

"Leonard!" the forgemaster called out. "Master Zephyrus would like to speak with you!"

An ancient Beastrunner poked his head out of a small alcove carved into the stone, then shuffled over to Cael and the forgemaster. Leonard's thick white hair was brushed back from a tanned face lined with deep-set wrinkles. A long, scraggly beard cascaded over his protruding belly and a pair of spectacles perched on his nose.

He wiped his hands on his leather apron, then reached one toward Cael. Before Cael could grasp it, Leonard looked down and squeaked.

"Back up, back up!" He pulled Cael backward and pointed to a line carved into the stone beneath their feet. "That's the range of her chains. If she catches you inside that line... Chomp. Crunch. Dragon lunch." Leonard doubled over with hooting laughter and Cael couldn't help his own soft chuckle.

The forgemaster turned to Cael. "If you don't mind, Master Zephyrus—"

"Just Cael is fine."

"—I'll leave you here. Need to show my face in the forges. Can't afford any slacking right now! Leonard can escort you out when you're finished." The forgemaster grabbed Cael's arm, then leaned in, his sour breath coating Cael's nostrils. "I trust you'll give a good report to your father? Tell him how hard we're all working? Would be nice to see a little bonus in this month's pay."

Cael nodded as the forgemaster retook the stairs. Though he doubted his stingy father would honor such a request. He turned to Leonard. "I'd like to hear about the dragon's care, please. What's her routine like?"

Leonard cocked his head. "Really? Why? Is Arran asking?"

Cael was a bit taken aback that Leonard had used his father's first name so casually. But he didn't probe as he took a step forward, towering over the male.

"*I'm* asking." He speared the male with his stormcloud glare and flared his wing.

Leonard chuckled. "Don't need to get all dominant with me, lad. I've dealt with far more dangerous creatures than you." He darted his gaze toward the dragon, then let out a sad sigh. "I begged him not to do it, you know. A magnificent beauty like that doesn't deserve to be in chains." He lowered his voice to a conspiratorial whisper. "A tragedy, if you ask me. But your father always gets what he wants, in the end." The male eyed Cael's wing. "As I'm sure you can imagine."

"Her care?" Cael probed, not bothering to correct Leonard's assumption that Arran had something to do with Cael's missing wing.

"You saw the livestock fields when you arrived, yes? She's fed a head of cattle once a day to keep her strength up, keep her fire productive."

"Does she ever leave the mountain?" Cael asked casually.

"Yes," Leonard answered, brows knit warily. "Every day, if I can manage it. After dusk. She's frightening enough if you catch a glimpse of her shadow in a darkened sky. If I let her out during the day, the Fae in the surrounding villages would probably shit themselves."

Cael glanced toward the dragon. Her horned head rested on the stone floor, eyes closed, tendrils of smoke curling up from her nostrils. Cael could sense her pain, as if he could feel it in his own body. In his own blood.

I'm sorry they have done this to you, he thought.

One of her lids cracked open, revealing a slitted pupil inside a kaleidoscopic iris. Aimed right at him.

He cocked his head, holding her gaze, but her lid closed and she released a heavy sigh. Soft flames glowed behind her gargantuan teeth.

"Why does she come back?" Cael whispered.

"How's that?" Leonard asked, and Cael finally turned away from the dragon.

"When you let her out. How do you get her to come back?"

Leonard shrugged, pulling at his beard. "Arran never told me how he achieved it. Think it might have something to do with their bond, but…"

Something about Leonard's tone piqued Cael's curiosity. "But you don't believe that."

Leonard leaned in, glancing around to ensure the other keepers weren't watching or listening. "Sometimes, just before she leaves the mountain, she has this look on her face like…" Leonard trailed off.

Cael turned back toward the dragon, and his heart lodged in his throat. Her reptilian eyes were wide open, glued to Cael's back where his other wing should have been. He could have sworn he felt sympathy in her perusal. And other than Xenia, it was the only sympathy he'd ever been offered that didn't make him want to tear off a head or two.

"Like what?" he asked.

Leonard's whisper shivered through Cael's chest.

"Like she's waiting for someone."

CHAPTER THIRTY-THREE

DID YOU BEHAVE YOURSELF today?
Cael's silky voice reverberated through Xenia's body thanks to the cuff around her wrist.

"Always, pterodactyl." She yawned against the back of her hand, balancing a plate of food in the other as she walked toward her room. "You'll never believe what I learned in the library tod—"

Where are you? Cael asked, and Xenia's heart soared. Was he going to come fetch her? Had he returned from his trip to Typhon Mountain?

"Staff hallway," she said, crunching on a glazed carrot.

Cael grunted. *It's late. We'll speak tomorrow. I'll come find you in the library once your shift starts. I had an interesting day as well.*

Xenia sighed, shucking off her disappointment. She hadn't spoken to him in person, only via the cuff, for the past few days. He'd been too busy doing the High-Gods-only-knew what for his father, plus had been dragged into several wedding planning meetings with Zosime, Petra, and Elodie.

"See you tomorrow, then," she said, a bit more petulantly than she was proud of.

Sleep well, Cael purred, his voice lush and dangerously sexy. Her limbs shivered so violently she nearly dropped her plate. Bastard wasn't playing fair.

So she wouldn't either.

"You sleep well, too, *my lord.*" She imbued the title with all the *want* his voice had inspired.

He chuckled, that deep, low rumble that was pure Cael. Rolling storm clouds and distant thunder. *Take the cuff off and hide it as soon as we're done. I don't want anyone seeing you with it. You should've waited until you were in your room to use it.*

And just like that, indignation replaced her desire. "Why? Everyone's asleep."

He sighed, exasperated, but not without a hint of mirth. As if he liked it when she talked back. *Just do it, Blondie. For me. Please.*

She smiled, hoping he could hear it in her voice. "Only for you." She tapped the stone, cutting off another of his rumbling chuckles, then slipped the cuff into her apron.

It was late, nearing midnight if she had to guess. And though her eyelids drooped and her limbs were heavy, her mind buzzed with everything she'd learned today. She could hardly wait to tell Cael.

As she approached her door, an unmistakable moan emanated from the room across the hall.

She snickered. She'd seen those stolen glances between the pretty kitchen assistant and the handsome stablehand over staff breakfast this morning. She was happy they'd found some little spot of joy in this place. Though High Councilor Zephyrus strictly forbade relations between his human staff and the Fae, he didn't seem to care if the humans were fucking each other.

A piercing cry arrowed past the stablehand's door, followed by a laughing *shhhhhh*.

Xenia's thighs clenched, remembering what Cael had done to her in his room last week. Thinking about how badly she wanted him to do it again. Thinking about how she wanted him to do *so* much more.

He hadn't touched her since. And she knew he wouldn't risk that final step, either. Any Fae on the estate would be able to scent him on her afterward. But sweet Amatu, she couldn't help fantasizing about how it would feel to have Cael inch his perfect, and frankly enormous, cock inside her. How he might talk her through it...

Heat rose to her cheeks as she opened the door to her room, then froze.

Her plate fell from her grip, meat, gravy, and carrots splattering across the plaid rug.

She turned to run, but Tomas was too fast. He snatched her arm and pulled her into the room, then pushed her up against the door, closing her in with his bulk.

He dipped his nose to her throat, and when she tried to scream, he slammed a rough hand over her mouth. "High Gods, what *were* you thinking about? You smell fucking incredible." He sucked down a deep breath and Xenia was horrified to feel her lust increase as he began to feed from her.

She kicked his legs, shoved his chest, but it was like trying to fight a statue. He slammed her head against the door and spots swirled in her vision.

"Do *not* fight me, you little human slut," he growled, pushing his hand up under her dress. "If you obey, I might even make it good for you. It's been a while since we had such a pretty mortal on staff. Has no one tasted you yet?"

She bucked and thrashed, and his hand at her mouth slipped. Enough for her to get her teeth around it and bite down. *Hard.*

"Fucking *cunt*," he yelped, slamming her against the door again and holding her in place with his hips. "The more you fight, the worse this will be for you."

Unwanted heat pulsed in her veins as Tomas drew out her lust. She bit her tongue against the involuntary moans threatening to push past her clenched teeth. Like fuck would she give this bastard any kind of satisfaction.

"That's it," Tomas crooned, his face buried in her neck. "High Gods, there is *nothing* sweeter than fresh human lust."

She slackened in his arms, pretending she'd given up the fight, then slipped her hand into her pocket. Her fingertip brushed over the mentrite speck, and the cuff warmed as she said Cael's name in her mind.

Tomas heaved and grunted as he sucked down her stolen lust. "You wanna be my pretty pet?"

Cael's voice exploded into her ears, fierce and savage and guttural. *What the fuck is happening right now? Is that* Tomas?

Xenia stayed perfectly still and silent, not wanting to give Tomas any hint of what she'd done. Who she'd summoned.

Another unwanted wave of sensation rattled Xenia's body, and a shuddering whimper slipped through her lips.

"You're enjoying this, aren't you? Needy bitch." Tomas laughed.

A snarl ripped through Xenia's mind before the door behind her swung open and she toppled to the floor, rolling away as Tomas crashed down next to her.

Cael's handsome features were twisted with ferocious rage. Xenia silently begged him to wipe the look away, terrified of what it might reveal to his brother.

Cael snatched Tomas's arm and pulled him to his feet. "What. Are. You. *Doing?*"

Tomas tried to shove his brother away, but Cael held firm. Tomas's years of gluttonous excess were no match for Cael's powerful, Vestian-trained body.

"What do you care?" Tomas hissed, his gray eyes flicking between Cael and Xenia. "What, have you already claimed this morsel for yourself? Thought you didn't feed from humans."

"I don't," Cael snapped. "Just get the fuck out of here and leave the staff alone. Father doesn't want any *incidents* while we have so many guests staying with us for the wedding."

Xenia pulled herself upright, then stumbled into her room and onto her bed. Her limbs trembled as the false lust faded, leaving her cold and empty and numb.

Tomas raked a hand through his golden strands. "You can't protect her forever. It's my right as a male of this household to take whatever I want from *any* human I want."

Cael spun his brother's shoulders, then planted a booted foot in his ass. Tomas stumbled down the hallway, out of Xenia's view. "Fuck off, Tomas. And don't think I'm not going to tell Father about this."

Tomas's response chilled Xenia further. "I could say the same. Seems you've gotten a bit too soft on the humans while you were in the colonies. Or maybe you're just soft on one in particular…"

Tomas's footsteps faded, and Cael watched his brother go with a look promising swift and violent death.

Xenia sat upright, whimpering as she brought her hand to the bump on the back of her skull.

Cael's eyes darted right to her, his face softening. He gripped her door frame so tightly that his knuckles whitened. "Use the cuff in five minutes," he whispered.

"The other stone, the opal. You know how it works right? Just picture where you want to be.

"And come to my room."

CHAPTER
THIRTY-FOUR

"Come," Cael said, gesturing to the plaid armchair in front of the lit fireplace in his bedroom.

Xenia limped toward him, her exhausted limbs spent, then sunk into the chair.

Cael stepped up behind her and ran his fingers through her hair, examining the lump. "What the fuck happened?"

Xenia choked back tears. "He was... he was in there waiting for me. As soon as I opened the door, he—"

"It's okay," Cael whispered, placing ice cubes into a towel and holding the compress against the back of her head. She winced as it made contact with her scalp, and Cael ran soothing fingers down her neck.

She didn't know what helped more: the ice or Cael's soft touch. "You don't have to tell me the rest. I can guess. He's done this before. He fixates." Xenia looked up at him. "You'll stay in here with me at night from now on."

Joy frothed through her. But she schooled her features. Didn't want Cael to know how much the thought delighted her. Despite how it had come about.

"Lock your door behind you every night, then use your cuff to come to my room," Cael said, lifting her hand and putting it in place of his own to hold the ice-filled towel. "It'll be safer for us to discuss our findings here every night instead of the stable loft. I can put a windshield on the door to make sure no one hears us."

"Okay," she said, with a nervous little giggle, looking down at her crumpled dress. "I don't...I don't have anything to sleep in though." She cocked a playful eyebrow at him.

Cael laughed, shaking his head. "I'll go back to your room and get your nightclothes and a clean pair of stockings. Were you able to eat anything or are you still hungry?" As if on cue, her stomach grumbled. "I'll grab us some food as well. Let me borrow your cuff. I'll lock your bedroom door behind me, then use it to come back here."

Cael turned to leave, but Xenia grabbed his wrist, stroking her thumb across his racing pulse.

"Thank you," she said, peering up at him. "You're always saving me. I wish I wasn't such a burden. That I was stronger. That I could—"

"Hey." Cael rounded the chair, then knelt at her feet. "None of that. There are many kinds of strength. Just because yours doesn't come with a wicked right hook or the ability to summon the wind doesn't make it less powerful. Your *mind* is your weapon, Xenia. You've used it to bring me to my knees a time or two, remember?" She blushed. "And I'm happy to be the brawn to your brains."

She smiled. "Still, that was a tremendous risk you took for me. Exposing yourself to your brother."

He stroked his thumb across her cheekbone. "Keeping you safe is *never* a risk. I feel half responsible for getting you into this mess in the first place."

"Only half responsible?"

Cael smirked, then leaned down to place a gentle kiss on her forehead. "Wait here for me. And try not to make any more poor decisions while I'm gone."

Xenia huffed. "*You're* a poor decision."

Cael pulled back, sadness spearing through his eyes, as he muttered, "I know," then turned away and left the room.

Xenia blew out a breath, wanting to shout after him that it was just a stupid joke.

He wasn't a poor decision.

He was the best one she'd ever made.

One she'd keep making forever.

If only he'd let her.

"It was the most magnificent thing I've ever seen," Cael said to Xenia, who was seated in the armchair across from him and munching on a slice of roast chicken.

Well, second most.

A profound sense of peace settled upon him as he trailed his gaze over her halo of golden curls, the chunky knit blanket wrapped around her delicate shoulders, the smooth skin of her thighs above her wool stockings.

Those fucking stockings.

"I can't even imagine," Xenia said around a bite. "But it sounds completely barbaric, what your father has done to her. Keeping a creature like that locked up, only allowing her out to fly for a short time each day."

"I need to figure out how my father forged his bond with her. How he not only used her for the war, but how he's managed to keep her captive. She doesn't even try to escape when they let her out to fly. As if her spirit is that broken. I'm going back in a few days to observe her for a longer period of time. It was... It was strange. While I was there, I said something to her in my mind and I could've sworn she heard me. I want to try again."

Xenia's lips thinned. "What do the Teles Chrysos have planned for her?"

"As far as they've told me, they'll be using her against Eamon. Flying her to Delos to take the Imperial capital."

Xenia scoffed. "So she'll be just another weapon again? Same story, different masters?"

"*I* will be her master," Cael said softly, and Xenia's brows rose. "It'll be a stipulation of my helping them. That I'll be responsible for her care and that she'll only be used when I allow it. At least until I can figure out how to free her from the bond altogether."

"Why, Cael Zephyrus, are you telling me that you want to try to heal a broken thing?"

Cael scrubbed a hand down his face, trying to hide his grin. "Someone is wearing me down."

The smile she aimed at him stole his breath. He buckled beneath its force, changing the subject. "What did you learn in the library today?"

She placed her plate on the table, then plucked up the glass of Nephian red he'd brought up with her meal. She swirled the glass, the liquid casting ruby shadows across her collarbone.

"It was all *fascinating*." Her emerald eyes glittered with excited curiosity. He knew reading, consuming new knowledge, was her favorite thing in the world. If there was a happily ever after waiting for them, he'd get her a house and fill every room with books. Well, every room besides the bedroom.

He shifted in his seat, adjusting his pants and trying to stop his natural pessimism from crushing his fragile dreams. For a future where he'd be lucky enough to bed this gorgeous woman every night.

"How much do you know about how your father came to be the High Councilor of Brachos?" she asked.

Cael picked at the fabric on his armrest. "Not much. In case you haven't noticed, my father's not really one for friendly family chats around the dinner table."

Xenia snorted. "There's a whole section of that library dedicated to his rise to power. What the territory was like before the Empire. You were never even the tiniest bit curious?"

Cael shrugged. "Reading's not my thing."

Xenia playfully slapped her forehead. "Right! You're more into brooding and fighting and fucking."

The word *fucking* falling from those lips had his pants growing tighter.

Her gaze darted to his lap, as if she knew. Little tease. "Well, good thing you've got me to do your research for you."

"Delegation is the key to any successful venture," Cael crooned.

Xenia let out a breathy little laugh that wrapped delicate fingers around his heart before she plowed forward. "Before your father was declared High Councilor of Brachos, the land was ruled by disparate clans of Fae—some Beastrunners, some Deathstalkers, some Windriders—each led by their own warrior-king. The clan that controlled Typhon Mountain and the surrounding hills were called the Cynn Drakan. Their leader was a Windrider male named Aedelmar Burkhardt. They worshiped the mountain itself, which, according to them, was the most powerful source of divine magic on Ethyrios. They made sacrifices to the fire and the resulting Typhon steel was seen as a gift from their gods by way of the dragon."

Cael jolted. "I thought my family invented that steel. At least, that's what Arran has always claimed."

Xenia shook her head. "It was the Cynn Drakan. In the century preceding the war, when Leonin Erabis was campaigning to solidify his power, he tasked your father with uniting the clans in the northwest corner of the continent. Leonin wanted Arran to consolidate them into a single territory, hold dominion over it in the name of his burgeoning Empire. Most of the clans went along with it, didn't want to risk slaughter by Arran and his Imperial-backed forces. But the Cynn Drakan held out. They were a proud, militant people, and they clung to their land fiercely."

Cael grunted. Of course, Arran had never told him any of this.

Xenia continued, "Arran was relentless. Fought the Cynn Drakan for years. Not only for his precious Empire, but because Leonin had promised that if Arran could defeat them, he could take control of the mountain and oversee the booming Typhon steel business. Reap its profits."

"*That* certainly sounds like my father," he grumbled.

"But in order to do so, he'd need to defeat the Cynn Drakan and gain control over the dragon. Leonin gave your father that flute, claimed he could use it to summon the dragon away from the Cynn Drakan." Xenia rubbed at her nose. "But the flute can't be the only part of the equation. If it was, your father never would have sold it."

Cael jerked upright. "He *sold* it?"

Xenia nodded, thinning her lips. "To a billionaire in the Northern Territories named Jurgev Otto. About three centuries after the war. Arran's weapons business was bleeding *drachas* at the time and he needed the infusion of capital to stay afloat."

Cael raked a hand through his ash-brown waves. "Still… To give up an object like that? He's either extremely short-sighted or extremely greedy." He sat back. "Scratch that. My father is *both* of those things."

Xenia tapped a finger against her lips. "There's got to be some other piece we're still missing. How did your father defeat Aedelmar Burkhardt and capture the dragon? How did he wipe the Cynn Drakan from the face of Ethyrios?"

He looked at Xenia. Really *looked* at her. High Gods, her intelligence was such a fucking turn-on. If he'd been the one researching, he was sure he never would have pieced together a tenth of this information.

How different would her life have been if Leonin Erabis had never come into power, hadn't started his war against the humans? Xenia would never have been taken from her parents. Would never have been forced into servitude with the Shrouded Sisters.

Would never have even met him.

He used to think that she'd be better off, but now…

He rested his forearms on his knees, clasping his hands between them. "Keep searching. There's got to be more in there about my father's time with the dragon during the war. How he commanded her. How he forced her to obey him. How I might be able to break their bond. And have you found anything about the tracking device?"

Xenia shook her head, gazing thoughtfully into the fire. "Might be faster if I had some help? Why don't you join me? We were pretty good research partners in the Temple library."

He dipped his chin, frowning. "I'll try. But it would look suspicious if I started spending hours a day in the library. I'm still needed for wedding preparations and I'm going to use the excuse of overseeing weapons production to travel to the mountain as often as possible."

Xenia lifted a nonchalant shoulder, but he could tell she was disappointed.

He rose from his chair, then plucked the wineglass from her fingers and placed it on the table. He reached out a hand. "It's late. And we've both got a lot of work to do these next weeks."

She placed her small, soft hand in his, and his blood sang at the contact. She shot him a coquetteish smile. "And where will I be sleeping?"

He took the blanket from her shoulders, then draped it over the back of the chair. "You take the floor. I don't like sharing a bed." Xenia laughed and smacked him on the thigh. "With me, Blondie," he said, guiding her toward the bed.

Always with me.

He wasn't ready to give voice to that fledgling wish yet.

Xenia nestled under his blankets, propping herself against the pillows and staring at him as he stripped down to his underwear. He was a hot sleeper, never slept in anything *but* underwear.

"You're so beautiful, Cael," she breathed out, as if the words had been ripped from her involuntarily.

It had been a very long time, maybe his entire life even, since Cael had blushed. But heat rose to his cheeks. To other places as well.

This was probably a bad idea.

"Even though I'm a little lopsided?" Though his words were teasing, pain simmered beneath them. The adoring look on her face eased it slightly.

"Even more so." She smiled, patting the bed beside her.

He climbed in, then turned toward her and adjusted his wing over the side of the mattress.

He ran a hand down her cheek, toying with her curls. "No funny business."

She rolled her eyes. "You really know how to kill a mood, pterodactyl."

He laughed, low and sultry, and she ran a foot along his shin beneath the covers. "I wasn't aware I was creating a mood in the first place."

"You always are," she murmured, pressing her cheek into his hand.

"How have you been sleeping?"

Xenia sighed, her soft, sweet breath kissing his lips. "Terribly. You know how much I hate sleeping alone."

"I know, Zee," he whispered. "I'll fix it."

He pulled her into him, wanting to explore her so fucking badly he could barely think straight. He wanted to run his tongue and teeth along every inch of her golden skin. Wanted to bury his hands in her hair, between her legs. Wanted to hear those soul-shattering noises she made when she came, the soundtrack to his very best dreams.

But she'd had a terrifying encounter tonight. He would *never* use her the way his brother had. A different kind of comfort was in order.

"Thank you," he whispered, his breath stirring her curls against his neck.

"For what?"

"For seeing me for the fool that I was." He kissed the top of her head. "For getting off that boat."

She nestled in closer. "We escape together or not at all, remember?"

CHAPTER
THIRTY-FIVE

"PLANT YOUR CREATOR-DAMNED FEET!" Mireille shouted.

"I'm...fucking...*trying!*" Cassandra snarled back, swiping her feathers off her shoulder. High Gods, it was nearly impossible to spar with these wings.

Was nearly impossible to do *anything* with them.

They'd resumed training three days ago and this morning's session had started with Cassandra teaching Mireille and Ronin a few poses from the Flow—those slow stretches accompanied by deep breathing that she'd loved performing as a Sister. A way to still her thoughts and awaken her muscles.

But when she'd tried today, she couldn't keep her balance and had toppled into the dirt, dislodging a memory of Tristan doing the same in the Temple training yard.

She'd shoved down the vision—had been trying not to think about Tristan at all. She was on the edge of a precipice. If she pictured Tristan and Ione together, she'd plunge back into bone-deep despair and lose all the motivation she'd gained during her Kennel visit.

Mireille stabbed her practice sword in the dirt and swiped her wrist across her sweaty forehead. She grabbed Cassandra's hips and angled her sideways.

Ronin called out from his position against the wall. "Your stance is still all wrong. Angle your body, left foot in front. When you thrust, put your entire torso into the movement, not just your arms."

Mireille nodded, then stepped back as Cassandra planted her feet and tried again. "Better."

"Now do the arc I showed you," Ronin added, picking at his fangs with the point of a practice dagger.

"Must be fucking nice," Cassandra grumbled, "standing against the wall and barking orders while the females do all the work."

Ronin blew her a kiss.

Cassandra lifted the sword over her shoulder and sliced down across her body. It felt good—*powerful*—right up until her momentum slammed her wings against her back and she stumbled forward. A frustrated roar tore through her clenched teeth and she threw her sword to the ground. "This is *useless*! I'm never going to be able to—"

Mireille cut her off. "I know you're frustrated and feeling like this is impossible. But if you give into those destructive thoughts, you're never going to make any progress." She slapped her hand onto Cassandra's chest, right between her breasts, pressing wet, sweaty fabric against her skin. "*Use* it, Cass. Hone your anger into the sharpest weapon."

Cassandra tore away, then stalked to the side table where Ronin handed her water bottle. "No offense to you both, but I need to be trained by someone with *wings*. It's impossible for you to understand. I need to know which muscles to hold, which to relax, and when to do it. How to use the power and momentum of the wings themselves." She shook her head, knocking back another sip. "I've *seen* Windriders fight with them before. Especially—" She swallowed.

Stop being a baby, she scolded herself. What, now she couldn't even say his name? If she ever got out of here, she might even have to *see* him again, Amatu save her.

Her gaze bobbed between the two wolf bi-forms, wondering how in Ethyrios they were dealing with that agony. Forced into proximity despite the cleft between them.

If they could handle it, she could handle it. She tucked damp tendrils of hair behind her ears, put on her big girl mask, and said, "Especially Tristan."

Mireille assessed Cassandra with a curious stare as Ronin twirled his dagger.

"I imagine it's quite a sight to see an Imperial Prince turned Vestian Guard fight," Mireille said.

"It's incredible," Cassandra answered, and Ronin grunted his agreement. "His wings act like a third set of limbs. Rooting him to the ground, knocking his enemies off-balance, swatting away weapons."

Mireille bowed her head, dejected. "I wish I could teach you to fight like that." She perked up. "What about Silas?"

"The half-human Windrider?" Ronin asked at the same time as Cassandra said, "I was thinking the same thing."

"He's powerfully built," Ronin said. "Looks like he knows his way around a fight."

Mireille narrowed her eyes. "He's survived Harvest Night five times."

"Fuck," Ronin breathed out, brows raised.

"We'd have to tell him the truth about what I was," Cassandra said. "What I am. Do you trust him?"

"I do." Mireille nodded, without a moment's hesitation.

"Then it's a risk I'm willing to take."

"I'll talk to him tonight."

"Why are you seeing him tonight?" Ronin asked, his clenched fist betraying his nonchalant tone.

"We're on rotation at the Kennel," Mireille answered, oblivious. "I've got a fresh batch of healing tonic to deliver."

"I'll go," Cassandra offered. "I can deliver the tonics and meet Silas there. I'd like to ask him myself."

Not to mention she couldn't stop thinking about the words that old woman had thrown at her.

Acting like you're better than the ones who did this to us.

"Sure, if you'd prefer." Mireille bent down to pick up Cassandra's sword. "No more stalling. Here's what I want you to do for the rest of the day." She kicked Cassandra's feet to shoulder-width apart, right below her hips. "Plant yourself. Firmly. Grip the ground with your toes. That's it. Now, raise and spread your wings."

Cassandra did as she was told, her back muscles protesting fiercely.

Mireille flipped the sword, then thrust the handle toward Cassandra. "Grip it. I want you to hold your arms up, at shoulder height, and keep them there for an entire minute. Once the minute is up, do that arc Ronin showed you thirty times on the left, then thirty times on the right. Keep your hips forward and only turn your torso. Once you've done the sixty arcs, pause for a minute and repeat."

"How many times?" Cassandra asked, panicky.

"Until you can do it ten times in a row without failure or without slamming your wings into your back," Mireille said with not a hint of sympathy. Fucking *ruthless.* "And don't think Silas is going to go any easier on you if he agrees to help."

Cassandra wanted to cry. Wanted to curl up on the dusty floor and lay there for eternity.

But then she thought of those humans in the Kennel with no light and barely any food or water.

Thought of the humans in the colonies, especially the obliviates who'd had their minds and memories stolen by the Empire.

Thought of the mixed-heritage Fae here in Tartarus, torn away from their loved ones for centuries.

Thought of Borea and her Sisters, bruised and bloodied on that platform outside the Vicereine's palace, Imperial broadswords shining at their necks.

Thought of Tristan's terrified, tear-stricken face as Eamon had pronounced Cassandra a traitor to the Empire.

Thought of Ione claiming Tristan's lips.

She'd use it. All of it. Every dark emotion that clouded her mind. Grief. Anger. Jealousy. Desire, even. Tristan may have thrust her aside, but she couldn't deny her heart still pleaded for him.

She'd catalyze the feelings into the fuel she'd use to power this step in her journey.

She gripped the sword tighter, brought her arms to shoulder level and began to count.

"Good," Mireille said, nodding. "*Good.*"

Ronin pushed off the wall and ambled over to Mireille. "Can I speak with you privately?"

Cassandra's arms dipped slightly as she lost her concentration, wishing they'd stay in here so she could eavesdrop.

But as Mireille and Ronin left the training room, she lifted her arms back into position.

And continued to count.

CHAPTER THIRTY-SIX

Mireille took Ronin to another room down the hall with the same dirt floor and rack of weapons.

Ronin paused in the center of the room, hands on his hips, and tilted his head back, sucking his lip between his canines. The sight of his sharp fangs sinking into his plush lower lip did nothing to Mireille.

Nope.

Not a *thing*.

"She's going to die," Ronin whispered.

Righteous fury pulled Mireille from her ogling. "You don't know that. We still have time. *She* still has time."

"To get skilled enough with a sword to defeat the Koenig? A hardened male who has an entire city of Fae bowing to him? And not only that, but can wield a hammer imbued with divine magic? Yeah, a recently Turned human who's barely past twenty can take him on and win. Sure."

Mireille squared her shoulders. "We'll help her. Silas will help her."

Ronin scoffed, pushing a hand through his messy white hair. "A half-blind, dried up old warrior, a she-wolf with snuffed out fire magic, and a sad-sack, half-human Windrider. If there have ever been worse fucking odds, I've never seen them."

Mireille exploded. "Then why did you agree to help when Cassandra called upon you? If you think this is pointless, why are you even here?"

"I'm not the type to back down from a fight," he snarled. "Neither is my wolf."

"Yes," she spat back, fists clenching, "I remember that *quite* well."

Ronin's face crumpled, the first real emotion she'd seen from him. A crack in his armor. "I *begged* him, Mireille—" her heart stuttered at her name on his lips "—*begged* him not to shift and go after you."

She stepped forward, invading his personal space. "I'm glad he did."

Ronin's eye blazed, anger radiating off his powerful body as a growl built in his throat.

She went in for the kill.

"At least he was willing to pay the price for my father's death."

His hand shot for her throat, but he stopped himself at the last second. Pivoted on his heel and bolted toward the weapons rack.

He tossed a practice sword at her feet, gripping another in his massive hand. The words tattooed across his knuckles—*Inom Than,* Become Death in Aramaelish—felt almost too appropriate. "Pick it up."

"No," Mireille said, taken aback. "Why?"

"Because we're going to do this right. This fight between us has been a *long* time coming. Not between you and my wolf. Between you and me. And if we're going to help Cass win her appeal, then we need the practice, too. You certainly haven't gotten in any sparring with her."

Mireille crossed her arms over her chest. "I'm not fighting you, Ronin."

He choked up on the hilt of his sword, circling her. "Why? Afraid you'll lose, little she-wolf?"

She scoffed, something kindling within her. As if she'd been waiting for this moment for centuries. A chance for her and Ronin to work through their shit on a level playing field without her fire to give her the advantage.

And even though a more rational part of her knew that talking it out, *hearing* him out, might be a better way to resolve things, that wasn't at all what she wanted right now.

She picked up the sword and shot him a savage smile. "Oh no, Matakos. I'm not afraid." She twirled the weapon, the tip whizzing through the air and lighting a fire in her blood. "Not for me, at least. I'm afraid *you* might lose another eye."

He bellowed and she barely had time to get her sword up before he was upon her. Their stone blades crashed together, the force reverberating through her bones.

"Say that again," he growled, his breath hot on her face, blades crossed between their bodies.

She pivoted away, then darted behind him and braced her sword in front of her.

He traced a large circle into the dirt with the tip of his weapon. "There's going to be rules this time. If you can handle that. A fair fight. No wolves. Just you and me and these blades. If you step outside the circle, I earn a point and vice versa. If the sword touches flesh, that also earns a point. First to three points wins."

No wolves? Her wolf whined. *That hardly seems fair. I've been waiting to spar with him for centuries.*

You'll get your chance, Mireille soothed. *But right now, he's fucking* mine.

"What are we playing for?" she asked.

His golden-blue eye met hers with what she swore was an audible crack. "Truths."

Mireille swallowed. Was it worth the risk? She couldn't begin to imagine what kind of truths he might request, but...

She had plenty she wanted from him.

"Deal," Mireille said, choking up on the hilt, her muscles tensing as she tracked his every move.

"I'll even make it easier for you to aim." He placed his sword in the dirt then grasped the back of his collar. He hauled his shirt over his head and tossed it aside.

She'd love to say she'd forgotten the thigh-clenching spectacle of a shirtless Ronin. That the memory had faded after two centuries.

But that would make her a filthy, filthy liar.

And the sight of him, vividly in the flesh, brought to mind a torrent of other memories.

Her body pinned against that spectacular chest. Those shapely fingers digging into her hips as he fucked her. Those intricate ice-blue tattoos pulsing in tandem with his thrusts.

A section of the tattoos had been burned away by his sentencing brand—a travesty.

Still, the faintest hint of a smirk grazed his stupidly tempting mouth.

Fuck *that*. Two could play at this game.

She leaned her sword against her thigh, then whipped off her own shirt. Her training pants hung low enough to expose the curve of her hipbones and her breasts were bound with a length of cloth. The only poor excuse for a bra in this time-forgotten city.

A shiver of satisfaction ran down her spine as Ronin's gaze blazed a trail across her newly exposed skin. Though his smirk melted into a pained grimace when it traced along her own sentencing scar—plus the myriad others she'd earned in here.

Was he upset by the evidence of her incarceration? Or that the sight of her bare flesh still turned him on? Did he hate himself a little for it?

Because she sure as shit did.

She wanted to be done with all this *useless* longing. For her one-time friend and lover. For her long-time enemy. For the male who had killed her father.

Hate and passion—two sides of the same fiery coin.

Which would it land on?

"Better be careful, *Butcher*," she taunted, raising her sword, her heart pounding a mad beat. "I've had nothing but time in here to hone my skills. I've gotten even better with a sword than I was outside that cabin."

He grinned, his eye glinting with feral delight. "Then let's see how you do when you face a *real* threat."

He didn't give her a chance to respond. He rushed forward with an arcing strike that she barely had time to counter, their swords cracking together.

It took all her effort to shove him away. He was bigger and more powerful than any male she'd ever fought. Ever *known*, really.

They volleyed blows, blades crashing, neither making a hit. He executed a series of swift swipes, an aggressive assault that had her shuffling backwards.

He barked out a victorious laugh. "One point to me."

She glanced down to see her heel raked through the circle. She snarled, thrusting out again and forcing him back into the ring.

He retreated to the other edge, twirling his sword in a single hand.

She scurried toward him, her blade up like a spear.

He knocked the tip away with his own, then grabbed her wrist and spun her against his body, folding her arm until her own blade was at her throat.

She struggled to break out of his unyielding grip, her back flush with his naked chest. Her skin flooded with electric heat, and she tried to push away, but he held firm.

The cool edge of his sword dragged across her stomach, and his chin grazed her shoulder as he whispered, "That's two points for me now. What were you saying about having plenty of time to practice?"

She swallowed a frustrated growl as she squirmed against him, unable to break free.

But there were other ways to retaliate. And she wasn't above using them.

She melted back against him, pushing her ass into his groin. A long-dead part of her lit up at his responding groan. One he desperately tried to stifle. He may not *want* to want her anymore, but his body betrayed him.

His cock twitched against her ass before he shoved her away. "Dirty fucking tactic," he growled, holding his sword in one hand as he adjusted himself with the other.

She shot him a lupine smile, her wolf panting and yipping within her. "You used to like it when I played dirty."

He bared his fangs and rushed for her again, though his focus was rattled. He broadcast his move well before he made it, and she ducked beneath his sword, angling her own and smacking it across his rock-hard abs. He grunted in pain, and satisfaction pulsed through her veins.

"One point for me," she sang out, then planted her foot in his ass and knocked him out of the ring. "And now that's two points. Seems we're all tied up."

He huffed out a laugh as he stood, brushing the dirt off of his knees. "Don't threaten me with a good time, Valette."

"Get back on your knees for me, and it'll be more than just a threat."

Unguarded hunger flashed through his eye, and she realized how foolish it had been to taunt him, to poke the beast.

He tossed his sword aside and barreled toward her, tackling her at the waist and snaking a hand behind her skull to protect her head as they crashed to the ground. He pinned her body down, then snatched her wrists and pushed her hands outside the ring.

He chuckled. "Looks like that's three points to me."

She scowled and bucked her hips up into his cock. Terrible idea.

Really terrible idea.

He dragged a fang along the edge of her jaw, and fucking Faurana spare her, she couldn't help the bone-deep shudder that trembled through her body.

"I win," he whispered against her neck.

"Get off."

"Not until I get my prize." His voice was a silken caress. "I believe I'm owed a truth."

His weight on top of her, his breath on her skin, his fingers wrapped around her wrists—she had to bite her tongue to keep from moaning. Or begging. "Fucking *ask* it, then."

His teasing expression melted into heartbreaking vulnerability. "Why did you take the fall? After the Cathedral of Bones? Why did you protect me?"

She clenched her hands into fists and squeezed her eyes shut. "Ronin, I—"

"Ah, ah," he whispered. "The *truth*. You promised."

"Because I was still in love with you!" The answer wrenched out through gritted teeth, and she popped her eyes open. Ronin's own looked shocked. As if he hadn't expected that.

He pushed up off her, couldn't get away fast enough.

"Mireille, I…" he stuttered. "That's…"

He didn't say another word. Didn't even look at her as he walked out of the room.

She curled into a fetal position, unable to stop the hot, salty tears that flowed down her cheeks.

He still wants us, her wolf whispered.

I know, she answered.

He still hates us, too.

Obviously.

But, he might not forever, her wolf whined.

Don't hold your breath, Mireille said as she pushed up off the floor, replaced the swords on the rack, and tried to put the pieces of herself back together.

CHAPTER
THIRTY-SEVEN

"I WAS WONDERING WHY MIREILLE asked us to talk with you the other day," Silas said, the rustle of his dove-soft wings the only sound in the midnight-cloaked streets.

Cassandra had just finished telling him her history.

And all he'd done when she'd finished was raise his thick, dark eyebrows and say, "Huh. Never met a Turned human before."

Unflappable.

No wonder Mireille had suggested he help with training.

He offered her a wry smirk. "She did mention that you needed some additional motivation to take down the Koenig. I would've thought your own survival would have been enough."

"I would have, too," Cassandra offered with a weary laugh. "It's been a rough few weeks." She cringed. "I'm sorry, how thoughtless of me. When you've—"

"Trauma's not a competition. Feel however you need to feel, Cass. Can I call you Cass?" She nodded.

They walked a few more steps in silence, Cassandra contemplating the wisdom in his words. He had a graceful countenance and a quiet depth. She might have even appreciated how handsome he was if her chest wasn't still tied up in knots over—

"So what happened to the male who Turned you? He waiting for you outside the wards?" Nothing colored Silas's questions but simple curiosity. There was no *I'm interested in you* subtext. She was grateful for that.

But she also didn't feel like talking about it with a total stranger. Regardless of how calming his presence was.

"No comment," she answered, as kindly as she could.

And Silas, bless him, didn't push.

When they reached the Kennel, Cassandra adjusted the linen bag of healing tonics and the glass vials tinkled as she opened the door. "After you."

Silas shook his head. "I'll stay out here on watch. You distribute the tonics."

"Why?"

"The Brethren don't like us coming here. They claim we're spoiling the humans by giving them extra food and additional care. Insist the humans need to *know their place.*"

Rage glowed fierce in Cassandra's chest. "But that's… High Gods, that's absurd. They're being kept in fucking *cages.*"

"I also think they don't like to be reminded that so many of us share ancestry with them. That the main difference between our species is the gift of magic. Especially when none of us can wield it in here. In its absence, the Koenig and his Brethren find other ways to maintain their dominance."

"And what will happen if they catch us?"

"They'll find some clever way to punish us. Sometimes, it's a week-long stay in the castle dungeons. Sometimes it's…something else."

He's survived Harvest Night five times.

She rolled her shoulders, ruffling her feathers. "I'm not scared of them. I've got the protection of the blood vow."

Silas grimaced. "Don't fully depend on that. The Koenig and his steward are cleverer than they seem. If they wanted to do you harm, they'd find a way around it. Best to be safe. If anyone approaches, I'll come in and fetch you."

Cassandra's nerves prickled, but she wouldn't let fear stop her from doing even a tiny bit of good.

She walked into the Kennel, and Silas shut the heavy metal door behind her.

"Back again, eh, do-gooder?"

The old woman's raspy laughter snaked out of the corner cell as Cassandra approached. She'd dispersed all but one of the healing tonics, her cheeks flushed with pride.

The old woman's greeting took her down several notches.

Cassandra tucked her wings and settled cross-legged onto the floor. She held out the last vial of tonic, swirling the clear liquid within.

Tremors wracked the old woman's body, and her pupils dilated. She wrung her hands in her lap, as if she were fighting against shoving an arm through the bars and snatching the vial.

The old woman wanted the tonic, *needed* the tonic. And it was abundantly clear she'd rather die than ask for it.

"Fresh batch," Cassandra said, rolling the vial between her fingers. "The apothecarist just finished brewing it today."

The old woman huffed, pulling her knees against her chest and wrapping her threadbare blanket around her shoulders. "I don't need your fucking Fae potions coursing through my system."

"You sure? It'd help ease your aches. Might help you get a good night's sleep for once."

"What makes you think I have trouble sleeping?"

"Because you look like the dog shit someone scraped off the bottom of their boot."

The old woman blinked, the silence stretching between them for a long moment before she exploded into body-shaking, limb-trembling laughter.

It turned into a hacking cough so phlegmy that Cassandra fought an urge to run a soothing hand down her back.

The old woman composed herself, coughing lightly and rubbing at her wet eyes. "At least you're honest. I'll give you that. But like I told you the other night, I don't need your fucking charity. Bugger off."

Cassandra shrugged, trying to maintain her nonchalant facade while her insides were churning with guilt and shame and anger. There was *nothing* that separated her from this woman, other than the wings on her back that she hadn't asked for. She could easily be looking at some alternate version of her own future.

"It's not *fucking charity* if you pay me for it," she said.

The old woman sat up a little straighter, then she laughed again, a bitter hiss, as she swiveled her gaze around the cell. "Oh yes! Let me pay you with all the *drachas* I have laying around my palace." She lifted her tattered bedroll, then smacked her palm against her forehead. "Darn, forgot I'm fresh out. Spent it all on these gorgeous rags. I'd offer to feed you some of my emotions, but I think you'll find they're a bit rotten."

The old woman moved closer to the bars, grasping at her hem with knobby fingers and hitching up her filthy skirt. "Or maybe you've got another payment in mind. It's drier than the fucking Desolation down there, but if you've a taste for some desiccated human flesh…"

The old woman stared Cassandra down, her rheumy eyes daring Cassandra to flinch, to show any sign of disgust, any small tell of anger.

But Cassandra wouldn't do it.

This woman had been enslaved, locked up, malnourished, sleep-deprived, and the-High-Gods-only-knew what else during the time she'd been here.

A tear crawled down the woman's face as she flicked her skirt down and turned away, folding herself into a fetal position.

"Like I said, do-gooder, kindly fuck off. Leave an old woman her dignity. It's all I have left."

"Your name," Cassandra whispered.

"What?" the old woman said, not bothering to lift her head.

"That's all I want. For the tonic. Just tell me your name."

"This some kind of Fae trick? I give you my name and then you control me, make me do whatever you want?"

"Fae can't do that."

"Can't they?" the old woman murmured.

She remained silent for what felt like hours. So long that Cassandra thought she'd fallen asleep.

Cassandra placed the vial through the bars, about to give up and leave, when a small croak came from the pile of blankets.

"Ana."

"What?" Cassandra whispered, afraid of scaring the woman back to silence.

"Ana," she repeated, slightly louder. "My name is Ana."

Cassandra bit back a thousand responses. *That's a beautiful name. Thank you for sharing it with me. I'm so sorry that this has happened to you. I'm not terrible, not like* them. *Please don't hate me.*

But Cassandra's guilty conscience was her own burden. Ana was already shouldering enough of her own.

So Cassandra pushed up off the floor, and left Ana to her peace.

As soon as Cassandra stepped outside, all the grief she'd held back in Ana's presence spilled over.

Silas pinched closed the leather journal he'd been drawing in and slipped it into his bag. "Well? How did it—" His brows crashed together when he saw her face. "That bad, huh?"

Cassandra swiped her wrist under her nose. "Why has no one tried to get them *out* of there? To at least free them from these cages?"

"Where would they go?" Silas asked gently. "Back through the mists? Take their chances in the moat? Hide away in the houses of sympathetic prisoners? We've tried all of it. And when we've failed, who do you think suffers the most? Not the Fae, I assure you."

Cassandra ran her fingers down her braid, trying to soothe her bleeding heart. She needed to calm down or she wouldn't be able to sleep tonight. Would be a mess for training tomorrow.

"I just..." she breathed out. "I just don't understand why the Brethren treat them like this."

Silas let out a ragged sigh. "I don't understand it either." He reached out a hand and gripped her shoulder. "And I—"

The cobbled street around them disappeared as the memory overtook Cassandra.

A lovely Windrider female in a soft peach dress sat in a cheery, sunlit kitchen. Auburn curls tumbled down her torso as she pitted cherries, singing softly toward her belly.

Cassandra, through Silas's eyes, looked toward the bump and an arrow pierced her heart.

She was ripped through space and time, rainbow shards and strings of light swirling until she came to a jolting stop.

And was looking through a different pair of eyes.

Female eyes, though she didn't quite understand how she knew that.

She was walking down a noisy, crowded avenue, arm-in-arm with another female.

She caught a glimpse of her reflection in a shop window—auburn waves, thick brows, dove gray wings—before pausing to examine a pair of shiny golden sandals.

Her friend tugged her arm. "Come on, Sofia. You do *not* need another pair of shoes." She lowered her voice. "Rebels need more sensible ones, anyway."

"Rebels wear whatever shoes they fucking want," Sofia said with bubbling, infectious laughter.

"Let's *go*," her friend cackled, pulling her away from the window. "The meeting started two minutes ago."

As the memory faded, Cassandra struggled to ascertain what city she was in. Obviously somewhere on the continent, based on the cars whizzing past and the height of the buildings. Plus, it was warm enough for Sofia to wear a skirt and no jacket.

She jolted out of Sofia's mind, and returned to Silas.

"—don't really want to understand it," he finished. "What's wrong? You look extremely pale all of a sudden."

She braced her hands on his forearms.

"Silas, I… I think I just saw your daughter."

CHAPTER
THIRTY-EIGHT

RONIN LAID ON HIS bed, his hand behind his head and his knee bobbing with restless energy.

He needed something to do. Something to distract his overactive mind.

Cassandra had left with Silas about forty-five minutes ago to head to the Kennel. Ronin had offered to accompany them, but she'd waved him off. Said one hulking male bodyguard was suspicious enough.

Then had made some smarmy comment about Ronin helping Mireille down in the shop instead.

But today's training session with Mireille was the *source* of his restless energy. Sensations overwhelmed him: her soft body pressed against his chest, her tortuously perfect ass grinding against his cock, her silky hair gliding over his shoulder.

Not to mention the confession he'd wrung from her when he'd had her pinned beneath him.

Because I was still in love with you!

She was so fucking cool and collected all the time. Even back when they'd been at the Otto estate together. Getting her to admit to any vulnerability was a challenge.

So for her to admit that she'd still loved him, despite what they'd done to each other...

It was the most vulnerable thing she could have said.

And he had no idea how to feel about it.

Didn't even know what in the name of the Creator had inspired him to ask the question in the first place. It was like the touch of her skin and the scent of her arousal combined with the sight of those terrible new scars had short-circuited his brain.

He'd scrambled out of that training room like a coward. He'd avoided dinner with her and Cass like a coward. And now he was hiding in his room.

Like a coward.

Wanna go for a run? he asked his wolf

No, thanks. The creature licked at a paw. *Why don't you take Cassandra's suggestion? Go downstairs and help Mireille. That must be more interesting than running circles around the city wall.*

Ronin grunted. *More interesting for who?*

Exactly.

You're worse than Cassandra.

His wolf hissed out a laugh. *She and I have similar objectives.*

Ronin groaned, then rose from his bed.

And clomped down the stairs to Mireille's shop.

Ronin leaned a hip against a shelf, arms crossed, and watched Mireille wipe down her mortar and pestle with a white cloth.

Her confession hung like a poisonous fog between them, gathering in the shadowed corners, ready to strike.

"Need help with anything?" he asked, trying to keep his tone bored. Disinterested. Nonchalant.

He hoped she couldn't sense his pounding heartbeat.

Focus glued to her cleaning, Mireille jutted her chin toward an iron pot at the end of her work table. "That's cooled and ready for bottling. Vials and corks are in the cabinet behind you."

He nodded, then turned around and opened a wooden door to reveal a gleaming row of glass bottles. "How many?"

Mireille assessed the liquid in the pot. "Ten should do it."

Ronin grabbed his supplies, then settled in beside her. The table was small, barely enough space for one person. As they worked, their elbows bumped, heat simmering his veins at each and every touch.

He ignored it as he ladled the liquid into a funnel. Once the vial was full, he brought it to his nose and sniffed. Lavender. "What does this one do?"

"Calming draught." Mireille didn't look up, but she didn't move away from him either.

"Where do you get the ingredients to make all this?"

Mireille's eyes glazed over, and his protective instincts flared. "The Brethren put in special requests with the Koenig for me."

Ronin went preternaturally still, his fingers stilling on the vials. "Like Jonas? That dark-haired Brethren who was bothering you on Harvest Night?" He failed to keep the bite out of his tone.

So much for nonchalance.

She slammed down her pestle. "You have no interest in me anymore. So I don't know why you care."

He steeled his spine. He didn't care. Of *course* he didn't fucking care. He'd had plenty of females since they'd parted. It would be hypocritical of him to assume she'd been celibate while he hadn't.

Still, he couldn't stop the surge of intense jealousy. The thought of that disgusting beast—fucking *Jonas*—putting his meaty paws on Mireille, rutting into her, using the body she'd taunted Ronin with today…

The body that had once belonged to him.

He smothered his possessiveness. If he involuntarily shifted right now, his wolf would wreak havoc through

Mireille's tiny shop. The creature was already howling and scratching at his insides. He attempted a few deep breaths to calm him.

He reached across the table and clasped her hand in a silent apology. He ran his thumb across the back of her knuckles, and she shuddered, then pulled away and gave him her back. He could've sworn he heard a small hiccup. Like she was choking back a sob.

"Don't," she whimpered.

"Don't what?" He stepped up behind her. Not touching, but close enough to feel her heat through the black silk of her robe. Close enough to lean down and sniff her hair. His eye nearly rolled back in his head at the sweet, floral scent.

"You ran out of that training room today like you were on fire," she whispered, seething.

"Mireille, I—"

"I don't need your fucking *pity*, Ronin!" she roared, rounding on him. "I didn't say I *wanted* to still love you. It's been the worst burden of my fucking life. If I could claw this feeling out of my chest, I would have done so two centuries ago."

She charged forward, backing him into the work table and clattering the vials. His wolf was a howling cyclone within him, and he clenched the edge of the table to keep himself under control.

She dipped in closer, and the table edge groaned under his hold. "Or better yet," she crooned, her petal-soft lips ghosting over his flesh, "I never would have made the mistake of *you* in the first place."

He couldn't handle it. He wanted to bend her over the table, rip up her robe, smack his palm across her perfect ass. One blow for every single lie she'd just thrown at him and a few more for good measure.

He was about to snap when the shop bell jingled and Silas and Cassandra barreled in.

Ronin and Mireille careened away from each other and Cassandra gave them a knowing look before Mireille barked out a sharp, "What?"

"You two need to come upstairs," Cassandra said.

"I have something to show you."

"It was like I was in her mind, seeing through her eyes," Cassandra said, fiddling with her mug.

Mireille had brewed a pot of chamomile tea while Cassandra told her and Ronin what had happened at the Kennel.

"It was similar to when I was upset the other night and you touched me," she said, nodding toward Mireille, who'd finished stirring her own tea and had taken a seat on the couch. As far away from Ronin, who was seated at the dining table, as possible.

Cassandra had no idea what the two wolf bi-forms had been up to when she and Silas had burst into the shop. For a split second, it looked like they were on the verge of devouring each other. But they'd bounced apart faster than opposing magnets, and hadn't said a word to each other since.

"One minute, I was in Silas's memory, looking upon his pregnant wife, and the next second, I was in his daughter's mind. In the present." She took Silas's hand. "I think she might be a member of the Teles Chrysos. Her friend mentioned something about rebels? About a meeting?"

Silas himself had lost a touch of his calm composure when Cassandra had told him his daughter's name. He hadn't known it. Hadn't even known that Penelope had given birth to a female. He'd been dazed and quiet for the entire walk back to the shop. Some color had finally returned to his cheeks, thanks to the tea.

"She was in a large city," Cassandra said. "Tons of Fae, streets packed with cars. The buildings were so tall I couldn't even see the tops of them and the window she was looking in had a golden sheen. It was still warm outside, so I'm guessing she was somewhere in the southern part of the continent?"

Ronin tapped the table. "Sounds like Rhamnos. The Teles Chrysos leadership, not to mention a majority of their forces, are stationed in Lebaedia, not too far from there. They often journey down to the city to recruit new members. What did you say her name was again?"

"Sofia," Silas said, testing out the syllables. Like he might never stop saying it. "Sofia Hershon. Her mother's name is Penelope."

Ronin shook his head. "Sorry, I don't recognize the name. Doesn't mean anything though. The movement is growing rapidly. She could have joined after I left for the colonies."

"It's okay," Silas said with a soft smile. "Just to know that she's alive, that she exists." He squeezed Cassandra's hand. "Thank you."

"You'll meet her," Cassandra said. "As soon as we get out of here."

"Well, there's something to look forward to." He pulled his hand away and scratched at a bushy brow, overcome.

Cassandra turned to Ronin. "I want to try it on you."

Ronin startled. "Why?"

"Because I think the jumping occurs between blood relatives. Mireille's father. Silas's daughter."

Ronin's face paled.

"Maybe we can find Selene." Cassandra reached a hand across the table, palm up.

"Okay," Ronin said, glancing toward Mireille who offered a sympathetic nod. "What do I... Is there a specific memory I need to conjure?"

Cassandra shook her head. "Any memory will do."

Mireille pushed up off the couch and ambled over, reaching into the pocket of her robe and placing a chess piece on the table.

The white queen.

He shot Mireille a rueful smile as he said, "I've got a few that might work."

Ronin's memories of his sister did work.

They were sweet. Playful, even. Cassandra could tell how deep their bond ran, even in the few memories where the twins had been at each other's throats.

Yes, the memories worked fine.

What did *not* work was the mind jumping.

They'd tried recent memories. Like the last time Ronin and Selene had seen each other before she'd been arrested. That one was a tense affair at Ronin's sleek, modern, and very official-looking townhouse in Delos. They'd been arguing about Selene's work with the Teles Chrysos. She was getting in with some of the more unhinged factions of the movement, taking unreasonable risks. According to Ronin, at least. Lethaphyll-powered trips to the Halfway. Studying chronomancy, that long-suppressed seer's practice. Attempting to commune with the Fallen Goddess. And distributing Teles Chrysos propaganda throughout Imperial-leaning northern Nephes.

After that memory, they'd gone back further. Selene tending to Ronin's wounds when he'd returned to their family cottage in Denevrae after he'd acquired his injury. Mireille had gotten up to make more tea during that one.

Then even further and further back until they reached one of Ronin's earliest memories. Two fluffy white wolf pups napping together, the smaller resting her black-nosed snout atop the larger's neck after an exhausting morning of shifting practice.

But every time Cassandra attempted to leap into Selene's mind, she was jolted back into her own by a solid white wall. As if something was blocking her entry.

"Shit." She slammed her hand down on the table, making Ronin and Silas jump. "I don't understand why it's not working."

Ronin dipped his head into his hands, rubbing at his patch, his voice quaking. "What if she's dead?"

Cassandra pinched the bridge of her nose. "That can't be it. Mireille's father has passed, but I was still able to travel into whatever part of his mind remains in the Halfway. If Selene were dead, I'd be able to see her there, too."

"Unless..." Mireille piped up from the kitchen, walking over with another steaming mug of tea.

"Unless what?" Cassandra asked.

She shot a nervous glance at Ronin. "Unless she was killed in the mists. And her soul is still trapped there."

Ronin heaved out a shuddering sigh. Mireille placed her hand on his shoulder and he clutched it tightly. As if her touch were the only thing tethering him to this planet.

Cassandra frowned. "I don't know. I'm not... I don't think that's it either. Whatever it is that's keeping me from penetrating her mind feels intentional. Like someone has put up a barrier."

"There's one way to know for sure," Silas piped up from beside the fireplace. "Wormwood keeps ledgers in his office above World's End. Records of every single prisoner—their name, number, and sentence—that has ever breached the wards. The wards themselves provide the information."

"What are you saying?" Mireille asked for Ronin, who was currently incapable of speech.

Silas looked to Ronin, compassion glowing in his moss-green eyes. "If we can get a look at those ledgers, we'll know whether you need to keep searching the city and the mists.

"Because if her name isn't in there, then she never passed through the wards."

CHAPTER
THIRTY-NINE

"INCREDIBLE THAT SOMETHING SO small could cause so much damage," Tristan mused, pinching the small metal tracking device between his fingers.

Toeing his boot through the dust on the church floor, Cael rumbled out, "My father's business motto."

"He's not... He can't track this right now, can he?"

Cael shot Tristan an annoyed glare. "I lost half my wings, not half my brains. I'm sure *Trophonios* of all people can still crack the secrets of an inactive device."

Tristan chuckled. "High Gods, I've missed your grumpy ass, Zephyrus."

Cael leaned forward, placing his forearms on his thighs. "No one to put you in your place among the rebels, huh? No wonder you need me to join."

Tristan perked up, his wings rising over his shoulders. "You ready?"

Cael shook his head. "Not until you tell me how to deactivate that thing. How was your trip to Delos?"

Tristan pocketed the device, gnawing on his lower lip. "It was... odd."

He told Cael everything that had happened to him there. About retrieving the Compendium. About the elemental magic he'd been temporarily gifted after Ione had kissed him. About Eamon's cryptic parting words.

"She *kissed* you?" Cael asked, brows rising.

"That's your only comment?"

"That's the only thing you said that makes me scared for your future. If Cassandra ever finds out..." Cael chuckled, slashing his hand across his throat. "Ethyrios can say goodbye to its new Emperor. Or hello to its new eunuch Emperor. She'll have your balls."

Tristan laughed, a loud thunderous sound. It felt good to laugh like that. He hadn't felt such unburdened laughter since... well, he could barely remember. Maybe the battle up in the Staurien Pass when all his anxieties had faded into the sole focus of slaughtering his enemies.

"I suspect she would," he said, his amusement fading. "But... What if Ione is right? How could we have created that storm together if we *weren't* fated to one another?"

"I didn't think that was a thing," Cael said. "Just some romantic nonsense children read about in story books."

"That's what I thought, too. But she's adamant. And all the evidence supports it. The Goddess blessed our union by Turning her. We enhance each other's power. She can Ghostwalk, for fuck's sake. It's just…"

Cael listened in silence, without judgment. Letting Tristan talk it out. He'd always been good at that.

Tristan blew out a long breath. "How could my fate be bound to Ione while I'm still pining for Cassandra? It doesn't make any fucking sense."

"Whoever said love was supposed to make sense? Have you and Ione talked about it since Delos?"

Tristan shook his head. "As soon as we got back and I gave Trophonios the Compendium, she took off to visit the rebels in Cernodas. Said she'd return when the interpretation was complete. She doesn't even know I'm here with you."

"Sneaking out to meet your boyfriend, huh?" Cael taunted. "Better be careful, handsome, she already thinks she has to fight off Cass. What would she say if she knew I owned a piece of your heart as well?"

Tristan snickered, regarding his friend in the orange afternoon glow. There was a lightness in Cael that he hadn't seen last time. That maybe he'd never seen.

"Your *yet* happened, didn't it?"

"What?" Cael said, taken aback. "No, we can't. It's the same problem you had back at the Temple when you were chasing Cassandra. If anyone scents me on her…"

"So the woman you're in love with—" Cael shot him a look "—don't fucking deny it, you've been mooning over her since Thalenn. The woman you're in love with is in your house, you see her every day, and you haven't touched her yet?"

The corner of Cael's lip twitched. "I didn't say *that*."

"You dog," Tristan snickered, even as a pang of the fiercest longing stole through him. He did a mental calculation; how many days had it been since Cass had been locked up? Nearly a month, surely. He'd gotten used to the panic. That ever-present anxiety lurking in the back of his mind that he wasn't with her, couldn't protect her.

And he couldn't explain why, but… He *knew*, deep in his heart, that she was alive. As if the blood they'd shared, the blood that connected them, still sang to each other. He would know if she'd been killed. Wouldn't he?

He turned back to Cael. "What have you discovered about the dragon?"

"Well, I've seen it, at least. I've been visiting the mountain every chance I can get."

"Does Arran suspect anything?"

Cael huffed a sarcastic laugh. "He's beside himself with joy. Thinks I'm finally taking a keen interest in the family business."

"Have you figured out how he's been controlling it?"

"Not yet. Xenia's been searching, though. Hopefully we'll find something soon."

"How's the wedding planning coming along?" Tristan smirked and Cael shot him a sharp glare. "I need to get going. There's a feast down at camp tonight to celebrate our retrieval of the Compendium. Rouse the forces and all that. You wanna come?"

Cael shook his head. "I need to get back to Stoneridge. I don't like leaving her there alone."

Tristan slapped a hand on his friend's shoulder. "Whipped, Zephyrus." But a frown stole across Tristan's face. If he had *any* chance to get to Cass, he'd be gone in a heartbeat.

Cael read every nuance of his expression. "You'll be with her again. And in the meantime, you're doing the right thing. Protecting your people. Ensuring the survival of the rebellion. Raising an army—with a dragon—to free her."

"Do you really believe that?" Tristan asked, needing to hear his friend confirm it.

"I do. Hold on to a belief in the most positive outcome."

Tristan smiled wryly. "She really is rubbing off on you, isn't she?"

Cael tilted his head back, eyes hooded, and bit his lower lip. "She's rubbing all *over* me."

Tristan released another hoot of laughter, grateful for the distraction from his own shit, then stood from the pew and rustled his wings. Cael pulled an opal from his pocket. "Why aren't you using the cuff?"

"Xenia has it. I want her to be able to get in touch with me in case… I want her to be able to get in touch with me."

Tristan nodded. "Same time Friday?"

"See you then, Your Highness." Cael's voice dripped with wry amusement as he winked out in a rainbow flare.

Tristan muttered *asshole* under his breath, then tapped his own cuff and portaled out of the church ruins.

CHAPTER FORTY

"You've been avoiding me."

Ione's voice tiptoed over to where Tristan was seated beneath the clocktower in Lebaedia. He'd finally gotten a moment alone to eat after the raucous night of celebrating with his rebels.

"Says the female who spent the past week in an entirely different territory," Tristan teased.

Ione's face fell.

"I'm not avoiding you." He dug into a grilled turkey leg, savoring the smoky flavor, then waved it at her. "Just trying to fit my meals in where I can. Everyone wants a piece of me." He cringed as the words left his mouth. Especially when Ione cocked her head, confusion passing over her face. He sighed and patted the rough bricks. "Sit. Have you had a chance to eat?"

Ione sat gracefully, a respectful distance away, though her feathers brushed against his. "Can't eat. I'm too nervous."

"About what?"

"About what the Compendium might reveal tonight."

As soon as Tristan had returned this evening, Trophonios had informed him that the translation was complete. That he was ready to reveal the end of the prophecy.

Tristan's stomach had been tied up in knots since. It seemed Ione was feeling the same.

"Oh," was all he said.

"Oh, indeed," she said with a small, secretive smile.

"You already know what it says."

"I do not." Ione snatched a grilled thigh from his platter and sank her fangs into it. She raised a hand to her mouth, hiding her chewing. "But I'm scared of how you will react, regardless of what it says."

"You're scared of *my* reaction?" Tristan asked, incredulous. "Why?"

Ione huffed out a laugh, wiggling her fingers toward Tristan's bottle of wine. He handed it to her, and she took a long pull, bolstering her courage.

She removed the bottle from her lips with a smack, then rested it on her knee, rolling it between her fingers. "I'm not so blinded by my faith that I can't tell when a male has no interest in kissing me, Tristan."

Her quiet, broken words stirred that guilt he couldn't manage to smother.

"Ione, I—"

"No, it's okay. I've been telling myself these past few days that it doesn't matter. That of course the kiss was awkward. We haven't seen each other in centuries. Passion doesn't rekindle that quickly, and rebuilding what we had will take time. And *effort*. On both our parts. The only thing I need to know before we hear that prophecy tonight is this." She turned to face him, her indigo eyes gleaming in the bonfires scattered throughout the village. "I need to know that you will do what's right for Ethyrios. No matter what."

His stomach twisted, but he vowed, "I swear it." With what he hoped wasn't a noticeable hesitation.

If the prophecy confirmed that he was fated to Ione, that it was their union that would save this world, was he strong enough to give up Cassandra?

He felt a disorienting mix of fear and shame. Because his heart already knew the answer to that question.

Ione nodded, placated, then polished off her grilled turkey thigh and tossed the bones onto his platter. "Come then. They're ready for us."

His mind raced as they walked toward the leadership building. This meeting would be a turning point for the Teles Chrysos, illuminating the final shape of the puzzle they'd been piecing together for centuries.

They encountered Layla at the entrance, her white and black hair twisted in two buns atop her head and her throwing knives glittering at her waist. Always ready to leap into action. Tristan couldn't remember if he'd ever seen her *without* them.

"General Fetar," Ione nodded. "A momentous night."

"It is that, indeed," Layla purred, her brown eyes roving over Tristan. "Bless the Creator."

The rest of the group were gathered around the table already. Felix tried, and failed, to keep the sneer from his face when Tristan and Ione arrived together, but Seraavi offered a warm smile as they took their seats.

Trophonios was as still as a windless night, his long fingers resting on the cover of the Compendium. As if he alone were the keeper of the book's mysteries.

Tristan's anxiety rose.

How drastically was his life about to change?

Trophonios waited until everyone had settled, then signaled to the recruit at the side of the room. The young Deathstalker darted over and placed a bottle of Aguaver and a stack of shot glasses in the center of the table.

"For after," Trophonios said.

"Well?" Felix barked, stirring his persimmon feathers and fidgeting with a shot glass. "Out with it. What does the prophecy say?"

He seemed just as nervous as Tristan to hear these words. Ione had said that whatever had happened between her and Felix was a mistake. Perhaps Felix didn't see it that way.

Tristan nodded to Trophonios, giving him permission to proceed.

Trophonios opened the Compendium and traced a fingertip down the page. The room was so dead silent that Tristan could hear the male's skin scrape down every fiber of the paper.

The gathered leaders held their breath, then Trophonios began to speak in his deep, measured voice:

"Two futures sown, one future known.
Born from phantom wings and mortal bones,
a new Delphine will rise to light
the way.
A story told ten thousand fold,
has but one ending to be told,
until the eight can interweave
their play.
A journey drowned, again is found.
To long-lost power, their fates are bound.
A crown exchanged, divine, will win
the day."

The words echoed until the only sound Tristan heard was the rush of his own blood pounding through his head. He glanced across the table, ensnared by Trophonios's teal gaze before shouting erupted.

Exclamations piled atop one another, tripping and tangling until Tristan couldn't even tell who was speaking.

"...could mean *anything*..."

"...very clear what the next path is. Isn't it obvious..."

"...eight could be the..."

"...I think the journey drowned is referring to..."

"STOP!" Tristan's command shook the room. "One at a time. Let's go around the room, please. I'd like to hear from everyone. Layla?"

"*The eight.*" Layla rubbed her fingers over the hilts of her knives. "That could refer to the six continental territories plus the northern and southern colonies. Eight territories interweaving their play." She glanced to Tristan.

Beside him, Ione nodded. "Yes, that was my interpretation of that line as well."

"*To long-lost power,*" Felix said, eyes glowing. "That's the restored elemental magics, surely?"

"If so, who's *fates are bound* to it?" Seraavi asked. "All of us?"

Felix waved her off, then looked to Trophonios. "Are you sure they got the translation right?"

Trophonios cocked an eyebrow, but didn't say anything as he returned his penetrating gaze to Tristan. It was fucking unnerving. Like the male didn't want to share his interpretation until he heard Tristan's.

Seraavi cut in again. "*A journey drowned.* That must be Adelphinae's own journey, her history. Drowned by the Empire, then found again by our members."

"It could also be a reference to Tristan and Ione." Layla's gaze bobbed between them. "They lost each other and then found their way back."

A soft smile parted Ione's lips as she brushed her wing across Tristan's feathers. It was all he could do to not leap away from her. "Yes. It could certainly be that." She turned to face him. "What do you think?"

"I..." Tristan squared his shoulders as the group stared at him expectantly. "Yes, I suppose it could be."

The corners of Ione's mouth dipped ever so slightly.

In truth, he had no idea *what* to make of the full prophecy. The words were far more vague than he'd anticipated. He'd been hoping for something more concrete.

And no one had yet dared interpret the line that had his heart battering his ribs.

A crown exchanged, divine, will win the day.

Whose crown? And what day?

Finally, he turned to Trophonios. "What do you think?"

Trophonios folded his hands atop the book, thoughtful. "I think that regardless of what we all believe these lines mean, if we cannot agree on an interpretation, we will fail."

Ione ruffled her feathers, her face pinched with distaste. It was clear to Tristan that she knew exactly what that prophecy meant. Both for the movement and for her and Tristan.

Tristan, meanwhile, was even less sure of his path than he'd been when he walked in here.

"Prince?" Ione said. "What do you think it means?"

The ringing in Tristan's ears grew louder.

Should he admit to his confusion, his uncertainty? Or would doing so crumble everything the Teles Chrysos had built?

The only thing he *was* certain of was that he needed more time to think. Away from the Fae around this table.

And certainly away from Ione, whose indigo eyes raked over him with such pleading intensity he could barely breathe.

"We should take some time to think on it," he said. Ione's wings drooped. "Let's regroup in a few days."

He abruptly pushed away from the table, and the group stood.

He didn't dare look back to see the judgment on their faces as he fled the increasingly claustrophobic room.

CHAPTER
FORTY-ONE

"ALRIGHT, CASS," SILAS SAID, tossing a practice sword across the ring, "show me what Ronin and Mireille have taught you."

Silas had met Cassandra and Mireille at the training room this morning just after breakfast.

After he'd left the shop last night and Ronin had shuffled off to bed, Cassandra and Mireille had stayed up for another hour or two, making plans about how they were going to sneak into World's End to infiltrate Wormwood's office and get a look at those ledgers.

They'd come up with what Cassandra thought was a pretty brilliant, albeit risky, plan. She was starting to think that none of her friends were capable of anything other than risky plans. She and Mireille planned to reveal it to Silas and Ronin this morning.

But Ronin wasn't here yet. And Silas wasn't about to let Cassandra wait for the white wolf before they started training.

So, Cassandra bumbled her way through the thrusts and arcs and swipes she'd learned these past weeks. Her wings bounced against her back and made her steps falter.

Silas's tentative smile turned into a grimace.

Cassandra planted the tip of the sword in the dirt and swiped her wrist across her sweat-soaked forehead. She hoped she didn't look as discouraged as she felt. "Well?"

"No offense—" his eyes darted to Mireille "—but I can tell you've been instructed by someone without wings."

"None taken." Mireille crossed her arms, annoyance darkening her silver eyes.

"You're fighting against them," Silas said.

Cassandra's own annoyance rose. "No shit. How do I fix it?"

Silas plucked the sword from her fingers and tossed it out of the ring. "We start from square one."

Cassandra rolled her eyes. "The appeal is in eleven days. I'm not sure that we—"

"Do you want to keep doing things *wrong* and get yourself killed, or start doing them right?"

She squared her shoulders, not so stubborn that she wouldn't try things his way. "Alright. Where do we begin?"

"Wing exercises."

Ronin entered the room right at that moment, then aimed a pointed smirk at Cassandra that said, *Told ya so.*

She grumbled, but obeyed, lifting and stretching and lowering.

"At least someone taught you how to do those right," Silas said.

She sent Ronin a big, fake smile. He leaned a hip against the water table, not even trying to hide his smug expression.

After Cassandra had done several repetitions, she tucked her wings against her back and looked to Mireille. "Now that we're all here, should we tell them?"

"Tell us what?" Ronin asked, stretching an arm across his chest to warm up.

"About how we're going to get our hands on those ledgers," Cassandra said, looking Ronin up and down in a way that made him pause his stretching and send her a questioning look. "You are going to be our distraction."

Mireille sidled up to Ronin and smacked a hand on his shoulder. "Rumor around town is that Wormwood was hitting on you outside World's End the other night. You're going to take him up on his offer of a drink. And I'm going to help."

"How?" Ronin asked.

"By doing something they've been begging me to do since I arrived here two centuries ago. A special performance by the former prima ballerina of the Kheimos Company."

Claws punched through Ronin's knuckles and he released an audible snarl. "No."

Mireille barked out a laugh. "It's funny that you think it's your decision."

"Wormwood will be suspicious that I suddenly changed my mind. He'll know something's up," Ronin said with a victorious little grin.

Mireille grinned right back. "We'll plant some rumors around the city that Cassandra's training is going poorly. That we think she's going to lose and are looking to switch sides."

Ronin shook his head, stepping into her. "I'm not asking you to do this for me."

Mireille stepped closer as well. "And I'm not asking for your permission."

"You two wanna take your tiff to another room?" Silas cut in. "Cass and I have work to do."

And Cassandra nearly huffed in annoyance as Ronin and Mireille left the room together. She wanted to see how this played out.

But she turned to Silas and said, "Now what?"

"Now," he answered, "*we* dance."

"When did you and your crazy winged co-conspirator come up with this plan?" Ronin asked, tossing his shirt next to the weapons rack in the room down the hall.

No matter how many times he'd shucked it off these past few weeks, the pulse-quickening sight never got old.

It was one of Mireille's few moments of unadulterated joy, a distraction from her anxiety over Cassandra's abysmal progress.

Mireille twisted out of her own shirt, ignoring the little thrill that shot through her when Ronin's eye darkened. She plucked two practice daggers from the rack and handed one to him. "I'll tell you after I kick your ass."

Ronin sighed, pulling long fingers through his white strands. The tousled result combined with his roguish eye patch made her want to throw herself against his deliciously bare torso and not come up for air for hours.

What's stopping you? her wolf purred.

Sanity, Mireille scoffed.

Nonsense. We used to be his preferred brand of crazy. Let's remind him.

Ronin's jaw tightened. "No fucking way am I letting you dance for those assholes, Mireille. They don't deserve you." Her chest clenched. "We'll find another way."

"You don't even—"

"I don't want you putting yourself in any more danger for me."

Mireille crossed her arms, her dagger dangling from her fingertips. "If Cassandra loses, we will *all* be in even more danger than we are now. Did you forget about that?"

Ronin stepped forward, towering over her, anger pulsing. "That has nothing to do with looking through those ledgers. We focus on the training, and when we get out of here, I'll have all the time in the world to figure out what happened to Selene."

His voice broke on his sister's name, and Mireille couldn't stand it.

"Those ledgers could be your only chance to learn the truth, Ronin."

"Wanna bet?" he snarled, pressing in closer.

"Actually, that's an *excellent* idea. Care to make a little wager on our sparring session? If you win, I'll drop this idea. But if *I* win, I dance. And you seduce Wormwood. And Cass and Silas sneak into his office to peek at those ledgers."

"I'm not fucking betting on your safety."

Mireille grazed the tip of her dagger along the muscled grooves of his stomach, and he hissed in a sharp breath. "Sounds like someone's afraid to lose."

He snatched the dagger from her grip. "If we do this, we're fighting with real weapons." He replaced the false daggers with real ones, testing the blade's sharpness with his thumb. "First to draw blood wins."

Mireille cocked an eyebrow, desire a ferocious throb in her veins.

Damn, her wolf cut in. *I'd nearly forgotten how good savagery looks on him. But I'm still rooting for you.*

Gee, thanks.

Make him bleed, girl. Her wolf loosed a vicious howl as Mireille plucked the dagger from Ronin's proffered hand. "Deal."

They took to the center of the ring, prowling in a circle, daggers raised. Her adrenaline spiked. Though blows from the practice swords always smarted, there was no real danger. Perhaps *that* was what had been missing from her sessions with Cassandra—a true threat. She made a mental note to begin training with real weapons to add some stakes.

Ronin rushed forward and she knocked away his blow before darting under his arm. "Aim's a little off today," she taunted.

"One good shot," he grumbled. "That's all I need. It's all *you* needed when you gave me this—" he gestured to his eye patch "—wasn't it?"

Guilt stilled Mireille's feet, and Ronin rushed her again. She barely got her dagger up in time to stop him from nicking her shoulder. "Creator save me, are you still harping on that? It was two-hundred years ago! Let it *go*."

"And my own crime was even further back than that." Regret quieted his voice. "Have *you* let it go?"

Mireille snarled, thrusting her dagger toward Ronin's oblique. He caught her wrist and spun her, holding her against his chest and forcing her dagger down to her hip.

He brought his mouth to the shell of her ear, his warm breath inspiring unwanted shivers. She didn't want him to be gentle. Didn't want him to be kind. She wanted his *anger*, his brutality. Wanted to prod it and provoke it. Wanted him to punish her for the harm she'd caused him.

She'd been punishing herself for centuries.

"It kills me that I was the cause of your father's death." His grip tightened. "I have no excuses. And it matters little that I hadn't even met you yet, or that I didn't know who he was at the time—"

"Those sound an awful lot like *excuses*." She wriggled within his arms, trying to pry herself loose. His words were too soft, too intimate. And though she'd ached to hear them for years, she couldn't bear them. Not now, not here. Not when the only reason they were even fighting in the first place was because he refused to put her in any more danger.

"I am sorry for the pain I caused you," he sighed. "I would take it back if I could. I'm sorry, Mireille. I'm so sorry."

Mireille's eyes burned and her throat closed.

A genuine apology.

His arms loosened. "I think we should—"

She hooked a leg around his calf and toppled him to the floor. She pounced, straddling him, and angled her blade up under his jaw.

His eye blazed with renewed anger—plus a healthy dose of lust—and he threw his arms above his head, dropping his dagger. "Yet again, I'm at your mercy, little she-wolf. What are you going to do about it this time?"

She wanted so much more than an apology. She wanted an admission that he felt the same as she did. Wanted him as raw and vulnerable as she'd been when he'd forced her to admit her truth the other day.

It was the only way to regain some semblance of power. To level the lopsided playing field between them.

She kept her dagger at his jaw while she scooted back to sit on his thighs.

He tried to lift his chin. "What are you—"

"Shut *up*," she snarled, pressing the blade in harder. Not hard enough to break skin. Not yet.

She trailed her other hand down his torso, running her fingers down those perfectly symmetrical muscles, across his swirling ice-blue tattoos. She reached his pants and his stomach quivered.

"M-Mireille."

"Hold still," she whispered. "You said you were at my mercy, right?"

His cock was already half-hard when she dipped her hand below his waistband. And it stiffened further when she wrapped her fingers around it.

His eye snapped shut as he sucked in a breath through gritted teeth and kicked his head back.

She began to stroke, light grazes of her fingers over his warm, smooth length. But no pressure where she knew he needed it the most—the taut skin of his head.

His hands fisted in the dirt as he tried to still his hips. She squeezed him harder, savoring her power. He may still hate her, hate how turned on he was. But he didn't stop her. And she knew it wasn't just because of the dagger.

They'd had a safe word, once upon a time. Spiders. If he wanted to utter it, he could and she'd stop immediately.

No, a part of her knew he wanted this, *needed* this, as much as she did.

She continued to stroke him, twisting and squeezing as she passed over his head then coasting back down his length.

High Gods help her, what she wouldn't give to tug off her pants and slip him inside of her. To impale herself on his glorious cock and ride him as hard as she used to.

An unbearable ache pulsed between her thighs, followed by a rush of damp heat. She knew he could scent it. She didn't fucking care.

He groaned then opened his eye, staring at her as he lost control of his hips and thrust up into her fist. "*Fuck, Mireille. I'm about to—*"

His thunderous growl bounced off the walls and beads of sweat gathered in the grooves of his shuddering abs as he came—*hard*—in her hand, his muscles tensing and releasing beneath her.

She rubbed his spend on his pants as he laid back, staring at her with some of that vulnerability she'd been craving.

She flicked his jaw with the edge of her blade, drawing a tiny line of blood.

She leaned down to lick it, and his cock hardened again beneath her as she whispered in his ear.

"I win."

CHAPTER
FORTY-TWO

"RONIN AGREED TO THE plan," Mireille said as she sank into the warm, bubbling water.

Cassandra, who'd already been up here in the bathhouse for thirty minutes after her punishing session with Silas, could tell there was more to the story. "Did he?"

She and Silas had spent hours in the training room, long after Ronin and Mireille had left. Cassandra had spent most of it frustrated. It was hard work, unlearning her bad habits.

She felt almost *too* aware of her wings. Silas had told her not to beat herself up about it. Said he couldn't even imagine how she felt. As if she'd grown a third pair of limbs overnight. Limbs with a mind of their own.

He'd shown her a few moves—how to use them as a counterbalance during kicks, how to harness their momentum to power her punches, how to flatten them against her back so they wouldn't interfere with evasive maneuvers.

He'd told her she'd made progress today. Much more than he'd expected. But she could hear the subtext.

She still had a long, *long* way to go.

She tried to ignore that depressing thought as steam sighed over her face and droplets peppered her chest and shoulders.

A long shallow pool filled with cooler water ran down the center of the main room. Lining either side were a series of semi-circular alcoves hidden behind privacy curtains, containing large, heated tubs. Within the alcoves, an array of oils perched on shelves carved into the black tiled walls. Today, Cassandra had scented the water with bergamot and mint.

Mireille seemed to appreciate it, releasing an audible groan as the water climbed to the base of her neck. She leaned her head back against the edge of the tub.

Cassandra sunk down deeper as well, keeping her wings angled up and out of the water. She'd made that mistake before, submerging her wings along with the rest of her body. While it had felt divine at the time, dragging water-logged feathers the whole way home had been a royal pain in the ass. She'd almost asked Mireille to shift into her wolf and give her a ride.

She chuckled at the memory, then probed again when it was clear Mireille was playing coy. "How did you get him to change his mind?"

Mireille cracked an eye open. "I used a bit of feminine persuasion."

Cassandra drew her knees up and rested her chin atop them. "Do tell."

Mireille sat upright, sending a wave cascading across Cassandra. "It's not important. What *is* important is that he agreed. We'll pick a night to do it and I'll get the promoter at World's End to spread the word about my performance."

"Good," Cassandra said, though she couldn't help being a bit disappointed in Mireille's answer. Not the part about Ronin agreeing—that was great news, obviously. But the first part. That Mireille didn't want to open up to her.

Cassandra thought back to the many baths she'd taken with Xenia at the Temple. Long hours surrounded by wobbly candlelight and relaxing scents, chatting about their days, scheming Cass's robberies, gossiping over the dramas in their supplicants' memories.

Cassandra's life had been so, *so* different back then. Not only had it been hundreds of years shorter— Creator willing—but it had been contained. She'd resigned herself to a quiet existence with her Sisters, pulling memories and helping families, with no aspirations grander than surviving to see the next day. Sitting here now, months later, with a very different female by her side and the fate of an entire city on her shoulders, she ached for a little bit of that normalcy. That connection.

She wouldn't go so far as to call Mireille her friend. Not yet. She didn't even know if Mireille wanted that from her. Sure, they were distantly related and sure, Mireille had some kind of cosmic mandate to help Cassandra. But Mireille didn't seem to want to share personal details.

And maybe it was Cassandra's desperation for *any* type of friend, since she'd lost so many of her own, that had her whispering, "You can talk to me about it, you know."

Mireille ran her fingers through the bubbles. "Talk to you about what?"

"About whatever is going on between you and Ronin."

Mireille's silver eyes shot to Cassandra's, then narrowed. "There's nothing going on between us."

Cassandra leaned back against the stone tub, the downy feathers at her shoulder blades wet and warm against her back. "It helps, you know. To have someone you can unburden yourself with. That's what my—" her voice cracked "—my best friend Xenia and I used to do for each other. In fact, we used to do *this*." She gestured around the alcove. "We'd spend hours together in our bath at the Temple, letting our fingers wrinkle and our worries fade."

"Is she still there? At the Temple?"

"I think so." At least, Cassandra *hoped* she was. She hadn't been able to confirm it. Had been arrested by

Eamon two days before Xenia was scheduled to return to the colonies. If Xenia had indeed returned to the Temple, then Borea would have told her what happened. Zee was probably sick with worry. The thought only strengthened Cassandra's resolve to get the fuck out of here and reunite with her friend.

High Gods, what would Xenia say when she saw what Cassandra had become?

If Cassandra knew her friend at all, she knew that it wouldn't matter. That their bond would remain, even across species. And she would do everything in her power to keep Xenia out of whatever mess waited outside these wards.

"I've never... I don't really have any friends," Mireille said. "Didn't have many before I was locked up either."

"Why not?"

Mireille shrugged. "Because I..." Her features hardened. "Because I can handle my shit on my own."

Cassandra leaned forward. "How's that working out for you?"

Mireille vented a bitter laugh. "Really fucking well, obviously."

Cassandra took the risk, grabbed Mireille's hand. "You can tell me. I promise I would never betray your trust or say anything to him. And to be perfectly honest, I could use the distraction from my *own* shit."

Mireille laughed again, then dipped her lashes, murmuring to the water. "I gave him a hand job while holding a dagger to his throat."

Whatever Cassandra had been expecting to hear, that was certainly not it. Buoyant, cackling laughter boomed out of her, bouncing off the tiled alcove.

Mireille hissed out a *shhhhhhh*, glancing nervously to their closed privacy curtain.

"That's…" Cassandra chuckled. "Wow. Feminine persuasion. Okay, I get it."

"I couldn't help myself. He apologized."

Cassandra cocked her head. "Why do you seem disappointed by that?"

"Because I didn't want him to! Not really. I mean, maybe I did. Who the fuck knows?" Mireille threaded her fingers behind her neck. "It was so much easier to hate him when I didn't have to see his stupid gorgeous face and his perfect tempting body every day. He didn't apologize on the day I found out. He just made all these excuses and—"

"Would you show it to me?"

"Show you what?"

"The memory."

"Why?"

"Because you've been living with your own interpretation of that event for centuries. Maybe it's time for a second opinion?"

Mireille's eyes widened, like she'd never considered such a thing. That someone else might see what had transpired between her and Ronin and help her figure out what to make of it.

"Okay." She closed her eyes and blew out a long breath. "Go ahead."

Cassandra closed her eyes as well, then placed her hand on Mireille's wet shoulder. Her power sparkled to life, tingling through her veins and concentrating at the base of her skull.

And though she no longer needed to say her chant out loud, she said it in her mind; a mantra to focus her power and draw the memory forward.

Lui ganeth, lui cathona. Lui ganeth, lui cathona, she chanted. Out of mind, out of body. Out of mind, out of body.

The scent of fallen pine needles surrounded her, and a cool breeze caressed her limbs, stirring her feathers.

"You. Fucking. KILLED HIM!" Mireille roared, the sword in her hands shaking violently as her fire swelled, crawling up the blade in a crackling blaze.

Ronin backed up a step, pleading. "I didn't know," he choked out. "I didn't know, Mireille."

"You slaughtered him before I even had a chance to—" Her voice broke, and she was furious to see that Ronin was echoing her tears. How dare *he.*

"Please. I didn't..."

"You're a fucking monster," she whispered, pain and regret stealing her breath.

He crashed to his knees. "What can I do? How can I fix this?"

"You can't." She towered over him. "Bring out the beast so that I can have my vengeance."

She angled the flaming steel so close to his face that sweat pebbled across his forehead, and he squinted his eyes against the excruciating heat.

Ronin's wolf burst forth, a violent shift so swift that he vomited.

The colossal creature crouched back onto his hind legs and sprang for her.

She pivoted away, calling upon her dancer's grace, and Ronin crashed through the porch, the stairs crumbling to shards beneath him.

Mireille regained her footing and brandished her sword as a crazed smile tore across her face.

She would make him pay for this. She would make him suffer. Anything. Anything at all to stop this terrible, soul-shredding grief tearing through her.

It was the last thought in her mind as the white wolf stood, shook off the wooden shards, and rushed—

Cassandra stopped the memory right before Mireille drove the sword into the wolf's eye.

Across the tub, a single tear tracked down Mireille's cheek. "I called him a monster that day. But *I* was the monster."

"You were devastated. And angry."

"Do *not* excuse what I did to him."

Cassandra lifted her palms, placating. "Do you know what I saw in that memory?" Mireille raised her head, shame and agony crawling through her silver eyes. "I saw a male desperately in love, looking for any way to right the wrong he did. He was fighting the shift. Trying to call off his wolf. He didn't want to hurt you."

"He already had." Mireille broke Cassandra's gaze, staring at the damp tiles. "And the only thing I wanted to do in that moment was make him feel an ounce of my pain. How could I have fallen in love with someone who would ruthlessly slaughter humans like that?"

"He regretted it, though, didn't he?"

Mireille nodded. "It haunted him. What he'd done on that battlefield in Aethalia. How the Empire had used him. He'd admitted as much to me when we were at the Otto estate together."

"Seems like maybe you were lashing out at him because of what you'd just learned about yourself. Maybe even lashing out at a world that had branded your father a second-class citizen. And using Ronin as a scapegoat." She softened her voice. "When he didn't deserve it."

Mireille dipped her head into her hands. "Creator, what a mess. What do I do?"

"You do what he did today. You apologize."

"And what? Just admit that what I did was wrong?"

Cassandra smirked. "Yes, that's usually how apologies work."

"What if...what if it doesn't change anything? What if I apologize and he still hates me?"

"That's a chance you're going to have to take. You can't control his reaction."

"I don't know. I think I'd rather just let him hate me. If I open my heart to him again, who's to say we wouldn't cause each other more pain?"

Mireille's fears mimicked Cassandra's own tangled mess of a love life. Since the moment she'd met Tristan, it had been one pain after another, her heart bruising the more she'd exposed it to him.

"That's the risk we all take though, don't we?" She smiled wryly. "We delude ourselves into thinking it's worth the pain. You take the bad along with the good. What's the other option? To never experience love at all?"

"Do you regret it?" Mireille's face was more open and raw than Cassandra had ever seen it. "Falling in love with Tristan, now that you know his fate may be tied to someone else?"

Cassandra's chest constricted. "No. I will never regret it. The night I finally gave myself to him, I was done trying to protect my heart. I'd take as much time as he could offer me. I'd hoped it was going to be a little longer." She shrugged. "Even though I only felt it for a short amount of time, I wouldn't give up that love for anything. And perhaps…perhaps I will find it again."

Cassandra didn't know who she was trying to convince, herself or Mireille. The she-wolf was staring at her, brows pinched, like she didn't quite believe it either.

But Mireille sighed, her face softening. "You are very wise for someone who's only lived two decades."

Cassandra snorted. "I've dealt with a lot in those two decades. Hopefully the next hundred will be a bit less dramatic."

Mireille laughed. "And how are you so good at interpreting memories?"

"I lived a thousand different lives as a Shrouded Sister." She leaned in, conspiratorially. "I used to keep the sexy memories."

Mireille cocked an eyebrow. "Pervert."

"You have no idea." Cassandra snickered. "Though obviously nothing compares to the real act. It sounds silly, given that I've only had it a few times, but High *Gods* I miss sex."

Mireille blew a breath through pursed lips. "Me too."

Cassandra's brows rose. "Have you not... I mean, you've been here for... Not once in—"

"Oh, I've had it. No, I miss *good* sex. The kind that leaves your body hungry and aching for *days* afterward." Mireille sighed. "So, this is what girlfriends do, huh? Sit around in a bath and talk about their feelings?"

"Pretty much. It's fun, right? Do you feel better?"

Mireille tilted her head, assessing. "I'm not sure. Let's talk more about sex. That was helping."

Cassandra chuckled. "I told you, I don't have much experience with it."

"Oh please," Mireille waved a hand, splashing through the water. "You went to bed with an Imperial Prince. From the oldest and most powerful Fae bloodline in Ethyrios. I highly doubt the experience gets much better than that."

"Well, *that's* depressing." Though deep down, Cassandra suspected Mireille wasn't wrong.

And now it was Mireille's turn to comfort Cassandra. "You don't know for sure what that vision means. And even Ronin admitted that the Teles Chrysos only *think* that Tristan and Ione are fated. Your Turning might have changed everything."

Cassandra rubbed her wrinkled fingers, shrugging, trying to snuff out the cruel ember of hope Mireille had just planted in her chest. "I guess we'll see when we get out of here."

"*That's* the spirit. So, details?"

Cassandra laughed again, despite herself. "He... It wasn't even so much about the mechanics—though he was very, *very* good at those—it was the way he made me feel. Like I was his most important person. Like he worshiped every inch of my body. And he really paid attention, you know? To the things I liked. Every time he..."

"Don't get shy on me now," Mireille prodded. "You can say it. Every time he made you come?"

"Yes," Cassandra blushed, some of her innate Sisterly primness returning, "every time he made me come it was like he won something. Like he was playing my body as his own personal instrument. Making me sing just for him. My pleasure was even more important to him than his own. And I wanted to give that to him, too, you know? I'm not saying that meaningless sex can't be pleasurable. Maybe when we get out of here and I find the courage to move on, I might even want some. But right now, I just... I can't imagine it."

"I know what you mean," Mireille said, sadness snaking through her silver eyes. "But I will say this— don't knock hate-fucking until you've tried it."

Cassandra sputtered. "Is *that* what you and Ronin have been doing during your sparring sessions?"

"Not yet," Mireille squirmed along the bench. "But honestly, this conversation has me seriously considering it."

"I don't think it's a very good idea."

"Why not? I can tell he still wants me. Quite badly based on how quickly I finished him earlier. Maybe if we bang the hatred out, we could go back to normal? Go back to being friends? Like we were up at the estate before…before everything went to shit. Maybe if we hate fuck each other, all this tension and angst will go away."

"When in the history of the world has that *ever* worked?"

"We could be the first."

Cassandra patted Mireille's hand. "Sure you could."

Mireille pushed up out of the tub, then grabbed a rolled towel from the shelf. "Come on, we should get going."

Cassandra sat in the churning water a moment longer, gazing up at Mireille. "This was…nice."

Mireille smiled, one of those rare genuine ones that lit up her whole face. She was unearthly beautiful. Cassandra understood why Ronin had never gotten over her. "I agree."

Cassandra climbed out of the tub, shaking out her feathers.

Mireille handed her a towel. "But next time we do this, I'm going to need a *lot* more intricate details about *your* sex life."

Cassandra laughed, wrapping herself up in the plush towel and wiping down her limbs.

And for the first time in the High Gods knew how long, she could actually feel some of her burden lifting.

Maybe this was the help that the Goddess had intended for Mireille to give her after all.

A friend to offer some gentle laughter on a rough day.

CHAPTER
FORTY-THREE

"I CAN'T BELIEVE I LET you talk me into this," Cael grumbled, leaning against the back of a leather couch in the Stoneridge library.

Xenia dusted off the shoulders of his pine green jacket. "Come on, pterodactyl. How hard could it possibly be to spend an afternoon reading love poems to your fiancée?"

"*Love* poems?" Cael groaned. "Since when was that part of the plan?"

"You need to get close enough to swipe the necklace without her noticing. And how do you expect to do that unless she's a pool of melted butter in your lap?"

Cael narrowed his eyes. "You are alarmingly okay with this."

Xenia shrugged. "I'm not above using your dashing good looks and charm to get us the intel we need."

"And what if *I* am?"

She smiled, baring her cute, blunt teeth. He wanted to feel them on his skin. "Then you'll stoop to my level. Because we have no other choice."

"Don't we?" He moved in as close as he dared without touching her. There were a few other patrons scattered about the hall, not close enough to hear their conversation but close enough to read their body language. "We could always, I don't know, do what I suggested in the first place and *ignore* this little side quest? I fail to see how opening that box will help us get the tracking device out of your neck or figure out how my father ensnared the dragon?"

She shook her head, her curls wafting her sweet, orange blossom scent and his cock twitched in his pants. He woke up to that scent each morning and it lingered long after they parted. Having her in his bed every night was torture. Pure, blissful torture.

"I'm working on that," Xenia promised. "I've only read through about three-quarters of the literature in here on your father's history. I plan to spend the entire day today searching through the rest. We're close, Cael, I can *feel* it. Just like I can *feel* Elodie is hiding something. I walked past the dining hall the other day and she was standing in there staring at those stuffed animal heads on the wall. Like she was hypnotized. Who does that? I've seen her skulking around the library, too. She startles every time I turn the corner and catch her. And remember how I caught her walking into your father's office? What if *she's* the one who's been feeding intel on the rebels to the Emperor?"

He let out a long sigh, and even though he suspected this was a time-wasting distraction—if Elodie wanted intel on the rebels, there were certainly better places to find it than Stoneridge—he was helpless to deny Xenia anything. A small part of him maybe even agreed with her.

Elodie's behavior did sound odd. And if the contents of that box could illuminate her motives, perhaps it was worth a try.

Besides, if there *was* something damning in there, maybe Cael could use it as leverage to get his father to call off the whole damn thing.

Xenia straightened his lapels, then gestured to a stack of thin volumes on the table.

He plucked up the top one. "*Odes on the Seasons of Love?*" He frowned. "I think you're seriously overestimating my acting skills if you think I'll be able to get through this drivel."

Xenia placed her hands on her hips, glaring adorably. "Laetitius is one of the most celebrated wordsmiths in all of Ethyrios. He was the official poet for the Imperial Court for centuries until he passed. Only an uncultured beast would call his work *drivel.*"

Cael laughed despite himself, unable to resist when she sassed him. He lowered his voice, using the tone he knew worked best to tame her. "You like that I'm an uncultured beast."

She stared at his lips, sinking her teeth into her own. "That. Right there. That's the voice you need to use on Elodie. Don't forget the goal—pool of melted butter in your lap."

He chuckled. "All business today?"

"No distractions. I've got my eyes on the prize. The *real* prize."

"Which is what?" he asked, unable to drop his smile. Happened a lot when she was around.

"You and me, far away from Stoneridge," she whispered, sending heat down his spine. "So you can finally show me exactly how uncultured and beastly you can be."

He nearly snarled with desire, had to shove his hands into his pockets to keep from bending her over the back of the couch. "You know, a male might question why a female who claims to be interested in him is pushing him into the arms of another."

She cocked her head, surveying him with a knowing smirk. "You're in a playful mood today. The affirmations are helping, aren't they?"

He snickered, remembering the one she'd left for him this morning: *I am capable of achieving greatness.*

He still felt stupid saying them, but he'd promised her he would. And as crazy as it sounded, he *did* think they were helping bolster his mood.

But was it the affirmations? Or was it the daily proximity to the woman who'd provided them?

He grinned. "Not sure I would classify stealing a necklace from my fiancée as *greatness*, but we'll go with it."

"Good," Xenia said, just as the door to the library opened.

Elodie stepped in, her hazel eyes landing on Cael and Xenia as soon as she crossed the threshold. She frowned as she wended through the couches and armchairs. Xenia stepped aside, clasping her hands and bowing her head.

"What is *she* doing here?" Elodie sneered, curling her fingers into the skirt of her lemon yellow dress.

Cael lifted Elodie's hand and pressed a soft kiss to her knuckles. "She works in the library now, my darling. She was reassigned per your request. Stays hidden within the stacks all day so she doesn't bother anyone else with her incompetence."

Xenia, head still bowed, shot him a look out of the corner of her eye that said, *Asshole.*

He shot her one back that said, *You asked for this.*

Elodie's lip twisted as she raked her gaze down Xenia, who shrank further beneath it. "Doesn't explain why she's here talking to you." Cael fought the urge to growl at her. She raised her hand to her throat, running the tiny brass key along its chain and letting out a little huff.

Cael gestured to the poetry books. "She collected these for us. I thought we could read them together."

Elodie squealed with delight. "I *adore* Laetitius's work!" She placed a hand on his chest. "Oh, Cael, you know me so well already."

Xenia stiffened, shot him another look that said, *See?*

Cael tried not to roll his eyes as he addressed Elodie. "I look forward to getting to know you even better."

Xenia rolled *her* eyes at Elodie's giggle, and Cael bit back a laugh.

Elodie turned to Xenia, leaving a possessive hand on Cael's chest. "You're dismissed."

Xenia curtsied, then shuffled toward the stacks, leaving Cael with his preening fiancée and a pile of love poetry.

Stygios fucking *take* him.

But before she slunk into the aisles, Xenia turned back, gifted him one of her glorious, sunshine smiles and mouthed *I am capable of achieving greatness.*

He kept his face neutral, didn't want Elodie—who was still staring up at him—to read anything across his face. But he sent the thought toward Xenia anyway.

With you, I am.

It was much harder than Xenia had anticipated, trying to concentrate on all this boring historical literature knowing that just beyond these stacks, Cael was cooing sweet nothings into his fiancée's ear.

She hadn't checked on them.

Much.

She was the one who'd encouraged Cael to woo Elodie, after all. And she'd known without a shadow of doubt that Laetitius's romantic words read in Cael's deep, sultry voice could soften even the most hardened female.

But seeing the successful results of her scheming in the form of Elodie draped across Cael, cheeks flushed and eyes shining, had Xenia *seething* with envy.

She'd thought she'd seen Cael's dark gray gaze flick her way when she peeked out of the stacks, a tiny smirk curling his sculpted lips as she'd huffed and ran back to her own table.

She hadn't gone to check on them again. But the image was burned behind her eyelids.

How long did it take for someone to steal a necklace from a distracted female anyway? Surely, Cael could have done it by now.

Or was he *enjoying* his time with Elodie? Xenia knew how powerful Laetitius's words were. She'd read his poetry plenty of times, had swooned at the passion captured within the simple stanzas.

Maybe reading them aloud was causing Cael to feel the same. Maybe he was out there right now, staring down at Elodie's graceful Fae features and thinking to himself that he'd like to marry her after all.

"You're the one that caused this mess," Xenia grumbled. "Stop being so silly and *read*."

I am capable of achieving greatness, she thought to herself, taking a long, deep breath through her nose and pushing it back out through her mouth. *I am capable of achieving greatness.*

"All by myself and without the help of an uncultured beast with adorably floppy hair and the voice of a sinful god," she muttered.

Then laughed at herself. She was being utterly, *utterly* ridiculous. She *knew* Cael. Knew him in a way that Elodie never would.

Unless…

Unless their plans failed.

It was that thought that allowed Xenia to push her jealousy aside and focus on the task in front of her.

She'd just finished reading through the last book in her current pile and hadn't found anything useful, so she decided to peruse the shelves. She kept her gaze carefully *away* from the reading couches and the couple entangled there.

The library was well organized, topics arranged by floor. Fiction on the top, history, religion, and folklore on the second. The sciences—engineering, biology, chemistry, magical arts, and mathematics—made up the main floor stacks.

She'd already searched the history and folklore shelves. Maybe she could find something in the engineering and magical arts sections. The dragon was used to craft weapons, after all.

She strolled the silent aisles, examining titles. Many were written in Aramaelish—Xenia had a passing understanding of the language thanks to her studies at the Temple—but she was surprised to see many in the common tongue as well.

As she passed a section on battle strategy and fighting techniques, her heart squeezed. What was Cassandra enduring in Tartarus? Xenia cursed every corny joke she'd ever made about the prison back when Cass was performing robberies in Thalenn. Cassandra Fortin was the strongest, bravest person Xenia had ever known. She had faith that her friend would survive.

Xenia had always believed that when one was uncertain of a future outcome, it was best to assume the most positive one.

She held onto that hope as she left the section, and an awareness prickled at the back of her neck.

Someone was watching her.

She pivoted, but the aisle was empty. She gazed through a row of books into the next aisle, but it was similarly unoccupied.

She shrugged off the prickly sensation, continuing her review of the titles. When she came to the end of aisle, she turned and slammed into a hard body.

"Careful, little human," Erik smirked, placing a steadying hand at her hip before crunching his fangs into a ripe green pear. "You never know who you might run into in here." His jaw worked as he chewed, juice shining on his full lips. "You looking for something in particular?"

Xenia's chest constricted. She couldn't get a read on Erik. He'd seemed kind the other night when he'd found her outside Arran's office. But he'd also seen Cael marching Xenia toward his bedroom the other day. The

High Gods only knew what assumptions Erik had made about *that*. Best to be careful around him.

"Not looking for anything. Just…taking a stroll."

Erik regarded her with a bemused expression as she cleared her throat and rubbed at her neck. The movement drew his attention to her scar. He brushed her hand away, then trailed light fingers across it. Goosebumps pebbled across her skin. He was just as handsome as Cael, and Xenia couldn't help her reaction. When an attractive, powerful Fae male touched one's throat, it was hard to *not* have a reaction.

"Such a barbaric practice," Erik muttered, taking another bite of his pear. "Does it hurt?"

"Not anymore. Though I'm not sure why you would care? You don't know me. And I'm a *human*. Your father has made it quite clear what he thinks of us."

Erik smirked again, offering her a bite of his pear which she waved away. He shrugged, then lowered his voice. "Not everyone in this household shares my father's disdain for your kind. Though I will admit, I certainly thought my brother did."

From the gleam in his chocolate eyes, she knew precisely which brother he was talking about.

Xenia held his penetrating gaze, aware that he could hear her accelerating heartbeat. "He's been nothing but indifferent toward me. Not sure why you would assume otherwise."

"Do you know that I intercepted the most interesting letter today? It was from Ohan Stolia. And it was addressed to Cael, of all people."

Xenia's stomach plummeted, but she tried to keep the shock off her face. "Oh?"

"It's a good thing I found it before my father had a chance to pry it open." Erik finished off his pear, then sent the core floating on a gust of wind toward a trash bin at the end of the aisle. "It mentioned that Cael had lost something in Rhamnos. And that Ohan had orchestrated its return to him. I wonder what he was referring to?" He grabbed her hand with sticky fingers. "Come. I want to show you something."

Xenia barely had a chance to protest before Erik dragged her past the stacks and into a dim corner between two shelves.

Erik muttered something, words Xenia didn't recognize. Not Aramaelish, and certainly not the common tongue.

A plain wooden door with a brass handle materialized in the bare wall, and Xenia emitted a tiny gasp.

"Concealment spell. My father thinks he's the only one who knows the incantation, but he underestimates just how sneaky his waste of a fourth son can be when he puts his mind to it." Erik winked, then pressed the tab atop the handle and opened the door. "Have fun in there, little human." He leaned down to whisper in her ear. "If I were you, I'd start with my father's journals. Enlightening stuff." He dipped his fingertips under her shirt sleeve, tapping on her hidden cuff. "Call me on this when you're done and I'll come let you out."

Xenia pulled her head back, searching Erik's gaze for any hint of why in Ethyrios he was helping her. "Why would you show this to me?"

"I've seen the way he looks at you," Erik said, softly. Wistfully. "As if you're the warmest ray of light parting the clouds of his lifelong gloom." He nodded toward the open door. "My brother could use some sunshine."

She turned toward Erik, but he was already gone. She'd barely felt him move.

Xenia took a deep breath, then crossed the threshold into the hidden section of the Zephyrus family library.

And after several hours of pouring through Arran's journals, Xenia could say two things with absolute certainty.

First, they were just as enlightening as Erik had claimed.

And second, Cael and Xenia were going to need a *miracle* to have any chance of freeing that dragon.

CHAPTER
FORTY-FOUR

"So, how did your research go today?" Cael asked, holding a glass of whiskey on his knee. A crackling fire warmed his room, enough that Cael had shed his jacket and left the top few buttons of his shirt undone.

Xenia froze at his question, nibbling her shortbread biscuit. Even his distractingly handsome presence—the tiny sliver of muscular chest, the messy hair, the relaxed smile—couldn't chase away her disappointment at what she'd learned in that hidden room.

"How did *your* research go?" she asked, trying—and failing—not to sound as petulant as she felt over his afternoon with Elodie.

Cael smirked, then took a sip of his whiskey. "Do I detect a hint of jealousy? From the unflappably positive Xenia Cirillo?"

She scoffed, then choked on biscuit dust and waved him off, coughing.

Real smooth, Cirillo.

"May I remind you," he purred, "and I quote '*I'm not above using your dashing good looks and charm to get us the intel we need.*' Those were your exact words, if I remember correctly."

"Did it work?"

He pulled something from his pocket, then held up his hand. Xenia's heart leapt as a chain unfurled below his fingers. "I am capable of achieving greatness."

She crowed a victorious laugh that dissolved when she noted the material the key was made from. Tin, not brass. "Is that the right key?"

"I had one of the stablehands make a copy for me, then 'found' the real one on the floor at Elodie's feet during dinner. She was so grateful, she nearly mounted me at the table."

"Gross," Xenia sneered, then reached for the key.

He curled his fist around it. "I'm not sure if I should give you this."

"Why not?" An indignant squeak.

He leaned forward, brows furrowed over storm-cloud eyes. "Because I don't trust that you won't go dashing to Elodie's room this very second to open that box."

"Come on. I'm not *that* stupid."

"I would *never* call you stupid. Recklessly impulsive. Maybe delusionally optimistic. But never stupid."

She crossed her arms and leaned back in her chair. "I'm not sure either of those are better."

"Elodie has fittings all next week for her wedding dress," Cael said, the words slicing past Xenia's ribs. "She'll be in downtown Diachre every day. You can go then. But *only* then. Don't try anything beforehand."

"I *won't*," she said, reaching out her hand.

He tossed her the key, and she slipped it into the pocket of her cardigan before returning to the biscuits. "So how many poems did it take before she was distracted enough for you to grab it?"

Cael lowered his voice to the octave that inflamed her blood. "She was putty in my hands from line one."

Xenia huffed. "Well, how fortunate for you to learn you have a skill to tame your future wife."

Cael snickered, not taking the bait. "Recklessly impulsive. Delusionally optimistic. And a complete and utter fool." Xenia recaptured his gaze and the look on his face was the softest she'd ever seen it. "Especially if you think for one minute that I would choose to share my *skills* with anyone other than you."

Her jealousy melted away, leaving something warm and frothy in its wake. At least until the reality of their situation frosted over it.

"But that's the problem," she whispered. "You may not *have* a choice. And after what I learned today..."

Cael pushed a hand through his strands, spreading his legs as he slumped in his chair. "Do I want to know?"

Xenia shook her head, rolling her lips together. "I found the piece of information we were looking for. The other thing, besides the flute, that your father used to summon the dragon. And how he's been controlling her since."

"What?"

"He's the only person in Ethyrios who knows the dragon's true name."

Cael rocked back against his chair, his limbs going numb. "The *only* person in all of Ethyrios?"

"Well, it depends on what you consider Ethyrios."

"What does that mean?"

"There is someone else who knows it. But he's been locked away in Tartarus ever since your father pried the dragon's name from him and used her to slaughter his people."

The information clicked together in Cael's mind. "Aedelmar Burkhardt, the leader of the Cynn Drakan."

Xenia offered him a wan smile. "Glad *someone's* been paying attention."

"How did my father get the name from him? I can't imagine Burkhardt just gave it to him willingly."

Xenia raised her palms. "There were no specifics within the journal, just the date when it occurred."

Cael perked up a bit. "Was the name in there?"

Xenia shot him a glare, like *Duh*. He nearly chuckled at the sight of it. Xenia was the rare human who was wholly unafraid of him. He loved it. "I wonder if Leonard knows it."

"Who?"

"Leonard. He's the dragon's main caretaker. Has been since the war."

Xenia cocked her head. "I doubt Arran would have been that careless."

"Why do you say that?"

"Once Arran used the flute and uttered the dragon's name, a powerful bond was created between them. One that's kept the dragon within his thrall for centuries. Do you think…" Xenia hesitated. "Could you ask your father for it?"

Cael snorted an incredulous laugh. "And what do you think his first question would be? He'd want to know how I even knew to ask in the first place. Then he'd want to know *why* I want to know. Can you come up with any possible reason—other than me trying to steal the dragon from right under his nose—why I would be asking?"

"Professional curiosity? You *have* been visiting the mountain a lot. You could say you want to know for when you eventually take over the business?"

"No way," Cael said, shaking his head. "It's too big of a risk. We'll need to find the name some other way."

Xenia scoffed. "What, like break into Tartarus to ask Aedelmar Burkhardt?"

Cael smiled slyly. "Well, *I'm* certainly not going to. But I know someone who might be desperate enough to try."

"Tristan?" Xenia blurted. "How would he even get in? And even if he could, how would he get back *out* to tell us the name?"

Cael rested his chin on his knuckles. "I don't know. I'll talk to him about it when I see him tomorrow. In the meantime, keep searching my father's journals. Maybe there's some kind of hint about the dragon's name. I'll ask Leonard as well."

Xenia nodded slowly, her thoughtful gaze glued to the fire.

"What are you thinking about?" he asked.

She grazed her fingers along the scar on her neck. "Nothing, I..." She sucked in a breath. "This just all seems so...*hopeless*."

He couldn't stomach the despair in Xenia's voice, a tone he hadn't heard there in...well, *ever*. She was supposed to be the effortlessly positive one. The one who always saw the silver lining, no matter how bleak the situation.

And before she'd barreled back into his life, he might have even let her despair drag him down as well.

But his bucket of positivity was well and truly full, thanks to her sunny presence. And he was determined to do for her what she'd done for him.

Drag her back toward the light.

By any means necessary.

Xenia hadn't felt this despondent in...well, *ever*. Every piece of information she uncovered just led to more mysteries. And they only had a little over two weeks until Cael would be taken away from her forever.

And she would be stuck here. In this lodge. With Arran.

And Tomas.

Her breathing went shallow, but before she could give in to the impending panic, Cael strode over to the bed and pulled a thin volume from underneath his rumpled jacket.

She recognized the gold-embossed title instantly.

Odes on the Seasons of Love. By Laetitius.

A small smile crept onto her face as Cael settled into his chair, spreading his legs wide.

She cocked an eyebrow and he chuckled. "What? I tortured myself with this shit all afternoon. Now it's *your* turn." He ran his fingers along the cloth cover. "Do you know why my performance with Elodie this afternoon was so convincing? Convincing enough that she didn't notice me slipping off her necklace?"

"Why?" Xenia asked, her breath trapped in her throat.

Cael tilted his head down, peering at her through his dark lashes. A rare, toe-curling appearance from shy Cael. "Because I was thinking about you."

Warmth prickled across Xenia's limbs, settling between her thighs.

"Come over here," he whispered, patting his knee, "and take off your cardigan."

She obeyed, perching herself in his lap and nestling her head against his shoulder. His arms encircled her as he flipped through the pages, then held the book open with one hand as he placed the other at her hip, rubbing in idle, soothing circles.

Her eyes slid closed as Cael began to read.

"She is the summer storm that drenches parched fields.

"Her love is relief.

"She is the autumn wind that strips away dried death.

"Her love is remedy.

"She is the winter snow that shields barren land.

"Her love is protection.

"She is the spring sun that coaxes fledgling green.

"Her love is renewal.

"All the seasons of my heart, from coldest stone to warmest growth,

"Belong to you, and you alone.

"My lady. My love."

Lulled by the silky cadence of Cael's voice and the beauty of the poem, Xenia laid against him and matched his breathing. In this moment, she didn't care where they were or what danger they were in or what lay ahead of them.

All that mattered was that she'd found her way back to him. And had somehow helped him find a way back to himself. Despite everything, the Cael she'd known these past weeks had been light, upbeat. Teasing, even. She hadn't even broached the subject of his missing wing.

But maybe she'd never needed to. Maybe just showing up here, having risked her life and her safety, had proven to him what she'd always known. That he was worth something. Worth *everything*. If only to her.

Was it enough? To be everything to just one single person? She knew it was for her.

But she'd never dared hope that it would be enough for him, too.

He closed the book and placed it on the table, then turned her in his lap to face him. Her thighs parted around his as he wrapped an arm around her waist and tangled his fingers through her curls.

She placed steadying hands on his firm chest and stared into his thundercloud eyes.

The side of his lip quirked up. "Did my performance pass muster?"

Her own rose in response. "I suppose it will do."

"Cruel little human." He tugged on her hair, a reprimand. "Laetitius certainly does have a way with words, though. Said it better than I ever could." His eyes bounced between hers, their faces close enough that she could taste the wind on his breath. "I've wanted you since the moment you flung this finger in my face and called me a pterodactyl." She laughed as he plucked up the offending finger and placed a gentle kiss upon it. "But I'm a stubborn, foolish bastard, and it took me far, *far* too long to admit it. After I lost my wing—"

"You don't have to—"

"No, let me finish. After I lost my wing, I convinced myself that I wasn't good enough for you. That you deserved more than a broken male. And when you kept needling me to talk about it, you played right into my assumptions. I thought you were trying to *fix* me.

And I couldn't bear the thought of disappointing you. But I think...I think I've finally realized that you weren't trying to fix me at all. You were just trying to show me that I was worthy of love and acceptance. Broken pieces and all." He brushed a strand of hair behind Xenia's ear, his fingers trailing over her scar. "I *will* find a way to get this out of you, Xenia. And afterwards, you're *mine*. Where I go, you go. I will never leave you again."

She surged against him, kissing him so fiercely she nearly tore her lower lip open on his fangs. His rumbling groan lit up her entire lower body, and she rocked her hips against his growing hardness. Weaving her fingers into the soft waves at the base of his neck, she pulled him closer. But not close enough. She wanted to consume him, to be consumed by him.

"Cael," she moaned as he kissed across her collarbone, "I want you so badly."

"I know, sweetheart," he whispered. "As soon as it's safe, you'll have *all* of me."

She grumbled a protest that he silenced by plunging his tongue into her mouth. She sucked it down greedily as he tucked his fingers into the straps of her chemise, then peeled them down slowly. His mouth was wet and impossibly warm as he swirled his tongue around an aching nipple, then bit down gently. She cried out, arching into him, and he caught her around the waist. He lifted her from his lap, then placed her down on the shaggy rug, nearly as warm from the fire as her heated skin. She laid back against it as Cael spread her thighs and knelt between her legs.

She reached up to fist his shirt. "Take this off. I want to look at you."

"Demanding," Cael smirked, pulling his shirt off and tossing it onto a chair.

Cael's reverent gaze crawled over her exposed flesh, her chemise bunched around her middle with nothing but her panties and stockings covering her lower half. She studied him as well—his lean, sculpted torso, his broad shoulders, those insane cuts of muscle that dipped below his waistband.

"Turn around," she whispered.

He cocked an eyebrow, and for a moment, she thought he was going to protest. But he merely closed his eyes, and turned, tucking his wing to avoid smacking her with it.

She sat upright, then began to rub his shoulders. He relaxed under her ministrations, moaning softly. An encouraging sign. She moved her hands lower.

Toward his scar.

She rubbed a tentative finger over it and he tensed.

"Xenia," he bit out. "You shouldn't—"

"Shh. It's okay."

He dipped his head forward, hanging it over his chest. "I haven't even looked at it since it happened."

Xenia used two fingers to caress the puckered skin, mimicking the movement with her other hand at his intact wing. Right where it met his shoulder blade. The most sensitive spot.

"*Fuck*, Blondie." Cael's breath went ragged as Xenia continued to stroke him.

"Do you want to know what I see when I look upon this scar, Cael?"

"If I say no, I suspect you'll tell me anyway," he chuckled, and she removed her fingers from his wing. "Wait, don't stop. You can tell me whatever you want as long as you keep touching me there."

She huffed a small laugh, then stroked her fingers down his wing and scar again. His responding moan was so addictive she wanted to inject it into her veins.

"I see bravery," she said. "I see the male who butchered my captors. The male who rescued me. The male who healed my wounds and made me feel safe."

She stroked her fingers harder, faster, trying to form the connection in Cael's mind and body—the damaged part just as capable of bringing him immense pleasure. His muscles tensed and his breathing grew ragged.

"I see the male who is *everything* to me. A male who is not nearly as broken as he thinks he is." She pressed her breasts against his back, then tucked her chin over his shoulder to whisper in his ear, "I see the male who makes me come hard enough to see stars."

Cael's restraint snapped. Snarling, he turned, then speared his hand into her hair and fused their mouths together. He pressed her back down onto the rug, curving over her and settling between her thighs. He was hard as a fucking rock.

He twisted her panties in his fist and tore them clean off. She yelped, slightly from pain, but more from delight at Cael's base, feral state. And the knowledge that *she* had brought him there.

He thrust against her, running the hard length behind his thin black pants up through her soaked core and along her swollen clit. He peppered her jaw, her neck, her breasts with kisses, nibbling softly with his fangs. His rough hands mapped her body, holding her against him as he stroked her with his cock.

"You're fucking soaked," he breathed around a nipple. "Is that all for me?"

She arched upward, shoving her chest toward his mouth. "The poetry helped."

He laughed, then clamped down on her breast nearly hard enough to break skin as he drove his hips into her harder.

"*Taste.*" The word was a guttural, primitive growl, but she knew what he meant. She dipped her hands between their bodies, pushing into herself, then brought her fingers to Cael's lips.

It was simultaneously too much and not enough. His cock grinding against her clit, his slick tongue sliding between her fingers, the weight of his powerful body crushing her into the rug.

His muscles tensed, his grunts accelerated, and she could tell he was close.

"Come with me," he commanded when she removed her fingers from his mouth, then wrapped her arms around him, stroking his scar and wing in tandem again.

"Yes," was the last word she managed to say as Cael drove against her, a final, mighty thrust, and her body broke into scintillating shivers of heat. She sank her teeth into his shoulder, screaming his name against his sweat-slick skin as he came apart with a shuddering groan, his release soaking through his pants. He gazed down at her, his fangs glinting between parted lips as he fought to catch his breath.

He rolled onto his back and dragged her on top of him. "Holy fucking High Gods, if I don't get to do that for real soon, I might die." He tangled his fingers through her curls, kissing the top of her head.

"Dramatic," she said, then yelped when he nipped her earlobe.

"Promise me," he whispered.

"Promise you what?" She nuzzled in closer, aftershocks of her orgasm quivering her thighs.

"Promise me you didn't just do all that because you pity me. That you're not with me because you're trying to *fix* me."

Xenia's heart constricted. He was such a fool. She didn't know how he could even *think* that.

She pushed up onto an elbow and poured every ounce of sincerity she could muster into her gaze. "Cael. There's only one reason I'm with you." She trailed her hand up his thigh, finding him still half-hard beneath her fingers. "Your enormous coc—"

He rolled back on top of her, laughing and biting her neck.

There was so much more she could have said. But she didn't want to spoil this moment of peace. This calm eye in the storm of their circumstances.

But as Cael rolled over and tucked her against him, his breathing growing soft and shallow, Xenia thought to herself that even though she was his light, he was *her* light, too.

And that maybe, just maybe, he was starting to believe it.

CHAPTER
FORTY-FIVE

THE DOOR TO TRISTAN'S room creaked open and he turned from the window where he'd been watching Ione laughing and drinking with the rebels down by the clocktower.

They hadn't spoken since the Teles Chrysos leaders had met on the prophecy. In fact, tonight was the first night Tristan had spent in Lebaedia in four days. If Ione could tell he was stalling with his visit to Lodesvale to check on the displaced hospital patients—many of whom had finally begun to heal, thank the Creator— she hadn't pressed him on it.

"Thought maybe you could use an ear to bend." Trophonios flashed his white fangs and waved a bottle of Aguaver. "You left the other night before we had a chance to toast."

Tristan gestured to a canvas chair, encouraging Trophonios to sit. "What, exactly, were we supposed to be toasting?"

Trophonios crossed a long leg over his knee and thunked two tumblers onto the table. He poured several fingers of the translucent spirit into each glass, then handed one to Tristan and clinked it with his own.

"To uncertainty." His teal eyes twinkled. "A more powerful force than absolute knowledge."

Tristan lifted his glass, letting the liquid burn down his throat. It did little to soothe his jangled nerves and simmering anxiety. "I thought hearing the full prophecy would make me feel better. Would make me more sure of my next steps."

Trophonios regarded him carefully, resting his own tumbler on his knee. "And I'm guessing the exact opposite occurred."

Tristan nodded, picking at the feathers of the wing folded over his lap. "It doesn't seem the other leaders agree. Especially not Ione."

"You must not judge her too harshly. When one has been walking a path for as long as she has, it's difficult to notice it branching."

Tristan's ears perked up. "So you don't agree with her then? That she and I are fated to one another? Supposed to unite the territories under our rule?"

"I maintain precisely what I said in that room. That what those words actually mean matters little if we cannot all agree on their interpretation."

Tristan took another sip of aguaver. "So if I disagree, our cause is doomed. Is that what you're saying?"

Trophonios put down his glass, then folded his hands in his lap. "Allow me to tell you the story of another male, a younger male, who was so certain of his own decision that he was blind to the consequences.

"The day I worked out the formula for Delirium was simultaneously the best and worst day of my life. Though I didn't realize it was the worst until much, much later. Willem tried to warn me, but—"

"Willem?" Tristan asked. He'd never heard Trophonios mention the name before.

"My husband." A sad smile crept across Trophonios's face. "My conscience."

"What happened to him?"

"The same fate that awaits us all, Creator willing," Trophonios murmured. "A peaceful goodbye at the end of a long, well-lived life." He cleared his throat and continued, "But decades before that, he was the sole individual whispering in my ear that Delirium may *not* be the miraculous solution that I thought it was. I couldn't be bothered to listen, of course. The arrogance of youth, and all that.

"No, I *alone* would fix what was broken in the world. I would facilitate peace between the species. End all the senseless killing of humans during emotion feedings and their violent retaliations. I thought surely, once the human and Fae leaders discovered what I'd achieved, that if each side gave just a little bit, we could share this world as Adelphinae intended."

Trophonios sat back, his attention drawn out the window by the buoyant laughter. "What I was *not* prepared for was Leonin Erabis using my invention to subjugate an entire species." Long-simmering anger filled Trophonios's eyes. "Your father forged my knowledge into the chains in which he bound the humans. And I was so blinded by my need to succeed, by the *certainty* of my path, that I failed to see what was right in front of me."

"And what was that?"

"That those with immense power will do anything to cling to it. And that abundance does not guarantee generosity. Willem was only smug about the whole thing for a year or two."

Tristan chuckled softly before his brows furrowed. "But you must not believe *all* leaders are like that? Otherwise, what are we fighting for?"

"No, Prince. I do not believe all leaders are like that. In fact, it's those who crave power the least that often wield it best."

"If you're talking about me—"

Trophonios huffed a genial laugh. "Of course I'm talking about you. This whole speech was intended for you. Didn't think I could have made that any more obvious."

Tristan echoed the laughter, holding out his empty tumbler for another round. "What makes you think I don't want to be a leader?"

Trophonios shook his head. "It's not that I think you don't want it. It's that I can tell it's a burden you wish to share. Leonin, for all his faults, was similar. Had a team of advisers whose counsel he sought regularly. Unfortunately, a few spoke in poisonous tongues and your father, swayed by their loyalty, often went along with them."

"You speak as if you knew him well," Tristan said, not without a hint of heartache. But whatever filial affection he'd held for his father had been blasted apart by his exile, leaving only hatred in its wake.

Trophonios continued. "I met him when he was a young leader during the war. A bit different than the male who sired you, one tainted by his own power and the greed of his Imperial court. There were two sides to him. It seems as though you've gotten his best qualities while your brother…" Trophonios trailed off, taking a thoughtful sip of his drink. "Power corrupts, is my point. Unless one has the proper checks and balances in place—and is willing to accept them."

Tristan sniffed. "And what makes you think I'm capable of that?"

Trophonios's eyes gleamed. "I knew it the moment I heard you'd Turned a human. To love across species signals an open heart. A willingness to accept *everyone* who populates this planet. Ione herself is evidence that you will be a great leader."

Tristan ran a hand through his hair. "How did you do it?"

"Do what?"

"Let go of the guilt. Stop being haunted by the unintended consequences of your decisions."

"You planning on making some bad decisions?" Trophonios smiled, then tapped his chest, right over his heart. "You do what you just said. You let it go. You forgive yourself. If you spend too much time fretting over the past, your future will never find you."

Tristan grimaced, pitching forward and resting his forearms on his knees. "I don't want to hurt Ione."

Trophonios nodded, swirling his tumbler against the table. "What would hurt her more? For you to reject her now, or for you to keep her eternally bound to a male whose heart yearns for another?"

Tristan pulled upright. "How could you possibly—"

"I've lived nearly seven centuries, Tristan. Heartache is an old friend."

Tristan sighed, collapsing back against his chair. "But if I don't choose Ione, this world fades into darkness. *A new Delphine will rise to light the way.* That's what the prophecy said."

Trophonios cocked an eyebrow at Tristan. "That may be what it said. But is that what it means?" Trophonios took a slow sip of his aguaver. "We learned much from the Compendium. Even more than we'd anticipated. We're still trying to discern how the wards were created. But we *have* learned how to dismantle them. There's a single substance on this planet that can do it. The same one that can deactivate that tracking device you brought me."

Hope stirred in Tristan's chest as he leaned forward, ensnared by the whisper that parted Trophonios's lips.

"Pure dragon-fire."

CHAPTER
FORTY-SIX

"Tell him what you told me," Tristan said, flaring his blue-black wings.

The midmorning light in the church ruins glimmered across his feathers and cast shadows in the folds of Nemosyna's marble robes.

Cael turned toward Trophonios—fucking *Trophonios himself*—and tried to keep the awe off of his face.

High Gods, he wished Xenia were here. The journals they'd poured through in Thalenn had showcased the ebony-skinned male's quick, exacting mind. Cael could only imagine the conversations Trophonios and Xenia might have together.

"Aedelmar Burkhardt," Cael began. "You know who he is?"

Trophonios sliced cunning teal eyes toward him. "The leader of the Cynn Drakan?"

Cael told Trophonios—and Tristan, who'd already heard this news via windwhisper this morning when Cael had arranged the meeting—about how Arran had kept the dragon captive all these years.

Trophonios's eyes had grown wider and wider as Cael spoke, and at the end of the tale, he turned to Tristan with a smirk. "Now I know why you wanted to come see him so badly."

Cael shot a confused look at Tristan, who spilled everything the Teles Chrysos had learned from the Compendium.

"This is all well and good," Cael said, "but even *if* you wanted to break into Tartarus to find Burkhardt— and Cassandra—how in Ethyrios do you hope to do it?"

Tristan pulled two lidded graphite crucibles from the pocket of his leather jacket.

"Do I even want to know what those are for?" Cael asked.

Tristan nodded. "You do. Because one of these is for you. Dragon-fire is the solution to both our problems. It will allow me to temporarily breach the wards of Tartarus *and* will help you de-activate the tracking device in Xenia's neck."

Hope blazed bright in Cael's heart, then dimmed slightly. "Will it hurt her?"

"Badly," Trophonios grimaced. "But if you share some of your blood, she'll survive it."

Cael smiled—a broad, goofy grin. He couldn't help it. They could remove the device. And Xenia would survive. They could finally escape Stoneridge.

Together.

He could still feel her soft, delicate fingers stroking his wing, could feel her lips and teeth at his neck as her perfect body shuddered beneath him. An imitation of the act he'd been waiting to perform with her since, well, since he'd met her, if he were being honest.

"So," he said to Tristan, "what's the plan?"

Cael sat before the rusted metal desk in Leonard's office, the two crucibles heavy in his pocket.

The two males were sharing a simple lunch—cold meats, cheese and bread, plus mugs of ale. It had become something of a routine for them. Every time Cael visited Typhon Mountain, he'd meet with the administrative staff first, then tour the forges, then spend the afternoon with Leonard and the dragon.

Outside Leonard's office, the keepers sat along the cave wall eating their own lunch, their shouted conversations mingling with the clang of the forges. In the center of the pit, the dragon rested, smoke puffing from her nostrils with each exhale.

"So," Cael said, breaking off a piece of cheese and popping it into his mouth. Trying to seem casual, though his palms were clammy and his voice was tight. If Leonard noticed, he didn't say anything. "Tell me more about how you came to be the dragon's caretaker. How did you meet my father?"

Cael thought if he asked about Leonard's history, he might be able to lead him toward the subject of freeing the dragon. It was an insane thought, but something about the chats they'd had these past weeks told him it wasn't completely off the table. But he didn't want to press the issue too quickly. Wanted to ease the old Beastrunner into it.

Leonard sipped his beer, froth catching in his white moustache. "Fought with him during the war." Pride brightened his wrinkled face. "In every single battle leading up to that final one in Akti, after he'd summoned her. I was the only of his commanders brave enough to help him care for the beauty." He huffed out a laugh, then leaned in for a conspiratorial whisper. "Don't tell him, but I think she's always liked me better."

Cael chuckled. "No offense, but that's not a hard contest to win." He flared his sole wing, and Leonard's sympathetic glance passed over it. Cael still hadn't corrected Leonard's assumption that he'd lost the wing to Arran. Nor would he do it today. His plans hinged on exploiting the lingering animosity between Leonard and his father. "Why did you stay with him after the war? Didn't you have family to get back to?"

"Nah." Leonard waved knobby knuckles. "*She's* my family. And she needed an advocate. No one else was clamoring for the job." Affection crinkled the corners of Leonard's eyes as he gazed out to the pit floor.

Cael's heart squeezed. If he achieved his goal, was able to bond with the dragon, he'd be stealing Leonard's family. His *purpose*. And though Cael felt guilty about that, a part of him wondered if Leonard wouldn't welcome such an outcome.

"How has my father been able to control her all these years?" Cael asked, as nonchalantly as possible. "I've always wondered. He's never talked to us about it."

Leonard quirked a bushy, skeptical brow. Cael kept his own expression neutral, then tried to fake a semblance of surprise when Leonard confirmed everything he already knew. "Emperor Leonin gifted him a relic that he used to summon her from deep within the mountain. A flute, imbued with the power of the Fallen Goddess. Heck of a show, that."

"You were there when it happened?"

Leonard nodded. "Thought the mountain itself was going to crumble to dust. Half the forges were destroyed when she burst through the rock that day." Awe stole across Leonard's ancient features. "Never saw anything so beautiful or magnificent in my life. All those shimmering white scales, wings that spanned nearly the entire cave."

"So, Arran summoned her using the flute, and then what?"

Leonard frowned. "He whispered something into his palm and sent the gust toward her. I could see the fight leave her body. After that, she obeyed any order he gave. Like he'd woven some kind of spell over her."

"Did he ever reveal it to you?" Cael asked. "What he'd whispered?"

Leonard shifted, uncomfortable with the question.

Cael placed his forearms on the table. "I would never tell Arran any of this, you know. I appreciate everything you've shared with me on these visits. I feel a kinship with her. I know what it's like to wish for the sky." Leonard softened at the wistful look on Cael's face. "I can't help but wonder if there isn't some way to free her."

Leonard shook his head sadly. "Oh, lad. If there was any way, I would have done so myself *centuries* ago."

If there was any better segue, Cael hadn't heard it.

Time to reveal his hand.

What other choice did he have?

"What if I told you there *was* a way?" Cael glanced toward the pit. The keepers were chattering amongst themselves, none paying a lick of attention to Leonard and Cael. He pulled the flute from under his shirt and laid it upon the table.

To Leonard's credit, he didn't make a single sound. But he did go preternaturally still. Whiskers unfurled at his cheeks, tangling in his beard and twitching. As if he were sniffing the relic.

"Where...where in Ethyrios did you get that?" A croaked whisper.

Cael told Leonard everything. About how the Teles Chrysos had given him the flute and assigned him this mission. About the dragon's name and how they intended to learn it. About their desire to use her to take back Delos from Eamon Erabis and install his brother Tristan—the rightful heir—on the Crystal Throne.

Leonard twisted his whiskers, contemplative.

Cael leaned back in his chair. "I don't think I need to tell you how much I've just risked to share all this with you. And I wouldn't have done so if it wasn't vitally important. *Everything* is at stake here. Not only the dragon's freedom, but the survival of our world. Males like my father, like Eamon Erabis, have been hoarding power for far too long. It's time us broken, scarred misfits had a chance to rise up, don't you think?"

Cael held his breath as he waited for Leonard to say something, *anything*.

The old Beastrunner swiveled his attention toward the dragon, his lips quirking up into a sly smile. "To the misfits. Long may you reign."

Cael closed his eyes, exhaling a long, relieved sigh.

"I wish I knew her name," Leonard said apologetically. "I'll do everything in my power to help you free her if you're able to learn it."

Out in the pit, the dragon awakened, and the keepers gathered around her for the afternoon session, readying their rods.

Cael turned back to Leonard. "Thank y—"

A strident cry rumbled through the cave. Not a roar. A wail of agony.

Leonard burst from his seat, his knees knocking the desk and rattling their mugs. He rushed out into the pit, Cael on his heels.

The dragon lay on her side, nosing at her belly and straining against her chains as she tried to shield herself with her wings. Her goopy, iridescent blood pooled out beneath her.

Icy rage frosted Cael's veins as the keepers laughed.

"What happened?" Leonard barked, his voice firmer and more authoritative than Cael had ever heard it.

One of the keepers turned, a Windrider male with fleshy charcoal wings and a braided mohawk. He held up a rod with an iridescent white scale the size of a dinner plate skewered on the end. "Sorry, boss. My aim was a little off."

Leonard fisted the male's shirt, fury distorting his features. And despite the keeper's height—a good eight inches, at least, above Leonard—he had the sense to look cowed. He raised his palms, and the rod clanged to the pit floor.

Leonard seethed, "How many *fucking* times have I told you to be more careful? That's the third scale you've pulled off this month. If it happens again, you're fired."

The keeper held Leonard's stare, jaw hardening, and his eyes flicked toward Cael. Likely worried about what Cael might say to his father.

"What does it matter?" the keeper grumbled. "She's a machine. She'd still breathe fire if we stripped off *all* her scales."

Leonard shoved the keeper in the chest. "Pick up your rod and get back into position."

The keeper grunted, but did as he was told. He plucked up his rod and wrenched off the scale, then tossed it aside as he retook his place in line.

Leonard turned to Cael, his hands trembling. "These keepers... Sometimes I think they forget she's a living, breathing being."

Cael pulled Leonard into a pocket of shadow. "I *will* learn her name and break the spell." He pulled the crucibles from his pocket. "But in order to achieve that, I'm going to need a few samples of her fire."

Leonard glanced at the graphite containers, then sauntered to a metal cabinet from which he grabbed a pair of long-handled pliers. "Take some when they prod her again. Do you need gloves?"

Cael shook his head, reiterating what Trophonios and Tristan had told him. "These containers keep the fire alive while the outside remains cool."

Leonard chuckled. "Do I even want to know where you got them?"

Cael smirked. "The less you know about the intricacies of our plan, the better."

Leonard clapped a hand on Cael's shoulder and squeezed. "Let me know what else I can do to help."

"I'll be in touch."

Cael took a position on the line between two keepers, placing both crucibles into the pliers. He eyed the dragon, swore he could feel her pain and anxiety as she awaited the next prod.

A plan coalesced in his mind.

Be ready. He sent the thought drifting toward her. Her muzzle twitched and her eyes cracked open, understanding glowing with them.

A keeper started a countdown, at the end of which the entire group poked the dragon with their rods.

She didn't roar this time, merely spewed a long jet of flame. Cael angled the pliers into the stream, then pulled them back, flicking the crucible lids closed to keep his samples secure.

The flames dissolved and the dragon slumped back down to the floor. But Cael could sense the tension priming her muscles.

She was waiting for his signal.

Cael gave Leonard a two-finger salute, then slipped the crucibles into his pocket. They were warm to the touch, but certainly not the skin-melting temperature of the seeds of dragon-fire now contained within.

Cael strode for the metal stairs, and as he passed the mohawked keeper, he stumbled into his back.

"Oof," Cael said, louder than necessary. "Sorry, mate."

"Watch yo—" The keeper turned, then bowed his head. "My fault, Master Zephyrus."

Cael looked down at the same moment the keeper did.

At the same moment the keeper realized he was well beyond the carved line.

"Oops," Cael whispered, flicking his gaze over the keeper's shoulder.

Pebbled lips pulled back from massive white teeth.

She'd moved so quietly, despite her chains.

Cael took to the stairs, his clomping footsteps silenced by screams as the dragon ripped the keeper apart.

CHAPTER
FORTY-SEVEN

ROPHONIOS'S WORKSHOP WAS SILENT, but not empty, as Tristan entered.

A lone figure bent over the Compendium at the far workbench, her tucked white wings glowing in the moonlight.

Tristan had just returned from Typhon Mountain, where Cael had slipped him a crucible full of dragon-fire. He'd known the instant he'd touched the warm graphite that his choice was made.

It took every ounce of his integrity to not portal straight to Tartarus.

But he needed to tell Ione first. In person. He owed her that much after all she'd done for him, for the rebellion.

A floorboard creaked beneath his foot and she turned, her honeyed hair sliding over a shoulder.

Her smile died when she met his gaze.

What expression was he wearing? He'd never been great at hiding his true feelings.

And right now, despite the difficult conversation ahead, effervescent joy and molten desire coursed through him at the thought of reuniting with Cassandra.

"Does Trophonios know you're playing with his toys?" Tristan asked, an attempt at lightness.

Ione didn't bite. Merely gestured to the seat across from her.

High Gods, why was this so strained? Why was *everything* between them so strained? As if the bond they'd shared in youth counted for nothing.

What a cruel trick of immortality—to age a friend slowly enough to mask centuries of change.

"I don't need the jokes and the small talk, Tristan." Ione rubbed her temples. "I can tell you've made your choice."

"I have," he said, taking his seat. Her hand lay on the table between them, but he didn't reach for it.

"*Born from phantom wings and mortal bones, a new Delphine will rise to light the way.* I don't think those words could have been any fucking clearer."

Tristan flinched. He hadn't heard Ione swear once since they'd been reunited.

"Delphine," he whispered. "Not Empress. You could be one and not the other."

Silence crackled between them, kinetic and combustible.

"Why do you want me?" he asked.

She jolted, her brows jumping. "I—"

"No, honestly. Why do you want *me*, specifically? Is it just because some Goddess says you should?"

She flattened her palms on the table, sneering. "Love is a luxury. One that people like us don't enjoy unless we're extremely lucky. We were, once. And we could be again if you'd just give us a chance. I've always known you were idealistic, but I never thought you'd be stupid enough to risk your people for some *woman*."

Tristan huffed out a bitter laugh, leaning back in his chair and crossing his arms. "Adelphinae's principles in action."

Ione's face went stony. "If you breach those wards and enter Tartarus, I cannot guarantee the Crystal Throne will be waiting for you when and if you're able to come back."

He sat up straight, looming above the table. "Are you *threatening* me?" He spoke in a low, powerful voice. A Prince's voice. An *Emperor's* voice. "It will be waiting for me because I am its true and rightful occupant. You may have built this movement, but you did so using *my* name. It would be very dangerous for you to forget that."

To her credit, Ione remained calm. Looked a little impressed, even.

"There's the leader we need," she whispered, resignation settling over her features. "So, what's your plan then?"

He pulled the crucible from his pocket. "I'll burn a temporary hole in the wards, slip into the prison, and get the dragon's name from Aedelmar Burkhardt."

Ione perked up. "If that's all we need, why can't someone else go? Send Layla. Or Seraavi. Why does it have to be *you*?"

"You know why," was all Tristan said. End of subject.

He told Ione the rest of what he, Cael, and Trophonios had discussed. That once Tristan learned the name, he'd pass it along to Cael via the cuff.

Trophonios had said the devices were far more powerful than regular commstones. Powerful enough to be used beyond the wards, though the connection might be spotty or difficult to achieve. And would likely only work to send a single communication.

Tristan had asked why the mentrite speck would work beyond the wards if the opal wouldn't, and Trophonios had answered that it was far easier to transfer sound waves than an entire body of flesh and bone.

Fair point.

"This still seems like a tremendous risk," Ione said. "If anything goes wrong, if you're not able to get the name from Aedelmar, or if the cuff fails, you're stuck in there. Maybe forever."

Tristan sent her a rueful smile. "Well in that case, I suppose it would be smart to have a plan B, wouldn't it?"

Tristan signaled through his cuff, and Trophonios entered the workshop.

To bear official witness.

Tristan took Ione's hand and led her toward the tall, elegant male.

"She doesn't look too angry." Trophonios grinned.

"Oh, she was furious a few minutes ago," Tristan said. "Cursed her head off. Threatened to steal my throne." Ione laughed as he turned to her. "But I'm hoping she'll make the same promise I made a few nights ago. To protect our people at all costs. No matter what happens to me in Tartarus."

Fierce determination shone in Ione's indigo eyes. "I will. Always."

Tristan nodded, relieved. He'd made this plan shortly after he'd heard the prophecy. A way to honor Ione's sacrifices and dedication in a manner that didn't require him to give her his heart. Which he didn't have the authority to give away, anyway.

It belonged to Cassandra.

"Ione Saros," he said, grasping her hands, "until I marry or produce an heir, I officially name you my successor. If I die before either of those events take place…"

He rested his palm upon her forehead, where her opal normally rested when she wore the Delphine's circlet.

"…then you shall be Empress of Ethyrios."

CHAPTER
FORTY-EIGHT

"I REALLY DON'T WANT TO give you the satisfaction, do-gooder, but High-Gods-damn, that feels nice."

Cassandra smiled softly as she rubbed healing salve into Ana's stiff ankle joints.

It was well-past midnight, the Kennel dark and quiet. She'd come with Silas again, but had sent him home a few minutes ago when she'd poked her head out the door and seen him sleeping against the wall.

Some lookout.

They'd been getting up earlier than normal to train for a few hours each day before Ronin and Mireille joined them. And the cost of her sleep was worth it; her balance, her aim, the force of her blows—they were all improving.

Before Cassandra had left tonight, Mireille had tried to convince her to stay home. With the appeal less than a week away, not to mention Mireille's performance at World's End tomorrow night, Cassandra shouldn't be risking exposure at the Kennel. There were plenty of other volunteers, so Mireille had said.

But none of those Fae had ever gotten through to Ana. And after several visits, the woman was finally opening up. Letting Cassandra deliver extra food. Letting Cassandra heal some of her chronic impairments.

Ana vented a contented sigh against the side of the cell as Cassandra's hands moved over her joints.

"So, what're you in for, then?" the old woman rasped.

Cassandra tried not to squeal with excitement. This was the first personal question Ana had ever asked her.

"You're going to laugh."

"Try me." Ana's eyes remained closed.

"I was arrested in the colonies," Cassandra said, not clarifying that she used to be human. She'd let Ana draw her own conclusions. "I used to hunt through people's memories, looking for things to steal and sell. Then I'd re-distribute the *drachas* to the poor. They called me the Savior Sister."

Ana grunted. "'Course they fucking did. And you ate it up, didn't you? Martyr."

Cassandra chuckled. "Why, what are you in for? Being a crotchety old bitch?"

Ana's wheezing laughter caused several humans in the neighboring cells to stir. "You're not far off." Her laughter died in her chest and her eyes danced with long-simmering anger. "I killed a Deathstalker. Down in Primarvia. Bastard had been following me for months. He tried to feed from me and wasn't he surprised when I poked him in the chest with a Typhon dagger. I was arrested the next day, then thrown in here. Ironic, really, since as soon as I arrived, I became the favorite meal of the Koenig and his Brethren." She ran a hand through her tangled hair, down her filthy dress. "They've since lost interest, praise Anaemos."

"How long have you been in here?" Cassandra asked, her heart in her throat.

Ana's rheumy eyes locked on Cassandra's. "Fifty-seven years. Since the day after my eighteenth birthday. Longer'n anyone else."

Cassandra choked back her horror, her sorrow.

Ana hobbled over to her bedroll, wrapping herself up in her threadbare blankets. "And Stygios willing, I won't make it to fifty-eight."

Cassandra didn't know what else to say. And she didn't think Ana would be pleased to hear what she *wanted* to say. That she shouldn't lose hope. That there was always something to live for.

She pushed the tub of salve through the bars. "Rub a pea-sized amount into each ankle morning and night. You should start to feel more permanent relief in a day or two."

Ana didn't answer as Cassandra brushed up from the floor, swiping away a useless tear.

Fifty-seven *years*.

She would get Ana out. She would get *all* of them out.

And then make sure no human was ever treated this way again.

She took some small comfort knowing that Tristan was still out there fighting for that dream. And though his absence hadn't become any easier to bear—nor had the thought of him fated to Ione—if that's what it took to change this world, then her scarred heart mattered little in the grand scheme of things.

She opened the door to the Kennel, distracted by her thoughts of revenge and revolution.

The Brethren was on her before she had a chance to run.

He grabbed her upper arms and slammed her against the door. The rough metal pulled at her feathers as she tried to fight back, use some of that new Fae strength she'd been honing with Ronin, Mireille, and Silas. But it was late, it had been a long day, and she'd been taken by surprise.

She recognized him: a Windrider with dark brown wings and shoulder-length blond hair. One of the Koenig's crueler Brethren. A feat in itself. He often had the youngest human females trembling in his lap when Cassandra had seen him around the city.

His rancid breath was hot against her cheek as he crowded her further against the door. "What are you doing in here, challenger?"

Cassandra snarled back, fear dissipating as she remembered he couldn't harm her, not really. Not thanks to the protection of her blood vow. "What does it look like?"

"These humans are *not* to be cared for without the Koenig's permission."

She gave him a smarmy smile. "And what are you going to do about it? You can't hurt me. Only the Koenig will have that privilege during my appeal."

His vicious smile caused her own to falter. "You should have listened more carefully to the words of that vow. No *Fae* within Tartarus can harm you."

He heaved her up over his shoulder, and her stomach dropped when he didn't turn up the main avenue that led to the castle.

Instead, he turned south.

To the city gate.

To the moat.

Cassandra scrambled backward, her feet slipping on the edge of the stone bridge. The waters of the moat were smooth onyx glass beneath her.

She knew they wouldn't be for long.

The Brethren—fuck, she didn't even know his name, couldn't curse it to the High Gods—was a solid wall at her back, gripping her shoulders and inching her forward.

"Someone should've done this weeks ago," he snarled into her ear. "The Koenig is too honorable to do it himself. He hews to the old ways. Not to mention, I think he actually *wants* to cut you down himself."

"You'd better let him," Cassandra growled, fighting against the ice-cold fear paralyzing her limbs. "If he finds out that you—"

He slapped a hand over her mouth. "Quiet, little pixie. They'll find you faster if they hear you. They're most active at night." He uncovered her mouth and placed his hands upon her back.

Then shoved her off the bridge.

Her body shut down when she plunged into the frigid water. She could no longer tell which way was up or down, could barely move her limbs. And she swore her wings were working against her, dragging her further into the depths.

She scrambled upward, aiming for the faint glow of the city lights above her. Breaching the surface, she hauled in a razor-sharp breath, then clenched her chattering teeth, treading as quietly as possible to stay afloat.

A loud clang thundered through the night—the iron portcullis falling into place. The Brethren saluted her through it, then turned and wandered back into the city.

Fucking *bastard*. If she left this moat intact, she would skin him ali—

A splash echoed to her left.

She whimpered. The wall of the moat was less than fifty feet in front of her. So close, yet so far.

She swiveled her head, then tried not to piss herself as a brown-and-green-scaled back crested the surface on the other side of the bridge.

It was moving.

Fast.

Far faster than she was capable of. Her heart stuttered and her lungs seized.

She took a nanosecond to calm herself—she would *not* go out like this. A snack for some mindless creature in the middle of fucking nowhere.

She hurled herself forward, arms flailing and legs kicking. Making an obscene amount of noise, but she didn't care. The creature had already homed in on her.

She needed to *move.* Her shoulders burned as she pulled her heavy wings through the water. If she could just make it to the wall—

Another wave crashed to her right and a second pair of reptilian eyes blinked above the surface.

Adrenaline flooded her veins in a tingling rush, and she surged forward.

Something brushed her foot and she screamed, swallowing a mouthful of brackish water. But she didn't pause, didn't turn, didn't look back.

She pushed harder, limbs straining, teeth gritted. Her vision was blurry, and she could barely feel her frost-bitten fingers and toes as she dragged them through the water.

One thought and one thought only blared through her mind.

Survive. Survive. Survive.

After what felt like an eternity, her hand cracked against stone, and she bleated a relieved cry.

The relief was short-lived; she turned to find the two beasts closing in and snapping their jaws. Taunting her. Toying with their food.

She swiveled around and pushed herself up, reaching for the top of the moat wall. Her fingers didn't even make it halfway.

A frustrated howl tore up her throat, and she glanced over her shoulder.

An open maw hurtled toward her, water sluicing between enormous, razor-sharp teeth.

Time slowed. She thrashed upward and for one heart-stopping second, the edges of her fingertips grazed the top of the wall.

Hope surged in her chest, then died a swift death as her fingers slipped. She splashed down into the water.

Pressing her wings against the wall, she froze as the beast's jaws raced closer.

And closer.

And *closer*.

So close she could smell its rotten breath, feel the warmth on her face.

She squeezed her eyes shut and sent three thoughts out into the ether.

One to Mama.

One to Xenia.

And one to Tristan.

Telling them all how much she loved them. How much they'd meant to her. She'd uttered the sentiment to Mama and Zee plenty of times.

But she'd never said it to Tristan.

He'd been about to say it before she was arrested, but she'd stopped him. And right now, as she waited to be eaten alive, she regretted it more than any decision she'd ever made.

She hoped he'd known. That she'd loved him all along.

A wave of water splashed her face, a surge from the approaching beast, and she braced herself for life-ending pain.

It never came.

Two strong hands curved beneath her armpits and wrested her from the moat. The beast's teeth closed onto the toe of her boot and yanked it from her foot.

Her heel dragged against the rough wall as she was pulled backwards and laid out on the cold ground. Her rescuer pushed wet strands from her face.

She opened her eyes, and the world fell silent.

She must have had died after all. She was in that beast's belly having some kind of post-death dream.

Because staring down at her, his amber eyes ablaze with fear and anger, was Tristan.

Tristan.

Her throat was raw, and she tried to speak, but only managed to cough up foul-smelling water.

Tristan's fear and anger turned to shock as his gaze snagged on her dirty white wings. He cupped her cheeks, a relieved smile brightening his handsome face, then choked out an incredulous laugh.

"Daredevil?"

Cassandra smiled back at him—or what she thought might be a smile, her senses too addled to truly tell—then beckoned him to lean in closer.

When he obliged, his lids sliding closed and his lips parting for a kiss, she pushed up onto an elbow.

And clocked him across the jaw.

CHAPTER
FORTY-NINE

TRISTAN RUBBED HIS ACHING chin, unable to corral his astonished laughter.

Cassandra was…

Holy fucking Creator.

She was *Fae*.

He'd always thought she was beautiful—the most beautiful woman he'd ever met.

Obviously, he'd never known the meaning of the word.

She was still Cass, still his Daredevil, but her facial features were slightly sharper, her pale skin glowing as if lit from within.

And those *wings*.

Even mud-caked and water-logged, they were stunning. Gorgeous, soft white feathers with a hint of rainbow iridescence.

As he gaped, she stood upright, cocking her arm back for another blow.

He laughed again, snatching her wrist and pulling her into him. She squirmed in his grip. He had no idea why she was trying to fight him, but he didn't care. And soon, his laughter dissolved into relieved tears.

She was here. *Alive.* In his arms.

She could beat him bloody and he'd beg for more contact.

"Let me *go*," she snarled against his chest.

"Cassandra," he exhaled, releasing her and stepping back. He raised his palms, trying not to melt into a puddle at her feet. She wore her fury like a crown. Wore it like a queen.

Like an *Empress*.

She lifted her fists, a proper fighter's stance—someone, likely Ronin, must have been training her—and his gaze snared on her biceps. She'd gotten stronger. Much stronger. She was all lean, lithe muscle, her body angled to deliver another punishing blow to his jaw. The first still smarted.

She was even holding her wings perfectly. Lifted slightly off her back, ready to strike out when needed. Tiny jolts of jealousy tingled through him that someone else had taught her to use them.

He smirked. "If I put my palms down, are you going to punch me again?"

"Probably," she growled, her brows pinched and her breathing heavy.

He shrugged, delighted. "And here I thought you'd be so thrilled to see me you'd fall into my arms and weep with joy."

"You'll be the one weeping as soon as I get my hands back on you."

"*Please* put your hands back on me."

She emitted a furious scream, then rushed for him, fists flying. He lowered his arms, didn't fight back as she landed a wicked jab to his stomach. He crumpled in half, his breath whooshing out.

She puffed out questions between each blow.

"Why did you come here?" *Punch.*

"You should be out there winning your throne!" *Jab.*

"With High-Gods-damned *Ione!*" *Cross. Cross. Uppercut.*

The strike knocked him off his feet, and he landed on his back, baring blood-stained teeth as he cackled with manic pride.

She leaned over him. "What the fuck is wrong with you?"

He shot up, then gathered her close and wrapped his wings around her, entwining their feathers. They fit perfectly. And the feel of them gliding together...

Holy *fuck.*

He pulled his hips back, didn't think she'd be happy to know how hard her thrashing had made him.

"How do you know about Ione?" he whispered against her hair as her angry breaths stuttered into choked sobs. He brushed a hand down her back, tucking her head under his chin.

She made to push out of his arms, but he held firm. "The Goddess showed me a vision of the two of you. *Kissing*. Ronin said… He said you're fated to her. That your union will save our world."

As grateful as Tristan was to Ronin for protecting Cassandra in here, his annoyance smothered it. Why would Ronin have filled her head with unconfirmed speculations?

He cupped her face and almost wept at the texture of her skin. So soft, so familiar. And the fire, the *vitality*, in her blue-gray eyes…

"Ione and I aren't… And now that you… I'll explain everything soon. I swear it. Including how I got here. But before you beat me with your tiny fists again—" she scoffed "—I need to say something to you." He stroked his thumb along her cheek. "Something I've been waiting to say since the day I lost you. I don't care what the prophecy says. I don't care what Ione thinks the Goddess wants for her and I. I don't care if choosing you means I'm damning this world to destruction.

"I love you, Cassandra."

She snorted out a wet laugh, her eyes shining. "Did you really get yourself locked behind the wards just to say that to me? You're a fool."

He chuckled, tucking a wet strand of hair behind her ear. "A fool for *you*. For eternity, remember?" He pulled aside the collar of her shirt, tracing an *M* with the tip of his tongue over his mark and whispering *unbreakable* against her skin. She shivered.

He barely had a moment to react before she looped her arms around his neck and captured his mouth.

The kiss was messy and urgent, a tangle of lips and tongues and teeth. Like they couldn't get close enough, couldn't touch each other fast enough. He ran his hands down her wet clothes, then breached the hem of her shirt. He groaned into her mouth as his fingertips coasted over her naked skin.

She stroked her tongue along his, clawing at his shoulders, her hips straining forward.

Her scent filled his nostrils and he nearly wept with joy. Honey and rosewood and something…new. Something sparkling and effervescent. The magical scent of her new Fae body. There was a faint taste of the wind on her tongue as well. He imagined it would be much stronger outside the wards.

He breathed in the life brimming within her, every tremor of restless energy, every quiver of anxiety he'd felt since she'd been taken from him melting away.

She pulled back, then kissed him gently, gazing up at him as if he were the most precious thing in the world.

"I love you, too, Tristan." She smiled, and his chest cracked open, spilling radiant warmth through his veins. Until she punched him in the chest again with enough force to send him staggering backward. "But fuck you *so hard* for kissing Ione."

He wanted to scream back, *She kissed* me! *There were dire circumstances afoot!* But he didn't want to make excuses. He'd make it up to her. Many, *many* times over. His grin went feral. "Haven't lost that filthy mouth, I see. Damn, I was hoping to give you more reasons to use it."

"You're going to be using yours first." Her eyes twinkled with mischievous intention and his cock, still rock-hard from their kiss, twitched against his zipper. "For groveling. So. Much. Groveling."

Fuck, he'd take her right here atop the wet ground if she'd let him.

She pushed past him, aiming for the city gate. "We need to get back to Mireille's. You've got a lot to catch up on."

"Who's Mireille?"

"Long story."

"And where the fuck are we? Is that a *city*?"

Cassandra chuckled, grabbing his hand. "Like I said, Birdman. You've got a lot to catch up on."

He ran his thumb across her knuckles, awe stealing his breath again at the sight of her beautiful wings.

"So do you. Birdwoman."

CHAPTER FIFTY

TRISTAN WAS *HERE*.

Cassandra almost couldn't believe it. She still wasn't convinced that she hadn't been eaten by those beasts and that his arrival wasn't some crazy, afterlife vision.

Especially since she couldn't even see him right now. She'd insisted he hide beneath his camouflaging feathers as they trekked back to Mireille's shop. Cassandra had no idea what the Koenig's policy was on individuals breaking *into* Tartarus without an official sentence. And she wasn't about to find out.

It was late, a few hours from dawn, so she didn't pass many other prisoners. And the few she did dipped furtive glances toward their feet. They didn't want to be caught out this late any more than she did.

The apothecary sign creaked and the bell jingled as Cassandra pushed the door open, then led Tristan up into the small apartment.

"Mireille? Ronin?" she called out as they stepped into the living room.

"Cass?" Mireille strode down the hallway, pushing her arms through the sleeves of a black silk robe, then fluffing her copper waves over her shoulders. She frowned as she drug her silver gaze over Cassandra's wet hair, clothes, and feathers. "By the Creator, what happened to you?"

Ronin tugged his eye patch into place as he emerged from his bedroom, shirtless in loose gray sleep pants. His eye darted to Mireille's bare legs then quickly back to Cassandra. "Everything okay?"

"You can come out now," Cassandra said.

Tristan unfurled his wings and Mireille shrieked, pulling her robe tighter. Ronin stumbled, catching himself on the arm of the couch and releasing a long, drawn-out curse.

"Nice place," Tristan said, nodding his head and surveying the tiny apartment.

Mireille snapped her mouth shut, then bowed at the waist. "Your Highness, welcome." She rose, blinking furiously, as if she had a million questions and couldn't decide where to start. "Can I...get you some tea?"

Ronin shot her a glare. "*That's* what you landed on?" Mireille sneered at him. "How about *what in the name of the Creator are you doing here? Or how did you get past the wards and through the mists? Or why is Cassandra soaking wet?*" He turned back to Tristan. "Or *what in the actual* fuck *are you doing here?*"

Tristan laughed, clapping a hand on Ronin's muscled shoulder. He squeezed it with an appreciative murmur. "Training time's paying off." He settled into a chair at the dining table, angling his wings over the back and resting his elbows on the surface. "A cup of tea would be wonderful, Mireille. I assume you're Mireille?"

"Yes, that's me," Mireille answered, dazed, as if she had no control of the words coming out of her mouth. "I'm Mireille. Been Mireille my whole life. My last name is Valette. Actually, it's Valois, but I changed it when I was twenty-one and I have no idea why that's important right now. It's not really, I… Right. Tea." She padded into the kitchen, filled a teapot, then hung it over the hearth and used a match to light a fire.

Ronin sank into the chair next to Tristan. "What *are* you doing here?"

"I couldn't leave Cassandra to face the terrors of Tartarus alone. No matter how much companionship she had." Tristan speared her with a pleading glance. "I'm only sorry it took me so long to figure out how to breach the wards." Cassandra gifted him a watery smile.

Ronin glanced toward Mireille, shame tugging down the corners of his mouth. "No one knows how to get through the wards except the Imperial delegation that comes for sentencing. Trust me, I've looked into it." Mireille's back stiffened, but she didn't turn, focused her attention on sprinkling tea leaves into the strainers. "How did *you* find out?"

"It has to do with the second reason I'm here." He motioned to Cassandra. "Come over here, Daredevil, you need to hear this, too."

Cassandra pulled out the chair next to Tristan.

"Nope." He pulled her into his lap, tucking her wings against her back and wrapping an arm around her waist. "This is your seat for the foreseeable future." He planted a kiss on her temple.

Ronin groaned, dragging a hand down his face. "There are going to be *rules*. This apartment is really fucking tiny *and* the walls are thinner than paper."

"Is that a challenge, Matakos?" Tristan grinned wide enough to expose his sharp canines and Cassandra fought an urge to slide her tongue down one.

Mireille joined them at the table, passing around mugs of tea, while Tristan regaled them with the incredible story of how he'd breached the wards. Of who the Koenig actually was.

And of the information they needed to pull from the male's memories.

"So, you had no problems at all in those mists?" Ronin asked, sipping his tea. It was deliciously bitter, just the way he liked it. Mireille hadn't forgotten his preferences. His chest squeezed.

"It was a little disorienting, but I never lost track of my direction." Tristan held Cassandra's chin and kissed her lips. "Like a divine presence was guiding me exactly where I needed to be." Her feathers rustled.

Ronin fought an urge to roll his eye. Like this shoebox of an apartment needed *that* kind of fucking energy.

He looked toward Mireille, seeking backup to protest this disgusting display of affection, but she was all starry-eyed over the Prince and his Turned lover. Wistful in a way he'd never seen before.

It twisted him up inside.

"Pure dragon-fire to burn through the wards," Ronin marveled. "How did no one know of this?"

Mireille scoffed. "There's only one dragon in all of Ethyrios, and it's been chained within Typhon Mountain for centuries. That's how."

Her snarky tone heated his blood, but he ignored it as he recounted Tristan's crazy-ass plans. "So, we grab the name from the Koenig's memory, you use that fancy cuff to tell Cael Zephyrus, and then he and the dragon come here with the Teles Chrysos to burn down the wards and free us? Any chance we can make this happen before Cassandra's appeal in six days?"

Mireille cut in. "Don't forget there's still the blood vow to consider. Even if Cassandra's free of the prison, she'll be connected to the Koenig until the bargain is fulfilled. One of them must die by the other's hand."

"I wouldn't leave here without killing him anyway," Cassandra said with a murderous sneer.

Ronin knew she was thinking of those humans down in the Kennel, knew she wouldn't abandon them to torture and captivity. He admired her for it. Her training had been steadily progressing—especially since they'd added Silas to the roster—but she'd still need a miracle to defeat the Koenig.

Though, Prince Tristan fucking Erabis was sitting in their living room. If *that* wasn't a miracle, then they didn't exist.

Tristan grimaced. "I hate the idea of you fighting him, Cass. But if we can bring down the wards beforehand, at least you'd have access to your wind."

Cassandra bit her lip. "I don't even know how to use it. It snuffed out as soon as I was Turned."

"That might help, actually," Tristan chuckled. "Untamed elemental magic from a newly Turned Fae? Creator help him."

"So, we stick to our training plan." Mireille nodded toward Tristan. "With the addition of a fourth instructor."

She wrapped slim fingers around her mug, and Ronin's cock stirred. Not for a single moment these past few days had he forgotten how they'd felt on him. That glorious madness that had overtaken them during the sparring session. What he'd let her do to him.

I win.

She'd won something. But fuck if he knew what.

"We can use your camouflaging wings as well," Mireille added, then told Tristan about the dance she'd arranged at World's End tomorrow night. She turned to Ronin. "He can sneak into the office and search those ledgers while you're downstairs distracting Wormwood.

And you and I—" her gaze shot to Cassandra "—can take advantage of the night for a new purpose. I'll lure the Koenig into the back room for a private dance. Where I'll dose him with a sleeping tonic so you can hunt through his memories for the dragon's name."

Ronin slammed his tea down, hard enough to spill and burn his fingers. "Absolutely not. A private dance? No way."

Mireille threw her shoulders back, matching his fury. "Do you have a better idea of how to get Cassandra access to him before her appeal?"

Ronin doubled down. "He could hurt you—or worse—if you get caught. I don't want you to do this."

"I told you before and I'll tell you again," Mireille seethed, "it's not your decision."

Cassandra swiveled toward Ronin, Tristan's fingers tangled in her hair. As if the Prince couldn't stop himself from touching her. It ignited Ronin's already combustible fury. "Ronin—"

"Do whatever the fuck you all want!" he roared, and they flinched.

He was done with this fucking day, this fucking week.

This fucking *life*.

And if he had to be subjected to Tristan and Cass for one more second... The sight of them, reunited and so disgustingly in love, made him want to stab his other eye out.

He pushed up from the table, then stomped to his room, throwing the door open before Mireille's voice stilled him.

"You're bunking in my hallway now," she called out. "We're giving your room to these two."

He whipped his head over his shoulder. "Are you serious?"

Tristan waggled his eyebrows. "Unless you want to sleep with me? Though I will warn you, friend, I've finally got my female back in my arms after too much time apart and I am *ready*. I can't promise I won't roll over in the middle of the night and go to town on your leg."

Cassandra and Mireille's uproarious laughter only made Ronin angrier.

He may have come to Tartarus as a commander, but these females were showing him just how little power he actually had. Maybe it was better to play the obedient foot soldier and let them lead.

That sounds good to me, his wolf offered. *Especially if Mireille keeps giving you rewards like the one she gave you in—*

That wasn't a reward, Ronin snarled into his mind. *That was a power play.*

She can play with our power all she likes.

You're the fucking worst.

He stalked into his new bedroom and slammed the door shut.

CHAPTER
FIFTY-ONE

"THIS BED IS VERY tiny."

Tristan angled his wings, trying to get comfortable in the, admittedly, very small bed in Cassandra's new room. She wondered how Ronin had fit in it.

Cassandra scrunched her wet hair with a towel, another wrapped around her body. "Don't worry, I'll fit."

"That's my line." He smirked.

"The shower's even worse. Good luck washing your wings."

He swept his gaze across hers. "You do look quite filthy."

She smirked over her shoulder. "That's *my* line."

He laughed—a Tristan special. Loud and hearty enough to inspire a growl from Ronin's room across the

apartment. "Come here and give me your towel. I'll clean them off for you."

She crossed the room and handed him her hair towel, keeping the other wrapped around her naked body. Though she wasn't sure how long Tristan would stand for that.

She sat at the edge of the bed, spreading her wings, and Tristan rose up on his knees behind her. She closed her eyes, relishing the gentle drag of the towel along her feathers. Zaps of pleasure sparkled through her every time his fingertips brushed one.

Ronin, Silas, and Mireille had all touched her wings—accidental brushes or entanglements during training sessions—but *nothing* compared to the heady sensation of Tristan's touch.

Heat pooled between her thighs when he stroked a finger along the downy feathers at her shoulder blade. His lips grazed her earlobe. "I could make you come this way, you know. Could have you soaked and screaming my name in seconds."

She breathed out a ragged laugh. "I don't think Ronin would appreciate that. Thin walls, remember?"

Tristan ran his fangs along her neck and she shuddered, her nipples stiffening. "If you think that I breached the wards of Tartarus, smashed open that gate, braved those mists, fought off the beasts in that moat—"

"I did most of that fighting."

"—defended myself against a tiny Fae female's wicked fists—"

"A tiny Fae female's *legendary* fists."

His breathy laugh tickled her skin. "If you think I braved all those dangers to return to you and *not* have you writhing beneath me in this ridiculously small bed tonight, you are sorely mistaken." He abandoned the towel, running his hands along her wings. The feeling was exquisite; like each and every feather connected to a nerve ending in her clit. She moaned and he wrapped a hand around her mouth. "I do remember—vividly and quite often—how hard it is for you to be quiet."

"I'll try my best," she whispered against his palm.

He removed his hand. "Or we could just go to sleep." He yawned, fake and obnoxiously loud. "I am pretty tired."

She turned and pushed him down onto the bed, then straddled him, pressing her bare sex against the loose gray pants Ronin had let him borrow. "I will beat you with these legendary fists again if you don't get inside me *right fucking now.*"

He cocked an eyebrow, folding an arm behind his head and popping his biceps. Sweet Amatu, he was a *spectacle.* She traced her fingertips down the sculpted planes of his torso, savoring the warm, hard perfection of him.

She'd missed this. Missed him. Missed his teasing and his laughter and his *presence.* She could surely conquer anything, even the Koenig, now that they were together again.

He peeled her towel off and tossed it to the floor as her fingers scrabbled at his waistband.

He stilled her wrists. "Wait. Let me look at you for a moment."

She placed her arms at her sides and threw her shoulders back, fluttering her wings behind her.

Awe shone in his honey-brown gaze. Awe and adoration. He stroked up her thighs, over the curve of her waist, then cupped her breast and ran a thumb across her nipple. She arched into his touch, never tearing her eyes from his as his cock thickened beneath her.

"Bless the Creator," he breathed. "You're devastating. I can't believe she gave you to me. *Turned* you for me."

Cassandra cocked her head. "What do you mean?"

"The only way a human can be Turned is if the Goddess herself blesses it. I was able to Turn you for a reason. Though fuck if I know what that is right now." He thrust up into her and she rolled her hips in answer, whimpering. "Or care."

"Don't distract me with your dick magic." He barked out a laugh. "Tell me what this means. Does it mean you're *not* fated to Ione?"

He sat upright, bringing a hand to her cheek and looping an arm around her waist, pressing their chests together skin-to-skin. Utter bliss. "I don't know what else it *could* mean. Though I have no idea why the Goddess would have Turned two females for me. The prophecy—"

Cassandra placed her hands on his shoulders, pushing back. "You saw it? You retrieved the Compendium?"

He rolled his eyes and released an annoyed sigh. "Because I really want to be talking about some dusty old book when I finally have you naked in my lap again… But yes, we did. And though it's not entirely clear, my interpretation is that it's my choice to make." He leaned forward and the whisper-soft graze of his mouth across her lips rustled her feathers. "And I choose *you*, Cassandra. Only you."

"Fuck fate," she whispered against his mouth, then tangled her hands into his silky hair and slid her tongue past his lips.

He kissed her back, ardently, reverently, then flipped her underneath him, her silky feathers cool against her back. He tugged his pants off, then settled between her thighs and wedged a hand between their bodies, positioning himself at her entrance.

Concern furrowed his brows. "Is this okay? We don't have to. I know you've had a terrifying night. Despite all my teasing, I really can wait."

"Well, *I* can't. Please, Tristan. I need you." She angled her hips, enough for his tip to slide into her.

He groaned, pressing their foreheads together and his eyes blazed molten. "Thank fuck" was all he said before he thrust in fully, his hand over her mouth to stifle her scream.

This. This was her favorite part. The initial penetration, that delicious fullness as her body stretched around him.

They melted into one another, and her senses heightened. Tristan's beautiful face above her in vivid clarity. His every breath tickling her cheeks. His scent and touch more intense than ever before.

Sweet fucking Amatu, is this how sex had always felt for him? She almost wished he'd Turned her sooner.

He ran a hand down her torso, along the side of her breast, then over her hip and under her thigh. He folded her leg up and thrust in harder, fucking her deep and slow. Savoring her.

She matched his rhythm, marveling at how well their bodies fit together.

As if the Goddess had crafted them specifically for each other.

"*Fuck*, Cassandra, you feel so good. Perfect. Made for me."

She kissed his jaw, dragged her teeth along his neck, angled her hips so he'd brush her clit with every downstroke.

Release coiled low in her belly, tensing and tightening, and this was all she wanted. Didn't ever want to leave this bed. Didn't care about the city or the mists or the wards or the world beyond. All she needed was him. Tristan. Her Rebel Prince. Moving inside her, filling her.

She could spend eternity beneath his powerful body and still beg the Creator for one more second.

"I'm close." She brought his hand to her lips, nipped his callused fingertips.

His muscles tightened, his pace faltering, but he grinned down at her and wrapped his palm over her mouth, hooking his thumb under her chin. "Loud as you want, Cass. I've got you."

He slammed into her and she erupted, cursing, her fangs grazing his rough skin. Waves of liquid heat radiated from her core, shuddering her limbs and rattling her feathers. Her inner muscles clenched and released, prolonging her pleasure and she was sure that nothing in her entire life had ever felt this good *ever*.

Tristan followed shortly behind, grunting against her neck as he spent himself inside her. He made to roll away, but she pulled him closer. Wanted his weight and warmth on top of her for as long as possible. She wrapped her arms around his shoulders and her legs around his waist, stroking his feathers.

"I choose you, too, Tristan," she whispered into his ear.

"Naturally."

She laughed into his hair, his cock still buried inside her.

They stayed that way—joined in every way possible—until they fell asleep in each other's arms.

CHAPTER
FIFTY-TWO

XENIA'S HEART THUNDERED IN her chest as she stood outside Elodie's room clutching the small tin key.

Cael had already informed Xenia that Elodie would be down in Diachre all day for her final dress fitting. And Xenia had seen Elodie leaving the lodge this morning after she'd laid into Mistress Ostere in the foyer, yelling about the thieving household staff and a missing key that had magically turned up at dinner two nights ago. Demanding that *no one* go into her room until after the wedding.

Xenia had watched from around the corner, smirking. Mistress Ostere assured Elodie that the staff would never dare steal any of her belongings. That perhaps Elodie herself had left the key in her dinner dress and not realized it? And was she *sure* she didn't want her room cleaned?

From the clipped tone, Xenia knew Mistress Ostere was hinting at Elodie's perpetual messiness.

Elodie had been about to strike the woman before Erik strode in. He'd warned that Elodie would miss her appointment if she didn't leave soon, then swept her through the front door. Xenia could've sworn he'd winked at Mistress Ostere over his shoulder on the way out. The head of the household staff, believing herself alone, had shuffled up the stairs muttering *Slovenly, cold-hearted bitch.*

Xenia had to clap a hand over her mouth to stifle her laughter. She'd untucked herself from her hiding place and slipped up to Elodie's room, excitement and fear warring in her chest.

Excitement, because she was about to find out what was in that box. And fear, because she was about to find out what was in that box.

She opened the door to find the room just as filthy as the first time she'd been here. Maybe more so.

Dresses and slippers and undergarments were strewn across every surface, as if the closet had spit out its contents. The bedsheets were crumpled, the pillows scattered, and every single drawer hung open and askew.

Xenia snickered, imagining an Elodie whirlwind tearing through this room two days ago, searching for the key her very own *fiancé* had stolen.

Worry cinched Xenia's gut as she padded to the closet. What if the box wasn't there? What if Elodie had gotten spooked and hidden it somewhere else?

She knelt down, loosing a relieved sigh when she found the box tucked into the back corner. She pulled it into her lap, then fitted the key into the lock.

The latch gave with a satisfying click, and the lid popped open.

Confusion wrinkled Xenia's brow.

The box was filled with small vials, maybe twenty in total. Two-thirds were empty while the rest were filled with clear liquid.

Xenia placed the box on the floor, then plucked up a full vial. The liquid was crystal clear, no flakes or particles suspended within. It looked like water. But when she angled the vial, it coated the sides of the glass. Water wasn't that viscous.

She pulled off the cork and sniffed. It was nearly odorless with a hint of bitter green at the finish.

She knew better than to taste it. The High Gods only knew what kinds of potions the Fae brewed with the enchanted flora here on the continent. For all Xenia knew, she might knock back this vial and turn into a frog.

All the adrenaline she'd felt since she'd walked into the room fled her body in a tingling rush. So disappointing. She was hoping to find something scandalous. Something unspeakable. Evidence that Elodie had a secret lover or a hidden child or was already married. Not these tiny vials of mystery liquid.

Did she dare take one? If she did, surely Elodie would notice it missing. And Xenia didn't want to be responsible for the wrath Elodie would unleash upon the innocent staff if she did.

Perhaps she could take an empty one. There were enough in the box. Surely, Elodie wouldn't be keeping a close count on those? She wasn't nearly that organized.

Xenia picked up an empty vial, removed the cork, and sniffed. That same leafy bitterness lingered within. Maybe Cael would know what it was? The scent seemed distantly familiar, but Xenia couldn't place it.

She slid the empty vial into her pocket, then relocked the wooden box and slipped it back into its hiding place.

As she stood, her gaze snagged on the gilded clock on the wall.

Shit. Her shift in the library had started eight minutes ago.

She rushed out of Elodie's room, then down the stairs, through the foyer, and out into the crisp brightness of an uncharacteristically sunny day in Diachre.

She bit her lip, lost in speculation as she hurried down the path to the library.

What in Ethyrios was in those vials?

Was Elodie sick? Were they some kind of healing treatment?

High Gods, were they *poison*? Was she planning to off Cael on their wedding night? Though that didn't seem likely, since so many vials were already empty.

She slammed into a hard, male chest.

Cael caught her shoulders before she could fall back on her ass. He was wearing the biggest, most joyful smile she'd ever seen grace his gorgeous mouth. Rays of sunshine backlit his wing, illuminating the pink within the gray. He reached into his pocket and pull out a small, dark container.

"What's that?" she asked.

She didn't know how it was possible, but Cael's smile widened.

"Our ticket out of here."

"It's going to hurt," Xenia said, more a statement than a question, as she paced in Cael's bedroom, wringing her hands in her apron.

Cael's concerned eyes tracked her. "Yes."

"A *lot*."

The small graphite crucible perched menacingly on the low table before the fireplace.

"Yes." Cael stepped in to grip her shoulders. "But you will heal. As soon as it's out, I'll give you my blood and you *will* heal. I promise."

She pressed her cheek against the top of his hand, spearing him with a fearful, hopeful gaze as she sucked in a shaky breath.

"Okay?" he said, his face soft.

"Okay." She steeled her spine, glancing toward Cael's packed bag on the bed.

As soon as he'd stolen her from outside the library, he'd whisked her to his room. Inside, he'd been a flurry of activity. Packing, cleaning, talking. More words than she'd ever heard leave his mouth at once.

She suspected he was trying to keep her distracted from what he was about to do—burn the tracking device out of her neck using dragon-fire.

He'd explained the process while slinging clothes and weapons—two Typhon steel daggers and a stun pistol—into the bag along with a pouch of *drach*as. Not much, he'd explained, but enough for them to get by while they awaited a message from Tristan. Who Cael had informed her was heading to Tartarus, High Gods fucking spare him, to seek the name from Aedelmar Burkhardt. And to find Cass, no doubt.

Cael hadn't told her where they would be waiting, but she honestly didn't care. They could be staying in a lean-to in the woods, and it still wouldn't dampen her effervescent excitement.

They would be away from Stoneridge. Away from Elodie and Tomas. Away from Arran.

Away *together*.

She'd shown him the vial she'd found in Elodie's room, and he'd distractedly slipped it into his bag, muttering something about looking at it later. It didn't even matter anymore, but Xenia's hamster wheel mind insisted she solve the mystery eventually.

"You should probably sit." Cael guided her to the armchair, then gathered up her curls and began re-pinning them atop her head. "Wouldn't want to burn all your hair off, Blondie."

She shot him an annoyed look.

"Come on. You'd look so fucking hot bald." He kissed the back of her neck, and she let out a ragged chuckle.

He came around the chair, then knelt at her feet, plucking the crucible from the table.

"We'll do it as quickly as possible," he said, as if he could hear her heart slamming against her ribs. "Scream if you need to. I've put a windshield around the room." He bit into his wrist, breaking the skin, then lifted it to her face. Tiny rivulets of blood trickled down the corded muscles of his forearm. "Grab hold. As soon as the fire touches your skin, I want you to suck and suck *hard*. Don't worry about me. Take as much as you need until the pain subsides."

She was beyond words, her emotions a confusing mix of terror and exhilaration. This was really happening. She and Cael were about to be *free*. She tried to focus on that rather than the impending pain.

She positioned his wrist at her mouth and licked up a drop of his blood. The taste—pure Cael, all rain-drenched mountains and greenery—calmed her.

"Ready?" Cael's thumb was poised on the lid of the crucible by her neck. Heat wafted through the thick material.

She sucked in a deep breath. "Do it."

Cael didn't hesitate. Flicked the lid off and pressed the opening against her scar.

The pain was unlike anything Xenia had ever felt. Like an angry god had driven a hot spike through her neck.

She dug her nails into Cael's forearm, holding on for dear life as a gut-wrenching scream tore past her teeth. Cael held her in place, his thighs bracketing her knees as she thrashed. Her instincts were roaring at her to flee, to buck him off, to make it stop.

Her skin was *melting*. She could smell it—a charred-flesh scent that was almost worse than the pain itself.

This was no ordinary fire. It was so white-hot it was cold. She shivered as a feverish sweat burst across her body, beads running into her eyes.

"Hurts." Her words were garbled screams. "Fucking *hurts!*"

Cael whispered something soothing, but she couldn't hear him over the blood pounding through her ears. He pressed his wrist to her mouth again, encouraging her to drink. She could barely concentrate enough to seal her mouth over the cut.

Small zaps prickled her neck—the device sputtering out its final gasps.

She pushed through, sucking down a mouthful of Cael's blood. No instant relief, but the pain's sharper edges dulled.

"Almost there," Cael whispered. "Just a few more seconds."

A pop sounded and she was certain her jugular had ruptured. She nearly passed out from a fresh wave of agony.

"Got it!" Cael's victorious shout cut through her haze, and she heard a soft ping. "Keep drinking."

She did as he commanded, though it was hard to swallow. She pushed his wrist away, then cracked her eyes open. Cael picked up the tracking device from the table, hissing as it burned his fingers. He dropped it at his feet, then stomped on it once, twice, three times for good measure.

He stared down at the charred remains, chest heaving, then looked to Xenia. Wonder flared through his storm-cloud eyes as he crashed to his knees and peered at her wound. "You may be the first human in the history of Ethyrios to survive being burned by dragon-fire."

She huffed out a weak laugh. "How does it look?"

He grimaced. "Bad."

"Great bedside manner, pterodactyl."

He gripped her hand and interlaced their fingers. "But it could be worse. You're *alive*. You did it." He peppered gentle kisses across her knuckles. "You're so fucking strong."

He strode to the bed, then fastened the cuff to his wrist and slung his bag over his shoulder.

He gingerly scooped her from the chair. She whimpered as a fresh bolt of pain shot through her neck. "It's okay," he whispered into her hair, cradling her against his chest. "You'll be okay."

And despite the hurt, despite the exhaustion, despite *everything*, she believed him.

They *would* be okay. Both of them.

It was the last thought in her head before Cael tapped the cuff and they portaled out of Stoneridge.

Together.

CHAPTER
FIFTY-THREE

XENIA RUBBED AT THE bandage on her neck, staring at the peak of Typhon Mountain through the window of the cottage.

A radiant peace stole through her as the setting sun dipped beneath the summit, several hundred miles away.

Behind her in the small but cozy living area, Cael spoke to an old Beastrunner with tanned skin and bushy white eyebrows.

Leonard.

"Thank you for letting us stay here." Cael's voice was drenched in the same relief Xenia herself felt. "The Teles Chrysos have promised protection for your assistance."

Leonard chuckled, a time-worn rasp. "I've been dreaming of this for centuries. To release her from her shackles. Hard to believe it's actually happening."

"Not happening yet," Cael said, a hint of his familiar pessimism sneaking into his tone. "Lots of things need to go right for us to have even a slim chance of freeing her."

Leonard smiled, tugging at his long beard. "A little optimism never hurt anyone."

Xenia liked Leonard.

Cael nodded. "I'll send you a message once I've gotten the name, and you can release her. Hopefully for the final time. You've still got that cuff I gave you, right?"

Leonard nodded, then creaked open the cottage door.

Xenia called after him, "We don't mean to put you out!"

"Nonsense," he said. "I barely use this cottage. Got a little cot in my office at the mountain so I can stay close to her."

Xenia's eyes stung. Leonard had cared for the dragon for centuries. She was his family. And if this all worked out, he would lose her.

Leonard curled his fingers around the door. "She deserves her freedom, lass. Not to mention the opportunity to rain down some fiery vengeance upon the Empire that used her. No old male's sentimental feelings should get in the way of that."

Cael clapped Leonard on the shoulder. "You're doing the right thing."

"I know it." Leonard blew out a resigned sigh. "There's not much in the pantry, but whatever's in there

is yours. Help yourselves. I'll wait to hear from you."
He saluted Xenia, then slipped out into the impending
dusk.

Xenia joined Cael at the window, then swiped away
a tear as she watched the old Beastrunner hobble away
from the cottage. Toward his final days with his friend.

Cael glanced down at her. "Sap," he teased, thumbing
her remaining tears away. "He'll be okay." He draped an
arm around her shoulder and led her back toward the
kitchen. "How are you feeling? Are you hungry? How
is your neck?"

She chuckled at his fussing as she took a seat
at the rickety table. "It's still a bit sore. But I'm fine,
Cael. Really."

He crept up behind her, then peeled back the
bandage. "It looks much better than it did earlier."

She grabbed his hand, kissed his knuckles. "I had a
good healer."

His wing rustled at the compliment as he began
opening cabinets. "There's not much in here. Crackers.
Couple tins of canned meat." He pulled out a jar with
a bit of sticky red...*something* topped by puffs of green
fuzz. "Whatever the fuck this used to be." He tossed it
into the waste bin in the corner. "Might make sense for
me to portal down to the village and grab some supplies."

"Not tonight. Crackers and canned meat will do.
I'm not that hungry anyway. And I'd rather have you
stay here where I can see you."

Cael chuckled low, amused. "Possessive."

Xenia stood and threw her arms around his neck, tilting her face up. "If you dared leave me again, I'd just hunt you down. Managed it once, remember?"

Cael ran his fingers through her curls. "My little predator." He leaned down to kiss her, a gentle brush of his lips, and she arched against him, sliding her tongue into his mouth. He indulged her for a moment, his arms tightening around her, before pulling back and whispering, "You're injured."

"Not too injured for this," Xenia breathed out, desperate, refusing to let him pull away. "Cael, we *made* it. For who knows how long. Don't you think we deserve a night to celebrate? Just one night."

He let out a rumbling purr as his hands traced up her body, scintillating heat following in their wake. "And how, exactly, would you like to celebrate, sweetheart?"

She ran the heel of her palm up the hard length straining against his pants. "With this. Inside me. As soon as humanly possible."

He tugged aside her collar, then grazed his fangs along her bare shoulder. "I'm not human."

Her core went molten, and he let out a sharp hiss as she squeezed his cock. Sweet Amatu, he was so fucking big. A tiny ember of fear blinked to life within her blaze of passion.

He reclaimed her mouth, a fierce, soul-searing kiss, then hoisted her up onto the table. The wood creaked and popped beneath her.

She tore her lips away. "Careful. Don't want to damage Leonard's table. Not after he was so kind to let us stay here."

"I'll buy him a new one," Cael growled, hiking up her skirt and kneeling beneath her. He slipped his fingers into her panties, then pulled them down over her stockings. She opened her legs, baring herself, and he groaned. "Fuck, I'll *build* him a new one."

She braced her hands behind her and the table squeaked another protest.

Cael trailed his nose along her inner thigh. "You have no idea how long I've wanted this again. Haven't been able to get the taste of you off my tongue since Rhamnos."

She stared down at him, wide-eyed and breathless. "I thought about it all the time. About how good your mouth felt on me. About how much I wanted you, too."

"You have me," he confessed, unblinking. "Always. Any part of me."

She grabbed his shirt, trying to tug him upwards. "I want *all* of you, Cael. No more waiting."

Resisting her tug, he grinned, a fang glinting in the waning sunlight. "Sorry, Blondie. You're going to have to wait a little longer."

He spread her thighs apart, then licked her from base to apex. A long, slow glide. Stars bloomed in her vision.

He shuddered a breath against her bare flesh. "*Fuck*, I could live off the taste of you."

Xenia threw her head back, rolling her hips as Cael licked and suckled her. Teased out her pleasure. Flicked his tongue through her flesh. Her thighs trembled, and staccato whines parted her lips. He sucked her clit into his mouth, and she nearly bucked off the table.

"Cael, please," she moaned, needing to be filled by something. And though she very much preferred his cock, right now she was desperate enough for his fingers, his tongue. *Anything.*

He huffed an arrogant laugh, licking her again slowly. Content to take his time. He circled his tongue over her clit, then speared two fingers inside of her, and her toes curled inside her stockings.

She gripped his shoulders with her heels, using the leverage to grind herself onto his fingers. He pumped them in and out, slow at first, then faster, lapping her clit in rhythm.

She fought against her rapidly approaching climax. She didn't want to come this way. Had been dreaming about coming on his enormous cock ever since she'd seen it gloriously in the flesh in Rhamnos.

He must have read her mind because he removed his head from between her legs, his lips swollen and glistening. He helped her out of her dress—but left her stockings on. Of course. He removed his own shirt and pants and then there he was. Towering above her with his sole wing kicked out. Utterly naked and breathtakingly beautiful.

They stayed like that for a moment, staring at each other. Studying each other. Wearing matching incredulous grins like they couldn't believe their luck.

She wished Cael could have been her first. She tried not to remember the last—and only—time she'd done this. But thoughts of Jaz the scholar, of that miserable experience back in the Temple library, brought a frown to her face.

Cael leaned down to kiss it away. "No thoughts of the past. It's just you and me. Tonight, and forever after." He fisted his cock, then dragged the blunt head through her wetness.

"Oh, is that so?" she teased, quivering with pleasure. "Not sure I've agreed to forever yet."

"I don't share, Xenia," Cael snarled. "You're fucking *mine*."

Her entire body throbbed at his possessiveness, and all she could manage was a strangled, "*Yes.*"

He grabbed her thighs again, spreading her wider, then notched himself between her legs.

She sucked in a breath. The head of his cock felt double the size of her entrance.

There was no fucking *way*.

Cael looked down between their bodies, ash-brown waves tumbling into his eyes. His muscles tensed and his brows furrowed adorably. As if he'd come to the same conclusion.

"You're gonna have to breathe through this." He recaptured her gaze, his lips curling into a sinful smile. "You ready?"

She nodded, biting her lip, trying not to squeal with delighted laughter as all her wicked fantasies came true.

Cael was about to talk her through it.

"Inhale," he whispered. She did. "And exhale." He stepped closer, his cock pushing against her, but not breaching her yet. "Good. Again."

When she exhaled a second time, he thrust in less than an inch. Just enough for her inner lips to wrap around his head.

"*Good girl,*" he sighed. "One more time."

She did as she was told, and he pushed in deeper. Her body stretched around him, pinching, and she yelped.

"Relax, sweetheart." He brushed her hair off her sweaty face and stroked his thumb along her cheekbone. "Relax. You can take it. Go again. Deep breath."

His cock was barely in her—two, three inches, at most. But it already felt so *fucking* good, pleasure edged in the slightest pain.

She stared into his stormcloud eyes, savoring the lust and affection in them. All for her. She sucked in another inhale, then let it out slowly.

Cael dipped a hand to her breast, running a callused thumb over her nipple as he continued spreading her, filling her, lubricating himself with her arousal. Working himself into her in small increments. He pushed in, then retreated. Pushed in, then retreated. All while cooing soft words of encouragement that had her trembling beneath him. "Good. Yes. That's it. Breathe. *Good* girl, taking me so well. Fuck, you're so beautiful." He speared his hands into her hair, folding himself over her and pressing their foreheads together. "Is this real, Xenia? Are you mine?"

"It's real, Cael. I'm yours."

He slanted his mouth over hers but kept his eyes open. Let her see every part of him, laid bare only for her.

Then he thrust all the way home and she could do nothing but scream with pleasure.

Cael's soul left his body.

That was the only explanation for the mind-erasing ecstasy he felt when he fully seated himself inside Xenia. Her perfect, tight heat swallowed his cock and he never wanted this moment to end. Wanted to spend the rest of his life trapped inside her, watching her pant his name, her curls askew and her cheeks flushed.

She wiggled her hips. A silent request for him to *move*.

She didn't need to ask twice.

He slid his palms under her thighs, then lifted them as he pulled his cock out to the tip and thrust back in again.

She kicked her head back, moaning his name and squeezing her eyes shut.

"Open them," he growled.

She obeyed, her mouth forming a surprised *O*. Like she couldn't believe he'd actually fit inside her. He almost couldn't believe it either.

He set a languid pace to start, priming her for his full force. "*Gods*, you feel perfect."

He dipped his chin to watch his glistening cock plunge into her, drunk on the slick sounds and her soft whimpers.

Her hands traveled up her slim, golden torso to play with her breasts, and the sight of her pinching her nipples while he fucked her sent electric pleasure jolting down his spine. His wing shuddered. As if it remembered how good those fingers had felt the other night. Good, but this was better.

It was so much fucking better.

He increased his pace, slamming into her so hard that his balls smacked her ass. She cried out again.

"Touch yourself," he demanded, digging his fingers into the flesh above her stockings. How many times had he imagined this exact scenario after he'd first seen her in them?

She brought two fingers down to her clit, rubbing in tight circles as she let loose a string of dirty babbling.

"*Fuck*, that feels so good. Yeah, right there. *Oh High Gods*... A little higher. Yes, right there, *yesssssss*... I'm so close. Harder. Never stop fucking me, Cael, please. Shit, yes. *Harder!*"

He bit his tongue to keep from laughing. Xenia had always been chatty. Of course she'd be chatty during sex. He loved it. Could listen to her stream-of-consciousness sex talk for eternity and never tire of it.

"Gods, you're so big." Her fingers circled faster over her clit. "I love your cock. Your monster fucking cock. Don't stop. Don't ever stop. I— *Fuck*, yes, right there. Right *there!*"

He did laugh then. A bubbling, joyous sound as he ran the tip of said monstrous cock across that spot just inside her entrance.

"Oh shit, *Cael*, I'm gonna come. You're gonna make me—"

He replaced her fingers with his own at her clit, then bent over and captured her wail with his mouth as she shattered. Her cunt squeezed him so tight, pulsed so fast, that he couldn't stop his own climax. He growled against her lips as he came harder than he ever had in his entire fucking life.

Just as his hips stilled and he finished spilling himself, the table let out a final groan of protest and disintegrated beneath them.

Xenia yelped, and Cael was quick enough to get one hand behind her head and to brace himself with the other before they crashed to the floor.

She clung to his neck, her uproarious giggles a balm to his soul.

This bright, sunny, sassy little human—with a mouth even filthier than his own—was *his*.

He eased out of her, then rolled over, arranging her atop his chest. He pushed sweaty curls off her face, kissed her rose-tinted cheeks and the tip of her nose, laughing right along with her.

Xenia caught her breath, and her eyes widened. "Leonard's gonna be so pissed at us."

Cael chuckled, running his knuckles down her cheek. "I think Leonard would agree that the table's sacrifice was well worth it." He saluted the broken shards beneath them. "Thank you for your service, friend. Thanks for holding out until she came."

Xenia cackled, then rested her chin on his chest, looking at him in a way that made his insides glow.

Like he was the brightest star shining in her sky.

"You're a *god*. That was incredible."

"I know," he said. She smacked him playfully, then nuzzled in and closed her eyes. "Should we get out of the pile of broken table?"

Xenia shook her head. "Not yet. Just let me stay here a moment and savor this."

He closed his own eyes and dipped his head back, profoundly content. Whatever Xenia wanted, he would give to her. For the rest of her life.

A small pang seized his chest as he remembered she was human. That her years on Ethyrios would be far less than his own.

But he let the thought rise, acknowledged it, and let it go.

I am in control of my happiness and my destiny.

And with Xenia here in his arms, safe and exhausted and sated and *his*, he knew it was true.

CHAPTER
FIFTY-FOUR

O N THE NIGHT OF Mireille's performance at World's
End, Cassandra peered out of the dark alley across
from the tavern, searching for snow white hair beneath
the gold-and-black striped awning.

"Wormwood show up yet?" Tristan's rumbled from
the shadows behind her.

"Not yet," she said, tucking herself back beneath his
camouflaging feathers.

The group had hashed out the minutiae of their
plan this morning, just moments after Tristan had lazily
woken Cassandra with his hands, mouth, and cock.
Ronin had been glaring from the dining table when
they'd emerged from her bedroom glowing and flushed.

"What?" she'd asked. "We were quiet."

"Not quiet enough," Ronin had grumbled into his tea. Behind his head, Mireille had winked, mouthing *details later* before handing Cassandra a plate of hard-boiled eggs, sliced melon, and toast.

The plan tonight was for Cassandra and Tristan to hide across from the entrance while Ronin waited for Wormwood to arrive. Once he did, Tristan would Ghostwalk himself and Cass into the tavern behind Ronin, then slink back to the private room where Mireille intended to lure the Koenig. And as soon as Mireille had knocked Aedelmar out, Cassandra would begin her hunt through his memories, and Tristan would head to Wormwood's office to review the ledgers.

The plan had become more complex and the stakes higher, but also remarkably easier since Tristan and his camouflaging wings had appeared in Tartarus.

"How do you do that?" she whispered, scanning the underside of his feathers.

"Do what? Be so charming? Look so handsome? Fuck so proficiently?"

Cassandra huffed out a quiet laugh, running a thumb over his plush lips. "My arrogant Prince. No, actually, I was talking about your wings. How do you activate the camouflage?"

Tristan, seated on a barrel with Cassandra in his lap, sat up a bit straighter. "Actually, you might be able to do it, too." He hesitated, brows furrowing. "Ione inherited my Ghostwalker abilities. You may have as well."

"Really?" Cassandra straightened, lit up by excited curiosity. "And you don't have to tiptoe around the subject of Ione, Tristan. I understand how much she means to you. But I'm your future. You told me that once. I believe you."

He kissed her temple. "I don't deserve you."

"Never forget it."

He pinched her side, making her yelp, before he began caressing her wings, which were tucked tightly against her back. She let out a breathy little moan. "Whatever you're doing back there, please don't ever stop."

"I'm trying to bring your awareness to each one of your feathers," he said. "You need to command each individual one in order to activate the camouflage."

"Dear wing feathers, please help me win the most epic game of hide-and-seek ever."

Tristan laughed. "Something like that. It's more like you need to believe it's possible. Give them a little shake and let's see what happens."

Cassandra did as he'd asked, half her feathers rattling and half remaining motionless. Her wings looked moth-eaten, covered in tiny holes.

"Shake it off, then do it again," he said. "Close your eyes and concentrate. Feel each feather."

She cracked her neck and shook out her feathers, managed to get a few more to activate.

"Not bad for a novice," Tristan said. "But you'll need far more practice before you can fully hide yourself. I'll still need to carry you into World's End."

"Oh, darn."

He chuckled, then pressed a soft kiss to her lips. "I'd carry you everywhere, Cass."

She kissed him back, then peeked through his feathers, resuming her watch on the tavern entrance.

A few moments later, Wormwood sauntered up to Ronin and Tristan scooped her up.

"Show's about to begin."

"I'm a bit surprised you finally took me up on my offer," Wormwood said, dragging dishwater brown eyes across Ronin's tattooed, muscled forearms. He'd purposefully left them on display tonight beneath the rolled-up sleeves of his white tunic.

Wormwood handed Ronin a silver goblet with creamy mist leaking over the rim. "It's called a Null & Void. House special. It's not quite Delirium, but still strong enough to make you shed your inhibitions."

Wormwood winked, slurping down a big, smoky gulp. Ronin took a small sip, then coughed.

The shit tasted like rubbing alcohol. Nothing like the pleasantly sour funk of Delirium. Creator, what he wouldn't give for one right now. To sink into temporary oblivion and forget about everything and everyone.

The tavern's main room overflowed with rowdy, hulking Brethren. They were crammed together at small, round tables, stacked three deep at the bar, and occupied every square inch of gilded wall.

The promise of leering at a half-naked Mireille drew quite a crowd.

And Ronin wanted to claw every single one of their eyes out before she even took the stage.

"Why *did* you take me up on my offer?" Wormwood asked, trailing a sharp nail down Ronin's shoulder and across his biceps.

Ronin vented an easy laugh. "Don't play dumb with me, Remy." Wormwood's pupils dilated as Ronin leaned in closer. "I know you've heard the rumors. About Cassandra's training? There's no way she's going to win. I've come to request a place among the Brethren." He lowered his voice to a whisper. "And to say I'm willing to throw the fight if he'll accept me."

"Well," Wormwood said, taking another sip of his cocktail and scooting his chair close enough that his thigh brushed Ronin's, "we'll see, won't we?"

Murmurs rippled through the room as the Koenig swaggered in dressed like a casual conqueror, poured into tight leather pants and shirtless beneath a black fur vest. His flaxen hair was tied back, and his eyes were bare of kohl. Absent also were his baldric of knives and the warhammer. Locked away at the castle, no doubt.

The Koenig sank into his seat, a veritable throne of carved black wood right in front of the stage.

The best view in the house.

Under the table, Ronin dug his claws into his palms, seething at imagined visions of the performance Mireille would give that asshole tonight. And grateful that he'd only have to witness a small portion of it.

A quartet of musicians perched beside the stage began playing a slow, sultry song full of indolent strings and hypnotic beats. The room quieted.

"She used to be quite famous, you know." Wormwood's breath stirred Ronin's hair. "The legendary prima ballerina of the Kheimos company. We've been begging her to dance for us since she arrived, but she has always refused."

Ronin glanced toward the Koenig, who'd just been handed a tumbler of aquaver from a scantily-clad waitress. "He never tried to force her?"

Wormwood shrugged. "She paid a price for each refusal."

Ronin recalled those scars he'd seen crisscrossing her body during sparring sessions. Recalled her stiff silence during Harvest Night, her improved fighting skills, that deadened glaze that often dulled her silver eyes.

Before guilt and self-loathing could fully consume him, Mireille sauntered onto the stage, her copper hair a braided crown atop her head, and…

Creator fucking *take* him.

Her firm, round breasts were barely covered by black triangles held in place with thin strings. A swath of black silk cradled her hips, no larger than a loin cloth. All her scars were on display, both old and new. That familiar silver gash down her right forearm. A slash up her left thigh. A jagged crescent from her ribcage to her belly button. The angry pink V of her sentencing brand just below her collarbone.

They were armor. They were art. The stories of her hard-won survival.

He'd never loved her more than he did in this moment.

She shimmied to the front of the stage, then smirked at the crowd. Shrill whistles drowned out the music, and her grin grew wider.

His wolf whimpered, then sucked in a breath like he was about to say something.

Not tonight, Ronin croaked. *Please. Not tonight. I can't bear it.*

Despite his wolf's obedience, Ronin could feel the creature growing restless as Mireille spent long minutes undulating her perfect body. The body Ronin had once mapped nightly with his tongue, his teeth, his fingertips.

The body that Aedelmar's gaze was currently devouring with presumptuous intention.

Fuck, this was so much harder than he'd imagined.

Mireille offered the Koenig an impish grin as her sinuous hips gyrated and her arms swirled overhead, and the blatant lust pouring off the male nearly had Ronin snarling.

He took a sip of his disgusting drink to smother it, and saw Wormwood regarding him curiously. Ronin plastered on a rogue's smile, then placed his hand on Wormwood's thigh, whispering, "She's a bit overrated, don't you think?"

Wormwood chuckled, eyes hooded, then threw back the rest of his drink. "Another?"

Ronin nodded and Wormwood rose, snaking through the mesmerized crowd toward the bar.

Ronin fought to control himself as he returned his attention to Mireille. She finished her dance with a deep bow, revealing the swells of her ass, and Ronin had to close his eye to keep from echoing the anguished howl his wolf let loose inside him.

Mireille floated upright, her attention landing on Ronin.

You were fucking magnificent, he thought. *You're always magnificent.*

And though he knew she couldn't hear it, her steps faltered as she approached Aedelmar, who wore a covetous, closed-lip smile as he clapped his meaty hands.

At his applause, the tavern burst into cheers and whistles. Mireille's cheeks flushed at the adulation before she settled into the Koenig's lap. He placed a hand on her hip, tugging her closer and she whispered into his ear.

Ronin bit his tongue hard enough to draw blood. It did nothing to mask the bitter taste of his ravenous jealousy.

Aedelmar nodded at Mireille, grinning like a deviant schoolboy, then rose from his seat as she took his hand. They walked across the stage and behind the black curtain. Heading to the back room for his private dance.

Ronin was grateful the room was dark.

So that Wormwood couldn't see the claw-marks gouged into the side of the table when he returned with Ronin's drink.

CHAPTER FIFTY-FIVE

"U M, WOW," CASSANDRA WHISPERED, her blood pumping, as Tristan unfurled his wings in the private room.

Tristan's hand was at his waistband, making adjustments, and Cassandra snickered.

"What?" he asked, innocently. "She's a *really* good dancer."

Cassandra couldn't disagree. She hadn't been able to take her eyes off Mireille when she'd slunk in here with the Koenig, sat him in the leather chair, and slithered across his body for what felt like an hour.

For the grand finale, Mireille had licked her magenta lips, activating the somnothian root and lethaphyll extract within her lipstick, then given the Koenig a sloppy, tongue-filled—on her end, at least—kiss.

That had been seconds ago and both Fae were out, Aedelmar slumped in his chair and Mireille collapsed at his feet.

Cassandra pulled out the antidote Mireille had crafted, wrapped an arm around her shoulders, and poured the thick amber liquid into her mouth.

Mireille came to immediately, goosebumps pebbling her skin as her eyes dilated. She gripped Cassandra's forearms, deep fear darkening her eyes. Reliving some private nightmare. She calmed when she recognized Cassandra, who stood and helped her up. Tristan was a looming, concerned presence behind Aedelmar.

"He looks so much...*smaller* than I expected," Cassandra said.

Mireille snorted. "Most males do."

"Hey," Tristan protested.

Cassandra blew him a kiss. "Never you, Birdman."

The Koenig's breathing was deep and slow, but extract-induced unconsciousness hadn't softened his face like real sleep might have. He looked tense, his eyes roving madly behind his lids. Like he might spring to life at any moment.

"Is he supposed to look like that?" Cassandra asked.

Mireille pinched her lips together. "Be quick. He won't remember anything when he wakes up. But I have no idea how long that will be. You need to be out of here by then. I'll give him another dance, then take him back into the main room."

"Where's Wormwood's office?" Tristan asked Mireille.

"Left out this door, then up the back staircase. Second door on the right."

Tristan wrapped himself in his wings, shook his feathers, and disappeared.

"I will never get used to that," Mireille said, blinking. She eased open the door, ducked her head out, then pulled back in. "All clear."

Tristan shot a hand through his feathers, giving them a thumb's up.

Mireille waited a beat for him to exit, then closed the door and turned to Cassandra. "Are you ready?"

"Ready as I'm going to be."

Cassandra glanced down at the Koenig, temptingly vulnerable with his bare chest exposed and the kohl cleaned from his eyes. She wished she had a weapon. Typhon steel, a shard of glass, a stone spike. Anything that she could plunge into his heart and end him right here, right now.

The mere thought sent a jolt of pain through her veins. Even if she'd been armed, the blood vow wouldn't allow her to harm him.

Cassandra leaned down to whisper into Aedelmar's ear, to encourage the memory she sought to the surface.

Before she opened her mouth, she glanced over to Mireille one final time, who sent her a determined nod of encouragement.

"Tell me the dragon's name," Cassandra whispered.

Then closed her eyes, grasped the Koenig's hand, and let the memory wash over her.

Aedelmar had failed.

He'd utterly *failed*.

How could he have been so stupid? To leave her here alone while he and his men had rushed to save that village? He should have known it was a trap from the moment that messenger had arrived.

But his warriors were spoiling for a fight after a week of unexpected calm in this on-going war against Leonin Erabis's Imperial designs.

Aedelmar's own clan—the Cynn Drakan—was the last hold-out in the northwest continent. And they would not be as easily taken as the others.

Though his certainty faltered as Arran Zephyrus paced before him. Aedelmar knelt on the floor, held up by two of Arran's soldiers. His jaw ached, his ribs smarted, and a trickle of blood ran down his chest where they'd slashed him with his own Typhon dagger.

He wanted to rip from their grasp and shred the room to pieces. But he didn't dare.

Not when two of Arran's other males were holding Priya at knifepoint on the bed. Terror brightened her eyes, but she kept perfectly still. Didn't cry or beg or wail for her freedom.

Creator, she was so brave. One of the many reasons he'd chosen her as his mate.

His clan had been against their coupling in the beginning. Wanted a Windrider for their queen. But Priya, a bear bi-form, had won them over with her skilled *hunting, her shrewd mind, her bawdy sense of humor. Plus her ability to drink every single one of his clansmales under the table. He was quite sure a number of them were just as hopelessly in love with her as he was.*

She'd helped him hold the Cynn Drakan together during these past months of battle with the conquerors. They had argued bitterly about her marching into battle alongside him. He did NOT want her putting herself in danger. One of them needed to survive.

He almost laughed at the irony now. The danger had come for her anyway. Right into their marriage bed.

"So," Arran drawled, his braided copper hair glinting in the moonlight, "it seems we are at an impasse."

Aedelmar grunted, and a soldier grabbed his bruised jaw and forced his chin up.

Arran plucked a small flute from his pocket, barely larger than a finger, and made a show of examining it. "Do you know how many times I have used this? Take a guess."

Aedelmar said nothing, and the soldier dug a finger into an open gash beneath his ribs. He hissed in pain, Priya snarling from the bed. "Answer him," the soldier growled, twisting his finger into the wound.

Aedelmar released a pained laugh, tasting blood on his tongue. "You could blow it ten thousand times and she would never come to you."

Arran nodded, flattening his lips. "You'd think I would have learned after the fiftieth or even the hundredth try that it wasn't going to work. But, what's that saying?" Arran directed the question to the soldier on Aedelmar's right, the one whose finger still gouged his side.

The soldier answered immediately, a pet wanting to please his master. "Hope springs eternal."

Arran snapped. "That's the one. Hope springs eternal. Yes, it certainly does." Arran's flinty steel eyes clapped onto Aedelmar's. "But not for you, I'm afraid." The two soldiers dragged Priya from the bed, then forced her to kneel beside her husband.

She turned to him, her pleading gaze begging him not to give in. She was a fool if she thought he had a choice. If the cost of her survival was his life, then he'd pay it a thousand times over.

"*Your* hope ends, but I will offer you one last piece of agency," Arran said, his dusty brown boots clacking across the floorboards. "Tell me the creature's name, and you will be the only one who dies tonight. Refuse, and I'll kill your mate instead."

Creator bless her, Priya steeled her shoulders and spat at Arran's feet. "He'll never give it to you."

Arran tapped a finger against his lips, his gaze trained on Aedelmar. "There are other ways I could wrench it from you, you know. Slowly and painfully, one strip of skin at a time. But that would require time that I do not have." Arran nodded at his soldiers and the tips of Typhon daggers appeared at both Aedelmar and Priya's hearts.

Priya strained against the soldiers' grips. As if trying to tear her hands away to protect him.

It shattered his resolve.

"Stop," he whispered, "I'll tell you."

"No!" Priya shouted, agonized. "Do you really think this monster will treat the Cynn Drakan honorably? If we *lose her, our way of life is over. There will be no coming back from this. If you damn our people to save me, I will never forgive you."*

His heart split as he took in his fierce, beautiful mate. This female he'd loved for decades. This female who'd helped him lead the Cynn Drakan, helped him keep Arran at bay. Arran, who was about to take everything from him.

Everything except Priya.

Aedelmar was strong, but not strong enough to survive that.

He poured all his love into his gaze. "My life is worth nothing without you. You must live."

Priya remained dry-eyed, even as tears bathed his own cheeks.

"So touching," Arran sneered. "I assume you've made your choice?"

He nodded once, sharply, ignoring Priya's bellowing protests.

"Muzzle the bitch," Arran bit out and a soldier clapped a hand over her mouth while the other maintained the dagger at her heart.

Aedelmar did not break his mate's gaze as Arran leaned down, so close their faces were nearly touching.

Aedelmar considered it for a moment. Smashing his forehead into the asshole's nose. Giving Arran a little taste of pain before the end.

But he couldn't muster the strength to do it. His fight was gone. He'd been bested. And now, he would bargain the only treasure he had left.

"Well?" Arran whispered. "The name. Now. Or she dies."

He blew out a long breath, then whispered into Arran's ear, to low for anyone else in the room to hear. "Her name is Signys."

Arran slid his eyes closed, shuddering with pleasure, as Priya wailed. A wicked smile formed beneath his long, copper beard as he stood. "Thank you, my old foe. You made the right decision."

He tucked the flute back in his pocket, and Aedelmar waited for the dagger to bite into his flesh. He brushed his fingers against Priya's. A final apology, though he regretted nothing.

Arran stalked to the door, then glanced back over his shoulder. "Unfortunately, you took too long to arrive at your decision. Pity." Arran nodded to the soldier holding Priya.

And Aedelmar's chest caved in as the soldier plunged the Typhon steel into Priya's heart.

His mate didn't make a sound as she turned toward him. And there was nothing accusatory in her stare, just deep, profound love as the light drained from her eyes.

Aedelmar roared, a volcano of agony erupting in his veins. He flared his wings, straining against the soldiers holding him. He tried to summon the wind, to tear the breath from these bastards' lungs, but the nessite chain around his neck prevented it.

"You fucking lying bastard," he bellowed.

Arran shrugged. "Didn't lie. Just changed my mind. Also, I'm assuming she knew the dragon's name as well.

Can't really have that now, can I?" Arran nodded to his soldiers again, and one pried Aedelmar's jaw open as the other dug fingers into his mouth, pinching his tongue. "You won't be able to tell anyone either, once they're done with you."

Aedelmar bit down on the soldier's fingers, tried to clamp his jaw shut. But the male was strong, and Aedelmar was fighting the greatest fatigue he'd ever known. Arran Zephyrus had destroyed his entire world in the span of seconds.

Aedelmar slid his gaze to Priya, who lay motionless at the other two soldiers' feet. Her life's blood drained away, seeping through the floorboards.

He sagged within the soldiers' hold, no energy left to do anything other than await his own death in the Eternal Fire to which all souls returned.

Aedelmar kept silent as the soldier gripped his tongue. Barely felt the pain when the other soldier began slicing through the muscle. Blood gushed into his mouth, choking him. It was not a quick, nor a clean, cut.

The soldiers released him and he crashed to the floor, nothing more than a sack of bones.

"The wings, too," Arran said. "Then throw him in the wagon with the others. Leonin can decide what to do with him."

Aedelmar wondered why Arran didn't just kill him. Zephyrus had gotten exactly what he wanted. In the cruelest way possible.

But there was his answer.

It was far crueler for Arran to let Aedelmar live with the choice he'd just made.

Aedelmar barely even felt the steel as the soldiers began sawing off his wings. He lay on the floor, his empty eyes traveling under the bed to where Lizbeth lay, hand clenched around her mouth and eyes red-rimmed.

His last movement before pain stole his consciousness was to place a single finger upon his blood-soaked lips, encouraging his daughter to stay silent.

She was the Cynn Drakan's last hope. If she lived, she could avenge her parents, her people. Someday.

She didn't know the dragon's name. Arran, the bastard, had guessed correctly. No one in Ethyrios save Aedelmar and Priya knew it.

But if Lizbeth lived, perhaps the memory of this terrible night could forge her into something.

The weapon that would finally excise Arran Zephyrus from this world.

As soon as Cassandra, looking through Aedelmar's eyes, had seen his young daughter under the bed, that piercing sensation stole her breath and she jumped into the girl's present.

Or at least, what Cassandra assumed was her present.

All Cassandra could sense around Lizbeth Burkhardt was darkness. Soft, endless darkness.

It was different than the solid wall of white that Cassandra had encountered in Selene's present.

Different than the diaphanous haze of Gareth's present in the Halfway.

Perhaps Lizbeth was asleep. A deep, dreamless sleep.

Cassandra savored the stillness, especially after that horrific memory. She felt the smallest twinge of sympathy for Aedelmar.

Something stirred Lizbeth's mind. A rap on a door. A clipped voice. An opened window letting in a damp, fresh scent…

Before Lizbeth woke fully, a hand shook Cassandra's shoulder and her eyes popped open.

"The somnothian extract is wearing off," Mireille hissed as she pulled Cassandra to her feet and pushed her from the room. "Go. *Go.* I'll meet you back at the shop."

Cassandra snuck through the back hallway of World's End, then out the door, hoping that Tristan had learned something from those ledgers and that Ronin had been able to shake Wormwood.

As she walked back to the apothecary, she couldn't stop thinking about Aedelmar's memory.

The Koenig was a monster.

But it was the Empire who'd turned him into one.

CHAPTER
FIFTY-SIX

Ronin's leg bounced beneath the dining table in Mireille's apartment. He was more nervous about tonight's outcome than he was about Cassandra's appeal.

Cass herself paced before the fireplace despite Tristan's calm presence beside him.

Ronin wanted to know what Tristan had found in those ledgers. What Cassandra had seen in that memory. But most of all, he wanted Mireille to walk through that door.

Right fucking now.

Creator, if that scarred, blond-headed fuck had put his hands on her in any way, Ronin would—

The bell tinkled, and Ronin released a relieved sigh at the same time as Cassandra breathed out, "Thank the High Gods" and raced for the apartment door.

She whipped it open and Mireille strode in, refusing to look at him. She pulled her cloak tighter. "I need a shower."

Ronin wanted to flip the table and slam his fists through the wall.

Twenty minutes later, Mireille was seated next to him, her eyes a bit less dead and glazed—a small mercy.

"Signys," Cassandra pronounced from Tristan's lap. "The dragon's name is Signys. And not that I want to feel any kind of sympathy for Aedelmar, but what Arran Zephyrus did to him, what your *father* did to him—" she looked at Tristan "—was pretty awful. He has a daughter who survived. I jumped into her present at the end of the memory, but she was asleep. Mireille pulled me out before I could see where she was."

Tristan tapped the cuff on the table. "I'll contact Cael right now."

"What did you find in the ledgers?" Ronin asked, bracing himself.

Tristan speared him with a hopeful glance. "Her name wasn't anywhere in those ledgers, Matakos."

Adrenaline surged through Ronin in a heady rush. He wanted to speak, wanted to ask another question, but he couldn't make his mouth work. Could barely hear his own thoughts over the agonized howling of his wolf.

"What does that mean?" Cassandra asked, her voice miles away.

"It means," Mireille said, "that Selene may have been arrested.

"But she was never sent to Tartarus."

After a blocks-long chase through moon-slick streets, Mireille finally found Ronin's colossal white wolf atop the wall at the city's edge, howling at the stars.

She shifted back into her Fae form, then ambled over to the wall. "Please come down from there."

His white muzzle swiveled down to her. Shadows hid his face, so she couldn't see his expression as he executed a three-story jump that would have injured a smaller creature. He walked toward her, claws clacking on the cobblestones.

Despite the hour, other prisoners roamed about, sending furtive glances their way.

The white wolf settled onto his haunches before Mireille, then lay down fully, resting his head on his paws.

Moonlight crawled over his scar, no longer hidden behind the patch Ronin wore in his Fae form, and Mireille sucked in a sharp breath.

It was *vicious*. A jagged, silver slash devoid of fur where his eye should have been.

She ran a tentative finger across it and the wolf whimpered, but made no move to retaliate.

"I'm sorry," she whispered, her voice choking with emotion. "I'm sorry I did this to you."

White fur rippled, then Ronin himself stood before her, one eye red-rimmed and the patch once again covering the other.

"She was never here," he croaked.

"I heard," Mireille responded. Pointlessly. She didn't know what else to say. She almost wished he'd stayed in his wolf form.

He staggered over to a bench and flopped down, dropping his head into his hands. Mireille sat beside him, close, but not touching.

"I'm the reason she's gone," Ronin whispered, so quietly that Mireille wasn't sure she'd heard him correctly.

"What?"

Ronin sat up and leaned against the bench, tipping his head back and rubbing at his patch. "I'm the reason she was arrested."

Mireille didn't respond. His tone was penitent. And she had a feeling he wasn't done confessing.

"She didn't tell me." Devastation crumpled Ronin's face, years of guilt and regret. "I had no idea she was going to be there. If I had, I never would have... I would have been the one to... It was the only way to protect my cover within the Imperial Defense Council. I gave up the name of the rebel cell's location and Selene was... She didn't have time to escape before they caught her. It's all my fault." He turned to face Mireille, his sensuous mouth twisted into a grimace. "I threw myself into Tartarus for nothing."

Mireille closed her eyes against the blow.

She'd already endured so much. Two centuries within this Creator-foresaken place, all those Harvest Nights she'd survived, the endless, unrelenting captivity. Not to mention what she'd done earlier. Putting her body and scars on display for those asshole Brethren, letting the Koenig himself paw her, kiss her...

Ronin's words were worse than all those atrocities combined.

She felt flimsy. Brittle. Bright hot. Like molten glass that might shatter at the smallest tap before it had a chance to fully harden.

And all she wanted to do was hurl the shards at him. To use what she knew of his and Selene's history to wound him as much as he'd just wounded her.

"Maybe if you hadn't been coddling Selene for her whole life, she might have had a chance of escaping that raid."

Ronin went preternaturally still. "What the fuck did you just say?"

She pushed the hood of her cloak back and shoved a finger into his chest. "You left her there in that cottage in Denevrae by herself for years. Living in her little bubble."

"That was her choice!"

"Was it?"

Ronin's hand was immediately at her throat. He dragged her off the bench and into a dark alley, slamming her into the wall.

Exactly the reaction she'd been seeking. Her thighs clenched even as her wolf whined, *This might not be the smartest way to get what you want.*

I thought you liked him dangerous and savage, Mireille responded.

Yeah, dangerously, savagely sexy. Not murderous.

Mireille huffed a laugh. *Same difference.*

He snarled, gnashing his fangs so close to her throat that they grazed her skin. "Say that again. I fucking *dare* you."

Mireille didn't back down an inch. Pressed her neck against his hold. She loaded her gaze with every ounce of her hatred, of her longing, of her hurt and anger. His fingers jumped with her pulse.

Pushing down her feelings, pretending they'd been nothing to each other, wasn't working.

Time to blow it all to fucking pieces and see where they landed.

She narrowed her eyes. "After two hundred years, you came here for your sister." Tears spilled down her cheeks. She didn't care that he saw it. "Not me."

She felt wretched and stupid and selfish and pathetic that she was *jealous* of Selene. A female who, by all accounts, was a good person. A kind person.

Far kinder than Mireille had ever been.

Sorrow cracked her voice. "Did you ever think about me? Even once?"

Ronin squeezed her throat harder, cutting off her breath as he leaned in closer.

His answer was a serrated blade, ripping through her vital bits. "I thought about you every minute, of every hour, of every fucking *day.* Kind of hard not to after the damage you did."

Salty tears dripped over her lips. "I told you I was sorry about your eye, Ronin, I—"

He slammed her into the wall. Hard.

"It has *nothing* to do with my eye!" His roar shook her bones. "You broke my *heart*, Mireille." Softer. Shattered. "You broke my fucking heart."

The words echoed off the cobblestones at her feet, the brick at her back. They died somewhere deep within her, buried beneath her ribs.

She lifted her chin, pushing her throat into his hand. Giving herself over to his wrath, she whispered, "Punish me for it."

His golden-blue eye blazed with rage and that simmering lust she'd seen so often this past month. His claws punched out, piercing her skin, and blood trickled down her neck onto her cloak. "Is that what you want, little she-wolf?"

"Yes," she breathed as her eyes slid closed.

His savage chuckle shivered across her limbs. "I don't think you have the faintest fucking idea what you're asking for. I won't be gentle with you. I don't give a shit about your pleasure. I'll take whatever I want, and you'll be a whimpering mess when I'm done with you."

Creator save her, liquid heat gushed between her legs. "Then do it." She wielded her words like a dagger. "You fucking coward."

He snarled and spun her around, shoving her face against the brick. It caught her cheekbone, splitting skin, and she welcomed the pain. He tore off her cloak, ripped down her leggings, then sliced a claw through her panties. The ruined silk settled at her feet.

Brisk night air cooled her bare flesh as he snatched her wrists in a single hand, then drove them up over her head. Metal clinked as he unfastened his belt and she began panting against the wall.

No one she'd been with had ever understood how much she needed this. How roughly she *wanted* to be treated. But Ronin had always known. Even now, at his mercy and with his foul threats ringing in her ears, her core was molten. Aching for this.

Aching for *him*.

She bit her lip to cage a groan as Ronin rubbed the swollen head of his cock up and down her slit from behind. He pushed in slowly, *too* slowly, hovering just inside her entrance.

"*Please*," she begged.

He licked up her throat, then bit down on her earlobe, his hot breath tickling her sensitive skin. A shudder pounded through her body as he growled a command into her ear, "Don't you dare fucking come until I say so."

He thrust into her. Hard enough that she nearly passed out at the delicious pain. She had just enough breath to support the moan that blasted up her throat.

"Louder." He set a bruising pace, then latched his fingers into her mouth, fish-hooking her cheek. Saliva spilled down her chin. "Fucking *louder*. Let the entire city hear you howl for me."

The fingers of his other hand dug into her hip as he bounced her off his cock, using her body to get himself off.

But this was not about pleasure. This was about possession. Ownership. Ronin staking his claim to what had been rightfully his for centuries.

Her clit throbbed at the thought, and she slipped her fingers between her thighs. He snatched her wrist and smacked her palm against the bricks.

"Don't," he snarled, pumping into her in time with his commands. "I told you—" *thrust* "—not to—" *thrust* "—fucking come." *Thrust.* "This pretty cunt is mine. I'll decide if she gets what she needs."

Footsteps of the city's night owls echoed beyond the alley. Maybe some were even lurking out there, watching them. Watching Ronin use her body. Her nipples tightened beneath her shirt and part of her wished he'd stripped her totally naked. Let everyone see her shame, see how wet and needy she was for the male who'd killed her father. The male who'd left her in this prison to rot.

The male who'd broken *her* heart as well.

Ronin's hand on her hip tightened, and his thrusts became frenzied. He was nearly there. He coasted a hand up her spine and grabbed a fistful of her hair. "Tell me you hate this."

"I hate it," she moaned, palms flat against the wall, hips arched to let him in deeper. "I hate *you*. So fucking much."

So much that she didn't hate him at all.

"I hate you, too, love," he whispered, then latched his fangs to the back of her neck, holding her in place as he drove into her.

He circled a gentle fingertip across her tender clit and she exploded. Came so hard that the entire alley disappeared. And moaned his name loudly enough that every prisoner within a hundred-foot radius likely heard her.

A strangled groan tore past his teeth, heating her neck as he spilled into her. He collapsed against her back, and she rested her face atop her folded hands on the wall.

The gossamer-light caress of his lips across the back of her neck was so gentle she wasn't even sure it was real.

He pulled out of her, a long, luxurious slide, and shoved away from the wall, his seed oozing down her inner thigh.

She didn't turn as he pulled up his pants, refastened his belt, then tossed her cloak against her back.

He slipped out of the alley, leaving her to stew in the mess they'd made. The mess she'd asked for.

She glanced down at her feet, at the ruined silk shreds that used to be her panties.

Once upon a time, she and Ronin had been two fractured souls who'd found comfort in each other's damage.

But how could they ever find comfort in the damage they'd done to each other?

CHAPTER
FIFTY-SEVEN

THE AUTUMN AFTERNOON OUTSIDE Leonard's cottage was as crisp and bright as Xenia's mood.

She and Cael had been at the house for several days awaiting word from Tristan through the cuff. Nothing yet, though Xenia was manifesting positive outcomes as she traipsed through the wind-swept fields picking wildflowers.

Cass and Tristan *would* succeed. Cael *would* get the dragon and burn down those wards.

Any anxiety she might have felt over the future had difficultly taking hold in her endorphin-flooded brain. Cael had made her come so many times in the past forty-eight hours she'd lost count. He was *insatiable*. Making up for lost time.

Not that she was complaining.

She smiled at the memory of this morning's session: Cael bending her over the kitchen counter, tossing her white cotton skirt up over her ass and taking her hard and fast from behind, the warbling birdsong mingling with her pleasure-soaked cries.

These hills were so remote, so peaceful. A part of her wished they could stay here forever. Forget about the dragon and the rebels and their cause.

But that would require a level of selfishness Xenia wasn't capable of. At least, not for long.

She bent to pick a flower with a black center and feathery orange-yellow petals, then glanced toward the empty cottage.

Cael had taken the cuff and portaled down to the village to meet Leonard for lunch and get a report on the dragon. And to apologize for the table before purchasing the supplies to build a new one.

Xenia had spent the morning with a book in her lap and a steaming cup of tea in her hand. Leonard didn't have much in his cottage, but he *did* have a surprisingly robust collection of historical romances. She preferred to believe the books belonged to Leonard himself and not to whomever had left the few simple dresses she'd found in his closet.

She'd blushed and giggled her way through the spectacularly filthy *The Windrider General's Prize*, then decided to get some fresh air. She'd tucked the flute—which Cael had left in her care—into her dress, then plucked up a basket and strode out into the meadows.

She was examining a white spray of baby's breath when a familiar scent tickled her nose.

Something soft and...*bitter.*

Xenia turned into the wind, trying to locate the source. Her gaze caught on a patch of tiny red blooms resting upon a sea of deep green leaves.

Dienswort. Named after Dienses the Jester, the human God of Merriment. Xenia had seen plenty of pictures, but had never actually encountered the plant.

She pinched a blossom off its stem, then brought it to her nose. It was most definitely the note she'd scented in Elodie's vials.

What was dienswort used for? Knowledge tickled the back of her brain but wouldn't materialize.

In the distance, the cottage door banged shut and she dropped the flower as a smile burst across her face. She rushed up the hill to welcome Cael home, her blood thrumming.

Sweet Amatu, she hadn't realized it was possible to want someone this much. And so frequently. A bottomless well of need that could never be filled no matter how many times she'd had him.

She whipped open the door. "What are you doing back so early, I—"

The greeting died in her throat, and her basket of wildflowers fell to floor.

Arran Zephyrus's dark gray eyes roved over the scattered stems before they landed on Xenia with the force of a runaway boulder. He flared his wings, stalked toward her, and she could do *nothing*. Couldn't run, couldn't scream, couldn't *breathe*.

"I did wonder what could have possibly inspired my son to stray from my plans." Arran's voice was as cold and hard as frost-bitten steel.

Arran whispered something into his palm, then sent the message gusting through the open window.

He grabbed her arm, his wicked smile even more terrifying than his typical stone-faced grimace.

"Help me get him back on track, won't you, little human?"

Cael was certain that every inhabitant of the remote mountain village had descended upon The Mottled Hog for lunch.

The crowd was jovial, the food delicious, and the ale refreshing. For one silly, selfish moment, Cael thought he might just stay in this tiny town of farmers and artisans. It was a rare refuge, unspoiled by the Empire. A place where he could remain spectacularly anonymous.

He could picture it so clearly: taking a job as a carpenter or fieldworker, wearing himself out with honest work, returning to the cottage every night to rejuvenate himself in Xenia's nourishing embrace. Maybe with a little half-breed or two running around his feet.

A simple life where his lost wing wouldn't matter. Where he'd have the space to heal.

A life he'd never wanted before he'd met her.

He smiled into his ale.

"What are you thinking about?" Leonard smirked, digging a fork into his meat pie and taking a large bite, crumbs flaking into his white beard. "Making good use of my cottage, are you?"

Cael huffed out a laugh, but didn't take the bait. He lowered his voice, though the restaurant was so loud it wouldn't have mattered. He could barely even hear Leonard across the table. And no one was paying them a lick of attention. Spectacular anonymity, indeed.

"How is the dragon doing? I still haven't heard from Tristan, but it could be any minute now. I'll send word as soon as I have it."

"She's ready," Leonard confirmed. "Been keeping her well fed. Making sure her fire is all fueled up."

Cael dipped his head in gratitude. "I can't thank you enough, Leonard. When this is all over—"

Leonard waved him off. "Don't worry about me. I'll be gone as soon as I see her flying toward Diachre. My niece lives over in Cernodas with her mate and children. They've been begging me to move closer. And I hear that territory is a pretty safe place for misfit rebels."

"Good," was all Cael said before polishing off his own meat pie and downing the rest of his ale. He tossed a *dracha* on the table, but Leonard chucked it back at him.

"Your money's no good here. Not after everything you've done for her. I'd never be able to repay you. Not even in three lifetimes."

You might not say that after what Xenia and I did to your table, Cael thought, chuckling. Aching to return to the cottage and drown himself in her again. Though he did have one more stop to make.

He waved goodbye to Leonard as he pushed through the crowded foyer and into the sun-drenched street. He turned down the main avenue toward the hardware store on the corner.

Cael was two blocks away from the small shop when the cuff began to glow and Tristan's voice floated into his mind.

—*ame is Si—ear me? Ca—ound it's n—*

"What?" Cael said, stopping in his tracks. "Tristan? I can't hear you. Say it again."

—*nys. Her name is Sig—*

"Fuck," Cael mumbled, holding the cuff up to his ear. Like that would make a lick of difference. "What did you say? Her name is Nys?"

—*o. Sign—on's name is Sign—*

"Signys?"

—*es! That's—*

The cuff went dead.

But Cael's insides were glowing. He'd heard the excitement in Tristan's voice when Cael had guessed correctly.

He turned away from the hardware store, sending a mental apology to Leonard for the now permanently broken table, his mind swirling with plans. As soon as he got back to the cottage to tell Xenia the good news and get the flute, he'd—

Arran's windwhisper stopped him cold and froze the blood in his veins.

I've got your pretty pet, boy. And if you do not come back to Stoneridge this instant to fulfill your duty to this family, I will end her. Time's ticking.

The village dissolved as fury blinded him, fiercer than anything Cael had felt in his nearly two centuries-long life.

Villagers flowed around him, throwing concerned, sidelong glances as his fists clenched and his chest heaved.

Cael didn't give a flying fuck who was watching as he lifted the silver cuff and tapped the opal.

And portaled straight to Stoneridge.

CHAPTER
FIFTY-EIGHT

THE VICTORIOUS SMIRK ON Arran's face whipped Cael's rage into a maelstrom as he exploded into his father's office. Cael scanned the space for a weapon, any weapon, he didn't care what.

Xenia had been taken from him, and Arran needed to die.

Now.

Cael wanted to see the life drain from his father's gray eyes. Wanted Arran to know it was his own son who'd ended him.

Arran was about to round the desk when Cael remembered he had his own weapon. He curled his fingers, calling the wind in an attempt to snatch the breath from his father's lungs.

Arran coughed, staggering only slightly before counteracting Cael's gust with a swish of his wrist. "Please."

Cael lunged across the desk, fisting his father's jacket. "What have you done with her?"

Arran was the portrait of silent, haughty confidence.

"Fucking *answer* me!"

Arran squeezed Cael's wrists nearly hard enough to snap bone, then threw them away and gestured to the chair. "Sit. Calm yourself. I'm sure we can come to an agreement."

Cael's chest heaved, his anger a wicked beast urging him to maim, to *kill*. To tear through everything and everyone in this wretched estate until nothing was left but blood and bone and dust. He propped his fists on the desk and leaned forward, snarling through clenched teeth. "What. Have you. Done with her?"

He should have been afraid of his father. Should have been cowering and begging for forgiveness. It was the only way he'd ever known to survive Arran Zephyrus. And some small internal voice pleaded with him to do it now. To back down. To obey. To protect himself.

Arran looked shocked by Cael's defiance before his eyes narrowed. "Sit. *Down*. And we will discuss this civilly."

Cael scoffed. But what else could he do? He had no idea what Arran had done with Xenia. So, Cael would sit and listen. Would learn what his father wanted. And would then decide precisely how to end the male.

He sank into the leather chair, gripping the armrests tight enough to crack a fingernail.

Arran nodded curtly. "Better." He took his own seat and intertwined his fingers atop the desk. "I am curious. How were you able to remove the tracking device? They're supposed to be tamper-proof."

Cael glared at Arran. Wasn't about to confirm *anything*. "*I'm* curious, also. How the fuck did you find us?"

Arran cocked his head. "You made some enemies among the keepers at Typhon mountain, boy. Including one whose mistress lives in some backwater village up in the Icthians. She wouldn't shut up about the one-winged male who'd just arrived and was staying in a little cottage outside town."

Cael kept his face blank, relieved that Arran didn't seem to realize that it had been *Leonard* who was harboring them, nor what they'd been plotting.

Arran waved a hand. "None of that is important. What *is* important is this. I have her. You won't find her. And if you don't marry Elodie Laskaris, I won't merely kill her." Arran's eyes glittered with sick glee. "I'll give her to Tomas."

Bile crept up Cael's throat, along with such a blinding wave of fear and panic that his vision blurred.

"Why are you doing this? I'm *useless*. You said so yourself. What does it matter if I marry Elodie?"

Arran shook his head. "You're so naive, Cael. What does a male have in this world outside of his legacy? I have spent *centuries* buttressing mine. Ensuring the name

Zephyrus means something in this world. Something powerful. Something *pure*. And you think I'd let my own son sully that with a piece of human trash?"

"How is offering Xenia to Tomas any different?"

"Because he will use her how nature intended! Feed from her, break her, discard her. Not fucking fall in *love* with her!"

The moment the words left Arran's mouth, Cael realized he *was* in love with Xenia. Had been for months now. And he was about to lose her. Was about to get her tortured and assaulted and killed because of his love.

It was the exact scenario he'd always feared. It was why he'd left her on that ship in Rhamnos. Why he'd never wanted her to love him in the first place. Because he knew, on some level, that his love was too dangerous for her.

He slumped in his chair, every ounce of fight draining from his limbs.

He'd been such a fool. All this madness with the dragon and the rebels and Tristan. He'd dared to hope for an escape from Stoneridge, from Arran. Where had that hope gotten him?

Outmaneuvered.

And now Xenia would pay the price for his failures.

He couldn't fucking bear it. He would do anything, agree to *anything*, to ensure Arran would not snuff out Xenia's light. The world deserved it.

Even if he didn't anymore.

"If I agree to proceed with this marriage, I want you to swear you will not harm her," he whispered, broken.

Arran ran his thumb along his jaw. "How will I ensure you won't flee your wife after the ceremony and run off to rescue your pet?"

"And how will *I* ensure you won't kill Xenia after I'm married?"

"We'll make a blood vow," Arran said, opening a drawer and pulling out a dagger. "Breakable only by death. I will promise to send your human back to the colonies, and you will promise to marry Elodie and never see the woman again."

Cael held his hand out over the desk, palm up. "Do it then."

He didn't so much as flinch as Arran dragged the blade across his palm. A line of red bloomed, and Arran did the same to his own before clasping Cael's hand.

"I promise to send the human—"

"Say her fucking name. Xenia Cirillo." His voice faltered as her name crossed his lips. His Xenia. His Blondie.

Fuck, she may hate him for this forever, but at least she'd be *alive*.

Arran rolled his eyes. "I promise to send Xenia Cirillo safely back to the human colonies. She shall not come to any harm by my hand nor my command after Cael Zephyrus says his wedding vows to Elodie Laskaris."

Cael squeezed his father's hand. "And I promise to say my wedding vows to Elodie Laskaris and afterward to never interact with the human Xenia Cirillo ever again."

A tingle swept up Cael's forearm as the blood bargain sealed, and something within him settled.

Xenia would be safe from his father.

Forever.

And the only thing Cael had to do to ensure it was to give away his life.

"The wedding will take place tomorrow," Arran said.

Cael blanched. "It's not scheduled until next week."

Arran glared from beneath furrowed brows. "Thanks to your little *vacation*, it's being expedited. Fortunately, the Laskarises have no idea why you disappeared. I told them I'd sent you on a business trip, then informed Elodie you missed her so terribly that you wanted to get married the moment you returned."

Cael stood. "Fine. The sooner we get this over with, the sooner Xenia will be safe."

Arran smiled. "I'm so glad you see it that way. And mind the words of our bargain, boy. If you try to leave before tomorrow to seek help or escape, I *will* be able to harm her. I am not bound until you say your vows. Remember that."

Cael squared his shoulders, choked down the urge to wail and scream and thrash, and walked to the office door.

"Enjoy your last night as an unmarried male, Cael," Arran crooned from his desk.

"Your bride will be waiting at the altar tomorrow."

CHAPTER
FIFTY-NINE

Arran Zephyrus's tiny, hidden room within the Stoneridge library was far more claustrophobic than Xenia remembered. And she couldn't help feeling an odd kinship with the trinkets, relics, and dusty books lining the shelves. Like her, they were locked away, forgotten, discarded.

Fortunately, she still had the flute. When Arran had deposited her in here this morning, he hadn't searched her person. Had merely shut her inside and left her some food—a loaf of bread, a few worm-eaten apples, and a wedge of moldy cheese.

She had no idea what he intended to do with her after Cael's wedding, which Arran had informed her was to take place tomorrow.

Xenia had nearly cackled in Arran's face. What would Elodie do if she knew how thoroughly Xenia had claimed her fiancé up in Leonard's mountain cottage?

Xenia had been frantic for hours, banging on shelves, tearing through books, searching for the hidden door Erik had revealed. She'd yelled so loudly for so long that her throat was raw.

But no one had come to check on her.

She'd come to the terrifying realization that no one could *hear* her. Whatever spell hid this room from view must be masking the sound as well.

She didn't even know what time it was. Maybe it was already tomorrow and Cael was stepping up to the altar at this very moment, promising himself to Elodie.

Xenia knew the only reason Cael would have agreed to go through with the marriage was to save her from Arran.

She wished she could see him, talk to him. Tell him to run away and steal the dragon and join the rebels. To forget about her. She was just a single human—a pittance in the grand scheme of things.

Tickling the back of her mind, also, were those hidden vials she'd found in Elodie's room. Especially with nothing to do in here but count down the hours until her death. She couldn't stop thinking about them.

She *knew* she'd read a description of something made with dienswort, some kind of potion, but the knowledge wasn't coming to her. She'd torn through the books in here, but hadn't found any botanical information.

Everything in this room was useless, including—

Arran's journals.

Perhaps he'd written the incantation to reveal this room in one.

She pushed up off the floor, then began searching the shelves. There were more than a hundred journals, many of which she'd combed through when she'd been in here previously.

But she dutifully checked each one again, hunting for Aramaelish phrases. As she removed each leather book from the shelf, not finding what she was looking for, she grew more and more frustrated. And that frustration led to mistakes. Like not bothering to put the journals back in the correct slot. She cursed herself for her inattention, especially after she began picking up ones she'd just reviewed.

She sucked in a deep breath to calm herself. She just needed a method, that's all. After she was done checking each journal, she'd put it on the desk instead of back on the shelf. So simple a child could have come up with it. But she offered her brain a bit of grace, given her circumstances.

Her hope dimmed as she failed to find the incantation after several hours of eye-straining perusals. Her hands trembled with fury as she picked up the last journal on the shelf.

This had to be the one. It *had* to. If it didn't have what she was looking for…

She said a silent prayer to Adelphinae—a Goddess she had *never* prayed to—then opened the journal.

Several minutes later, she launched it across the room with an audible growl.

Fucking *nothing*.

Despair and agony and helplessness brewed until she was a storm of heaving breaths and righteous tears.

She needed to attack something.

The shelves would do.

She kicked them, smashed her fists into them, shook their sides as furious screams tore past her lips. She kicked the unit so hard that the center shelf jumped off its pegs and fell to the floor.

Through her watery gaze, she noticed a small crack in the back wall where the shelf had been. She leaned in closer.

It wasn't a crack. It was a hidden compartment. She pushed on it and it sprang open.

She expected to find another journal.

Instead, she found a pile of letters, some white as fresh snow while others were stained with age.

Each was addressed to Arran in a ragged scrawl. There were ink splotches on many and physical tears on others.

As if the author had scribbled each one in an incensed rush.

And upon every single missive was the exact same message.

Death for death.

There was a date at the top of each letter. The same date, year after year. Xenia flipped through the pile—several hundred. One for every year since Arran had stolen the dragon.

The name at the bottom chilled Xenia's fury.

Lizbeth Burkhardt.

It also shook loose a piece of information from Xenia's subconscious mind.

The line from a book she'd read on herbology years ago in the Temple library: *Dienswort has an acrid, bitter scent and its dried leaves are the main ingredient in veiling potion.*

Those vials she'd found in Elodie's box. That bitter scent.

Veiling potion.

Oh, High Gods.

She needed to get out of this room.

She banged on the walls, clawing and kicking even more furiously.

No one came, no one answered. But she couldn't stop trying.

Cael was in more danger than she'd ever imagined.

CHAPTER SIXTY

THE KOENIG'S THRONE ROOM looked quite a bit more joyous than it had on the day Cassandra had arrived in Tartarus.

An arrangement of round black tables topped with lit candles ringed the room's outer edge. Beside the dais, a quartet of musicians were plucking out jaunty tunes that powered twirling couples across the dance floor.

Aside from the decorations, the other difference was the sheer amount of Fae in the hall. Nearly every single prisoner from the city below had been invited to tonight's pre-trial feast, it seemed.

The Brethren who'd delivered the invitation yesterday morning—just after Tristan had finally, after three days of trying, managed to contact Cael before the cuff's magic had sputtered out—had also dropped off two garment bags, one for Cassandra and one for

Mireille. Each held a dress with a note—a command really—to wear them tonight.

Cassandra, Mireille, Ronin and Tristan had spent a long hour debating what to do.

On the one hand, Cassandra felt she should spend tonight resting to prepare for tomorrow's appeal. On the other, to refuse the Koenig's invitation would be a grave insult. And he might very well send a few Brethren down to fetch her anyway.

They'd all agreed it was safer to play along. To keep indulgences to a minimum. And to leave as early as possible once they'd shown their faces. Well, three of their faces. Tristan would attend as a Ghostwalker only, hidden beneath his wings and a scent-suppressing potion Mireille had concocted. Cassandra had begged him to stay at the apartment tonight, to not risk exposure. Of course, he'd refused. She could feel his tense presence behind her now.

She spied Silas at a table in the corner in quiet discussion with a Beastrunner female from the Kennel volunteers. Cassandra nodded a greeting when they noticed her, then scanned the room for humans.

She breathed a small sigh of relief when she didn't find any.

As they pushed deeper into the hall, many heads swiveled toward Mireille. Not that Cassandra could blame them.

Mireille's burgundy silk dress featured a strapless, gathered bodice that hugged her shapely figure and cascaded layers of chiffon past her feet. She looked *stunning*. And when she'd emerged from her bedroom earlier, Ronin looked like someone had punched him in the chest.

Cassandra's own dress was lily-white silk in a halter-style to accommodate her wings. In a likely unintended consequence, it also showed off the results of her training: her sleek, muscled shoulders, her toned upper arms. Tristan had smiled appreciatively at her new Fae strength on proud display, then murmured something about the bastard having excellent taste.

The dresses *were* undeniably beautiful.

But that's all they were.

A blatant attempt by Aedelmar to put Cassandra and Mireille on display for him and his Brethren. To transform the females into decorations instead of the weapons they were.

Ronin hadn't received a costume from the Koenig, so he wore a pair of slim leather trousers and a sky-blue cotton shirt. To which he'd clipped a piece of maroon silk from the underside of Mireille's skirts in solidarity.

At the far end of the dance floor, just in front of the dais, long tables were piled with roasted meats, potatoes swimming in butter and rosemary, honey-soaked cakes topped with edible flowers—the Koenig showing off the bounty he'd provided with the hammer's magic.

In the center of the table, a large swan with pristine white feathers gleamed in the candleglow. Its wings were raised to expose a bulb of glazed meat from which several slices had already been removed.

Cassandra raised her chin and flared her own pristine white wings, fluttering her silk dress.

Wormwood scurried over, wearing a preening smile. He winked at Ronin, who offered him a fanged grin in return.

"Challenger Fortin," Wormwood said. "You look like a lovely, delicate blossom. Come." He plucked up her forearm and rested it atop his own. "I'll have someone fetch you some food." He snapped at a servant, then flicked toward the buffet. "Let us not be enemies tonight. We will dine, drink, and dance to honor Vestan."

Cassandra didn't bother responding. Stoic and strong, that was her mask tonight. She'd be a careful observer, would protest nothing, and wouldn't show a hint of nerves. She knew without a shadow of a doubt that Wormwood and nearly everyone else in this hall expected her to die tomorrow.

As Wormwood dragged her toward the dais, Ronin and Mireille slipped into the crowd. Cassandra sensed Tristan move away, as well. Likely to plant himself at the closest column to keep an eye on her—a silent sentinel ready to defend, maim, and kill for his female. Her lips twitched upward at the thought.

Anyway, she was more worried for Ronin and Mireille than herself. Cassandra still had the protection of the blood vow upon her; they did not. The Koenig or his Brethren might attempt to put them out of commission before the appeal tomorrow, weaken Cassandra's chances.

Wormwood led her onto the dais, then sat her down next to the Koenig.

Aedelmar didn't acknowledge her presence. Was signing toward a black-haired male on his left whose beard was bathed in juice from his roast pork.

A servant placed a plate before her—slices of swan and nothing else.

Excited speculations and critical gazes roved over her, prickling her flesh and ruffling her wings.

"...*will never defeat him...*"

"...*does look a* little *stronger than when she first arrived. I wonder who has been...*"

"...*not going to last more than a few minutes...*"

She ignored them as she dug into her meal.

Wormwood sauntered to the edge of the dais. "Dearest Brethren and our most esteemed challenger—" he aimed an oily smile at Cassandra "—welcome to our pre-trial feast! We hope you've enjoyed yourselves so far. Please, help yourself to the generous bounty of food and drink provided by our beloved Koenig. Tomorrow, life as we know it in our little city could change—if challenger Fortin is up to the task."

Snickers erupted, and Cassandra ignored them, keeping her wings and chin up.

Wormwood raised a bronze goblet toward her. "May Vestan the Warrior bless your appeal. May he guide your weapons and your heart. May he offer you grace in victory and dignity in defeat. To the warrior!"

Cassandra darted a side-eyed glance toward the Koenig, but the male wasn't even paying attention.

Had a dark-haired Deathstalker beauty with jade green eyes and ebony skin perched in his lap. His hand was crawling up the thigh-slit in her salmon dress as she whispered into his ear.

Couldn't even be bothered to pay attention to what could be his last meal. He was that assured of his victory.

As Cassandra drank from her goblet, a small sip of wine to take the edge off, she couldn't wait for tomorrow.

So she could prove him wrong.

"He's looking at you like he wants to eat you," Ronin growled, shoveling a forkful of potatoes into his mouth.

Mireille glanced up to the dais. The Koenig was indeed staring at her. Ravenously.

Let the fucker stare, her wolf piped up. *Maybe it will make Ronin so jealous that he'll take us again as roughly as he—*

Hush, Mireille hissed, not needing a reminder.

She hadn't stopped thinking about it since.

But whatever madness was going on between her and Ronin—the knife-to-throat hand job, the rough sex in the alley—they hadn't said a word about either since.

Maybe Cassandra was right about hate-fucking being a bad idea.

Mireille waved Ronin off, plucking up her goblet and gulping her wine. So much better than the vinegary swill they offered at The Other Place.

Ronin tossed his fork down, then stood and held out his hand.

She cocked an eyebrow. "What are you doing?"

"Dance with me," he said, voice tight.

"I don't dance anymore. Only when lives are at stake."

Ronin wiggled his fingers. "Lives *are* at stake. We could die tomorrow." He sent a shit-eating grin toward the Koenig. "And figured I'd stake my claim to keep that mouth-breather away from you."

Mireille huffed out a laugh, but didn't rise.

"Come on, Valette," Ronin coaxed. "One dance won't kill you. I've never shown you *my* moves." Mireille gave him an incredulous look and he rolled his eyes. "Never shown you my moves with a *partner*. That silly number in the woods doesn't count."

Mireille snickered, remembering Ronin botching those ballet steps to save her from Julius Kosera. The memory softened her.

High Gods, what she wouldn't give to go back to that time.

She didn't care about the sex.

Liar, her wolf purred.

Okay, fine, it *had* been mind-melting. The kind of sex that ruined her for anyone else.

No, more than anything, Mireille wanted her *friend* back.

So she let him pull her from her seat. Let him lead her onto the dance floor. Let him envelope her hand in one of his massive, tattooed mitts as he placed the other at the small of her back. He pulled her into him, crushing her bodice against his chest.

His iced pine and citrus scent washed over her, and her eyes welled up.

This was a terrible idea.

She stared at his plush mouth as he twirled her across the floor. She wanted to kiss him so badly, she could barely breathe. But was terrified of his rejection.

Sure, they'd fondled each other, fucked each other. But kissing was... Well, it was too intimate. Something they'd likely never do again. She bit her lip to stall her tears.

Ronin placed a knuckle under her chin and tilted her face up. "Hey. *Hey.* What's this all about? Am I that terrible of a dancer?"

She garbled out a wet laugh. "You're fine."

He smirked. "Glowing praise."

"I..." She didn't even know how to start this conversation. Didn't even know what she wanted to say. Her soft question barely parted her lips. "Do you still hate me?"

Ronin tucked her head against his chest, blowing out a long sigh that stirred her hair. "I never hated you. Though I had every reason to."

"*Have* every reason to," she murmured against his solid warmth. "Ronin, I'm so sorry about what I said about Selene. I didn't mean any of it, I—"

"Shhh," he soothed, running a hand down her hair. "Creator, I'm so sick of it."

"Sick of what?" She nuzzled into him. Savoring any contact she could get before he tired of holding her.

"I'm sick of trying to convince myself that we meant nothing to each other. I just…" He sucked in a shuddering breath, squeezing her closer. "I don't know where to go from here."

A tear stole down Mireille's cheek, wetting his tunic. "What if we leave the past where it belongs—the bad *and* the good—and start over?" She gathered her courage, then pulled back to look at him, heartened by the affection in his eye. "If we survive tomorrow, can we do that? Just start over?"

He released her and held out a hand. "Hi. Ronin Matakos. Pleasure to meet you."

She shook his hand. "Mireille Valois-Fortin." Her mother's true last name and her father's last name. An honor to both sides of her heritage. If she was starting over, she might as well do it right. "Would you like to dance, Ronin Matakos?"

He swept her back into his arms, then spun her around the dance floor for hours, asking her a bunch of questions to which he already knew the answers and making her laugh.

But it was nice. The hope that they *could* start over.

As long as they survived tomorrow.

She tried not to dwell on it. Tried to enjoy the first stress-free night she'd had with Ronin since he'd arrived.

She should have known it couldn't possibly last.

CHAPTER
SIXTY-ONE

CASSANDRA DRUMMED HER FINGERS on her chair, wondering what time it was. Wondering if she'd shown her face long enough to leave. She was anxious to get herself and her crew out of this dangerous room filled with their enemies.

No one had discovered Tristan's presence, bless the Creator. She didn't even know where he was. Probably still leaning against that column.

Ronin and Mireille twirled past her on the dance floor, laughing and smiling. It heartened Cassandra to see it.

She pushed up from her chair, intending to grab her friends and leave, when a gong sounded from the other end of the hall. The crowd stilled and the dancing pairs paused mid-step.

A hulking Brethren in a shaggy fur cloak banged the gong again. Four strikes. Eight strikes. Twelve.

Midnight.

Cassandra glanced toward Mireille, who shrugged. She didn't know what was going on either.

Wormwood slithered out from behind a column and joined the Brethren at the gong.

Cassandra's nerves prickled. Was he going to make another speech? Chant out a final prayer to Vestan? Close the festivities?

Her stomach fell when the Koenig appeared next to him.

With an iridescent white feather clenched in his fist.

Silence blanketed the hall.

"Well, friends," Wormwood said, "it seems our challenger has tested the boundaries of her blood vow. Challenger Fortin! Come down here."

Cassandra stepped off the dais, and a tense presence settled in behind her—Tristan. The Fae on the dance floor parted as she progressed toward Wormwood and the Koenig, her mind whirling.

She may have prowled through Aedelmar's memories, but she hadn't *harmed* him. She couldn't. The blood vow protected him just as much as it protected her.

She stopped in front of the two males, and Ronin and Mireille stepped up to flank her.

"Were you in that room at World's End with the Koenig and Mistress Valette?" Wormwood asked.

Several Brethren snickered, elbowing each other.

The clank of their weapons chilled Cassandra's blood. She didn't have a single one on her person. Neither did Ronin nor Mireille. Tristan had the Typhon steel dagger he'd arrived with, but surrounded by a small army of armed males, it wouldn't do much. And sure, Ronin and Mireille could call upon their wolves, but there were at least two dozen Beastrunner Brethren who possessed similarly powerful creatures.

Cassandra and her friends were severely outnumbered and underequipped.

"Answer me," Wormwood barked, his obsequious mask slipping.

"Yes." Cassandra squared her shoulders. "But he came to no harm by my hand."

"How can we be sure though?" Wormwood hissed. "The apothecarist addled him. Who knows what you may have done to him in that room? What stories you may have slipped into his mind?" The Brethren crowded closer as many of the regular prisoners—save Silas and the Kennel volunteers—retreated to the edges of the room. "A challenger without integrity does not deserve a fair appeal. And without a fair appeal, the Koenig is not obligated to honor his end of the bargain."

"Which means what?" Cassandra flared her wings, muscles tensed.

"It means that the Koenig may appoint as many of his own fighters as he wishes." Wormwood turned to the crowd. "Brethren! Are you with us?"

The roar that burst from the gathered males shook Cassandra's bones.

"And it means," Wormwood stepped back, spreading his palms wide, "that your appeal begins *now*."

Chaos exploded throughout the throne room as a blur of white wrapped around Cassandra, followed by a streak of copper.

Ronin and Mireille's wolves circled her, snarling and snapping at any Brethren who attempted to breach their line. They paused only once, to let in Silas, whose dove gray wings streamed behind him as he came to Cassandra's aid brandishing a stone sword swiped from a Brethren.

"This way!" Silas shouted over the din.

Ronin and Mireille held the line, dodging blows from swords, slices from daggers, and swipes from the paws of other beasts as Silas guided them toward the far corner of the room. To a slim, unguarded archway.

Cassandra peered through the circling wolves, searching for Tristan. He hadn't appeared yet. Was probably waiting for the most opportune moment to pop out and startle their enemies.

Cassandra tripped on the train of her dress, and as soon as her tailbone cracked against the stone floor, a sleek black panther with ice-blue eyes breached the circle.

Jonas.

His jaws snapped inches from her foot, and she kicked out, ripping her dress. She caught Jonas across the muzzle, and he roared, rancid breath and spittle bathing her as she scrambled backward.

Mireille pounced, tackling the panther bi-form out of the circle, but not before Jonas sank his substantial claws into her flank and tore out a chunk of flesh. Mireille howled, and Ronin's massive wolf bounded over, grabbing Jonas by the throat.

The violence that Ronin wrought upon the panther shifter was savagely personal.

Cassandra's only wish was that Mireille could have done it herself.

By the time Ronin was finished, Jonas was nothing more than chunks of shredded flesh and tufts of black fur.

Blood soaked the throne room floor.

Everywhere Cassandra looked, prisoners were fighting off Brethren, distracting them from going for her or Ronin or Mireille. A rush of gratitude overtook her as she shucked off her shoes then stood, her bare feet sliding across the red-stained stone.

Silas was at her side instantly as Mireille and Ronin reformed their circle, weeping wounds matting their hides.

Cassandra could tell they were all flagging, though they'd kept the Brethren at bay. They'd caused a fair amount of damage themselves, tearing off limbs and crunching through throats.

In a spectacularly vicious move, Silas used two swords to scissor a male's head from his shoulders, then roared, "Through the archway! *Now!*"

They'd managed to back themselves into the corner.

And escape was mere steps away.

But where the *fuck* was Tristan? Cassandra refused to leave the hall until she had eyes on him.

The Brethren didn't let up. Continued their assault and slammed into Silas and the wolves, who held firm, biting and slashing and slicing.

Each time a weapon was dropped, Cassandra scrambled for it. She managed to assemble an impressive little collection: several daggers, a broadsword, and even a double-headed axe.

She held the latter aloft, arcing into limbs and fingers when necessary, and scanned beyond the wall of fur in front of her for the Koenig.

Aedelmar was across the hall. Out of the fight. And smiling.

He raised a brow at Cassandra, then turned and *left the room.*

Wormwood was nowhere to be found either.

Cassandra's back hit the frame of the arch, and she turned to see a narrow stone staircase. If they could get inside, they'd only have to fend off one Brethren at a time.

Cassandra opened her mouth to call out to the wolves—flagging, tired, wounded—when Tristan materialized in front of them.

He flared his wings wide, wielding a dagger in one hand and a broadsword in the other. "Go!" he bellowed. "*Go!* I'm right behind you!"

Cassandra's stomach clenched as the remaining Brethren—at least twenty—swarmed Tristan, eyes wide as a few recognized the exiled Imperial Prince.

The recognition was a blessing, as a few hesitated, allowing Tristan to strike first.

Cassandra stood in the archway, helping Silas and the wolves—who'd shifted back into their humanoid forms—through. Ronin propped up Mireille, who'd taken the worst blow from Jonas. Her left leg hung limply, and her neck and shoulders were covered in blood from a deep gash on her neck.

Ronin's face was a cold mask of fury. Like he wanted to shift back into his wolf and go berserk on the remaining Brethren.

As soon as Silas, Ronin, and Mireille were through the archway, Cassandra hollered to Tristan, "Come on!"

Ronin scooped Mireille into his arms and covered her neck with a palm to staunch her bleeding. He turned to Silas. "Where does this lead?"

Silas grimaced. "Down into the dungeons."

"Great."

"But the entrance to the west tower lies beyond them. The *only* entrance to that tower in the entire castle. If we can barricade it, between the five of us we should be able to hold the door."

Ronin's terrified gaze darted down to Mireille. "We need to get out of here. Get back to her shop so she can heal."

Cassandra frowned. "If we leave, they'll be on us in an instant. We'll lose any advantage we'd have protecting ourselves within that tower."

"And what are we going to do there?" Ronin roared.

Tristan barreled into the narrow corridor. "Wait for our allies to come burn down the wards!"

Silas took the lead as the group raced down the staircase. Cassandra and Tristan were able to stave off the few Brethren who'd given chase.

The group barreled through the dank, empty dungeons and before long, they arrived at another archway.

The staircase beyond all but dead-ended upon the circular room at the top of the tower.

Tristan closed the door and Ronin dragged an empty bookcase in front of it.

And the crew settled in to wait for Cael and a dragon-sized miracle.

CHAPTER
SIXTY-TWO

ON THE MIST-COVERED MEADOW behind Stoneridge, the wedding guests gathered in their finery.

And in his groom's suite, Cael's hands trembled as he buttoned his suit.

It was less a suit and more a military uniform. The charcoal jacket sported a row of silver buttons down the right breast and the sigil of Brachos over his left—Typhon mountain bracketed by a pair of membranous wings.

Cael studied himself in the mirror, the dark circles beneath his bloodshot eyes. A result of the hours he'd spent last night searching the estate for any trace of Xenia. She hadn't been in her room. Neither Mistress Ostere nor any of the staff had seen her. He hadn't even found any trace of her scent. He'd gone looking for Erik, too, but couldn't find the little bastard anywhere.

As a desperate last resort, he'd visited Tomas's room. He hadn't found her there either, thank the High Gods. But when Tomas had licked his fangs and asked if Cael was sure he wanted to go through with the marriage, Cael had no doubt his brother knew exactly what Arran had threatened.

Cael had returned to his room tired and devastated. Had gotten a few fitful hours of sleep before Petra bustled in this morning, the picture of oblivious cheer on her baby's wedding day.

Petra had hustled Cael down to this small room off the kitchen, shoved his suit into his hands and told him to get dressed. Said she'd come fetch him when it was time for the ceremony.

The door creaked open and his shoulders sagged. She'd come back earlier than expected.

But his heart lifted, ever so slightly, when he saw not his mother, but Erik standing in the doorway dressed in a similar Brachian uniform. His brother's unruly hair was slicked back and he wore a weary frown.

"Fuck." Erik aimed the curse at the floor. "I had hoped maybe you were gone again. Escaped with your pretty human."

Cael rubbed at his temples. "That had been the plan until Father…" He couldn't even finish the sentence.

"He's been more smugly evil than usual today," Erik ground out, stepping up behind Cael in the mirror. "Not to mention the servants have been working around the clock to set everything up for the wedding."

"Where were you last night?" Cael ground out.

Erik shrugged, rubbing at what looked suspiciously like a bite mark on his neck. "Constance arrived."

"Tomas's fiancée?"

Erik had the good sense to look apologetic. Not about Constance, certainly. "I'm sorry, Cael. I was distracted. I had no idea you'd come back. What happened?"

"He's got her," Cael said, rage a thunderous echo in his chest. "He found us and he...he took her. Said if I didn't marry Elodie, he'd give her to Tomas."

Erik shuddered, his wings rustling. "Where is she?"

"I have no fucking idea!" Cael roared. Erik didn't even flinch, just let his brother release his anger.

Erik perked up, his dark brown eyes widening. "I'll help. I can help now."

"It's too late," Cael whispered. "I made a blood vow. Promised I would marry Elodie and never interact with Xenia again. And he promised to send her safely back to the colonies after."

"And you trust he'll do it?"

"Even Arran Zephyrus can't break a blood vow." Cael's nerves flared. "Can he?"

Erik's brows furrowed. "He's capable of many things that normal males aren't." He canted his head to the side. "But I have an idea of where he may be keeping her."

Cael sagged with relief, then pried the cuff from his wrist and handed it to his brother. "Then I need you to get her out of here. Give her this and tell her to portal to Akti. A town called Lebaedia. Tell her to find the Teles Chrysos and Trophonios and give him this name—"

Cael whispered the dragon's name into Erik's ear "—and they will protect her."

"What is this?" Erik ran his fingers along the silver cuff.

"Something I got from the rebels. Don't worry about it. Just..." He dipped his head. "Tell her I'm sorry. And that I love her."

Erik grabbed Cael's shoulder. "You can tell her yourself. Just get through this farce today, say your vows to Elodie and then leave her. Not like you'd be the first male in history to step out on his marriage."

"And what? Spend the rest of my life running from him? If I leave Elodie, I break my part of the blood vow which will release Father from his. He'll hunt Xenia for the rest of her life. Even if I'm there to protect her. I'm not going to do that to her. She deserves better than that. Better than *me*. I've known it since I met her." Erik stared at him, concern twisting his features. "Please."

"Okay," Erik breathed out. "Do you want to come with me? See her one last time?"

Cael looked upward, tears blurring his vision, and whispered, "If I see her, I'll never let her go. And I'll end up getting her killed." He steeled his gaze. "Go. *Go*. The ceremony begins in less than a half hour. You need to be back by then, or Father might suspect something."

Erik kept his mouth shut, though he looked like he wanted to shout at Cael. Not that Cael could blame him. But his little brother merely nodded, slipped the cuff into his pocket, and left Cael alone in his suite.

Hoping against all odds that Erik would find Xenia and get her as far away from here as possible.

Xenia paced around the claustrophobic room, frantic.

She wracked her brain as she stalked from corner to corner, trying to piece Lizbeth's motives together. Why marry Cael? Perhaps she was trying to acquire his last name? If she married Cael, became a Zephyrus, then murdered him and his family, that would give her dominion over Brachos.

Is that what she wanted? And once she had Brachos, what would she do next? High *Gods*, if Lizbeth got a hold of the dragon... Did she know its name? She didn't have the flute, thankfully. That was still laying against Xenia's sternum, tucked safely within her dress.

She needed to get out of here. Needed to warn everyone. How many hours, minutes, were left until the ceremony started?

She pulled at her curls, her anxiety a swirling tempest, when a door appeared in the wall to her left.

Erik stepped in, and Xenia collapsed with knee-shaking relief, catching herself on the desk. "Oh, thank *fuck*. How did you know I was in here?"

"This is where Father keeps all his secrets."

Xenia glanced over Erik's shoulder, hoping to see a one-winged male behind him. "Are you... Have you come alone?"

Erik frowned, sympathy glazing his dark chocolate eyes. "He's determined to go through with the marriage."

"Why?" Xenia wailed.

"He's convinced it's the only way to protect you," Erik said, pulling the cuff from his pocket. "He told me to give you this. Said you need to get yourself to the Teles Chrysos in Akti. Give them the flute and the dragon's name."

Xenia's head shot up. "How did he learn it? Did he hear from Tristan?"

Erik raised his palms. "I guess? Didn't have time to talk through all that."

"Tell me."

Erik told her the name, and Xenia ran her hands through her hair. "I don't even know where in Akti to go! How am I supposed to—"

"They're in a town called Lebaedia. He wants you to go there right away. He also told me to tell you he's sorry." His voice lowered. "And that he loves you."

Xenia nearly snarled. The *fucking* idiot. Saying those words through his brother. Sending her away because he believed she was safer without him.

Had he learned nothing in Rhamnos?

She refused to let him leave her behind again. And when she saw him, she'd make him say those three little words to her face.

She turned to Erik. "Listen to me. Elodie Laskaris is *not* who she says she is."

"What are you talking about?"

"I found a box of veiling potions in her room. She's been masking her true identity this entire time."

"If she's not Elodie Laskaris, then who is she?"

Xenia frowned. "A female named Lizbeth Burkhardt. She's the daughter of one of your father's enemies from before the war. Arran killed her mother, brutalized her father and had him thrown in Tartarus."

Erik blinked. "What's her endgame?"

Xenia shook her head. "I don't know. But I have a bad feeling you are all about to find out."

Erik scrubbed a hand down his face. "The ceremony starts in ten minutes. What should we do?"

Xenia's lips curved into a cold, cruel smile.

Cael had told her once that strength came in many forms. And a sharp mind could be even more dangerous than brute force.

She was ready to show everyone—Arran, Tomas, Phidion, Lizbeth—*exactly* how dangerous she could be.

"Go back out there and act like everything is normal," she said to Erik.

"I've got a plan."

CHAPTER
SIXTY-THREE

CAEL COULD DO THIS. Just put one foot in front of the other. He could *do* this.

For Xenia.

To keep her safe from the monster seated in the front row, spearing him with a steel stare and a disgruntled frown.

Brachos hadn't seen fit to offer any sunshine for today's occasion. Misty rain coated Cael's jacket, face and hair.

He didn't bother looking toward the guests. Couldn't bear to see the joy on their faces. Not on the day he was giving up his dreams.

Giving up *her*.

He choked back his nausea and just before he reached the altar, his father stood and embraced him.

"Smart choice," Arran whispered into his ear. Anyone watching would have only seen a proud father bestowing some final advice upon his son. "For a second, I was worried you wouldn't show."

"I honor my vows," Cael whispered back. "I trust you will, too."

"Play your part today, boy, and your little human will be safe."

Cael glanced over Arran's shoulder toward his three brothers. Viktor yawned, his wife Helena shooting him a sharp look. Tomas pouted next to his fiancée Constance, who angled as far away from him as possible, her thigh brushing Erik's...who winked when Cael caught his eye.

Relief slowed Cael's anxious heart.

Xenia was safe.

He pulled away from Arran, a weight lifting from his shoulders. As long as Xenia was out of his father's clutches, Cael could *do* this.

He stepped onto the altar, nodding to the priestess of Faurana, High Goddess of Land and Life, who'd be officiating the ceremony. The serene, dark-skinned Beastrunner bowed to him, shifting her sage-green robes.

The string quartet struck up a processional, and Elodie took to the aisle, resplendent in an ivory crepe-silk gown with lace sleeves. A bouquet of white peonies dotted with red tea roses bloomed between her clenched fists.

Cael swallowed his anger and disgust, schooling his features into some semblance of contentment.

And offered a shaky smile to his approaching bride.

Xenia waited a few moments after Erik had left, then streaked out of the library and back up into the main lodge. The foyer was empty, every single family member and guest, plus the household staff, gathered out back for the ceremony.

The flute bounced against her chest as she tore through the quiet, stodgy hallways, searching for a specific room.

"Come on, *come on*," she muttered, the plaid carpet swishing under her swift footsteps. She was still in the white cotton dress she'd borrowed from Leonard's cottage, the cuff tucked within her pocket. Her curls were a wild, bouncing spray around her head.

Because fuck them *all*.

She would not be invisible today.

The lingering scent of smoky licorice wafted up her nose as she turned a corner.

"*Yes*," she hissed out as she came upon the heavy oak doors of Arran's office. She reached for the handle, panic flaring. What if the doors were locked? She hadn't considered that.

She pressed on the brass tab, then pumped her other fist in the air when a click sounded and the door swung open.

The scent of lethaphyll was even stronger inside the office. Xenia crept along the forest-green damask wallpaper toward the desk, her gaze traveling out the two-story window overlooking the backyard.

The office was dark and the sky was overcast; no one would be able to see her through the window, but she had a clear view of the venue.

Nausea dizzied her as Elodie exited the main house, then turned onto the path that led to the seated guests and the altar.

Xenia had never been to a Fae wedding, but she'd read enough to know that Cael and Elodie's vows would come at the end of the ceremony. First, both sets of parents would say a few words, then there would be a blessing from the priestess.

Elodie began her procession, and Xenia's eyes bolted for Cael.

High *Gods*, he looked impossibly handsome. So elegant in his Brachian uniform, the talon at the peak of his sole wing polished to gleaming. She was too far away to make out his face, but his posture was stiff as Elodie approached.

And even though Xenia knew he didn't want this, knew how much he'd prefer to be *anywhere* else, her heart pummeled her ribs at the sight of him awaiting his bride.

"You High-Gods-damned moron," she muttered. "Why, *why* did you make that blood vow?"

She turned from the spectacle, then plopped into the leather desk chair and began rummaging through Arran's drawers. She crowed victoriously when she found what she was looking for. Placing it atop the desk, she slipped the cuff onto her wrist and angled her head toward the window to see how the ceremony was progressing.

In the meantime, she tapped the cuff and sent one final message to a concerned, frantic, and ultimately, relieved Leonard.

Then awaited her cue.

"In times like these, one thing is more important than all else. Family."

Cael fought an urge to roll his eyes as Arran began the final of the parents' four speeches.

Phidion's had been bawdy, Zosime's teary-eyed, and Petra's sincere. His mother's words were heartfelt, genuine, and contained a few nuggets of wisdom about how to maintain a centuries-long commitment to a single person.

The foundation, she insisted, was to never take one's vows for granted. To show up, always, with empathy and curiosity. To fall in love with every new version of one's spouse.

The entire audience was in tears by the end. Cael nearly had been as well. For the wrong reasons. All he could think was how much he wanted that with someone *other* than the female beside him, whose eyes remained dry.

He also wondered how in the name of Stygios Arran had convinced Petra to marry him in the first place. And how the fuck had he been able to keep her all these years? Did Arran do *any* of what Petra had just said?

Cael's cynical side thought maybe his mother hadn't meant any of it. More pretty lies for an ugly day.

He turned his attention back to Arran, who had climbed atop the altar.

"The bonds that created us, the bonds we were born with, the bonds we choose to forge. They are what matter most. And though there are forces in this world, especially now, attempting to break those bonds, if we stick by each other, honor the contracts we've made—" his eyes darted straight to Phidion, who nodded in recognition "—then we will all thrive. *Together.*"

As Arran continued his blowhard speech, Cael fantasized about slipping the ceremonial dagger from his father's belt, plunging it into his back, and ending him right here, right now, in front of everyone.

His fingers twitched and he was about to reach for it when Arran turned, hauling Cael to his side. The side opposite the dagger.

"Cael, my son," he said with false cheer. Cael wanted to punch the stupid grin off his fucking face. "Elodie is a wonderful female. I doubt you deserve her—" the crowd tittered "—but that's the secret to a happy marriage. Wake up every day and assume you don't. Then spend every single minute making it up to her."

Petra blew a kiss from the front row as Arran winked at her.

The crowd laughed louder.

Cael was going to vomit.

Arran slapped him on the shoulder, staring him directly in the eyes. "Hopefully, she'll be able to replace what you've lost."

Cael didn't know what Arran was talking about—his wing? Xenia? That empty pit that had been inside of him for centuries?

Either way, Cael heard the unspoken threat in his father's words.

And to replace what you've still got to lose.

Arran retook his seat next to Petra, who placed their clasped hands in her lap. The two of them looked every inch the proud parents of the groom and Cael couldn't fucking stomach it.

He turned back to Elodie, who was beaming at him, then took her hands as the priestess inched forward. She raised her arms at Cael and Elodie's backs, encouraging them to step into one another. "Gathered frien—"

"May I say something?" Elodie's soft voice cut in.

Wrinkles of confusion lined the smooth brown skin of the priestess's forehead, but she bowed her head and took a step back.

Cael scanned both families, found questioning looks on their faces as well.

Then he glanced at Erik.

His younger brother's chocolate eyes were narrowed on Elodie as he gave Cael a subtle shake of his head.

Wait. Listen.

Elodie regarded Cael expectantly. As if seeking his permission as well.

Cael released Elodie's hands and gestured toward the crowd. "By all means. Today is your day."

Elodie demurred, "I wanted to say just how very much I agree with High Councilor Zephyrus's speech."

"Please," Arran crooned from his seat. "Call me father."

A pained grimace clouded Elodie's face, there and gone in an instant. If Cael wasn't standing right beside her, he might've missed it.

"Father," she cooed, honey smooth, and inclined her head. When she looked up, silver lined her eyes. "Family *is* the most important thing in the world. During times like these, but also in the times to come. If civil war comes for our continent, bonds will be tested, families will be torn apart, and many of us will be forced to decide where our true loyalties lie."

Cael placed a hand on Elodie's bare back as the crowd twittered polite, nervous laughter. "My darling, why don't you—"

Elodie angled her arm behind her back, then elongated her claws and sunk the tips into Cael's knuckles. An unmistakable warning.

"Please, husband." A saccharine smile. "Let me finish." Elodie cleared her throat. "As I said, many of us will be forced to make choices. Especially when our families are inevitably wronged. How long would you wait to seek your revenge?"

The guests were deathly silent, no doubt wondering where in Ethyrios Elodie was going with this. Many on the Zephyrus side looked embarrassed for her.

"Weeks? Months? Years?" Malice glinted in her eyes. "Centuries?"

She removed her hand from Cael's, then lifted her bouquet.

"Where I come from, when someone harms your family, you harm them back. An eye for an eye. A tooth for a tooth."

The yard was silent enough to hear the drizzling rain splattering the leaves in the woods beyond.

"Or perhaps, a son for a mother."

Arran shot to his feet as Elodie turned to Cael, gifting him a glorious smile.

"*Per Ta Cynn Drakan*," she whispered, then slid the top of her bouquet off the stem with an unmistakable metallic hiss. She lifted the dagger up over her head, then arced it down toward Cael's chest.

Before he could yell or blink or step back, a flash of rainbow light bloomed behind Elodie.

"Don't *fucking* touch him," Xenia snarled.

She pressed the barrel of Arran's gold pistol—the one he used to implant tracking devices—to Elodie's neck, then pulled the trigger and tapped the cuff around her wrist.

Cael reached for Xenia, his fingers brushing her forearm, and the last thing he heard before he, Xenia, and Elodie portaled off the altar was the war cry that erupted from the Laskaris side of the aisle.

"*Per Ta Cynn Drakan!*"

CHAPTER SIXTY-FOUR

THE CUFF SPIT ELODIE and Xenia out at the base of a moss-covered tree deep within the woods behind Stoneridge. The damp ground soaked Xenia's dress as she spun away from Elodie's claws and frantically searched for Cael.

He'd grabbed her arm before she'd portaled with the cuff, but he must've slipped before they'd fully made the jump. Only Elodie and Xenia had arrived beneath the tree.

Well, not *Elodie*.

Lizbeth Burkhardt.

Lizbeth stood on shaky feet, pressing her palm against her neck. Inky crimson lines trailed down the ivory bodice of her elegant wedding dress, and wet leaves clung to her lace sleeves. Her bouquet was nowhere to found, buried within the layers of vegetation at their feet.

"You little *CUNT*," Lizbeth roared, lunging for Xenia, who tapped her cuff and reappeared several feet away. "Do you have *any* idea what you've just ruined? How many centuries of planning?"

Keep her talking, keep her chasing.

Those were the only thoughts in Xenia's mind.

Just a few more jumps, and—

Lizbeth's claw caught Xenia's shoulder and she yelped, portaling a few yards further.

All the jumping was making her nauseous. Though the distances were short, the frequency was jarring. Xenia's vision blurred and spots appeared in her periphery.

High *Gods*, where was Cael?

Xenia pressed a hand against a damp tree, trying to not to vomit as Lizbeth stalked toward her. "I'm sorry about your parents, I truly am, but—"

Lizbeth paused, startled. "How do you know who my parents were?"

"The Cynn Drakan. Aedelmar and Priya Burkhardt. Everything Arran took from you… the dragon, your people. I'm so sorry for all of it."

Lizbeth's face crumpled momentarily before twisting with fiery rage. "You have no idea what you've done. *No* idea! He was mine to end, and you took him from me, and—"

"I know the dragon's name," Xenia said, playing her final card.

Lizbeth's features went carefully blank.

Xenia continued, "Were you hoping to get it from Arran? That's what you've been searching for, isn't it? Were you hoping to ransom his son for it? Arran wouldn't have given it to you. He would have let you kill Cael before he'd give up that information."

"How do *you* know it?" Lizbeth crept closer and Xenia's fingers hovered over the cuff. Rain plinked against the leaves, puddling at her feet. Birds chirped overhead, and the wind whistled through the branches. The edge of the tree line—Xenia's final destination—was less than a hundred feet away.

"Your father is *alive*," Xenia said and Lizbeth's face fell. "He's in Tartarus. My friends were sent there, and they learned the name from him." Xenia reached out a hand. "We're going to *free* them. Lure the dragon, then take her to the prison to burn down the wards. You don't need to get your revenge today. Join us. Then take your revenge against the entire Empire."

Lizbeth tilted her head, considering, then rubbed at her neck wound again. She began to shake her head as brown fur fluttered along her limbs and her nose transformed into a dark brown muzzle. "I don't make deals with fucking *humans*."

Three things happened at once.

Cael burst into the clearing, shouting Xenia's name.

Lizbeth swiped a massive claw across Xenia's torso, shredding fabric and slicing her chest open.

And Xenia tapped the cuff one final time.

The two females disappeared, then reappeared inches outside the tree line.

Outside the edge of the Stoneridge property line.

Where Lizbeth Burkhardt's head exploded.

Xenia collapsed to the ground, clutching at her ruined chest. "No no no no *no!*" Cael wailed, skidding to his knees in the tall grass and pulling Xenia into his lap.

She was covered in blood, brain matter, and skull fragments. He couldn't tell which blood was hers and which was Elodie's. Lizbeth's? He thought he'd heard Xenia call her that.

Xenia's hands brushed feebly at the vicious, bone-deep slash in her chest. Her skin was paling. She was losing too much blood.

"Stay with me," Cael begged. "Stay with me, Zee."

Her eyelids fluttered and her limbs trembled as a laugh shook her thin, cold body.

Cold. She was too cold. Cael needed to warm her up.

"What did you do?" he whispered.

"Pretty fucking spectacular, right?" she croaked, gasping for breath. "I think my rescue skills might be even more dramatic than yours." She reached beneath her collar, stiff and coated with blood, and pulled out the flute. She pressed it into his palm. "Call the dragon. Leonard released her."

Her eyes slid shut and Cael patted her bloody cheek. "Don't you fucking die on me, Xenia Cirillo. Don't you *dare!*" He bit into his wrist, pressing the wound to her cold lips and trying to force his blood into her mouth. She coughed it back up, couldn't swallow a drop.

She cupped his cheek, pulling his face toward hers. Her voice was so faint he barely heard it above the pounding of his panicked heart.

"Tell Cass…" she sucked in a shuddering breath, blood oozing from her chest and staining her teeth, "…tell Cass that I wanted to see her again. So much. That I'm sorry I won't be there to watch her take down Eamon."

"You'll tell her yourself," Cael sobbed, clutching Xenia's hand on his face. "You're not going to die."

A soft smile parted her lips. "You're so much stronger than you think." Her emerald eyes hardened with determination. "This will *not* break you."

She pressed her lips against his, then whispered against them, "I love you, Cael. Every part of you."

And then she became very still.

"Blondie? Zee? *Xenia!*" He shook her shoulders, but he couldn't rouse her. His Fae hearing detected the faintest pulse of her heartbeat. She may have lost consciousness, but she wasn't completely gone. Not yet.

He slipped the cuff from her wrist and placed it on his own, then sent a frantic message as the sun slid below the horizon.

He placed the flute at his lips and blew into it. A single, piercing note echoed through the world.

"*Signys,*" he said aloud.

Then scooped up Xenia, tapped the cuff and portaled back to the lodge.

To fucking finish this.

Cael appeared in his bedroom with Xenia's limp body cradled in his arms, and prayed to every real and false God in Ethyrios that the message he'd just sent had reached its intended recipient.

And that the male was on his way.

Xenia was still unconscious as he laid her on the bed, but every few moments her chest shuddered upward.

He cursed himself for making that stupid blood vow. It hadn't even mattered in the end. He'd never said his vows to Elodie. She wasn't *Elodie* at all. Which meant he'd never been constrained by the vow. And Arran hadn't harmed Xenia. The little fool had led herself to death's door all on her own.

But Cael would be damned before he'd let her walk through it.

He stripped off her dress, then cleaned and bandaged her wound as he awaited his guest. He peered out the window and down into the backyard.

What he saw was enough to momentarily pull his attention from the woman slowly dying in his bed.

In the burgeoning twilight, the wedding guests were tearing each other apart.

Tomas, Viktor and Arran stood atop the altar, hands raised and striking out with gusts of wind. A large black bear—Phidion?—was fighting a golden mountain lion, claws and fur flying. Cael thought the lion might have been one of his mother's distant relatives? Had Phidion and Zosime known of this plan all along? And if so, did they even have a daughter named Elodie?

Cael didn't fucking care. He was about to end *all* of it.

He searched the chaos for Erik and Petra, but didn't see either of them. Cael hoped Erik had gotten their mother to safety. Hoped they were fleeing the estate at this very moment.

Cael would be fleeing as well. Soon.

Kaleidoscopic light flared behind him and he turned, relief shuddering his chest.

Trophonios strode toward him. "What happened? I got your message. You said Tristan was able to—"

"No time for that," Cael ground out, pointing to Xenia. "Fix her."

Trophonios reared back. "*Fix* her? What do you mean? I can't—"

"Fucking. *Fix*. Her," Cael snarled. "Or the Teles Chrysos doesn't get the dragon." He pulled the flute from his pocket. "I played the note. I said her name. And she's on her way to me now. I can feel her."

And it was true, he *could* feel Signys. Heat thrummed through his blood and colossal wings flapped in his mind.

His destiny racing toward him at several miles a minute.

Trophonios knelt beside the bed, feeling Xenia's wrist for a pulse. "She's still alive. For now. But her pulse is extremely faint. Any other mortal would have already died from the loss of blood." He sniffed her wrist. "You've given her yours."

"Yes," Cael bit out. "Several times. You told me to."

Trophonios cocked his head. "It may be the very thing that saves her." Cael braced himself against the bureau, his knees sagging. "*May* be, I said. Even I may not be clever enough to bring her back."

"Try." Cael gnashed his teeth. "Or I swear by your fucking Creator, I will—"

"Now, now." Trophonios flashed his own blindingly white fangs. "There's no need for blasphemy. Especially since she'll likely need Adelphinae's help." Trophonios wrapped Xenia in Cael's plaid blanket and lifted her into his arms.

Cael ran his lips across Xenia's forehead. "Please. She's… I cannot live without her."

Trophonios's teal eyes softened. "I will do everything in my power to bring her back to you. Once you have the dragon, message me on the cuff and I'll tell you where to meet us.

It's time to free our Prince."

CHAPTER
SIXTY-FIVE

"You."

Arran's voice was as terrifying as ever as it boomed across the killing field that had been a wedding celebration less than an hour ago. Wild strands escaped Arran's braided hair and a gash on his cheek spilled blood into his copper beard.

Bodies were strewn everywhere, piled among the red-and-green-smeared chairs that had been white at the start of the ceremony.

It was impossible to tell which side had won. Though Cael wasn't entirely sure victory could be claimed by either.

This had been a massacre—an explosion of senseless, avoidable violence fueled by a centuries-long feud that had chewed up far too many innocents.

Phidion and Zosime were nowhere in sight, neither live nor as bodies on the field. Cael wondered if they'd escaped.

Not important at the moment.

Right now, Cael's sights were set on the three males atop the altar using wind and Typhon steel to fight off the few remaining members of the Cynn Drakan.

Arran left Viktor and Tomas to the task and stomped down the aisle toward Cael, who approached with a casualness that belied his volcanic rage.

Arran had done this. Arran had forced this marriage. Arran had endangered them all for betrayals committed half a millennium ago.

And Arran was the reason Xenia was barely clinging to life and on her way to Akti.

Arran and Cael paused before each other in the center of the aisle.

"This is *your* fault," Arran ground out. "You and that meddling human bitch."

"Do *not* speak about her that way," Cael said, voice low and dangerous.

Arran stepped forward, attempting to loom over Cael. But Cael was far from the skinny youth he'd been, cowed by his father's beatings. Cael's shoulders were at least as broad as Arran's, his arms threaded with sleek, lean muscle where his father's were doughy bulk.

Even despite all that, fear coursed through Cael's veins.

Could he do this? Could he strike down the male who'd sired him?

Less than a month ago, even two weeks ago, he might not have dared.

But the world would be better off without males like Arran Zephryus. Arran didn't care about his family's wants or wishes. He had one goal in life: capture as much power as he could for himself and ensure everyone who bore his name got in line to maintain it.

Cael had barely been able to stomach it when he thought he had no other options.

But now, he *did* have options.

And he was ready to fucking exercise them.

Arran laughed. "What are you going to do about it, *boy*? Kill me?"

"With the greatest pleasure." Cael snapped his gaze toward the dagger in his father's hand. "And with my bare hands. No weapons. No back-up." Viktor and Tomas, having dispatched the last two surviving members of the Cynn Drakan on the field, ambled over. "Just you and me. You always preferred fists anyway, right?"

Arran sniffed, wiping the blood from his nose on the back of his wrist, then held up a hand to halt Viktor and Tomas. "You want to wrestle with your father, huh? Will that make you feel better? Make you feel big and tough for your little human slut? You've never been *half* the male I am. Even before you lost your wing."

Cael focused on his breathing. He would not let Arran bait him any longer. He'd taken his father's cruelty to heart too often. Believed it to be the way of the world.

But Xenia had taught him otherwise.

He grinned, a broad, dazzling smile full of joy. Despite the day's evils. Despite the day's violence and bloodshed. Despite the daunting road ahead.

Cael smiled, and he laughed.

Then he rushed for his father.

He caught Arran unaware, knocking them both to the ground. Viktor and Tomas stood off to the side, nervous glances bouncing between them. Unsure if they should intervene.

Arran twisted himself on top of Cael, who blocked his face with his forearms as Arran smashed down with massive fists. Cael swiped out his wing, slicing the talon across Arran's neck and drawing a line of blood.

Arran roared, clapping a hand over the wound, and Cael took advantage of his father's distraction to buck his hips and throw him off.

Arran shook out his wings and shot Cael a crazed smile. "Got some fight left in you after all. Maybe you're more like me than I thought."

"I am *nothing* like you," Cael spat as he tackled his father to the ground.

And beat him bloody.

Cael was a tempest of rage and joy and instinct that Arran could do nothing to counter. One blow delivered for every time his father had dared to lay a hand upon him.

Arran's face was a swollen, pulpy mess as he garbled out a wet laugh beneath his son. "You don't have the fucking balls to kill me, cripple."

Cael wrapped his hands around his father's neck and squeezed. "Wanna bet?"

Arran's choking gasps severed as a force stronger than a battering ram crashed against Cael's back.

His brothers dragged him to standing and held his arms behind his back.

"Get off," Cael yelled, struggling against their hold. "*Get off!*"

"You're not worthy of the name Zephyrus," Tomas hissed. "Father should have ended you as soon as he saw your pathetic wing."

"A disgrace to our family, to Brachos," Viktor echoed, ripping Cael's arm back so violently he might have dislocated it.

Arran staggered upright, wiping the blood out of his swollen eyes, then cocked his arm back and smashed his fist into Cael's stomach. Cael braced, but it still emptied the breath from his lungs. He would've doubled over if Viktor and Tomas hadn't been holding him upright.

Arran pummeled Cael in the face. Broke his nose, cracked his cheekbone, smashed his jaw. Blood poured from Cael's nose, his limbs sagging in his brothers' grip. Arran pulled back for another blow, and Cael spat at his feet, cackling.

"Go ahead." Iron-rich spittle dripped down his chin, his voice slurring. "Fucking teach me another lesson, *Father.*" He stared into Arran's eyes but there was nothing in them. No love, no pity, no compassion. As if his father was more machine than male.

Cael was all too familiar with his father's mechanical gaze—one he used to try to emulate. It was why he'd joined the Vestians, why he'd aspired to a position with the Vasilikans. Arran had always seemed so in control of his emotions. Like he'd solved the great mystery of survival.

Feel nothing, bury everything, don't cry, don't show affection, suck it up.

Be a *male.*

But that was no way to live.

Tristan had tried to teach that to Cael over the years, but Cael had been too stubborn to learn the lesson.

It was only when assaulted by Xenia's positivity, her compassion, that he realized how wrong his father had been. About *everything*. How wrong Cael himself had been.

And if Cael survived this mess, he'd spend the rest of his life becoming a better male. For her.

He held his father's gaze, the mad smile never leaving his mouth. "If you're going to end me, you'd better make damn sure to do it permanently. Because if you don't, I'm going to marry that *little human* and pump her full of half-breeds. And I will relish destroying the Zephyrus family name."

Cael howled, hysteria overtaking him at his father's horrified expression. He felt no terror, barely any anger. Only pure joy. Because in his heart, he *knew* that end was waiting for him. A staunch belief in the most positive outcome.

He was moments away from blissful unconsciousness when something slammed into the ground behind Arran, rattling the chairs like bloodied bones.

Viktor and Tomas's hands trembled as they looked over their father's shoulder.

Signys's horns and scales glistened in the twilight, her iridescent wings tucked against her back and her long, spiked tail swiping the ground behind her.

Arran turned and all the color fled his face. He whipped his petrified, furious gaze back to Cael. "*What* did you do?"

Cael caught the dragon's kaleidoscopic eyes. *What's the word for fire in your language?*

He wrenched his arm from Viktor's distracted grasp, then pulled the flute out from underneath his shirt.

"No," Arran whispered, suitably horrified.

The word was crystal-clear in Cael's mind, uttered in a deep, lovely female voice.

Fieyrtes.

Cael tapped the opal on his cuff and portaled out of Tomas's grip. Right to Signys's side.

And Cael stroked her scales, grinning as his bonded dragon roasted Arran Zephyrus and his two eldest heirs alive.

CHAPTER
SIXTY-SIX

TRISTAN STARED OUT THE tower window, trying to will the noonday sun to creep across the sky faster.

If the tiny band of soldiers in this tower—himself, Cassandra, Silas, Ronin, and Mireille—could hold out until Cael arrived with the dragon...

It had been forty-eight hours since Tristan had given Cael the dragon's name. How many more hours would his friend need?

Overnight, a few Brethren had tried to breach their door, but they'd been chased away by the massive double-headed axe Cassandra had picked up downstairs. Tristan had used it to slice off a few hands, smash a few shins, lop off a head. After that, the Brethren had stopped trying to break through their barricade.

Wormwood—as arrogant and slimy as ever—had stopped by this morning before dawn.

"You're going to have to come out of there eventually," the weasel bi-form had crooned through the door. "You have no food, no water. And you may have thought you were clever, barricading yourself into a room with a single entry point. But that *also* means you have only one exit point. Where you will find us waiting as soon as starvation forces you out. Or you could take your chances out the window. But know that we *also* have Brethren armed with bows and arrows in the courtyard and on the east wall. I'm sure they'd *love* to pick you off one by one should you attempt to scale down the tower. Not sure you all could manage such a thing, anyway. One of you is quite injured, yes?"

Tristan hadn't bothered answering.

That had been an hour ago, before Tristan had encouraged Cassandra to tuck up into a corner to get some rest. She'd cocooned her wings around her body with only her head poking through her feathers. Silas was snoring gently against the stone wall beside her.

Tristan was too antsy to sleep. Hence why he'd been pacing by the window.

Wormwood hadn't been lying; Tristan could spy the archers in the east tower windows, plus down in the yard and along the walls. He could also hear Brethren guards shuffling around on the stairs. He hadn't spied the Koenig yet. Wondered what the male was doing while Wormwood and his Brethren were executing this siege.

Tristan sighed, then crossed the room to sit down next to Ronin. Mireille had fallen asleep with her head in Ronin's lap, and he was brushing tattooed fingers through her hair.

She stirred when Tristan plopped down, and Ronin checked the makeshift bandage around her neck, torn from one of his shirt sleeves.

"How is she?" Tristan asked. "Is it healing?"

"It was much deeper than any of my wounds," Ronin whispered. "It's starting to heal, but it will likely take another day or so. And she needs to get some food into her system. Her body can't help without fuel. So, if you have any grand plans to take a stand against these assholes, we should probably do that soon."

Tristan snickered. "She means that much to you?"

"Too much," Ronin grumbled. "More than I'd like to admit." He leaned his head back against the stone. "But I fucked it all up."

"How?"

"I should have done something—*anything*—over the years to get her out of this place. I just... I *left* her in here." He turned to Tristan, his mottled blue-and-yellow eye bright with anguish. "For centuries, Tristan. I should have gotten myself thrown in here sooner. Could've been here to watch over her. Could have protected her. I could have—"

"A very wise male once told me that if we spend too much time fretting over the choices we made in the past, we'll never move forward. She's forgiven you, has she not?"

"Yeah, but only because she thought she *deserved* to be in here. Only because she's been punishing herself for this" He gestured to his eyepatch.

Tristan cocked his head. "And have you not been punishing *yourself* also? Atoning for your sins against the humans—including her father—by joining the Teles Chrysos? You've spent the past two hundred years fighting for a world where Mireille's half-human heritage won't make her a second-class citizen. A world where her father might not have been killed in the first place."

"I guess," Ronin said, scrubbing a hand down his face. "If we get out of here—"

"*When* we get out of here."

"—I'm going to make it up to her. All that time we lost. Restore our friendship and do this the *right* way." Ronin stroked a hand down Mireille's coppery waves, and she nuzzled in closer. "Enough about my shit. How are *you* doing? We haven't had a chance to talk since you arrived. I can't imagine Ione is pleased that you're here."

"She's not," Tristan said, without an ounce of guilt. "But as soon as Trophonios told me how to get through the wards, there was only one place in the world I wanted to be."

Tristan looked toward Cassandra, sleeping peacefully within her feathers, her dark lashes kissing her cheeks and her full lips parted.

Here. Here was where he was supposed to be. With her. Always. Anywhere.

He rested his head against the rough stone, listening to the soft breathing around him. Ronin's own joined the sleepy symphony seconds later.

Tristan had no idea how long he sat there savoring the peace and quiet and watching the sun move across the floor.

He'd nearly slipped into slumber himself when a shrill voice called out from the other tower. He looked out the window, and his stomach plummeted.

Ronin ambled up beside him, rubbing the sleep from his eye and readjusting his patch. "What's going on? What does that mean?"

Tristan glanced at Cassandra, a grimace pulling down his lips as she stirred, waking. He swiveled his gaze back out the window.

"It means we're well and truly fucked."

"I will not let him do this," Cassandra said, standing by the tower window next to Tristan.

"I was afraid you'd say that," Tristan grumbled, rubbing a hand over the back of his neck.

Mireille and Silas were awake now, too, the former allowing Ronin to check beneath the bandage on her neck. The wound still looked red and angry, but it wasn't infected, thank the High Gods.

Tristan turned Cassandra from the window, then brought his face level with hers. She hated the fear and worry crawling through his honey-brown eyes. Would do *anything* to erase it.

Just not what he was about to ask her to do.

"He's using them as bait, Cass." Tristan's voice wobbled. "Don't fall for it. Cael is coming. With Signys. And as soon as those wards are down, you, me, and Silas will all have our wind back."

"And I'll have my fire." Mireille pushed up from the floor.

Cassandra knew they were right. She *knew* it.

But a cry outside turned her attention back to Ana, who was trembling upon the ledge of an open window in the east tower. The old woman whimpered as a gust of wind billowed the skirt of her filthy dress.

Wormwood smiled wickedly behind her. "Don't make me do it! If this woman dies, her blood is on *your* hands. The Koenig is waiting in the throne room. You're late for your appeal."

Wormwood tightened his grip on Ana's neck, and she grappled for his hands. Her rheumy, terrified eyes caught Cassandra's across the expanse.

"Please," Ana rasped. "*Please.* I was wrong. I don't want to die in here."

Cassandra squeezed her eyes shut, tears coating her lower lashes.

"Clock's ticking!" Wormwood crooned. "And we have plenty more humans in here if you keep dragging your feet."

Cassandra peeled her attention from the window, then turned toward the others. Tristan's expression was pained, Mireille's determined, Ronin's furious, and Silas's resigned.

"I'm going to do this," Cassandra declared. "It's been my destiny since I arrived. To fight him."

"Yeah, but you were supposed to have *help*." Mireille winced as Ronin helped her to her feet. "Ronin and I were supposed to fight alongside you."

"Well, it seems the Koenig is changing the plan."

"What are you doing in there, challenger Fortin?" Wormwood's slithery voice called out, followed by Ana's panicked yelp.

Cassandra cupped Tristan's face. "I just need to stay alive until Cael arrives. I don't have to beat the Koenig. I just have to *survive*."

Tristan grimaced. "We have no idea when that will be. How long do you think you'll be able to hold out?"

Cassandra squared her shoulders, flaring her wings. "I'll—"

A scream pierced the air, followed by a crunching, squelching, splat.

She rushed to the window, and looked down upon Ana's frail body, broken apart on the stone.

Hatred blazed through her veins, blowing apart her grief, as she glared at Wormwood.

Another human life wasted, crunched beneath the boot of an indifferent Fae master. This could not stand. *Would* not stand.

"Oops." The weasel bi-form shrugged, then leaned out of the tower and shook his head. "I think she slipped. Better go get ano—"

"*DON'T!*" Cassandra roared. "I'm coming."

Tristan's head was bowed when she turned back. She stepped into him and lifted his chin with her finger, whispering, "If we let those humans die for me, how can we possibly claim to be their leaders in our new world? We'd be no better than your father. No better than your brother. Every being on this planet deserves a chance at life, right?"

Tristan's lips kicked up, despite his obvious anxiety. "You want to lead with me? What makes you think I'm offering you the job?"

She grabbed the back of his neck and kissed him fiercely, not giving a damn about their audience. She broke away, placing her hand upon his heart. "Because fuck fate, remember? There's no one else for either of us. And you can pretend all you want that you're not totally turned that I'm about to go down there and kick some Koenig ass, but we both know different." She winked. "So stay close, Birdman.

"You're not going to want to miss this."

CHAPTER
SIXTY-SEVEN

THE THRONE ROOM WAS eerily silent beyond the archway. As the group approached, Tristan paused and Cassandra tried not to read too much into the tension roiling off his muscled body. She knew it wasn't because he didn't believe in her abilities. He was just utterly terrified at the thought of any harm befalling her.

She glanced over her shoulder toward Silas, who gave her a firm, determined nod.

Mireille stepped forward, supported by Ronin. "Look, I'm not going to lie to you. The Koenig is the most skilled one-on-one fighter I've ever witnessed. But he's not *completely* beyond pain. Those scars on his back still bother him. If you can strike at them, it may disable him for a bit. Or at least distract him." She narrowed her eyes, violence filling her voice. "And use whatever you learned about him in that memory you saw. Be *vicious*. Throw him off psychologically. Do whatever you have to do."

Cassandra's brows rose, and she darted her eyes toward Ronin. "*Way* scarier than me," he snickered, kissing Mireille's temple, but the laugh didn't quite reach his eye.

Tristan pulled Cassandra toward him, then speared a hand into her hair, their faces inches apart. "You can do this, Cass. Make the bastard *work* for it. You're smart, you're cunning, you're agile, and you're so, so strong. The strongest person I've ever met." He planted a soft kiss on her lips. Not passionate and hungry. Not saying goodbye. Just a kiss that said, *I believe in you. I believe that you will survive. I believe that you will come back to me.*

Neither said *I love you.* They'd say it after.

"What are you all doing in there?" Wormwood rasped from the throne room. "Have you changed your mind, challenger? Do I need to have the Brethren make another trip to the Kennel?"

Cassandra steeled her spine, kissed Tristan again, then sauntered through the archway.

The crowd in the throne room was larger than she expected given the silence.

The space directly in front of the dais was empty, the black stone floor gleaming like an obsidian pool in the buttery, late-afternoon sunshine. But every other available space was occupied by not only Brethren, but many of the city's regular citizens. Several sported wounds and bruises, the results of their resistance against the Brethren.

Cassandra wondered why they weren't locked up in the dungeons, then realized the Koenig would never pass up an opportunity to showcase his strength.

The male himself was seated on his throne, his baldric of knives crossing his bare chest and his eyes ringed in fresh kohl.

"Aww, you did your make-up for me, Aedelmar." She winked. "I'm flattered."

His frown deepened, whether at the jab or her use of his true name, she couldn't tell.

From the floor before the dais, Wormwood offered Cassandra a mawkish smile, then gestured toward a cage of iron bars with a thick padlock.

"For your friends," Wormwood preened. "Can't have them rushing to your aid now, can we?"

Tristan tensed behind her, and she reached back to grab his wrist, running her thumb across his racing pulse. He didn't protest as he pulled away and walked into the cage with the others.

Wormwood clanged the door shut and closed the padlock. Ronin assisted Mireille to the floor, then sat down behind her, cradling her between his legs and against his chest. Silas joined Tristan at the bars, wrapping his hands around them.

Cassandra lifted and lowered her wings, then smiled at Silas. Thanking him for his assistance. He smiled back.

She looked to Tristan once more, emboldened by the pride and love and certainty she found on his face. She rattled her feathers, preening at him.

Unbreakable. She sent the thought toward him.

Wormwood stepped toward her, then beckoned the Koenig to join them. "Challenger Fortin, since you've so graciously agreed to handle your appeal alone, the

Koenig will allow you to choose which weapons you'll be fighting with."

Cassandra looked toward Mireille, who gave a subtle shake of her head. Cassandra wouldn't choose swords, no fucking way. A month was *not* enough time to gain the skills necessary to fight off a male who'd been wielding a broadsword for nearly a thousand years. If Mireille and Ronin had been fighting alongside her, then sure, she would have chosen swords.

But facing the Koenig alone, there was only one way she had a chance.

She announced to the crowd, "I choose no weapons at all."

The Koenig's shark-like grin appeared as he slipped off his baldric, an eyebrow raised in approval. A portion of the crowd laughed at Cassandra's decision, some out loud and some behind their hands.

And as the Koenig settled into his stance, at least a foot taller than her and far broader and stronger in every way, Cassandra wondered if she'd just made a terrible mistake.

The first move Cassandra made, something that inspired gasps throughout the hall and whooping cheers from the cage, was to activate her camouflaging feathers.

She didn't fully achieve it. She could tell by where the Koenig's eyes darted that pieces of her body were still visible—an area down by her legs and the upper half of her head.

But it was better than being completely exposed. Especially when the Koenig rushed for her.

She side-stepped, her body hidden enough to throw off his aim, and he skidded past her, smacking his palms against a column.

A snarl bubbled in his throat as he turned, his mad gaze glancing across her until he focused on her forehead.

"Come on, *come on*," she muttered, rattling her feathers and trying to activate each one like Tristan had told her.

It didn't work.

The Koenig barreled toward her again.

She swore under her breath and barely pivoted away in time to avoid his path. His fingers invaded her invisible feathers, coming close enough to her face for her to bite down on them—*hard*. He barked out a yelp, then jumped back.

She re-arranged her wings, shook her feathers to reactivate the camouflage, but even less obeyed this time. Many were askew due to the Koenig's assault.

Her entire torso was visible—she could tell by where the Koenig was staring, waiting patiently across the floor as if trying to discern her next move.

This was useless. If she couldn't activate all her feathers, she'd never be able to hide from him.

She took the chance, whipped open her wings, and faced down Aedelmar.

Tristan and Silas barked out protests from the cage, but she ignored them. This was her fight. Her choice.

The Brethren, Wormwood included, erupted into gleeful bellows as the Koenig stalked toward her.

She didn't back down, ran directly for him—hoping to surprise him—but before she could pivot, he wrapped an arm around her waist and slammed her to the ground.

Her skull hit the black stone, her vision swirling. The Koenig attempted to pounce on her, but she rolled away and popped to her feet. She darted behind him and raked her fingernails across the scars on his back.

The Koenig released a half-mad roar, then whirled, swinging out with his fists. Cassandra ducked out of the way, though not easily.

High *Gods,* this fucker was fast.

The fight stretched for long minutes, Cassandra getting in a few choice blows—mostly kicks to the Koenig's back, ribs, and legs—that had the male wincing in visible pain and Cassandra's hope soaring. But for every strike she landed, Aedelmar landed three.

Elbows to her chest, chops to the back of her neck, a fist across her jaw. The blows felt like running full speed into a brick wall.

After each one, the Koenig would back away, smirking down at her. Expecting her to give up.

And every time, she'd lurch to her feet, lift her fists, and beckon him forward.

Again.

For Ana.

And again.

For Xenia.

And again.

For Mama.

And again.

For the woman Cassandra had been at the Temple. A rebel wolf in sheep's clothing, waiting to tear her enemies apart with her teeth.

She wouldn't give up. She couldn't. No matter how broken she felt, no matter how disoriented, she would never let a male like Aedelmar Burkhardt—a male who thrived on violence and subjugation—defeat her.

She glanced toward the window as the last golden rays of dusk slipped away.

If she could keep this up, could just *survive*, until Cael and Signys arrived, then she, Tristan, Mireille, and Silas would regain their elemental magics and—

The Koenig's fist connected with the side of her face and her brain rattled in her skull. Searing pain radiated up her cheek and down her neck.

He'd broken her jaw.

She staggered back, but he captured her head, then folded her in half and crashed his knee into her forehead. A brow split, and a rush of hot red blinded her.

She tried to twist away, but dizziness overwhelmed her as she crashed to the stone floor, writhing in pain. The ringing between her ears drowned out every sound. All save agonized wails and groaning metal as Tristan pulled against the bars of the cage—desperate to reach her. Desperate to save her.

She could do nothing but crawl away from the Koenig, who'd retrieved his warhammer and was stalking toward her with it.

She rolled onto her back and he knelt above her, his thighs bracketing her hips, his knees crushing her feathered wings. She could barely feel them.

She was nothing but a bloodied face atop a pile of broken limbs and what the fuck had she been thinking, taking on this male without a weapon? Though to be fair, if she'd let him have a weapon, she'd probably be dead by now.

A victorious smile bloomed onto Aedelmar's terrifying face as he arced the hammer over his head.

She stopped him with a single word.

"*Priya.*"

The hammer stopped inches from her nose, and centuries-old sorrow dampened his sapphire eyes as his chest stilled.

"Priya," Cassandra moaned around her sticky lump of a tongue. "You…didn't…get…a goodbye. Let…me…have one."

The Koenig's arms fell to his sides as he sat back on her thighs, his weight nearly crushing her bones.

"Please…let me…say…goodbye." A tear dripped from the corner of her eye and trailed down her temple as she turned to toward the iron cage. Toward Tristan. His knuckles were bone-white as he clenched the bars hard enough to snap them.

The Koenig followed her gaze, then pushed off her. He snapped at Wormwood, his fingers dancing.

The weasel bi-form shuffled over wearing a confused smile. "Yes, but I… Well, that is very sympathetic of you, but… Do you really think… *Fine.*" He released a frustrated huff as he hustled over to open the cage, allowing Tristan— and only Tristan—to exit.

Tristan leapt through the door, but Wormwood stopped him, wrapping a clawed hand around his forearm. "Sixty seconds to say goodbye. Then it's over." He pushed his claws out, sinking the tips into Tristan's flesh and drawing blood. "And if you try *anything*, your friends die."

A line of Brethren poured into the cage, placing daggers at Ronin, Mireille, and Silas's throats.

Tristan didn't say a word, merely clenched his jaw and ripped his arm from Wormwood's grasp. Claret drops plinked to the floor as he stalked over to Cassandra.

The Koenig stepped back and swung his hammer over his shoulder. Waiting. Allowing Tristan and Cassandra a final moment together.

Tristan knelt down beside her, his hands hovering over her chest and arms. As if he wanted to pull her into his lap but was terrified of injuring her further. Her jaw was rapidly swelling and stiffening. She'd lost the ability to move it, to speak.

Tristan gently tucked his hand behind her head and ran his nose along hers. His honey-brown eyes were filled with devastated rage.

Good, she thought to herself. She wanted him to cling to the anger. Use it to reshape the world.

Even if she was no longer in it.

Their hot tears mingled as he pressed their foreheads together.

"Cassandra," he moaned.

Her lips tried to form those three precious syllables, but she couldn't manage it, couldn't move her jaw.

He trailed gentle fingertips across her lips. "It's okay, *ma'anyu*. I know you do."

She winced out a tear-choked laugh. The response was so him. So *Tristan*. And High Gods, what she wouldn't have given to have just one more anything with him.

One more year. One more day. One more hour. One more minute.

The edges of her vision darkened, and it was all she could do to focus on his perfect, beautiful face.

"I love you, too, of course." He traced his lips across his mark at the base of her throat. "More than any crown or any throne. In every world that's ever been and every one that's yet to come. Maybe I can find us one with a happier ending."

A sob bubbled past her lips and she squeezed her eyes shut against the tightness in her throat, the burning in her nose, the unbearable aches in her head, chest and jaw.

He thumbed her tears away. "Open your eyes, Cass. Look at me one last time."

She did. High Gods, she did.

And he was *breathtaking*.

She loved him so much she thought her heart might explode.

And wouldn't *that* be a gentler way to die.

It was the last thought in her head as Tristan cupped her cheek, and pressed his lips gently, so gently to hers.

A kiss to cling to as her breath dissolved and her life faded away.

CHAPTER
SIXTY-EIGHT

RAINBOW-COLORED LEAVES SWIRLED ABOVE Cassandra, stirred by warm, desert winds. There was silky sand beneath her feathers and a rough tongue lapping her cheek.

Her jaw was completely pain-free.

She struck out with an elbow and hit a fur-covered leg. "Alright, *alright*. I'm up. I'm awake."

As she sat upright, the tiger standing next to her rippled, orange and white fur transforming into light brown skin and auburn hair.

"Hey, Cass," Reena said with a sly smile, legs folded beneath a shimmering white robe. Identical to the one she'd worn in that picture Cassandra had found of Reena as a young female.

When she'd been an acolyte of Adelphinae.

"*Hey, Cass*," Cassandra snorted, surveying her body, which was bathed in an iridescent, multi-colored sheen.

She looked toward Reena, who was not glowing. "You're not dead."

"No. I'm not."

"But I... I am, aren't I?"

"Yes." Reena nodded. "You are. Again."

Cassandra jolted. "*Again?*"

Reena held out a hand, and Cassandra pulled herself to standing. The clairvoyant pool gurgled softly at her feet as a dramatic golden pink sunset kissed the dunes, a fiery sphere slipping beneath the miles-wide blanket of russet sand.

Reena stepped to the edge of the pool, beckoning Cassandra to join her. Her slinky confidence melted into nervous energy as she glanced out at the dunes. "I'm not supposed to be here. If she finds out..."

"She who? Adelphinae?"

Reena's brows lowered and her voice pitched low. "He does this every time."

"Reena, I don't understand what you're saying. You need to explain."

Reena gestured to the pool. "Watch. *See.*"

The second word faded with a sibilant hiss, Reena's voice multiplying a thousandfold.

The water churned, boiling and popping, then stilled. A scene crystallized upon the surface.

Cassandra's body broken on the floor of the throne room in the Koenig's castle. Tristan leaning over her, his lips pressed against hers.

Cassandra saw the precise moment of her death, the moment her soul left her body.

Tristan gathered her into his lap, letting out the loudest, most agonizing, most heart-broken wail she'd ever heard. She ached to return to him, to comfort him.

Wormwood approached, and Tristan tossed him aside like a rag doll.

Brethren swarmed Tristan, but he'd become a being of pure rage, ending his enemies with fists and feet, elbows and wings. In his feral state, no one could touch him.

His chest heaved, his features twisted into the cold, wrath-filled mask of a male determined to make the world pay for his bottomless grief.

A male with nothing left to live for.

He fought his way to the Koenig, who clutched the hammer against his chest. The centuries-old Windrider looked *terrified*. Tristan ripped the hammer from him, then swung it twice. Once into the Koenig's stomach, then once across his cheek, instantly breaking his neck.

Tristan approached the throne, then arced the hammer over his head.

"Don't!" Wormwood croaked from the floor. "Don't bring that hammer down! It doesn't belong to you! If you—"

Tristan slammed the hammer into the throne and a blinding white flash blanched out the pool.

"What just happened?" Cassandra asked, leaning over the edge.

"Tartarus is gone," Reena whispered.

The coldest fear trickled down Cassandra's spine. "What do you mean it's *gone*? An entire city can't just disappear."

"It can," Reena said sadly. "And it did. It has every time. In exactly the same way. Watch." She directed Cassandra's attention back to the pool.

Bile rose in Cassandra's throat as she watched the same scene play before her over and over again.

Small details changed. Sometimes Tristan's wings were another color—sky blue instead of iridescent black. Sometimes Cassandra's facial features were different—her nose wider, her lips thinner. Sometimes Wormwood was a Deathstalker and not a Beastrunner. Sometimes the Koenig was female.

But in every single instance, the ending was the same.

Cassandra would die. Tristan would climb the dais. Wormwood would issue his warning.

And Tristan would end them all in a flash of blazing white.

The scenes blended together until there were echoes of Tristan rampaging through that throne room.

"Stop," Cassandra whispered. "*Stop*. Please. I don't need to see any more."

Reena swept a hand across the pool and the water stilled, the churning boil giving way to soft ripples.

Tears blurred Cassandra's vision. "Why are you showing me this?"

Reena shook her head. "It can't end like this."

"Yeah, no shit."

"No—" Reena grabbed Cassandra's hand "—I mean it *will* not end like this. Not this time. The eight paths are coalescing. The specific convergence. You and I being here together proves it. He is coming for her. And it's not just our world that's at stake this time. It's *all* worlds."

Cassandra's anxiety skyrocketed. "He who? Reena, what are you—"

Reena cut her off with a *shhh*, then glanced back toward the dunes.

"I have to go." Reena gathered Cassandra into a hug and clutched tightly. Cassandra never wanted her to let go. "We'll see each other again. Sooner than you can imagine."

"How?"

Reena pulled back, her sympathy morphing into celestial confidence.

"Because I'm sending you back to change the ending."

She raised her palm to Cassandra's chest.

And pushed her into the pool.

The moment Tristan's lips met Cassandra's, they heated. Not the normal, intimate warmth of two mouths meeting, but something hotter. Something glowing.

Something divine.

The only time Tristan had felt anything remotely like this was when Ione had kissed him beneath the Imperial palace in Delos. But this was infinitely stronger.

He continued to press his lips against Cassandra's, but popped his eyes open.

Iridescent light shimmered across her body—whether it was coming from inside her, from inside him, or from somewhere else, he couldn't tell.

He pulled back, awe stealing his breath as Cassandra's bruises and breaks disappeared, her body instantly healing itself.

"Cass?" he whispered.

A drop of water plinked onto his hand and when he looked down, more droplets splattered. He touched his face, found wetness beaded there. It wasn't tears.

He was summoning water.

Beyond the wards of Tartarus.

A temporary gift from the Goddess due to the connection he shared with the female beneath him.

A rush of wind burst from the floor and Cassandra sat upright, placing a hand on Tristan's cheek. "Don't destroy Tartarus."

Tristan hugged her to his chest. "What?"

She snaked her hands under his armpits and clung to his shoulders, shuddering with fear. She pushed back and cupped his face. "Reena told me that we need to do it differently this time."

"Daredevil," he said, running a thumb across her blissfully intact jaw, "what the fuck are you talking about?"

Before he could interrogate her further, she pushed to standing, swiveling her gaze across the amazed crowd. Who'd just watched her rise from death.

Over at the cage, the Brethren holding Ronin, Mireille, and Silas had dropped their daggers.

Cassandra strode for the Koenig and reached out her hand. "Give me the hammer."

The hall was so silent Tristan swore he could hear pebbles rattling outside in the courtyard.

The Koenig cocked his head, signed something and Wormwood approached to help translate.

"He wants to know why he should give it to you," Wormwood said.

Lightning crackled through the throne room, snapping between the columns and arcing from floor to ceiling. Several Brethren screamed as a bolt cracked into Wormwood's chest and the male crumpled to the ground.

Dead.

"That was for Ana, you weaselly little prick," Cass whispered before turning to the Koenig and putting on a fake-sweet voice. "Oops. I slipped. I'm a bit new at this." She blasted an untamed gust of wind that blew back Aedelmar's hair. "Hand over the hammer. *Now.*"

There was a powerful echo in her voice. As if it had multiplied a million times over.

And High Gods, it was a thousand kinds of untimely, but all Tristan could think was how much he wanted her to use that voice while she stripped him naked and rode him into oblivion.

He'd always known his Daredevil couldn't be tamed.

Not even by death.

Aedelmar cautiously approached Cassandra, his footsteps the only sound in the hall. As if every one of his Brethren and each and every prisoner held their breath. He towered above her, clutching the hammer's handle and frowning deeply.

Tristan's protective instincts flared as Aedelmar grabbed Cassandra's hand and wrapped it around the handle.

He uttered a single word, a bit garbled without his tongue, but clear enough to interpret.

"Koenigin."

Queen.

Of Tartarus.

Cassandra had won her appeal.

CHAPTER
SIXTY-NINE

CASSANDRA HEFTED THE HAMMER into the air, grinning at the male who'd turned it over to her.

And though she hated Aedelmar for the cruelty he'd enforced here in Tartarus—she would never, *ever*, forgive him for how he'd treated the humans and the half-breeds—a part of her understood why he'd become such a monster. The loss of his wife, his people, his way of life… It was enough to drive a male past the brink of sanity.

She glanced over her shoulder at Tristan, those visions from the pool swimming behind her eyes.

Yes, she could understand it.

Silas shuffled over. "Hate to be the bearer of annoying news, but one of you must die by the other's hand. Or else ownership of the hammer will not transfer."

The hall tensed, and a flurry of sounds erupted: the hiss of unsheathed weapons, the pop of newly exposed claws, rumbling growls and snarls.

The Koenig grunted, then signed to Silas, who through a mix of intelligent guesses and pantomiming was able to interpret for him.

Silas addressed the hall, "He says she is the Koenigin now. Resurrected by divine force. He will die by her hand."

Cassandra passed the hammer to Tristan. "Careful with that, Birdman," she winked, lightning writhing up her fingertips.

Aedelmar made another series of hand gestures.

"I think…" Silas began, "he's asking about his Brethren. About what you intend to do with them."

Cassandra flicked her eyes toward the blond-haired male with the brown wings who'd thrown her into the moat. She had no desire to give him any kind of chance. She thought about Jonas, who'd taken advantage of his power over Mireille to use her for his own sick amusement. He certainly hadn't deserved more than the savage death Ronin had already delivered.

Could *any* of the Brethren be worthy of forgiveness?

There was only one person Cassandra trusted to answer that question.

"Their fates will be decided by Mireille Valois-Fortin," she pronounced, jutting her chin toward the she-wolf, who was still propped up by Ronin. Mireille offered the Brethren nothing but stone-cold indifference. Many trembled. "When she's ready."

Cassandra glanced up at Aedelmar. His eyes were closed, and his face was soft. Resigned.

Cassandra pointed the tip of a crackling finger at his left breast.

His eyes snapped open and he wrapped his hand around her wrist, his eyes saying what he no longer could.

Do it. Mercy. Please.

Cassandra gripped his shoulder for leverage, and just as she was about to unleash a bolt, a shuddering boom rattled the castle walls.

Followed by a bellowing roar.

Cael and Signys had arrived.

Cael was sitting astride a dragon.

A fucking *dragon*.

The only dragon in all of Ethyrios.

And though Tristan knew they were coming, it was still a shock to see the creature in the flesh.

Cael's ash-brown waves were tousled, his cheeks red and blotchy. He was bundled into a charcoal wool cloak, his sole wing rustling behind him.

From the exhilaration on Cael's face, Tristan knew his friend had left that wing out for the entire flight. Had relished the feel of the rushing wind and misting clouds. Sensations he'd thought he'd lost forever.

But there was something dark at the edges of Cael's expression. Something devastated.

Tristan's stomach dropped.

Where was Xenia? No way would she have let Cael leave her behind to free Cassandra.

He tried not to jump to conclusions, distracted himself by surveying Signys.

Her iridescent white scales glowed, beacons against the black stone castle. Her long neck ended in a massive horned head housing reptilian rainbow eyes and a mouth full of sharp, curved teeth. Tiny puffs of smoke curled out with each breath, a giant beastly bellows.

Two enormous wings hugged her back, though she draped one down to allow Cael to dismount. Before he did, he brushed a hand along her neck, and she chirped affectionately.

Cassandra, Tristan, and Aedelmar stood at the front of the crowd who'd amassed outside the castle to welcome their rescuers. Mireille, Ronin, and Silas gaped behind them. Tiny flames flickered at Mireille's fingertips. Testing out her magic after centuries without it.

Cael landed in the gravel and crunched toward the group, his eyes widening as he beheld Cassandra's wings. "Uh, wow." He swiveled toward Tristan, cocking an eyebrow. "Did you do that?"

Tristan glowed with pride, rustling his feathers. "We'll tell you about it later. Have you come alone?"

"The others are up at the intake tower."

Ronin's eye narrowed as he addressed Cael. "The intake tower is miles away through those black mists. Are you gonna give us a ride on your new pet?"

"Nice to see you, too, Matakos," Cael smirked, shaking his head. "The mists are gone. They dissolved as soon as the wards fell."

"The souls were freed," Mireille said reverently.

"And the intake tower is just beyond the hill across the moat." Cael nodded backward.

Cassandra stepped in front of the prisoners and called out in a commanding tone that heated Tristan's blood, "You're free to leave Tartarus. Free to return to the continent and take your chances with Eamon Erabis. But if you seek a different path, consider joining the Teles Chrysos."

"She's right," Tristan added. "Join us willingly, and you'll be given a chance at vengeance against my brother and the Empire who locked you away."

"What about us?" One of the Brethren shouted. Heads swiveled toward Mireille, seeking permission from their new master.

She raised a hand to her face, flames licking between her fingers. "I haven't decided yet. You'll be locked up by the Teles Chrysos until I do." She turned to Tristan. "Got any kennels in your rebel village?"

"We'll make some," Tristan said with a razor-sharp grin.

Aedelmar had fallen to his knees before Signys, sorrow and worship etched onto his face.

Cassandra strode over with Silas, and after a bit of back and forth, Silas relayed Aedelmar's final request. Shock widened her features, and Aedelmar grabbed her wrist, mouthing *please*.

Cassandra nodded, and Aedelmar nearly sagged with relief, but did not rise from where he knelt.

Cassandra returned to Tristan. "He says he wants the dragon to end him. It's the most honorable way for the Cynn Drakan to die. As long as I give the command, he will die by my hand and ownership of the hammer will transfer."

Tristan shrugged. "No reason to deny him."

Cassandra turned to Cael, who threw his arms around her and dipped his head against her neck, his shoulders shuddering violently.

Tristan had a very bad feeling.

Cassandra pulled back, scanning Cael's face with furrowed brows, but there were too many eyes upon them to discuss it. Plus, there was a centuries-old wingless warrior turned king of a warded prison turned loser of an executioner's appeal to deal with.

"Aedelmar wants to be ended by the dragon," she said. "Can you make that happen?"

Cael nodded stiffly, then walked back to Signys, who regarded Aedelmar with a slight tilt of her head. As if she recognized him.

Aedelmar closed his eyes, a tear tracking down his scarred cheek.

The ground shuddered beneath Tristan's feet as Signys crept forward until she was directly above Aedelmar. He lifted a palm, and she nuzzled it with her nose, her lids sliding closed.

Cael whispered a word to the dragon, too faintly for Tristan to hear, and Signys roared a grief-laden bellow to the sky.

Aedelmar signed to Silas, then opened his arms wide.

"What did he say?" Cassandra asked.

"To...Priya?" Silas said. "Who's that?"

Aedelmar opened his arms wide, then tipped his head back and closed his eyes, a faint smile curving his lips.

"His peace," Cassandra answered.

Signys's gigantic ribs pushed outward, and when she opened her maw, a column of flame poured out over Aedelmar.

The heart gem within the hammer, still clasped in Tristan's fist, pulsed. Faintly at first, then more intensely with each wave of Signys's fire.

The dragon closed her mouth, dissolving her fire, then turned her muzzle toward Cael. Seeking comfort.

When the smoke cleared, all that remained of Aedelmar Burkhardt was a smoldering pile of bones.

The gem pulsed once more, and a burst of red erupted from its center. The glowing light bathed Cassandra, then sparkled up her limbs and out across her feathers. Binding her to the hammer's magic.

The courtyard was grave silent, giving the Brethren a moment to say farewell to their erstwhile king.

And now that her ceremonial duties were over, Cassandra rushed over to Cael and cupped his face in her palms.

"Where's Xenia?"

CHAPTER SEVENTY

CASSANDRA'S SOBS CRASHED PAST Cael's ribs, pelting his battle-weary heart.

Stretched out beside Xenia in the narrow bed, Cass cried into her friend's shoulder as she maintained a vise-like grip on Xenia's limp hand. Cass's white wings—her fucking *wings*; High Gods, that was going to take some getting used to—were tucked against her back.

Cael knew exactly how Cassandra felt. He'd been in the same position—with less crying only because he was so fucking numb inside—the night after Signys had incinerated his father and he'd come down to Lebaedia to check on Xenia.

He'd spent the night here in the healer's quarters with his arms wrapped around her, begging the High Gods, the Lesser Gods, the Creator herself, to give her back.

None had listened.

So, he and Signys had left for Tartarus the next morning to burn down the wards with the rebels.

Tristan squeezed Cael's shoulder as Cassandra pushed up from the bed, circling the heels of her palms against her bloodshot eyes. "What happened?"

Cael grimaced. "She saved me. Elodie Laskaris, my fiancée, was Lizbeth Burkhardt disguised beneath veiling potions. Come to enact revenge against my father for what he did to her parents." Something like recognition flashed through Cassandra's eyes, but she didn't interrupt. "Xenia figured it out and crashed the wedding. Tried to get Lizbeth to join us, but she refused. Lizbeth died right after she swiped that fatal gash across Xenia's chest." Cael gestured to the bandage, visible above the woven cotton blanket.

"It wasn't fatal, though," Tristan whispered. "She's still alive."

"Only her body," Cael said. "She's got some of my blood in her system. Trophonios said it's keeping her stabilized. For now."

"How do we get her back?" Cassandra asked, resolve sharpening her tone.

"You journey through the Halfway and retrieve her soul," a deep voice said from the door.

Trophonios entered, then introduced himself to Cassandra. He sent Tristan an approving smile. "I get it."

"And how the fuck are we supposed to do *that?*" Cael asked Trophonios, who'd ambled over to the bed to check Xenia's vitals. She was hooked up to a bunch of magical machinery, all soft swishes and faint beeping. Cael had no idea what it all was, but he was grateful for it.

"That hammer you now control—" Trophonios's eyes glanced off Cassandra toward the black stone weapon leaned against the wall "—was gifted to a previous Delphine by Adelphinae herself. A tool the Creator once used to forge and end worlds. When Phaeban Erabis began his campaign against the Goddess, he slaughtered that Delphine. Though she had the last laugh when, upon her death, she erected the wards of Tartarus. A final sacrifice to protect our world from the warhammer's power. Phaeban's progeny decided to make use of her wards as a prison."

"They decided to lock up their criminals with a weapon that could end the world?" Cassandra asked, incredulously.

Trophonios shrugged. "Stupidity is the fuel of arrogance."

"What does this have to do with rescuing Xenia's soul?" Cael snapped.

"Legend claims that hammer can open a portal to the Halfway that allows the living to enter in corporeal form, not just as spectral visitors. And Adelphinae will want the hammer back. You may be able to use it to bargain for your friend's soul. If you can survive the journey to Palathea."

"Palathea?" Cassandra angled her head.

"The realm of the Creator," Trophonios answered. "An opalescent palace deep within the Halfway. Some call it the Singularity. The place from which all life springs. In this universe and the infinite others the Goddess has created."

"Let's go," Cassandra said to Tristan, stalking for the hammer. "Let's go right now."

"Cass," Tristan said softly, halting her. "Not yet."

Cassandra looked like she wanted to kick her lover in the balls. Cael would happily join her.

"There's an entire village of rebels out there waiting for us," Tristan said, then turned to Cael. "Waiting for *you* and your dragon. We need to keep our promise to them. March upon Delos and take back the Crystal Throne."

Cassandra slapped Tristan across the face at the same time as Cael snarled. If they didn't have centuries of loyal friendship between them, Cael might have ripped his future Emperor's fucking wings off.

Cassandra collapsed against Tristan's chest, sobbing. He wrapped his arms and wings around her, cooing soothing words into her hair.

Cael glanced down at Xenia. So fragile. So pale.

And so incredibly beautiful it nearly stopped his heart.

"He's right," Trophonios cut in. "The location of the portal remains a mystery. There may be clues within the Compendium, but it will take time for my team to find and translate them. And it will be smarter—and safer—for Tristan to approach an all-powerful Goddess as Emperor."

Cael brushed his hand through Xenia's soft curls. "How long do we have? How long does *she* have?"

"She's incredibly strong," Trophonios said. "Even discounting the blood you've given her. She's fighting. Clinging fiercely to this life." Trophonios turned to him. "Like she has something—or someone—to live for."

Cael pinched his eyes shut and sucked in a deep breath. He didn't rage against the terrible despair dissolving his insides. Just let it sweep over him. Just felt it. Welcomed it, even. It was better, somehow, than the numbness.

I am in control of my happiness and my destiny.

When he re-opened his eyes, Tristan and Cassandra had left the room, but Trophonios was still there. "You have time, my friend. *She* has time. Help your Prince secure Ethyrios. I will watch over your hum—"

"Wife," Cael barked out.

He pressed a kiss to Xenia's soft, warm lips. The hint of vitality in them lifted his despair ever so slightly.

"As soon as she wakes up, I'm making her my wife."

CHAPTER
SEVENTY-ONE

THERE WERE VERY FEW things in Cassandra's life—only one really—that could distract her from the heartache of Xenia's terrifying condition.

And that one thing currently stood atop a small platform in front of Lebaedia's clock tower, resplendent in his new uniform.

Cassandra hoped she looked as good in hers as Tristan did in his. While Tristan's leather armor was matte black, Cassandra's was a stunning opalescent white that shimmered in the fading sunlight. It not only cradled her curves, but also showed off her hard-won Fae muscle tone. She loved it. Felt sexy, powerful, and absolutely unstoppable.

Embroidered onto both of their chest plates—hers in white thread and his in black—was a sigil designed by Trophonios. The continuous, curved strip doubled back on itself and was bisected by a vertical line in a nod to the movement's original Teles symbol. It represented the connection between the four species and sub-species plus the four elemental magics gifted by the Goddess. Cassandra thought it resembled an infinity symbol.

Or a sideways eight.

Her feathers had prickled when she'd first seen it. She'd told both Tristan and Trophonios about what Reena had said in the Halfway. Something about *eight paths coalescing*. Trophonios had brought up the prophecy, the only other reference to eight that he recalled. His researchers were looking into it, but he didn't anticipate an answer until after the rebels' march on Delos.

Which was the topic of this evening's gathering.

Thousands of rebels blanketed the village and surrounding jungle, anticipating a rousing speech from their future Emperor.

Tristan regarded them with a broad, dazzling smile, looking so regal and powerful and, frankly, fucking hot, that she could hardly believe he was *hers*.

And High Gods help her, despite her grief, despite her worries, all she wanted to do was peel his new uniform off and take her prince for a long, sweaty ride.

She snickered to herself and Tristan's heated gaze shot to her, as if he could tell precisely where her thoughts had strayed.

He traced an M on his thigh.

Ma'anyu.

Unbreakable.

Truer now than it had ever been.

Lined up beside her in front of the platform were the rest of the Teles Chrysos leadership: Trophonios plus the three generals—Fetar, Pfania, and Tanius—to whom Cassandra had been briefly introduced this morning. The latter curved a bright orange wing around the back of a honey-blond female, then planted a kiss on her cheek.

Ione—who Cassandra had not yet officially met—offered Felix a strained smile before turning her attention back to Tristan, her expression indecipherable.

Tristan had insisted on meeting with Ione as soon as he'd returned from Tartarus with Cassandra in tow. He'd asked Cassandra to join him, told her that he had nothing to hide from her. But Cassandra wanted them to have their privacy for what she worried might be a difficult conversation. It's what she herself would have wanted were she in Ione's position.

The meeting had been tense, according to Tristan. Ione had threatened to leave, but he'd convinced her to stay, at least for tonight. Said her absence would be noted and that they needed to project a united front before undertaking their opening move against Eamon.

Cassandra hoped she and Ione would have a chance to speak soon. She didn't want there to be any awkwardness between them.

But some small, wretched, unkind part of her couldn't help holding her head a bit higher, her wings a bit wider, around the stunning female. Couldn't help thinking *he's mine now, and if you try to kiss him again I will rip out your fucking tongue.*

She wasn't proud of it, but there it was.

Behind the Teles Chrysos leadership, Ronin and Mireille laughed quietly, heads bowed together as they shared some secret joke. Though the two wolf bi-forms weren't touching, there was a lightness between them that Cassandra had never seen in Tartarus. Cassandra smiled. Mireille had finally gotten her wish. She had her friend back.

Cassandra was happy to see Ronin smiling, as well. He'd been anxious the past few days. Wanted to find out what had happened to Selene and was hoping to find clues in Delos—the last place she'd been seen after her arrest.

They'd tried reaching her through Ronin's memories a few more times after they'd arrived in the village, to no avail. Cassandra was met with that same solid white wall she'd encountered when she'd tried it behind the wards.

It *had* given them the thought to try it on Tristan, to see if they could jump into Eamon's mind, but that hadn't worked either. All Cassandra had encountered was a blurred haze with indecipherable sounds prickling at her ears. As if something was muddying the brothers' connection.

She tossed away thoughts of those failures as she glanced over her shoulder, scanning the faces spread out behind her. She smiled at some humans from Tartarus, those well enough to leave the healers' quarters. She waved at Hella and Aneka, then saluted Silas, who had an arm wrapped around the shoulder of a tall female with wavy, auburn hair and dove gray wings.

Sofia.

Silas had found his daughter. The tear-stained smile he aimed at Cassandra had her own eyes stinging.

Though her tears froze at the sight of the solitary figure beyond the edge of the crowd, his bonded white dragon curled up in a clearing behind him.

Cael looked murderous. The same expression he'd worn when Cassandra had first met him in the Temple atrium in Thalenn what felt like a thousand years ago. Tristan claimed Cael had softened these past months under Xenia's influence. But now that Cael was on the verge of losing her…

Cassandra shook her head. She wouldn't think about it. It wasn't possible. They *would* get Xenia back.

A purple disc of mentrite floated below Tristan's chin, amplifying his voice to the sprawling crowd.

"Rebel hearts!" he shouted, a deep boom that shivered through Cassandra's bones. "Are you ready to take back your continent?"

The roar he'd summoned shook the cosmos.

"Before we march upon Delos to tear my brother from a throne which he has no right to occupy, I have a few announcements. First and foremost, I'd like to offer my sincerest gratitude to our Delphine, Ione Saros. Not only did she rescue me from my brother's clutches, but she's worked tirelessly over the years to steer the movement toward this very moment. None of us would be here today without her."

He offered Ione a humble bow, which she returned, stiffly, then pressed her palms together at her chest and touched the opal on her platinum circlet.

"Next," Tristan continued, "I'd like to announce a few additions to my Imperial Council. Leaders who have pledged to uphold our values and to usher in a better world for you, your loved ones, and every living creature on this planet, regardless of species or status."

Applause rippled through the crowd, along with joyful laughter and shouts of agreement.

So different from the last time Cassandra had watched a powerful Erabis male address a crowd.

Back in Thalenn, on that fateful day months ago when she'd been arrested, Eamon Erabis had issued threatening decrees based on fear and hatred to his subjects.

Today, Tristan Erabis spoke in gratitude, in love, and in service to his people.

Cassandra's chest swelled with the deepest pride.

"First," Tristan began, "is a female that some of you have likely heard of, though you've only heard half her story. You know her as one of the greatest dancers in the history of Ethyrios. But at the same time as she was climbing those ranks, she was honing her craft as a spy and assassin. Now granted, it was for my father's backwards Empire, but we'll give her a pass on that."

Good-natured ribbing echoed, followed by a long wolf-whistle from Ronin. Cassandra could've sworn she saw Mireille blushing—an extremely rare sight.

Tristan encouraged quiet as his tone intensified. "We will give her a pass because she's spent the past two centuries in Tartarus, protecting half-breeds and humans from Fae who sought to harm and exploit them. She's got the scars to prove it." Tristan locked eyes with Mireille. "But though she is scarred, she is anything but broken. Please welcome our new Captain of Intelligence, Mireille Valois-Fortin!"

Cheers swept through the rebels, the loudest from Ronin, as Mireille sashayed onto the stage to shake hands with Tristan. True to form, she wore no smile, only that *fuck with me and I'll end you all* look that Cassandra remembered so well from their training sessions. She nodded toward the rebels, then retook her spot next to Ronin, who wore a big, goofy grin.

Tristan continued, "Next is a male you know quite well. He's been risking his fur-covered hide for centuries, feeding you vital information as a member of Eamon's Defense Council. And though his wartime history with humans is marred by blood and violence, he is living proof that we are all capable of great change if we can earn the forgiveness of those we've harmed. And learn to forgive ourselves. The new leader of my war committee—General Ronin Matakos!"

Ronin climbed the platform to shake Tristan's hand and showboat for the crowd, who'd leapt to their feet. When he rejoined Mireille, he muttered something that sounded like *they cheered louder for me.* Mireille elbowed him in the ribs.

Tristan went on, bestowing the title of General upon Hella and adding her to Ronin's war committee. Aneka welcomed Hella back into the audience by leaping into her girlfriend's arms and fusing their mouths together.

When the furious celebrations finally died down, he spoke up again. "I would not be standing here before you were it not for this next male. He saved my life countless times during our tenure as Vestian Guards. Plus, a few of us would still be stuck in Tartarus if he hadn't ended the reign of his maniacal father and won himself a *fucking dragon.*"

The crowd whooped and hollered while Signys preened, fluttering her giant wings and releasing a contented puff of smoke.

Tristan choked up on the next part. "He's taught me the true meaning of resilience. That your injuries don't define your limits. And that the deadliest weapon you can possess is a friend who isn't afraid to sit with you in your darkness. There's no one I'd rather have guarding my back. Meet the new Captain of my Imperial Guard—Cael Zephyrus!"

Signys shot a column of bright, crackling flame into the twilight sky as the rebels erupted. Cael portaled to the stage, his face slightly softer. Tristan curled a hand around the back of Cael's neck and pressed their foreheads together.

"We'll get her back," Tristan whispered to his friend. "We'll burn a path through the Halfway if we have to."

Cael grimaced, offered a stiff bow to the crowd with his wing flared, then portaled back to Signys's side. He was even less comfortable with the praise than Mireille.

"And last but certainly not least…" His eyes flicked to Cassandra and her heart kicked into a frenzied beat. "I have a shameful confession for you all. Up until very recently, I wasn't sure if I believed in your Goddess."

Low laughter and a few shocked gasps burbled through the crowd.

"I asked myself, if Adelphinae truly existed, how could she have allowed the beautiful, harmonious world she'd created to devolve into such suffering and hatred? How could a Goddess that purports to love all her creations equally and unconditionally allow them to cause each other such pain?"

Tristan dipped his head, rubbing his thumb into his palm. Across his original Turning scar.

"But then something miraculous happened." He returned his gaze to the crowd. "The Goddess gave me a gift. One I'm sure I'm not worthy of, but a gift nonetheless." He reached a hand toward Cassandra, encouraging her to join him on the platform, and her pulse skyrocketed further. "And the wonderful news is she's not just a gift for me. Well, in some ways she is." He winked and the crowd burst into laughter as Cassandra fought the urge to roll her eyes.

Tristan placed his hands on her shoulders and turned her toward his people.

"She'll be the greatest gift to you as well."

She flared her wings, incredibly moved by the openness, the joy, in the faces staring up at her. Tristan said he didn't know if he was worthy of her, but at this moment, she didn't know if *she* was worthy of *them*.

But Creator help her, she was willing to work for it.

Tristan continued, "She's borne many titles: Shrouded Sister, Savior Sister, Koenigin of Tartarus, Prince's Consort. But there's one more I'm hoping she'll add to her list."

The crowd sucked in a collective breath. Which was ironic because Cassandra had ceased to breathe.

Tristan knelt down on one knee, tucking his iridescent black wings down his back, and reached for her hand. Sensing how nervous she was, he ran a gentle thumb across her knuckles.

"Cassandra Fortin," he asked with tears in his eyes. "*Ma'anyu.*

Will you be my Empress?"

She wanted to burst into elated tears. Wanted to leap into his arms. Wanted to kiss his face off and scream with delight.

But the responsibilities he'd just asked her to accept—to forge this new world beside him, to uplift these people, to help them repair the rifts created by Eamon and Leonin—were so much larger than Tristan and Cassandra's own responsibilities toward each other.

They imbued their love with even greater importance. As if Adelphinae had brought them together for exactly this purpose.

So instead of answering Tristan, she turned her gaze upon the gathered rebel hearts. Windriders and Deathstalkers and Beastrunners and half-breeds and humans.

Her people. Each and every one.

And accepted them all with a resounding "*YES!*"

CHAPTER
SEVENTY-TWO

THE CELEBRATIONS CONTINUED WELL into the night. Cassandra was grateful her rebels would have a full day to recover before they marched upon Delos the day after.

Shouts and laughter and music echoed through the jungle as she made her way toward a small dwelling at the corner of the square. She knocked on the chipped red door. When no one answered, she tried the handle, found it unlocked, and pushed inside.

It was dark as pitch, the only light a triangular slice down the wooden stairs.

Rustling wings and opening drawers sounded as she crept up to the second floor, then turned into a large, spartan bedroom.

Ione froze in the midst of packing a leather sack, pain and sorrow mingling on her beautiful face.

"Creator, you're gorgeous," she said, tossing a square of folded white linen into her bag, then placing her hands on her hips.

Cassandra let out a nervous chuckle. "Uh, so are you." Then couldn't think of another single thing to say as Ione stared at her.

This was far more awkward than she'd hoped it was going to be.

She decided to cut the small talk and plow forward to the uncomfortable bits.

"I'm sorry, Ione. If I had—"

Ione expelled a bitter laugh. "No, you're not." She stalked over to a chest of drawers, opened one, then shoved the contents into her bag. "And if he'd chosen me, I wouldn't be sorry either."

Cassandra remembered what Tristan had told her. That since Ione had rescued him, he'd never felt like she really loved *him*. That any affection she'd shown was inspired by duty to the movement.

Is that why she was so upset? Because she thought she had to give up everything she'd worked for?

"You don't have to leave," Cassandra said, reaching for Ione who took a very purposeful step back. "Tristan doesn't want you to."

Ione snorted. "So magnanimous of you to deliver that message on his behalf." She opened her closet, her frown deepening before she fished out her opal-topped, platinum circlet. She regarded it with a sad, bitter smile before tossing it to Cassandra. "He didn't offer you a ring, but perhaps you'll accept a crown. Not like I need it anymore."

"But you're still the Delphine."

"Am I?" Ione asked, crowding into Cassandra. Ione had a few inches on her, but Cassandra didn't cower. Ione's indigo eyes flicked to the circlet. "The irony is they don't even need a Delphine. The Goddess herself blesses the Anointed, as long as they believe. But I guess my presence helped bolster their faith." Cassandra had no idea what Ione was talking about. "Did he tell you what he did?"

Cassandra swallowed, but didn't answer. She trusted Tristan with both her life and her heart, and braced herself for whatever anger-induced lies Ione was about to spew.

"He named me his successor. When he was worried he might not come back from Tartarus." Ione's laugh was cold enough to frost glass. "He vowed before Trophonios that if he died before he married or bore an heir, that I would ascend the Crystal Throne."

"Are you implying that you're a *threat* to me? If you think—"

Ione's cackle raked across Cassandra's feathers. "No, you stupid bitch. I'm saying you weren't supposed to survive. That's not how your and Tristan's story has ended. Ever."

Cassandra's head spun, recalling everything Reena had said in the Halfway before sending her soul back to Ethyrios.

About Tristan always choosing her.

About him cratering Tartarus with Adelphinae's hammer.

In every previous version of this world, Tristan and Cassandra had died before becoming Emperor and Empress.

"I don't want Tristan," Ione hissed. "I want what I was promised."

A chill prickled down Cassandra's spine.

Ione struck, but Cassandra was quicker. She grabbed Ione's wrist and the memory that overtook her made her sick to her stomach.

Atop a translucent throne veined with gold flakes, a younger, bare-backed Ione straddled a brawny male with two enormous, iridescent black wings.

"You love me," Ione demanded.

"I love you," Leonin grunted, *her long, blond hair wrapped around his wrist as he thrust up into her.*

"You'll never leave me." She gripped the armrests for leverage as she rocked her hips in his lap.

"I'll never leave you. Never," Leonin pressed his face into the side of her neck.

She fisted his shoulder-length black hair and wrenched his head back, unmistakable lust crawling through his obsidian eyes.

She stopped moving. A necessary manipulation. She needed to force him to agree. He hadn't during the Turning ceremony last night.

She wasn't Fae yet, though she knew she would be soon. She and Leonin had a plan for that, too. How they would hide it from Mila. The idealistic young Prince was so obviously in love with her. Bedding him would ensure no one knew who'd truly Turned her.

Leonin.

The male who'd promised her everything.

Well, almost everything.

She leaned down to whisper in his ear, "I will be Empress."

Leonin groaned, his fingers digging into her flanks. He was right on the edge, exactly where she wanted him. "Ione, you know I—"

She pushed herself up, then sank down his cock again. Very, very slowly.

"Fuck," he growled. "Yes. Alright, whatever you want just—"

The memory dissolved as soon as Ione wrenched her arm from Cassandra's grip.

Cassandra paled. "Does Tristan know? Does *Eamon* know?"

Ione's voice shook. "What did you see?"

But before Cassandra could grab her again, Ione tapped her cuff and melted away in a rainbow flash.

"Felix is gone, too," Seraavi said, stalking into the war committee room with murderous intent darkening her fuchsia eyes.

"Who else knows?" Trophonios asked, his long fingers massaging his ebony forehead.

Cassandra, seated beside Tristan and still trembling from shock, held her fiancée's hand beneath the table and ran her thumb across his Turning scar.

Referring to him as her fiancée helped ease the sting of Ione's betrayal. Slightly.

Tristan was taking the news surprisingly well. Or perhaps he was just trying not to fall apart in front of his Council.

"I haven't said a word to anyone outside this room," Cassandra promised. "As soon as Ione portaled away, I sought out Tristan."

"Nothing's spread through the village yet," Layla added from her seat next to Ronin and Mireille. Hella rounded out the Council—what was left of it—her tiny golden braids piled in a knot atop her head.

"I don't want to lie to them," Tristan ground out, squeezing Cassandra's hand. His lifeline.

Trophonios lifted his gaze. "I don't disagree with you, Your Highness, but...this is the worst possible timing. Might it not be wiser to wait until after we've marched and won? Ione is a powerful symbol within the Teles Chrysos. Knowledge of her dishonesty could shatter morale."

Tristan sighed, releasing Cassandra's hand and raking his own through his hair.

"He's right," she said softly, fingertips resting gently on his thigh. "We need to stay the course. I'm not sure our rebels could stomach such a blow right now."

"We need story for why Ione gone," Hella added.

"Like what?" Seraavi asked.

Trophonios sat up straighter. "Something that will *boost* morale. Even if it's not precisely accurate. We'll tell them Ione has journeyed into the Icthians, with Felix as protection, to commune with Adelphinae in the wilderness and solicit blessings for our fight."

"That would do it," Ronin nodded, fiddling with his eye patch.

"I don't like it," Tristan grimaced, tapping his fingers on his armrest.

"Sometimes a lie can be kinder than the truth," Mireille piped up. "In this case, what good would it do to tell them they've been duped by the female they'd come to trust above all others? You'll only distract them from their duty, open them up to harm."

Cael, who'd been standing in the corner with his wing tucked and his arms crossed, chimed in. "She's right," he said in a deep, ferocious grumble. Someone had fucked with his friend. His *brother*. "And once we win back your throne, there won't be a corner of the fucking continent Ione can hide. Signys and I will smoke her out ourselves."

Tristan dipped his head to his chest, blowing out a resigned sigh. "Remind me why I appointed you all to tell me what to do?" He turned to Trophonios. "What kind of threat does she pose? Not just once we march, but after."

Trophonios grimaced. "I suppose it depends on how much your brother knows of her truth. Or if her plans involve luring any of the membership to her side."

"What if she aligns herself with Eamon?" Cassandra asked. "He remains unmated. She could make a bid for him. Or, Creator forbid, show up with him in Delos."

"We find out in day and half," Hella grunted, rustling her crimson feathers.

Cassandra continued, addressing Trophonios. "Ione knew of things that I'd only heard from Reena in the Halfway. It was more than just an interpretation of the prophecy. Where would she have gained such knowledge?"

Trophonios shook his head, rubbing his jaw. "I don't know."

"Do you have any idea where she might have gone?" Layla asked, stroking her knives.

"I don't know that either," Trophonios answered.

"I could find out," Mireille said, and Ronin's head whipped toward her. "I can make a lot of things happen with a few vials of veiling potion and a supply of *drachas*. I'm guessing the network of information brokers I used as an Imperial Affairs agent is still thriving." She sliced her quicksilver gaze to Tristan. "Let me prove I'm worth that fancy new title you just gave me, Your Highness."

"I'll go with you," Ronin proclaimed, his broad shoulders tensing.

Sorrow and affection mingled in Mireille's expression. "You can't, General. Your Emperor needs you. Selene needs you, too. See what you can find in Delos, and I'll ask around as well. If I find any answers on my quest, I'll let you know."

She lowered her voice, but Cassandra was close enough to hear. "Save a dance for me. Maybe a game of chess, too. I need to kick your ass again."

"Be careful." Ronin clasped her hand, then pressed a long kiss to the back of it before whispering, "Come back to me."

Tristan turned to the group. "We all clear on the story, then?" They nodded. "Rest up. We march in thirty-six hours."

The group rose from the table, offering Tristan and Cassandra subtle bows on the way out.

Trophonios stood, pushing his chair back, but Tristan stopped him. "Not you. I've got a few more questions."

The Beastrunner retook his seat as they waited for the room to empty.

Once it had, Tristan gripped Cassandra's hand again. "So, all the evidence that proved my and Ione's connection—her Ghostwalking abilities, our ability to summon multiple elements together—that was possible because..."

"Because it was your father who Turned her," Trophonios said gently. "The commonalities in the blood. That's what forged the connection." He smiled at Cassandra. "You've only Turned one woman."

"The lines of the prophecy then. *Two futures sown, one future known?* Does that mean Cassandra is the Delphine?"

Trophonios pinched the bridge of his nose. "It's still unclear. Ione could still technically be the Delphine since the *phantom wings* could refer to Leonin. And she did *light the way* for the movement, even if upon a foundation of lies. Only the Creator will know for sure." He turned to Cassandra. "Has the Goddess ever spoken to you? Ione claimed to have received messages from Adelphinae that guided her path and kept her alive over the years."

Cassandra nodded. "She spoke through my mother in a vision. She told me to *find her*. At the time, I thought she was referring to herself, but now I think she may have meant Mireille. Then when I was behind the wards, she showed me a vision of Tristan and Ione together." Tristan squeezed her hand. An apology. She squeezed back. Long forgiven. "And after my appeal, after the Koenig killed me, Reena spoke to me in the Halfway. Though I'm not sure she'd been sent by the Goddess. Seemed like she'd gone rogue."

Tristan chuckled. "Of course she had."

"Well, stay open to her," Trophonios said. "Adelphinae may send you messages as our plans coalesce."

"Ione said something odd before she left," Cassandra pondered. "That the mixed-species rebels didn't need a Delphine. That all they need to become Anointed is to prove their faith to the Goddess herself. That no intermediary was necessary. But she thought that having a Delphine helped inspire that faith."

Trophonios cocked his head. "Are you willing to do that for them going forward?"

Cassandra raised her chin, squaring her shoulders. "I don't care *what* that prophecy means, whether I'm the Delphine or not. They're my people. I will be whatever they need me to be. And I will fight for them to the end."

Trophonios relaxed, revealing a slash of dazzling white teeth. "Then they couldn't ask for anything better." He stood once again. "We should get some rest, too. Long days are ahead of us." He bowed at the waist before exiting the room. "Goodnight, Your Highnesses."

Cassandra wondered if she'd ever get used to it, the titles, the deference. But perhaps she didn't want to be the kind of leader who would.

As soon as they were alone, Tristan crumpled, catching his face in his hands. "I'm such a fucking fool."

"Hey," Cassandra said, climbing into his lap and cupping his face in her hands. "This is *not* on you. Your father and Ione—" Cassandra shuddered, the sight of them fucking on the Crystal Throne burned behind her eyelids "—they manipulated you. They took advantage of your good nature, and the world paid for it. Don't you dare shoulder an ounce of the guilt that by all rights belongs to them."

"But that's the problem, isn't it?" Tristan frowned as he shifted beneath her. "I'm *too* trusting. It's what got us into trouble with Eamon down in the colonies. I failed to see what was right in front of me. And I've just gone and done it again with Ione. It's a weakness our enemies could exploit."

Cassandra stroked her thumb across his cheekbone, hating the self-loathing dulling his toasted-honey eyes. He wrapped his arms around her waist, holding her tighter against him. "Assuming the best in people is not a weakness, Tristan. It's your greatest strength. I wouldn't be sitting here if you hadn't assumed the best in a tiny thief who'd stolen a diamond necklace." She kissed his jaw. "A tiny thief who's about to become your wicked, suspicious wife, and who will be more than happy to help you sort your enemies from your friends. And then sort those enemies' heads from their bodies."

He chuckled, some lightness returning to his eyes as he plucked up her hand and kissed her fingertips. "My blood-thirsty Empress."

She lowered her brows. "We will make her pay for it. *I* will make her pay for it."

"Is it wrong that I can't wait to see that?" He squeezed her tight and tucked his head against her neck. "I love you, Cass."

She ran her fingers through the soft hair at his nape. "Love me so much you were willing to destroy a city for me. A thousand times over."

He pulled back, scanning her eyes, nothing but the deepest love and most ardent affection in his own. "I'd end the entire world if I thought I was going to lose you again."

She snickered. "A very responsible stance for an Emperor."

"How's this for responsible?" He stood from his chair, threw her over his shoulder and smacked her ass. "I know we should be resting, but I think I might keep you up for another hour or four."

After he'd lugged her out of the war committee room, he kept his promise. Had her up for more like five hours that night, making up for their lost time.

And as they drifted off to sleep, clutched sweaty and spent and satisfied in each other's arms, Cassandra couldn't help but think that the best version of this world would include a lot more trusting people like Tristan.

CHAPTER
SEVENTY-THREE

THE WIND OFF LAKE Phaeban ruffled through Tristan's feathers as he shook the hand of a gray-winged, brown-eyed male atop a hill overlooking Delos.

"I can't thank you enough for the support, Erik. Or should I call you High Councilor Zephyrus now?"

Erik cringed. "High Gods, please don't." Cael had abdicated the position to his younger brother, though nothing would be official until a seated Emperor decreed it. "Father would be rolling over in his grave. If he had one." Erik dipped his chin and snickered, but Tristan detected a layer of pain beneath the mirth. Surely not for Arran. Probably for all those who'd lost their lives during the Stoneridge wedding massacre. "Anyway—" Erik perked up and gestured toward a tight formation of lethal warriors with membranous wings in shades of black, brown, and gray "—a horde of Brachian soldiers. As requested, Your Highness."

"High Gods, please don't."

The two males shared a laugh.

Layla Fetar strode up, her black-and-white hair braided away from her face and her leathers polished to a gleam as sharp as her knives. She bowed to Tristan. "The last winged rebel unit has just arrived via cuff, Highness. We go on your command."

Tristan nodded. "Thanks, Layla."

The curvy, deadly honey badger bi-form strutted down the hill, and Erik's head nearly swiveled off his neck. "Who was *that*?"

Tristan smirked. "Nothing you can handle, lordling."

Erik pulled at the lapel of his uniform. "Hey, I'm a High Councilor now. Or will be as soon as you swear me in."

"You just balked at the title."

Erik clapped a hand on Tristan's shoulder, his gaze still devouring Layla's ass. "I'm not opposed to throwing it around for a good cause."

"She won't be impressed by it."

Erik ambled toward his warriors, throwing a two-fingered salute over his shoulder. "Never say never."

Tristan watched him go, then swept his gaze across the rebellion's aerial army. In addition to the Teles Chrysos themselves, official units from both Cernodas and Akti had joined.

Tristan clomped through the wet grass, seeking out his Council.

Ronin, decked out in a midnight-blue battle uniform with the sleeves rolled up to expose his ice-blue tattoos, was frowning beneath his eye patch as he assessed the assembled forces. Judging the lines, or missing Mireille already?

Seraavi, Hella, Trophonios, and Layla were rallying the troops, giving last minute pep-talks.

Cael and Signys were up in the sky, scouting.

Cassandra stood alone at the edge of the field, pensive. And looking so fucking gorgeous and powerful in her opalescent leather armor that Tristan wanted to bellow *she's mine* across the field. Her warhammer rested at her feet.

They weren't planning to use it. Not unless things got really dire. But he hoped the weapon would scare off anyone stupid enough to tangle with her. Especially since she couldn't fly yet.

He stepped up behind her, tugging on the end of her tousled braid. "What are you thinking about?"

She turned, worry pinching her features. "I don't know, Birdman, I just… I have this unsettled feeling. Like today is going to go horribly, horribly wrong."

"I feel that way before every battle. We'll be okay. We've prepared. We have thousands of fighters from three different territories on our side." He rubbed the back of her neck, and she relaxed slightly. "Do you want to try mind-jumping into Eamon's present again? Maybe it'll work this time." An attempt to soothe her anxiety and nothing more. He doubted it would work any better today than it had the past few times they'd tried.

Cassandra shook her head. "I can't stop thinking about what Reena said after she sent my soul back. That we'd see each other again sooner than I could imagine." The fear dampening her bright, blue-gray eyes wrecked him. "What if…what if I die again today?"

He pulled her into him, running his wings along hers and relishing the little shiver that coursed through her body. "You are not going to die today. Or ever again. I won't allow it."

She released a breathy little laugh, then parted her lips—probably to continue arguing with him. But before she could say a word, a boom echoed across the hill.

Signys landed in a clearing, then laid down a wing.

Cael climbed down and even from this vantage point, Tristan could see the shock and confusion on his Captain's face.

Tristan's stomach dipped as he rushed for Cael, meeting him halfway across the field. "What—"

"It's empty," Cael said. "The palace is empty.

"Your brother is no longer in Delos."

The Crystal Throne room of the Imperial Palace in Delos was the most beautiful place Cassandra had ever seen.

Crafted entirely of gold-veined white marble, the circular room was ringed by arches on the first floor and topped by a mezzanine of sculpted columns. Far, far above, a massive domed ceiling was decorated in gold filigree and sported ornate frescoes honoring the Erabis family's conquests. Scaffolding branched out beneath one stark white section bearing a spiderweb of sketched lines.

Eamon's unfinished addition.

But despite the room's undeniable beauty, the scene that awaited the rebels was gruesome.

A golden-haired Beastrunner male wearing an Imperial soldier's uniform sat atop the throne in a growing pool of blood. Rivulets of red trailed down the translucent crystal, and the Typhon steel spear pierced through his chest had a folded letter tacked to the end.

The male himself was motionless. Long-dead, Cassandra supposed.

And as terrible a sight as that was, the scene leading up to the throne was worse.

Piles of human bodies lined the aisle. Men and women of all ages, sizes, and races.

No children, praise Anaemos.

The bodies were intact. Preserved, even. Cassandra didn't scent a hint of rot.

Even so, someone retched behind her.

Tristan and Cassandra and their Council had entered the palace easily. *Too* easily. Not a single door nor gate had been locked, and there wasn't a soldier in sight.

"What the fuck happened here?" Cael breathed out, a step behind Cassandra.

A vein jumped in Tristan's jaw as he answered. "These are the obliviates that Eamon had shipped from the colonies. Darius—" Tristan's sad eyes flicked to the male pinned to the throne "—told me he'd seen them. But he didn't know what Eamon was doing with them."

"What *was* he doing with them?" Cassandra asked, her voice barely a croak. The level of devastation spread out before her was…numbing. A cold emptiness that frosted out every other emotion.

Tristan stepped onto the dais and leaned down to examine Darius.

The male awoke with a shuddering wet cough, his bloodshot eyes darting madly as the group jolted back.

"He's gone," Darius garbled out. "They're all gone." He grasped for the spear in his chest, attempting to remove it, but was too weak to manage it.

Tristan knelt down before him as Cassandra, Cael, and Ronin crowded in behind.

"Shh, Darius, it's alright," Tristan said, placing a hand on the male's leg. Darius was seconds from death. Cassandra couldn't believe he'd held out this long. But perhaps he'd been preserving himself for this very moment? "What happened to these humans?"

Darius coughed, blood bubbling down his chin. "He was using their bodies. Hijacking their obliviated souls to spy on her. To spy on *us*. He enslaved a chronomancer to help him."

"Who?" Tristan asked.

Darius's chin flopped against his chest, and with his final bit of strength, he ripped the letter off the spear and thrust it toward Ronin with a shaky hand.

Ronin furrowed his onyx brows, then plucked the letter from Darius's limp fingers as the male slumped back against the throne.

Ronin's golden-blue eye roved over the three simple sentences, and black claws burst from his knuckles as a savage growl rumbled in his throat.

"What?" Cassandra asked, feathers prickling, that terrible sense of dread returning as Ronin tossed her the letter.

She read the final sentence above the scrawled *E* of Eamon's signature.

Why rule just one world when I could rule them all?

"He's got Selene," Ronin ground out to Tristan. "He's marching his army through the Halfway. Toward Palathea.

"Eamon Erabis has declared war upon the Creator herself."

EPILOGUE

AT A TABLE IN the cozy cottage, Xenia arranged wildflowers in a vase of dark blue glass, humming to herself.

Every time she placed her elbow upon the surface, the table wobbled. As if the legs hadn't been installed properly.

It didn't really bother her. It was hard to be annoyed by *anything* in such a lovely place. The bluebird sky outside was always bright, the clouds always fluffy, the breeze always warm.

When she strode through the meadows every morning, the blooms she'd clipped the previous day had re-sprouted. So odd. But delightful.

The cottage was like that, too. The pantry and refrigerator restocked every morning. New books appeared on the shelves every few days. Firewood appeared underneath the mantle whenever she needed it.

She was never cold nor hungry nor thirsty. Never tired. Slightly bored.

More than a little lonely.

But she was safe, at least. She didn't know how she knew that. But she knew.

She couldn't remember how she'd gotten here. Couldn't remember her life before...

If she concentrated very hard, sometimes she'd catch small snippets of memory.

A low, sultry chuckle. Fingers caressing her curls. A fang grazing her collarbone.

A pair of thundercloud eyes.

The snippets never materialized into full memories. All they did was lodge a persistent ache in her chest for hours afterward.

So, she tried not to trigger them. Tried not to think of him.

Whoever he was.

Instead, she picked wildflowers. And made tea. And read smutty books. And ate shortbread biscuits by the fire.

She plucked up a poppy, then leaned her elbow across the table to place it in the vase. The table wobbled, nearly tipping it, and she cursed.

She should fix it. She'd always been so good at fixing things. Hadn't she?

She pushed out of her chair and crouched onto the floor.

Just as she was reaching for the offending leg, a knock sounded at the door. She was so startled she banged her head on the underside of the table.

No one had *ever* come to the cottage.

Rubbing at her sore crown—which faded immediately; she never felt pain for long in this place—she swung the door open.

"Hello?"

Her visitor—a little Fae girl—couldn't have been more than six. A beautiful child with ash-brown curls, bright green eyes, and the cutest, tiniest pair of dark gray wings Xenia had ever seen.

"You're glowing," the girl said.

"What?"

The girl giggled. "Like a rainbow."

Xenia looked down at her arms, but didn't see any glow. The girl wasn't glowing either.

"You're not."

The girl stretched out her limbs to make sure. "No, I'm not. I'm just visiting. He told me to come back here in my dreams. To where my story began. He said you might be lonely."

"He who?" A tear tracked down Xenia's cheek. When had she begun crying?

"He's only got one wing, but it doesn't matter because—" the girl beckoned Xenia closer, bearing a familiar sly grin "—he's got a *dragon*."

Something splintered in Xenia's chest.

"Who are you talking about?" Her voice was little more than a cracked whisper.

The girl laughed again. "Well, who *else*? Daddy, of course.

"He's coming for you."

ACKNOWLEDGEMENTS

Every time I finish one of these, I take a deep breath to relax and then—

FUCK. I forgot to write the acknowledgements.

After pouring every ounce of creativity in my weary body upon these pages, I hope you'll forgive the straightforward and slightly dull words below.

First and foremost and always, to Mark. My rock. Thank you for always being there to put me back together when I fall apart. I love you.

To Susan, who always knows exactly what questions to ask to whip these stories into fighting shape! I wouldn't dream of plunging back into this world without you.

To Noah, for giving the words a final polish and for the "nitpicky" (your words, not mine) comments that helped me wrangle some unforeseen plotholes!

To Rena, your artistry never ceases to amaze me. I say it every time, but this time I *really* mean it – FAVORITE COVER YET!

To the incredible artists I've had the privilege to work with these past few years—and a few who I'm anxiously awaiting upcoming commission slots—your work is incomparably valuable and irreplaceable. Fuck generative AI.

To the online communities of which I'm privileged to call myself a member—especially Bookstagram, BookTok, and BookThreads—your passion fuels me and your content inspires me. I might be lurking most of the time, but I promise I see you.

And lastly, to you, my dear reader. I am mind-blown every day that you exist. And that so many of you have joined Tristan, Cassandra, Cael, Xenia, Ronin, and Mireille on this journey. When I first wrote *The Memory Puller* (way back in 2021!), I assumed that no one would love these characters as much as I did. Thank you for proving me wrong.

ABOUT THE AUTHOR

Kris K. Haines is a fantasy romance author and lover of stabby, swoony stories. A Jeopardy!® silver medalist and self-proclaimed adrenaline junkie, Kris can be found barreling down mountains in the winter and hugging the turns on her motorcycle in the summer. That is, when she doesn't have her nose stuck in a book. She lives outside of Philadelphia with her supportive husband and two sassy pugs.

Made in United States
Troutdale, OR
04/02/2025

30291322R00412